Trouble
Don't Last
Always

Trouble
Don't Last
Always

FRANCIS RAY

ST. MARTIN'S GRIFFIN ✠ NEW YORK

www.stmartins.com

ISBN 0-312-32163-5

First published in the United States under the title *The Turning Point* by St. Martin's Paperbacks

10   9   8   7   6   5   4   3

*This book is dedicated to those who walk by faith
and to those who are almost there.*

Heartfelt Thanks and Gratitude

First of all, I want to thank God. With Him in my life all things are possible.

My gratitude also goes to the following:

LaRee Bryant and Angela Washington-Blair, who were with me in the beginning, two years ago, when the idea for this book came to me. I'm blessed to have you as my friends.

Bessie Lassiter, who called her son, Wright Lassiter Jr., who called Dr. Michael Harris, ophthalmologist, who answered question after question for over a year with keen insight and patient understanding.

Dr. Susan Parks, ophthalmologist/retina specialist, University of Texas Southwestern Medical Center at Dallas. A macula hole in my left eye could have meant permanent blindness. You and God deemed otherwise. Thanks also for the encouragement to write this book.

Dr. Eugene George, neurosurgeon/head trauma specialist, University of Texas Southwestern Medical Center at Dallas. Thanks for the medical expertise and the laughs.

ACKNOWLEDGMENTS

David Ondick, vocation specialist, and Shelly Smith, caseworker for the Texas Commission for the Blind. Thanks for giving me invaluable insight into the lives of those who view their loss of sight as an inconvenience, not a handicap.

Trisha Chandler, supervisor of Orientation and Mobility for the Dallas Lighthouse for the Blind. Thanks for the O & M lessons.

Glenda Howard, my editor. Your intuitive instincts are phenomenal. Thanks for helping me turn my dream into reality.

As always, to the home team, William and Carolyn Michelle Ray, husband and daughter, my biggest fans and supporters, thanks for not complaining about the house or uncooked meals. You make life meaningful. I love you.

Trouble
Don't Last
Always

Chapter One

"Death is inevitable. You can't hide from it, run from it, bargain with it. Each one of us has to accept that sobering fact. The best thing you can do is be ready."

Pastor Hezekiah Fowler's deep bass voice reached every person within the packed frame church without the help of the failing PA system. In the front pew, Lilly Crawford sat with her long legs demurely crossed at the ankles. Her hands clutched a flowered, tear-stained handkerchief as she stared at the white casket draped with a spray of white gladiolus. More sprays were at the head and foot and clustered around the casket and podium.

So many flowers, Lilly thought, *and so utterly useless. Mother Crawford couldn't smell them now.* She had loved flowers of any kind, loved to spend time in her garden, but she'd been bedridden for the past six months as her body fought a losing battle. Yet the only person who had thought to send her flowers while she could enjoy them was the one person who couldn't be here for her home going. If Rafe had come, there might have been two caskets instead of one.

To Lilly's left sat her husband, Myron, in his best black suit, his usually straight shoulders slumped, his callused hands clamped between his legs, his proud head bent in submission to a power greater than his. Next to him sat his daughter, Lilly's stepdaughter, Shayla, draped in black and misery, sobbing loudly. To her right was David, her husband, a shy, earnest young man with a nervous eye tic but, according to Shayla, a computer genius. Since David had been to his in-laws' house only a handful of times before their marriage three years ago and twice since, Lilly couldn't be sure.

"Hear me now; I said you can't run from it, hide from it, bargain with it," Pastor Fowler continued, and Lilly respectfully gave him her attention. "Each one of us in God's appointed time is gonna have to give an accounting of our sins and look God and death in the face. The best thing you can do is be ready."

Pastor Fowler's hands, work-worn from thirty years at the bottle plant lifting twenty-pound crates of beverages, clamped around the scarred wooden pulpit. Out of his mud-brown, heavily lined face his brown eyes sparkled with the fervency of his message as he leaned his robust torso over the worn, open Bible.

Shouts of "Amen" came from around the church. Lilly knew if she were to turn around she'd see heads nodding in agreement as well. The pastor was in top form. Mother Crawford would have been pleased, but a little sad as well. She had always said no one preached more earnestly than Pastor Fowler when trying to win lost souls; his fervent prayers could wrench tears from the eyes of the boldest sinner. Too bad, she'd once commented after a particularly powerful Wednesday night prayer meeting, that he didn't seem to be able to save himself.

Lilly hadn't asked for an explanation. She had lost faith in too much to add Pastor Fowler's sins, real or imagined, to the list. Besides, she knew how frightening and helpless it felt not to be able to save yourself.

"Our faithful sister, Minnie Faye Crawford, was ready," Pastor Fowler said, assurance in every syllable of his voice. "At eighty-one she had lived a long time. Was blessed with a loving husband who preceded her in death, a loving son and granddaughter who gave her countless moments of joy and blessings in her declining years. The Lord saw fit to take her first daughter-in-law, but He blessed her with another fine Christian woman in Sister Lilly."

"Amen" flared up again. Lilly closed her eyes against the looks she knew would be cast upon her. No one except Mother Crawford and Rafe ever let her forget she hadn't been the first Mrs. Crawford. To everyone else Lilly was still trying to measure up, still failing. Just as Rafe had failed.

"So, brothers and sisters, I come to you today asking this question." Pastor

Fowler paused, his hard, piercing brown gaze sweeping over the gathered crowd again. "When it's your time to lie in the arms of death as our beloved Sister Minnie Faye Crawford now rests, when it's your time to close your eyes and wake no more, when it's your time to lie in front of the pulpit, when it's your time to take that last final ride, will you be ready?

"Will you be able to look back on your life with no regrets as this sister did, to count your blessings instead of your woes, or will you bow your head and weep for all that is lost, for all that should have been done and wasn't?"

Lilly's head snapped up. Wide-eyed, she stared at Pastor Fowler. Had he guessed?

No, he wasn't looking at her. He didn't know that she lived with regrets, that her blessings were few, her tears many.

Lilly didn't know she was sobbing until she felt the brush of wind on her face and opened her eyes. Standing in front of her, in her starched white usher's uniform and black armband, was Sister Lawrence waving her fan. "Mother Crawford wouldn't want you to weep for her."

Tears rolled faster down Lilly's amber cheeks. She shut her eyes again. Guilt pressed against her chest like a heavy weight.

If only they knew.

Stepping back from the pulpit, Pastor Fowler lifted his hands and beckoned. "Undertakers in charge."

"Grandma! Grandma!"

Lilly shut her eyes tighter against the wailing sound of her twenty-one-year-old stepdaughter. No matter how unchristian it was, Lilly couldn't help thinking that Shayla should have come to see her sick grandmother. Houston was only a three-hour drive away from Little Elm, but Shayla always had an excuse.

"Grandma!"

The wail grew more plaintive, more demanding. As in the past, Shayla's father drew his only daughter and favorite child into his arms, murmuring words of comfort and reassurance.

"Hush, baby girl. Daddy's here."

"She's gone! Grandma's gone!" Shayla refused to be comforted.

Lilly turned to see Shayla being physically restrained by her father and her husband. David's eyes were wide behind his gold wire-frame glasses. He was as lost as Myron in his attempts to comfort Shayla, and just as concerned. No surprise there. Shayla wouldn't have married a man who wouldn't meet her many demands and go soft at her frequent emotional outbursts.

"Daddy! Daddy!" Shayla shouted as the spray of gladiolus was removed, the upper half of the coffin lid lifted.

Lilly faced forward thinking this was one time that Myron wouldn't be able to give Shayla what she wanted or what he thought she needed as he had done so many times in the past. The pain and heartache he had caused others hadn't mattered. No price was too high for Shayla to be happy. No one knew this better than Lilly . . . or felt the burden of it more.

The small white frame house on North Fourth Street was filled to capacity. The April day was unseasonably warm, with no clouds in sight. People spilled out of the eight-by-ten living room, cooled ineffectively by a window unit, onto the freshly cut grass in the front yard, careful of the borders of newly sprouting tulips on either side of the paved walkway that stopped in the middle of the yard.

The mourners were content now to mingle happily beneath the undisciplined mulberry tree in the front yard. Laughter came often. Funerals were a social event. People took the opportunity to mourn, but they also renewed acquaintances not seen sometimes since the last funeral and gave thanks that they were still among the living.

Inside the scrupulously clean kitchen there was barely enough room for the women from the church's auxiliaries to fit. Mother Crawford, the eldest member of the church, had been well respected and loved. The food had been accumulating for days. Most of the women over forty were known for their special dishes and took pride in bringing them to the home of the bereaved.

Lilly stood over the huge roasting pan on top of the electric stove and scooped out corn-bread dressing onto a paper plate. Sister Madison had a touch with dressing that made you want to savor each bite. When asked what her secret was, she'd only smile in that serene way of hers. She never told. Some of the women at the church thought that was selfish, but Lilly knew that some secrets could never be shared.

"Sister Crawford, are you all right?"

Startled, Lilly looked up to find Sister Madison staring at her with narrowed eyes in her ebony-hued face. "Y-yes."

"Don't look like it." Sister Madison glanced at the plate in Lilly's hand. "I know my dressing is good, but don't you think whoever you're fixing that food for wants more than dressing?"

Lilly jerked her gaze back to the plate in her hand. It was heaped with dressing and tilting dangerously. Flushing, she quickly scraped most of the dressing back into the pan.

"Maybe you should rest. Nobody would blame you." Sister Madison laid a broad, comforting hand on Lilly's thin shoulder. "You've been a good wife and stepmother to him and Shayla. Mother Crawford often said how blessed they all were that Myron found a good woman like you after Carol died."

Lilly flinched and grabbed the long-handled spoon in the green beans. Carol again. They didn't do it out of meanness, Lilly had finally decided, but as a compliment. Carol had been a fine, Christian woman. She'd worked tirelessly in the church. She never complained or had a cross word to say. Everyone said so. Myron most of all.

"Is that plate ready, Lilly?"

Lilly went completely still for the space of two heartbeats. Hands trembling, she quickly reached for the meat fork. "In a minute, Myron."

"Brother Small has a long drive ahead of him," Myron said.

"You go on out and talk with the men, Brother Crawford. I'll bring it to you," Sister Madison offered. "I don't think Sister Crawford is feeling well."

In the small kitchen, it only took Myron a few steps to reach Lilly. Sharp brown eyes studied her face. He took the plate out of her hand. "Go rest for a while. I'm sure the other women won't mind."

Immediately there was a chorus of agreement.

"I-I'm fine," Lilly protested.

He smiled in that old familiar way that used to make her heart turn over. "You've been on your feet enough. Go rest."

The words were spoken gently, but Lilly watched his eyes. They were cold.

Quickly untying her apron, she laid it over the back of the yellow vinyl-covered chair at the table. On her way out of the room she heard several of the women heap praises on Myron about how thoughtful he was and how blessed Lilly was to have him as a husband. They praised him for being a good Christian son, for the nice way he had put his mother away. He didn't bother to correct them.

If only they knew, Lilly thought, opening their bedroom door at the end of the short hallway. Mother Crawford had paid for her own funeral arrangements, and when Myron had learned she had paid cash he had acted so hurt that she hadn't trusted him that she had gone the next day to have his name added to her checking and savings accounts. By the time Mother Crawford died there was nothing left of the money she had done without to save.

Too nervous to rest, Lilly paced the carpeted floor and watched the luminous dial on the clock radio on the nightstand. When fifteen minutes had passed she returned to the kitchen, telling the protesting women she needed to keep busy. With looks of sympathy they let her stay.

Lilly was out of bed at first light the next morning. She never lingered. Before Mother Crawford's death it had been to check on her. Now it was to escape her husband. Easing out of their bedroom, she closed the door softly and went to take her bath. Walking down the narrow hall, she wondered how had she let her life come to this? How could she have been so wrong about a man?

She had had such hopes and dreams when Myron first asked her out. That he was sixteen years older, a widower with two children aged fourteen and sixteen, had made her feel somehow special that he had chosen her.

In the town of twenty thousand, he had a good job as a short-haul truck driver, and a neat little house, and was a respected deacon in the church. In everyone's opinion he was a good catch, and for the first time in Lilly's life women envied her.

She'd grown up being referred to as "that Dawson girl," and the reference had never been good. Marva Dawson, Lilly's mother, hadn't cared what others thought of her and certainly not what they thought of her daughter. To Marva's way of thinking, her life was her own to live as she pleased. It was her turn to have some fun after what she'd suffered. Her unwanted and unplanned pregnancy with Lilly had ruined Marva's life, just as her washout of a husband had.

Johnny Dawson was supposed to be the next great Jim Brown. Instead Johnny had been cut in spring training from the New York Giants. Marva had banked heavily on him being her ticket out of Little Elm.

If she hadn't been pregnant with Lilly, Marva could have stayed in New York and used her face and figure to be an actress or find a rich man. Instead she had to come back with a disgraced jobless husband who took off to parts unknown a year later.

Unemployed, Marva had used the face and figure she was so vain about to get "her due" from other men. She had no intention of standing in line for government cheese or having some social worker look down her snooty nose at her. If one man couldn't give her the things she thought she needed, she found another.

Lilly had grown up with people talking about her mother's lifestyle and speculating on how long it would take for her to turn out the same way. The girls of the good families didn't speak to her, and the boys who asked her out were mainly interested in how fast she'd take off her clothes. Even the girls with a reputation for being fast wanted nothing to do with her. Books became her friends.

At fourteen she lied about her age to get a job at the Dairy Queen in a wasted effort to help her mother so she wouldn't have to take money from men. Marva had looked at the fifty-six dollars Lilly had proudly handed her after two weeks of work and flatly told Lilly her perfume cost more than that. Lilly hadn't offered again.

She'd met Minnie Crawford when Minnie'd gone to JC Penney to buy a hat for Women's Day at Little Elm Baptist Church. Since Penney's was one of the few places to buy ladies' hats in town and elderly black women wouldn't think of setting foot in church without their hats, Lilly had waited on several women in her first three weeks of working in ladies' accessories.

However, Minnie Crawford hadn't looked at Lilly's name tag and stuck up her nose because some man in her family had biblical knowledge of Lilly's mother. Minnie hadn't taken her merchandise to another salesperson to ring up as a few of the women had. She'd looked Lilly in the eyes and asked her if she knew the Lord. Taken aback and sure Minnie was being condescending, Lilly had flippantly replied that He wasn't on her Christmas mailing list.

She'd always remember Minnie Crawford's reply: "Doesn't matter about your mailing list. I meant in your heart. Now, how much is this hat gonna cost me?"

Befuddled, Lilly had rung up the sale, thinking that was the last of it. It wasn't. Minnie Crawford kept stopping by, and before Lilly was sure how it had happened they were having lunch at the deli in the mall, then supper at Minnie's home.

Lilly had gone to church with Mother Crawford, as she liked to be called, out of respect for her and their growing friendship. Lilly went back because of the peace she'd found there—and because of Myron.

The first time she'd seen him, handsome and tall, in his black suit, his Bible clasped to his wide chest, her heart had beaten a mile a minute. She had been so nervous, she'd had trouble getting her words out. For the first time she had been conscious of people whispering about her and hadn't cared.

Myron had taken her home after Sunday dinner at Mother Crawford's and after prayer meeting that following Wednesday night. He and Lilly easily fell into a routine of him picking her up for church services and seeing her home. Always he was respectful and nice.

After a month of Lilly and Myron being seen together, people no longer whispered or speculated if she was as free with her body as her mother. They nodded cordially. Lilly could look people in the eye, hold her head up. Each time she was with Myron, she fell in love a little more and dared to dream that he loved her in return.

Thirty-six-year-old Myron Crawford was everything her naive twenty-year-old heart had wished for. He represented all the things she had never had: love, respectability, a family, and security.

Stepping out of the tub, Lilly grabbed a towel and rubbed it briskly over her body. She'd been starved enough for affection to believe he loved her, believe he wanted to share his life with her, believe he'd give her the children that, having been a neglected child, she'd always wanted.

Hanging up the towel, she stepped into her plain white cotton underwear and hooked her bra. If Myron had felt any love for her it had disappeared fast. He'd wanted her as a caretaker for his children and a convenient bedmate. Pulling the slip over her head, she shot her arms through the shirtwaist dress. All her praying hadn't helped them to grow closer. Then Mother Crawford had suffered a stroke a year after their marriage and come to live with them.

That had been five years ago. Lilly had been trapped by her devotion and respect for the woman she had come to love dearly, a woman who had become her surrogate mother. Trapped by the two lost children who didn't understand why their mother had to die in a senseless automobile accident on her way to a meeting at the church. Trapped by her dream.

Making her way to the kitchen, she put on the coffee. Arms folded, she stared out the window at the red roses climbing the Cyclone fence in the backyard. She and Rafe had worked an entire morning on the project as a birthday surprise for Mother Crawford. Rafe, intelligent, proud, and determined to butt heads with his overbearing, tyrannical father at every turn. Rafe, the son that Myron now refused to acknowledge. The son Myron had tried to beat and cower into submission.

Rafe had stayed because Lilly begged him to finish high school, but he had never come back to the dinner she had prepared after his valedictorian speech. His leaving had broken her heart. They were too close in age for her to think of him as her son, but he was the younger brother she never had. She wished she could have done more to shield him from Myron's anger.

She'd thought many times of leaving and taking Rafe with her before Mother Crawford's stroke, but since Lilly wasn't his legal guardian, it would have been considered kidnapping. Mother Crawford might have helped, but she had a weak heart and the doctors had already warned them that too much excitement wasn't good for her.

The first light heart attack Mother Crawford ever had was caused when Rafe and Myron's argument became physical shortly after he and Lilly married. Lilly had never seen that side of Myron, mean and hateful, spewing foul words meant to hurt as much as the belt in his hand. But Rafe had refused to bow down to his father's whipping because he hadn't mowed the lawn the way Myron liked. Mother Crawford's sudden illness had stopped that argument, but others followed.

Lilly did her best to protect Rafe, and when she failed it was as if her soul were being wrenched from her body. Before long Myron's meanness killed any love and respect she had for him. She couldn't leave Rafe, no more than she could leave Mother Crawford after Rafe left home.

Lilly understood Rafe's leaving; she just missed his easy smile, his laughter, in a house that had seen too much misery and hate. He'd been back several times in the four years since his graduation to see Mother Crawford, but he'd always called first to make sure Myron wasn't there. Lilly understood that as well. After Rafe left, Myron had turned his anger against Lilly. Just hearing the sound of his voice sent fear and loathing churning through her. She tried to hide her feelings, but apparently she wasn't always successful.

Mother Crawford wasn't blind to Myron's temper, but she was powerless to do anything about it. Lilly could see in her sad eyes the pain her son's behavior caused, but it was never discussed between them. Yet whenever she heard Mother Crawford praying and asking God to touch his heart, Lilly instinctively knew she meant Myron.

Although Mother Crawford never lost faith in God's power, she made sure Lilly went to the junior college in Little Elm to further her education. Myron hadn't liked it, but in that Mother Crawford had held firm. She'd known she wouldn't be around much longer and wanted Lilly to be able to care for herself. Mother Crawford had loved her son, but she had also loved Lilly.

Just as Lilly had loved her like a mother.

Hearing the coffee dripping, Lilly opened the cabinet for a cup. She didn't know how to contact Rafe to tell him about his grandmother. Somehow she felt he knew. The two had had a way of silent communication that had been as powerful as it was beautiful. Mother Crawford would say more than once, "Rafe's gonna call," and the words would barely be out of her mouth before the telephone would ring.

Their connection was something Lilly envied. She'd never been that close to her mother, a woman who was seldom home unless she was expecting one of her men friends. Lilly had never known the father who had walked out when she was six months old and never returned.

Sipping her coffee, Lilly stared back out the window, watched a bluebird light on the fence, then fly away. Wistfully, her gaze followed. Freedom. What a wonderful thing that must be.

Lilly was at the stove tending the bacon and sausages when Myron came into the kitchen. Immediately she went to pour him a cup of coffee. "Morning."

He rubbed his large hand over his unshaven face, then sipped his coffee, syrupy with sugar and enriched with condensed canned milk. "Morning. Anyone else up?"

"David came in a few minutes earlier. Shayla's hungry," she told him. "They're staying over another couple more days." Slowly she shook her head.

"I'm so tired from caring for Mother Crawford. I wish I could just rest." The words were out of her mouth before she realized it.

He was across the kitchen and on her before she knew it, his large frame looming over her. "This was Shayla's house before it was yours. If she's hungry, you better cook her breakfast or anything else she wants."

"Good morning, Mr. Crawford," David greeted Myron from the kitchen door.

Myron swung around with a quickness that belied his six-feet-two height and 200 pounds, his posture relaxing as he did so. "Morning, David," Myron greeted him cordially. "I understand Shayla's hungry."

"Yes, sir," David said, worry in his voice and on his clean-shaven face. "She didn't eat much yesterday. I don't want her getting sick."

"Me, neither. Tell her to stay in bed today and Lilly will bring all her meals today on a tray," Myron told him.

"Thank you, sir."

Myron didn't move until David left. He turned and stared at Lilly with dark narrowed eyes. "Don't make Shayla wait too long for her breakfast. You know what she likes. Cook it fresh. You know she don't like leftovers." Her orders given, he marched away.

Lilly was at the stove before he was out of sight. Removing the bacon and sausages, she placed them on paper towels to drain.

Rage almost choked her. Rage toward Myron, but also toward herself. She had been stupid and careless.

Rafe might have been his mother's and grandmother's favorite, but Shayla was her father's. Lilly had never understood why he felt that way unless it was because his daughter expertly played on Myron's need to feel important. He never seemed to realize that when Shayla fussed over him the most, she always wanted a new dress, a new pair of shoes, or money. Unlike her self-sufficient and loving brother, Shayla was usually out for Shayla. If it didn't benefit her, she wasn't interested.

Shaking her head, Lilly took down the plates. She had to remember Myron doted on his younger child and be more careful. She had to be as smart as Rafe until she left. And as God was her witness, now that Mother Crawford was gone, Lilly was leaving Myron.

————

"That will be three hundred and fifty dollars."

Lilly's jaw dropped. She stared in disbelief across the neat wooden desk at the lawyer she had hoped would take her case. Tied and tucked in her purse was all the money she possessed in the world . . . $394.33. "I thought it would be less."

His back straight in his leather chair, Kent Powell's expression didn't change. His long-fingered hands remained loosely interlocked on top of a manila folder with Lilly's name printed on it in neat black letters. "That's my fee. If you wish to seek another attorney for counsel, you're free to do so."

Lilly's flagging spirits sank lower. She had chosen Kenneth Powell because he was fresh out of law school and new in town. She'd hoped he would be hungry for business and charge less. She'd seen his sign hanging in front of the once-vacant house and memorized his phone number. Although his fee was twenty-five dollars less than the two other lawyers she'd contacted, it was more than she had allotted.

She moistened dry lips. "Can I pay half now and send you the rest?"

"You can, but I won't start proceeding with your case until I have the full retainer."

Hands clamped around the edge of her patent-leather purse, Lilly's stomach knotted. She had to leave today. As soon as Myron had left for work that morning, she'd thrown a few clothes in Mother Crawford's old suitcase, packed some food, and paced until ten minutes before Kent Powell's law office opened.

"I don't want to go back." Her voice sounded high-pitched and frightened to her own ears.

"A restraining order doesn't cost anything."

Her head snapped up. "It would be his word against mine. The pain and scars are on the inside."

"Don't you have a friend or relative you could stay with?" he asked, leaning forward in his seat.

Lilly shook her head. Five years ago her mother had finally hit it rich with a man who owned a furniture store in Dallas. Lilly hadn't seen her since she had stopped by her house briefly to show off her diamond ring and the Mercedes he had bought her. Lilly hadn't been invited to the wedding or to their home. As for the people at church, they were Myron's friends before they were hers.

"I don't want to be here when he's served," she finally said.

"Then pay half and send the rest when you find a job."

That would be the sensible thing, but Lilly was already opening her purse and picking loose the knot in the handkerchief. She didn't want to be married to Myron one day longer than she had to be. Counting out the full amount of money, she laid it on the desk. "I want my freedom."

Powell barely glanced at the crumpled bills. "If he contests the divorce, the cost will go higher."

Despite the fear and worry, she said, "I'm getting a job as soon as I reach New Orleans."

For the first time a flicker of doubt ran across the lawyer's young face. "New Orleans can be a difficult place for people unfamiliar with it."

"My stepson is there." At least that was the last place Rafe had said he lived. The telephone operator hadn't found a listing in the phone book. But New Orleans was as good a place as any to stay until her divorce was final. Myron would never think to search for her there. And look he would. Not because he cared, but because he saw her as a possession, just like the house or his dogs.

Standing, she held out her trembling hand. "Thank you."

"You have my card to keep in touch." The handshake was brief.

"I'll call you when I'm settled."

Lilly walked from his office and got inside her car. Fear and uncertainty dogged each step.

Forty-four dollars and thirty-three cents wasn't much to reach New Orleans and start a new life, but it was all she had. Worse, finding a job to earn more would be tough. Myron had never wanted her to work after they were married. Initially he'd used the excuse that he wanted her to stay at home to get Shayla off to school and be there when she came home. In reality, he'd used it as a way of controlling Lilly and keeping her dependent on him.

Lilly had been blinded by his true nature, a nature he hid so well from others that they believed he was just a proud man. What he was, was manipulative and possessive.

But she hadn't seen that. She'd only seen that finally she had a family she could love and who would love her in return.

She had been determined to show her appreciation for Myron's faith in marrying her, to show the people of Little Elm she was a decent woman. She had succeeded in gaining respectability but failed in her marriage. She'd stayed these last miserable years because she hadn't wanted Mother Crawford to spend her last days in a nursing home.

Starting the car, Lilly put it into gear. There was one last stop she had to make.

After parking on the shoulder, she wove her way through the stone markers to the fresh mound of black dirt. A double granite marker was already in place. Minnie Faye Crawford, beloved wife and mother, would rest forever beside her husband, Effraim.

Kneeling down, Lilly placed her hand on the withered gladiolus.

"I'm sorry, Mother Crawford. I tried to make the marriage work, but I couldn't. I know you understood and tried to help me and Rafe. That terrible fight between Myron and Rafe brought on your stroke. I wish I could have spared you that heartache and pain." Tears welled in Lilly's eyes, trickled down her cheeks.

"I'm going now, but I'll never forget you. I promise, just like I promise to always love you and never forget you were the first person to love me."

Standing, she walked to her car and drove away fighting tears, fighting fear.

Chapter Two

The car died without warning.

Over the faded grayish-blue dashboard that had once been an electric, eye-popping blue, Lilly's brown eyes widened in alarm as a thin spiral of gray smoke curled from beneath the battered hood. Clutching the steering wheel, she wrestled the aged Ford onto the short-cropping of weeds beside the two-lane blacktop on the outskirts of Shreveport, Louisiana.

Her heart thumping, she watched in growing fear as the smoke blossomed into a thick black cloud. This couldn't be happening to her. It couldn't.

Damp work-worn hands clamped and unclamped around the steering wheel. Why did her life always have more misery than luck? She tried to do right. She was a good person.

In despair, she slumped back against the seat. She was still a good six-hour drive away from New Orleans. She didn't have money to fix the car. After paying the lawyer she barely had enough money to buy food and gas. Closing her eyes, she dropped her forehead onto the back of her clutched hands and fought against panic and the useless tears forming behind her lids.

No matter what, she had to stay strong. She only had herself to depend on. "You can do this, Lilly. You can do this."

Opening her eyes, she lifted her head and brushed the heel of her hand against the outer corner of her eyes. Bone-dry. Feeling steadier and a bit more in control of herself, if not the situation, she got out of the car. There was no use opening the dented hood to look at the engine; she knew next to nothing about cars.

Shielding her eyes against the hot midday sun, Lilly stared ahead of her and behind. All she saw was the black winding two-lane road bordered by dense green trees, tangled weeds among waist-high bushes, and a creek filled with murky green water that snaked beside the road.

Reaching through the open window, she took out the three-state map that connected Texas, Louisiana, and Arkansas and studied it. The blunt tip of her unpainted nail raked over Shreveport, Louisiana, then paused. Obviously she'd taken the wrong exit off the freeway for New Orleans, but she had no idea how close she was to another town.

She bit her lower lip. Reading maps was something else she wasn't good at.

"I always told you you were worth next to nothing."

Myron's often-spoken words came out of nowhere, seeping into her brain, shaking her newly emerging confidence. For a long moment, as she had always done, she drew into herself, bowing her head, accepting her husband's accusations.

A gentle breeze tugged the map in her hand, reminding her of her promise to never let him dictate to her again. Her head lifted; determination instead of defeat shone in her narrowed brown eyes. Tomorrow or the next day he'd be served with the divorce papers and she'd be one step further to having her freedom from him.

"You're wrong, Myron."

Lilly spoke aloud the words she never could say before. There had to be something in this world she was good at. God gave everyone a special gift; she just hadn't found hers yet.

So, she'd taken a wrong turn off the freeway and ended up on some back road with her car now smoking like a freight train. She was a grown woman, wasn't she? She could figure out what to do.

But nothing came to her as one hour ticked into the next. A truck passed, followed by a late-model Chevrolet with three wide-eyed children in the back. Neither slowed despite her frantic waving. Doubt tinged with an escalating fear began to creep into her mind. Glancing back down the road from which she had come, she tucked her lower lip between her teeth. Nothing.

And if another car did pass, would they stop? People weren't as quick to help strangers anymore. Woman or not.

Opening the car door, she rolled up the windows, then slung the narrow black strap of her purse over her shoulder and locked the car. She'd do what she had done most of her life: rely on herself.

Without further hesitation, she began walking the way she had come. At least that way she knew she'd eventually reach a service station. If she continued, she wasn't so sure.

Less than two miles down the road she glimpsed the red slate roof of a house peeking through towering oak trees. With excitement rushing through her, her pace increased. When she stood in front of the wide arms of an intricately scrolled black iron entry gate, she realized why she hadn't seen the mansion when she passed. The two-story house sat at least 500 feet from the road at the arch of the curve. Her attention had been on maneuvering the sharp turn, not her surroundings.

Nestled beneath moss-draped oaks, the immense home was breathtaking. A balcony ran the length of the second floor. To Lilly it looked like something out of a movie of days gone by when the plantation owner took his ease while the slaves worked the fields.

As she walked closer, she saw that the house had a stucco exterior and was painted a pale yellow with white trim. Chastising herself for her wayward imagination, she continued up the tree-lined path. Her mother had always said she kept her head in too many books. But books had been her salvation then and now. Closer, she realized the house hadn't been here in the 1800s and the owners were probably very friendly toward black people.

But what if they weren't? Her steps slowed. She hadn't dealt with many rich people, black or white. In Little Elm the teachers and the funeral home owners were the rich black people and, although they went to work every day, they were in a different social group from Lilly and her truck-driving husband. She couldn't imagine the owner of this place having a nine-to-five job or worries about the mortgage.

Stepping off the paved road onto the thick green grass, Lilly cut across the yard to the back of the house. Some people didn't like the hired help or service people coming to the front door. She wasn't either, but she wasn't an invited guest, either. One thing Lilly knew was how to keep her place. Another lesson courtesy of Myron.

Rounding the corner of the house, she pulled up short. Two well-dressed black women stood at the bottom of the wooden steps leading into a side entrance to the house. They were deep in conversation. The older woman was of average height and appeared to be in her late fifties. She wore a cream-colored blouse and pants. Her stylishly short reddish-brown hair complemented her attractive cinnamon-hued skin. She kept wiping the corners of her eyes with a white handkerchief.

The younger woman's lips were pressed together as if she fought her own battle with tears. Model-thin and a head taller than the other woman, she wore a sleeveless black shell and trousers. Silver hoop earrings twisted with each movement of her head. Smooth bangs brushed the slim arch of her brows. The rest of her bone-straight hair fell to the middle of her back.

Behind them the screen door burst open. Both women turned. Out came a tall, beautiful woman in her early thirties wearing a tangerine-colored linen pantsuit.

The door banged shut. The wind had picked up, carrying with it the scent of magnolias, but Lilly didn't think it had caused the door to slam.

"He's impossible!" cried the woman coming down the white-painted steps.

The older woman clutched the handkerchief tighter. "Nicole, he still insists we leave?"

"Yes, Mrs. Wakefield." The answer was clipped and final.

Mrs. Wakefield's head lowered.

Wide-eyed, the youngest woman stared from one to the other, then back toward the door. "But we can't leave."

"Try telling that to Adam, Kristen," Nicole said, folding her arms, her heavily lashed eyelids blinking rapidly, her magenta glossed lips tightly compressed.

Mrs. Wakefield's mouth curved upward in a strained smile; then she took Kristen's agitated hand in hers. "Don't worry. We'll find a way."

"How?" Kristen cried.

The women traded glances, but none spoke.

"Excuse me. Maybe I can help," Lilly offered before she thought better of interfering.

Three pairs of startled eyes turned to her. Fear quickly gave way to other emotions in their faces. Kristen's was weary, Nicole's suspicious, Mrs. Wakefield's curious.

"Who are you and what are you doing here?" Nicole asked, stepping forward.

Lilly clamped her hands together to keep from retreating. This wasn't Myron using his size to intimidate and abuse for the simple reason that he could. This woman had a right to demand answers. Trespassing was bad enough, but Lilly had compounded her bad manners by eavesdropping as well.

"Lilly. Lilly Crawford. My car broke down about two miles from here. This is the first house I passed, and I wanted to see if anyone could help or if I could use the phone."

"Of course." The older woman visibly relaxed. "I'm Eleanor Wakefield. This is my daughter, Kristen. Ms. Ashe is a family friend." The nods of acknowledgment were brief. "Samuel, the groundskeeper, is off, but you can certainly use the phone."

"Thank you."

"I'll show you where it is," offered Kristen, quickly bounding up the four steps and opening the door.

Lilly clamped her hand around the frayed strap of her purse and pushed the words out. "I–I couldn't help but overhear some of your conversation." She knew what it was like to feel helpless and without anywhere to go or turn. The women looked as if they were well off, but she was a living testament on how looks could be deceiving. "If I can get my car started and you need a lift into town, you're welcome to come with me."

Surprise flittered across Mrs. Wakefield's face; then it was gone, to be replaced by a warm smile that erased the lines of strain bracketing her mouth. "Thank you, Ms. Crawford, but that won't be necessary."

Now it was Lilly's turn to be surprised. It was a rarity for anyone to address her as "Ms.," let alone her betters. Nodding, Lilly went up the steps after Kristen.

The house was as magnificent on the inside as it was on the outside. Yellow was here, too, but the mellow color of butter was mixed with the palest blue and green. Highly polished oak floors gleamed beneath the worn soles of Lilly's sturdy flat black shoes. Persian rugs were scattered throughout. Tall, wide windows were draped in blue silk.

Beautiful antique furniture, crystal lamps, and brass accents gave the home an air of subdued elegance and warmth. Picture-perfect. It would be like living in a little corner of heaven to stay in a place like this. She briefly wondered if the man the women seemed afraid of appreciated the beauty of his home.

"Here's the phone. The yellow pages should be underneath."

"Thank you." Squatting, Lilly opened the door of the cherry drum stand and pulled out the telephone book. Standing, she heard the back door close. Her shoulders stiffened. Myron had taught her early to avoid confrontations at all costs. She quickly began flipping the pages. Nicole had looked at Lilly as if she had crawled on her belly out of the slimy water that pooled in the ditch along the road. Lilly wanted to be gone as much as the other woman apparently wanted her gone.

Lilly's hand paused. What was she doing? She didn't have the money to pay for towing or repair. She'd hoped she'd find someone to help fix the car.

"Is there a problem?" Kristen asked, her pencil-thin brows furrowed.

"No." Turning away from the concern in the young woman's heart-shaped face, Lilly flipped another page. Lying was easier than telling the truth.

"Excuse me, then."

"Yes. Sure." She watched Kristen join her mother and Nicole in an adjoining room with a high ceiling and lined draperies that arched over the windows and pooled on the oak floor. It wasn't lost on Lilly that Nicole had positioned herself by the oak fireplace mantel so that she could see Lilly. She might be poor, but no one had ever questioned her honesty . . . until now.

Realizing she couldn't stand forever in the hall, she picked out a random garage number and dialed. If the towing cost was too high, she'd . . .

Her eyes shut. She had no idea what she'd do. She couldn't sleep in the car, not on a back road leading to who knew where.

She berated herself as she opened her eyes and punched in another number. Why hadn't she planned better? Why did she always make a complete mess of things?

"Did you decide what we are going to do?" Kristen asked as soon as she reached her mother.

"No, dear," Mrs. Wakefield answered, worry clear in her cultured voice. "We can't just leave him."

"Don't worry. Adam won't be alone," Mrs. Wakefield promised. "If he doesn't want us, I'll find someone else to look after him."

"How will we do that on such short notice?" Kristen sought reassurance as she always had. She was twenty years old and still unsure of herself despite being eight weeks away from graduation from Stanford with a degree in art history.

"Jonathan may be able to help find a companion for Adam," Mrs. Wakefield said, her attractive face thoughtful. It was up to her to keep the family together. "After all, Adam only needs a minimum amount of help with food preparation and cleaning his room. However, it will have to be someone who is completely trustworthy, someone who won't make him feel worse about his condition, and, of course, someone who is willing to live in."

"Finding someone to live here won't be a problem," Nicole said, glancing around the lavishly decorated room. "Adam has made this place a showcase. The problem will be keeping them."

"I know Adam has been difficult, but he has cause," Kristen defended hotly. "I get angry just thinking about what they did to him."

"I didn't say he didn't have reasons. But while we have an emotional connection to Adam, anyone we hire won't," Nicole replied. "People don't have the loyalty they used to have for their employer." She wrinkled her pert nose. "I know. They quit faster at my temp agency than I can hire new ones to replace them."

"Nicole's right, Kristen. We love Adam no matter what." Mrs. Wakefield laid a comforting hand on her daughter's rigid arm. "We love him now more than ever. We feel his pain as if it were our own. If we can't get a person to stay out of commitment to doing a good job, we'll have to offer them a financial incentive. For a thousand dollars a week, they shouldn't care if Adam is a bit cross with them."

The phone slipped from Lilly's hand, crashing down on the cradle and almost knocking over a small floral arrangement of sweet peas. She grabbed the phone and steadied the heavy cut-crystal vase.

Once again she found herself the focus of the three women's questioning gazes.

"I—I didn't mean to overhear your conversation," she stammered. "But . . . but I'm looking for a job. I'm dependable and hardworking, and since my car clunked, you don't have to worry about me leaving," she said, trying to make a joke out of the last comment, but none of the women smiled.

Since they hadn't said no, Lilly kept talking, "Up until a week ago, when she passed on, I took care of a woman after her stroke for five years. She was partially paralyzed on the left side, so I bathed her, read to her, took her for walks, her appointments, did her physical therapy. Dr. Mason always said I was the best caregiver he'd ever seen. I'm sure I could do a good job." She prayed she didn't sound as desperate as she was.

"We don't know anything about you," Nicole pointed out dismissively.

"She did offer to help us when she thought we needed it," Mrs. Wakefield said thoughtfully. "That showed a caring nature."

Nicole gaped, staring at the older woman in disbelief. "You can't honestly be considering her for the job?"

"We need someone immediately, and since she's here, why not let Adam decide?"

Nicole crossed her arms over her generous breasts. "He'll toss her out the same way he did us."

Mrs. Wakefield threw an irritated glance at Nicole, then crossed to Lilly. "Perhaps we should sit down and I can tell you about my son."

Lilly's eyes widened. "Your son owns this place!"

"Yes," Mrs. Wakefield answered, glancing around the high-ceilinged room as she led Lilly to the Chippendale sofa. "He bought it about five years ago. Although he's been back only occasionally, he always said he loved the beauty and peacefulness he found here."

Gingerly Lilly sat on the blue-green- and white-striped cushion, careful not to disturb the tapestry accent pillow by her elbow. "I can see why he'd never tire of being here. Everywhere you look there's beauty. Both inside and out."

Mrs. Wakefield's body jerked.

Nicole glared.

Kristen tucked her lower lip between her teeth.

"I'm sorry; did I say something wrong?" Lilly asked, apprehension sweeping through her: *Don't mess this up, Lilly. You need this job.*

"It's not your fault. You couldn't have known." Hands folded in her lap, her legs crossed sedately at the ankles, Mrs. Wakefield drew a deep breath as if fortifying herself and said, "Because of the senseless greed of others, Adam lost his sight."

"He's blind?" Lilly blurted.

"Oh, goodness." Nicole threw Lilly a look filled with derision and sank gracefully into a side chair. "I can see she's going to be fabulous."

Lilly flushed under the censure of the other woman. "I–I thought he was just sick." She gave her attention to Mrs. Wakefield. "If you're his mother, he can't be that old."

"He celebrated his thirty-eighth birthday just weeks before it happened."

Twelve years older than she was, yet he had accomplished so much while she had done nothing. Had nothing to show for her years but a broken-down car and a few pieces of clothes. "This must be hard on all of you."

"It is," Mrs. Wakefield admitted and leaned back in her seat. "Worse because it didn't have to happen. Adam stopped at a red light and two men ran up to his car and demanded he give them the keys. When he refused they pulled him from the car and severely beat and kicked him." Hands trembling, her voice unsteady, Mrs. Wakefield visibly fought to continue.

"If you'd rather not go on, I understand." Lilly understood pain and despair.

"No, it's all right," Mrs. Wakefield said, her voice noticeably stronger. "You have to understand the kind of person Adam was to not think too badly of how this has affected him. One brutal act changed not only his life but also those of hundreds of others."

"My brother was a well-known neurosurgeon specializing in head trauma injuries." Kristen sat down on the curved arm of the sofa by her mother. "He had a thriving practice and was sought after by several hospitals across the country. But no matter how tired or how busy he was, he always had time for me and Mother."

"Adam takes his responsibilities seriously," Mrs. Wakefield said, pride in her voice.

Nicole's expression thoughtful, she said, "Month by month his reputation grew. He was interviewed the day before the accident by the Associated Press. When asked what about his life he'd change, he said, 'Nothing. It is perfect.' "

Another silence stretched across the room until it was broken by Mrs. Wakefield. "The doctors aren't sure if the blindness is temporary or permanent. The X rays and other tests indicate a great deal of hemorrhaging. We're hopeful that, once the hemorrhage dissolves, Adam's sight will return to normal. If the doctors attempt to operate and remove the hemorrhage there is the possibility of causing other complications, including permanent loss of sight. The doctors thought it best to see if the hemorrhage will dissolve on its own."

"How long will that take?" Lilly asked, trying to figure out how long she'd have the job . . . if she got it.

The women traded worried glances again before Mrs. Wakefield answered, "At first they thought two to three weeks."

Lilly was almost afraid to voice the next question: "And now?"

Mrs. Wakefield reached up and clutched her daughter's hand. "They aren't sure. It's been almost five weeks and there's been no change in his sight."

Lilly wanted to ask Mrs. Wakefield if she thought the blindness could be permanent but didn't. From the worry in her face and the faces of the other women in the room, they were already dealing with that possibility.

"Adam is understandably having some difficulties adjusting," Mrs. Wakefield continued. "His medical training makes it more difficult, not easier. He's used to being active. Waiting has never been his strong suit. Now that's all he can do."

"Sometimes that's all any of us can do," Lilly murmured, thinking of her own problems. She'd waited and bided her time to leave Myron.

Mrs. Wakefield stood. "This way." At the foot of the stairs, she stopped and faced Lilly. "Adam's room is the third door on the right-hand side. He may not give you permission to enter, but go in anyway. I'd take you up, but my presence seems to upset him."

"Mother Crawford had bad days, too." Lilly felt compelled to try to ease the other woman's burden.

"Your mother?" Mrs. Wakefield questioned.

Lilly started to explain, then changed her mind. In every way that counted, Mother Crawford had been her mother. "Yes." Turning, she started to climb the stairs.

"Ms. Crawford?"

"Yes." Lilly paused, her hand wrapped around the mahogany newel cap.

"Adam is a wonderful man," Mrs. Wakefield said, Kristen and Nicole on either side of her. "But he's used to having his orders obeyed. Being thwarted is not something he takes easily. He's striking out because he's angry at what's happened to him. Please remember that."

Not sure of how to answer, Lilly nodded and continued up the spiral staircase, her hand sliding over the smooth polished wood railing. With each step she fought the trembling in her body.

Remembered thoughts of Myron towering over her, his rage-filled face inches from hers, caused her stomach muscles to knot. A man could do a lot of damage with a cane. She hadn't seen any bruises on Mrs. Wakefield or the other women. Maybe she meant "striking out" figuratively. Or maybe they were good at ducking.

Wiping her sweating palms on her dress, Lilly stopped in front of the third door. Taking a deep breath, she lifted her hand and knocked.

"Dr. Wakefield. Your mother sent me. May I come in?"

"Dammit. Leave me alone."

Lilly jumped at the venom in the deep voice. "Dr. Wakefield, I want to help."

"Didn't you hear me? Go away."

She'd like nothing better, but that choice had been taken from her when her car died. Following Mrs. Wakefield's instructions, Lilly twisted the brass knob and slowly opened the door and entered.

She barely stifled a gasp. The room was in chaos. Chairs were overturned. Food littered the floor. And standing in the midst by the foot of the king-size four-poster, head bowed and his right hand clutching one of the thick, spiral-turned posts, was Dr. Adam Wakefield.

He was tall and elegantly built. The fingers holding the post were long and tapered. His body was lean, conditioned.

The hair on his head was shaggy and black. He sported an unkempt beard of the same color. His gray silk shirt and linen pants were stained and wrinkled. In no way did he appear to be a prominent doctor, related to the two immaculately dressed women downstairs, or owner of this beautiful house. He looked defeated, lost.

How many times had Lilly stood with her head down, misery pounding at her from all sides?

To have so much and then to have it taken from you because of the senseless cruelty of others would fill anyone with rage and despair. Hadn't she felt the same way after Myron had done a number on her? Empathy swept through her.

Abruptly his head snapped up, then tilted, paused, moved only to repeat the jerk–pause motion over and over as he moved his head in a semicircle around the room. Gold-rimmed shades were perched on his aquiline nose.

"Who's there?"

Lilly took a small step forward. "My name's Lilly Crawford. Your mother said I should come in. She wants to hire me to sit with you if it's agreeable wi—"

"Get out!"

She jumped, tucking her head as she had always done when faced with conflict. Then she remembered again her disabled car and little money. Her head came up; she took another halting step farther into the room.

"Please, Dr. Wakefield. I need this job. I've taken care of ill peo—"

"I'm not ill. I don't need you," he said, cutting her off once again.

"I could keep your room clean and make sure you eat," she said, her words as desperate as her face. "I promise to stay out of your way."

"I don't want you or anyone else here!"

"Please, I have nowhere else to go. I could read to you, take you on walks. I promise—"

"If you won't get out, I'll throw you out!" he threatened and started for her.

Lilly instinctively shrank back, throwing up her arms. A cry of rage caused her to jerk her arms away from her face. Adam lay sprawled on the floor. His left foot and leg were hooked over the claw-and-ball leg of an overturned armchair.

"Why! Dammit. Why?" he shouted, pounding his fist repeatedly against the area rug.

Forgetting her fear, Lilly rushed to untangle his leg. She set the chair upright, then reached for his arm. "Let me—"

Adam snatched his arm away, came to his knees, and planted both hands firmly on the floor. Head down, his lean body trembled; his breath rushed out over his lips as if he had been running. His shades lay on the floor. "I don't need your help."

"I'm sor—"

"Get out," he ordered, finally turning his face to hers.

She cowered from the rage she saw there. Then she saw his eyes, black as onyx but with none of its brilliance or fire. They were . . . lifeless. The dramatic contrast caused her throat to dry. The full depth of what had been taken from him slowly sank into her. In that instant Adam Wakefield became a person instead of a job.

"I'm sorry. So sorry," she whispered, her voice unsteady. "How could anyone be so cruel?"

His shaggy head snapped back. His right hand lifted toward sightless eyes, stopped inches away, then curled into a fist. "I don't need your pity. Just leave me alone."

The soul-deep misery in his voice shook her as few things had. And she had put it there just as Myron had done so many times to her. Coming to her feet, she backed away, then turned and ran. From him. From herself.

Fumbling with the doorknob, she finally opened the door and raced down the hall. Rushing toward her were the three women and a distinguished-looking black man with wings of silver in his closely cropped black hair.

"What happened?" Mrs. Wakefield asked frantically.

Lilly moistened her lips. Guilt weighed heavily on her thin shoulders. "He—he tripped over a chair."

Mrs. Wakefield gasped and pressed the trembling fingers of both hands against the lower half of her face.

"Was he hurt? Did he hit his head?" the man asked. The drawl in his deep, authoritarian voice demanded an answer.

"No. I–I'm sorry. Forgive me."

Her back against the wall, Lilly quickly eased past them, then turned to run down the stairs and out the front door.

Chapter Three

On bended knees Adam found his glasses and slipped them on, then felt the cool, tufted cushioned seat of the winged leather chair that had tripped him. It was lying on the floor because he'd tripped over it earlier. She must have righted it. *Bully for her!* he sneered, coming unsteadily to his feet.

Could she possibly imagine how degrading it felt to flounder around, tripping over the slightest obstacle, while people stared at you as if you were on exhibit? No, she couldn't. No sighted person could. All she wanted was a job. Well, he didn't need anyone. He'd be fine until Samuel and Odette returned on Monday.

He had to be.

In the past he had always been able to overcome any obstacle he set his mind to, achieve any goal. He could do it again.

His anger turned inward. Why hadn't he given them the keys to the damn car? He'd just finished an emergency surgery on a young man with massive head trauma. Going in, the college student had had less than a 5 percent chance of survival. He might have been in a coma for the rest of his life. Thankfully, Adam's skill and that of his team had lengthened the odds. Once the marathon seven-hour surgery was over, the man's condition remained critical, but his chance of survival with normal brain function had increased dramatically.

When the unkempt man had come out of nowhere at a stoplight, Adam had first thought he was looking for a handout, a common occurrence in the San Francisco area. Adam had watched the man approach without apprehension. The night had been mild and Adam had the window down on the Porsche, unwinding with a Billie Holiday CD.

When he realized what was happening, he'd been tired enough after being at the hospital for almost twenty hours to tell the man and the one who suddenly appeared by his side to jerk off.

Adam would never forget the chilling sound of the windshield glass shattering. He'd thrown up his hands to protect his eyes. He had succeeded then. But he hadn't been able to protect them from steel-toed boots and fists.

His hands clenched. In one stupid, arrogant moment he had jeopardized everything he had worked most of his life to accomplish. He worried that the hemorrhage wasn't clearing up as fast as any of them had thought it would. But more so he was worried about possible damage to the optic nerve.

If the optic nerve was damaged, his blindness was permanent. He'd remain in a hell he had helped make.

Taking a sliding step, he felt the sole of his shoe smear across something soft and grimaced. Eggs from breakfast or mashed potatoes from lunch? He couldn't even feed himself without making a mess. He was as helpless as an infant. To urinate he had to almost get on his knees. Every waking moment of his life was filled with humiliation. Why couldn't they understand how it degraded him for the people he loved, people who had always seen him at his best, to see him at his worst?

The bedroom door opened. He pivoted. His hand connected sharply with metal. Frantically he grabbed for the object, only to hear it crash to the floor. Immediately he knew what it was: the solid brass trumpet lamp he had been so happy to find at an estate sale. His anger soared. It wasn't important. He'd find another reading lamp once his sight returned.

He straightened. "Enjoying the sideshow?"

"If you weren't blind, I'd knock you to hell and back," answered a heavily accented male voice that was just as biting as Adam's. "What if it had been your mother?"

His anger still high, Adam didn't back down. Jonathan Delacroix might be his godfather and a lifelong friend, but at the moment he was another reminder of what Adam had lost. "Get out, Jonathan."

"I'm staying."

Stalemate. Jonathan weighed in at 200 pounds and stood six-feet-two. He lifted weights to stay in shape. He was as solid as the trunk of an oak, and just as immovable if he wished to be.

In growing frustration, Adam ran his hand over his head and felt an inch of hair at the nape of his neck. He needed a haircut. Damn, he needed so much and was so helpless. His hand fisted. "Can't any of you understand? If I wanted company, I wouldn't have chartered a private plane to bring me here."

"It's a good thing you and your mother have the same travel agent and that she contacted her," Jonathan said, the words followed by a thudding sound.

Adam turned toward the sound. Another chair righted, probably the Chippendale armchair by the reading table. Leather creaked. Jonathan's heavy weight settling into the seat. Adam knew Jonathan had made both sounds on purpose. There wasn't a clumsy bone in his body. He might resemble a linebacker for the Forty-niners, but there the resemblance ended. His gentleness and concern for his OB-GYN patients was almost legendary.

He was one of the finest doctors Adam knew. In the operating room, there was no hesitation, only precise, swift movements that amazed and awed those seeing Jonathan's large hands do such delicate work for the first time.

The unnecessary noise had been his way of making Adam aware of where he was. Talking to where you thought the person was, was another reason Adam didn't like being around people. Still, he wasn't in a mood to forgive the man he had looked up to and admired for as long as he could remember.

"My ex–travel agent. She won't get any more of my business when I start traveling again." He'd see again and when he did he'd find another agency. It was just a matter of time before the hemorrhage dissolved.

"I'm sure her concern wasn't monetary, Adam," Jonathan told him. "A great many people think highly of you and sympathize with what you're going through."

Adam's lips curved into a snarl. "They pity me."

"A few."

Adam's hand clamped heavily on the back of the leather chair. Those who didn't pity him felt uncomfortable in his presence. They'd tried. He'd tried.

But sooner or later a word would slip out and a thick pervading silence would hang in the room. A word he no longer could associate with. *See.*

He couldn't *see* the game, *see* to read the article in the medical journal, *see* a beautiful woman, *see* the curb.

He'd never noticed before how, in even casual conversation, gestures and expressions conveyed just as much as words. He was as lost in carrying on a normal conversation as he was lost in a world of darkness.

And it was all his own fault.

"I was about to lie down. I'm sure you'll understand if I don't show you the way out."

Jonathan's weight settled heavier in the chair. "Eleanor says you haven't been out of this room since you arrived three days ago. What do you say we go for a walk and get some fresh air?"

"I'm fine," Adam snapped, then said more calmly, "I'm just tired." If they realized the real reason he didn't want to leave his room, he'd never get rid of them.

"That's debatable."

"I appreciate your concern, but it's unnecessary."

Adam moved in front of the chair, guiding himself by the back of his knees against the edge of the seat. His hand securely on the arm of the chair, he sat down, then pressed his back firmly against the cushion. In the past he'd always liked space and the ability to move freely. Now it made him feel helpless and lost. "Please tell Mother not to bother with dinner."

"You aren't fooling anyone, Adam, and I think it's time the kid gloves came off."

Adam stiffened, a sense of foreboding creeping over him. The reasons Jonathan was such a good doctor were his unshakable concern for others, his dogged determination to help those in need, and his keen intelligence. Once committed, he was unshakable. "What are you talking about?"

"Your stubborn refusal to listen to reason," Jonathan told him. "You have to realize that there is no way you can stay here by yourself."

"Odette and Samuel will be back Monday." Adam tried to get his tense body to relax and his voice to sound normal. He knew he accomplished neither.

"Today is Thursday," Jonathan said.

From the closeness of his voice and the faint whiff of the spicy Oriental cologne he always wore, Adam knew Jonathan had stood and moved closer. His nearness was oddly menacing.

"What," Adam's godfather finally continued, "do you plan to do in the meantime?"

"I'll manage." Somehow he had to.

"I'm looking at the way you've managed for the past three days. Not only is this room in shambles; you're in pretty much the same condition. You need a haircut, a shave, clean clothes."

The painful words were like a slap in Adam's face. It took all of his control to remain seated. Giving full vent to his anger and coming to his feet to defend himself might make him feel better . . . until he stumbled over some object and proved Jonathan right.

Adam's fingernails dug into the soft leather armrest. "If I offend you so much, leave."

"If I didn't care about you and your family I would, but I do and you're stuck with me." Jonathan's sigh was long and deep and filled with frustration. "I was there with your father the night you were born. I watched you grow into a man to be proud of. You're the son that I never had. You've been hurt and it's not my intention to hurt you more, but I will if you leave me no choice."

"Stay out of my life, Jonathan."

The older man continued as if Adam hadn't spoken. "If you insist on staying here by yourself I have a lawyer ready to start proceedings to declare you incompetent."

Fear came first, almost choking Adam before reasoning intervened. He eased back in his chair, dismissing the threat with a negligent wave of his long-fingered hand. "You'd need Mother's permission and she'd never give it."

"Don't bet on it, Adam. She'd fight until her last breath to keep you from the slightest harm, whether that harm was caused by you or another source."

Jonathan's deep bass voice grew quieter, yet infinitely more terrifying. "Insisting you stay by yourself in this huge house is insane. How the hell do you plan to find your way downstairs to the kitchen when you can't find your way around this room? What would you do if you were to fall and seriously injure yourself? I tell you what you'd do: not a damn thing, because you couldn't see how, and that's exactly what I plan to tell your mother."

Rage mixed with fear propelled Adam to his feet. "You bastard!"

"Never said I wasn't," Jonathan said calmly. "Your mother is outside this room worried to death. I don't care what you think of me, but she's suffered enough. She's not eating and Kristen tells me she's not sleeping."

"Once she returns to San Francisco, she'll be fine," Adam said, aware of his mother's concern yet unable to reassure her. How could he when fear was his constant companion just as guilt was?

"You don't believe that lie any more than I do. Your mother hasn't ever been nor will she ever be that shallow. She loves with all her heart. And now her heart is breaking because of you."

A heavy weight on his chest, Adam slumped back in his chair. He and his mother had always been close. His father had been a busy gastroenterologist and raising Adam and Kristen had fallen to their mother. She'd never faltered or complained. Losing her husband, their father, five years ago was hard enough on her. Now this.

"I don't want her here."

"I can understand your reasoning, Adam." Jonathan's voice gentled. "Eleanor probably understands it, too. All she wants is to be sure you're taken care of. How that's accomplished is up to you."

Adam's head came up, hope surging through him. "Then why put her through a painful court battle?"

"You're slicing her apart. What's one more cut?"

Adam flinched. His mother loved deeply and completely. She was fond of telling one and all that her children were her greatest accomplishments. And she'd walk through fire for him and Kristen.

Head bowed, Adam braced both arms on his thighs; his wrists and arms dangled over his knees. "How long will it take to hire someone?"

"I don't know."

Adam was already shaking his head. He wanted the women gone today. Especially Nicole. Each time he heard her voice, the shame and humiliation of that night he came home from the hospital and they went to bed together came rushing back. "There was a woman just here."

"She left running."

"Find her; then all of you can leave."

"Aren't you forgetting one thing?"

Adam's mouth flattened into a hard, narrow line. "Please."

Jonathan laughed, a robust, hearty sound that easily rolled from his deep chest. "That was nice, but unnecessary. I'm used to your high-handed way of ordering other people around. Comes from being the top in your field."

Adam flinched again. Once he had been the best. *Once.* No more.

"I meant, aren't you forgetting the young woman may not want to come back?" Jonathan explained.

"Then you'll have to convince her otherwise, won't you?"

Adam couldn't see the smile on Jonathan's ebony-hued face but heard it in his voice. "I guess so."

Their questions tripping over one another, the women swarmed around him as soon as he closed the door to Adam's room.

"Is he all right?" Eleanor asked, pushing ahead of her daughter and Nicole.

"Did he hurt himself?" Kristen asked, her eyes teary.

"Can I go in?" Nicole wanted to know.

Jonathan's gaze stayed on Eleanor. Hope, fear, desperation shimmered in her deep amber-colored eyes. He'd give anything, do anything, to keep the hope alive.

"We'll talk downstairs."

"Jon—"

"Downstairs." Jonathan glanced meaningfully behind him to the closed door.

Without another word, Eleanor turned and headed downstairs, her heels clicking rhythmically against the hardwood floor. She had never been a patient woman, less when it came to those she loved.

In two long strides Jonathan caught up with her, his large hand closing around her upper arm. She never slowed or indicated in any way that she was aware of his touch. His fingers flexed out of his own perverse need for her to acknowledge him. The need no longer annoyed or disgusted him; it simply was.

The glance she threw him was impatient at best, but for the moment it was enough. His fingers relaxed, but not before he noted the fragility of the bones beneath the silk blouse she wore. His brows bunched as they started down the carpeted staircase.

Eleanor's once-svelte body had gently rounded as the years and the births of two children altered her shape. To him the change added depth and dimensions to her maturity, not detracting from it. He could still easily sweep her off her feet if the occasion arose, still admire the easy sway of her hips. What bothered him was her not taking care of herself. Mentioning it now would only be a waste of time. Her every thought was on Adam, her firstborn.

"Well?" she asked, rounding on Jonathan the instant she reached the bottom of the stairs.

"The living room." Steering her in that direction, he led her to the sofa. "Sit down, Eleanor. Please."

With ill-concealed grace she sat, then crossed her ankles and clasped her hands, preparing herself for the worst. For a brief moment he stared at the thumb of her right hand absently rubbing the diamond-encrusted wedding band on her left hand. For a futile moment he wished she had reached for him.

Feeling every one of his fifty-nine years, Jonathan moved to the oak fireplace across the room. He stared at the woman he had always loved and could never have. "Adam will let the woman stay."

As Eleanor briefly shut her eyes, her shoulders slumped; her head fell forward. "Thank God."

Across from Eleanor, Nicole, her beautiful face a picture of disbelief, surged to her feet. She was tall, elegant, and, at the moment, enraged. "He can't do that!"

Jonathan dispassionately studied the beautifully polished woman in her early thirties. Not an auburn hair was out of place. She had flawless almond-hued skin and soulful hazel eyes. Once again he wondered why Adam never mentioned her name anymore. "It's his decision and he wants me to bring her back here."

"You can't seriously be considering letting that woman stay," Nicole retorted. "We know absolutely nothing about her. You can't forget she caused him to fall."

"Adam did that to himself," Jonathan said. He shifted his gaze to Eleanor. He'd expected Nicole's disapproval and outrage. Eleanor's opinion was the only one that mattered. "Even with my contacts in the medical profession, hiring another person on such short notice would be difficult."

"*We* could stay." Nicole glanced at Kristen for agreement.

Kristen, standing by the window, wrapped her arms around her waist. "It's Adam's decision."

Nicole's hazel eyes glinted; the lush, sensual mouth flattened in annoyance. "Adam hasn't been making the best decisions in the past weeks."

Kristen's slim body tensed. She stared at her mother as Jonathan knew she would. Adam was the strong, independent son; Kristen, the tender-hearted daughter who remained unsure of herself. Asthma as a child coupled with an overprotective family hadn't given her the opportunity to find her way as healthy, robust Adam had. Losing her father when she was fifteen had left her floundering even more. Just as she was beginning to come into her own, the brother she worshipped had to learn a hard lesson about invincibility. Regrettably, she had to learn with him.

"Uncle Jon?" Kristen asked, finally bringing her troubled gaze to him.

Despite his own doubts, Jonathan smiled. She'd been three years old when she announced to him and her family that she wanted him to belong to her, too, just like he did to Adam. From that day on he was "Uncle Jon." He loved her fiercely. "I'd say it's about time for Adam to get one right."

The small smile that flittered around Kristen's mouth was worth hearing the inelegant snort from Nicole. Sitting down in the overstuffed wing chair, she crossed her long legs and swung her right foot impatiently.

From what Adam had told Jonathan, Nicole wasn't the type of woman who liked losing at anything. She was a self-made woman. With a college scholarship to Old Miss she'd been able to shake poverty and the red clay of Mississippi from her bare feet, and now she wore three-hundred-dollar shoes and thousand-dollar designer suits. Nannette became Nicole. She owned a successful temporary employment service in Marin County specializing in office skills.

She and Adam had been together six months before he was injured. With their busy schedules, he'd said they suited each other perfectly. The arrangement had sounded businesslike rather than loving to Jonathan, who, given a choice, would want the woman he loved with him even if it wasn't convenient.

But Adam had never been the romantic, sentimental type. Neither, apparently, was Nicole. Their loose relationship had suited them . . . until he lost his sight.

"You can go if you want," Nicole announced, her small nose tilted upward. "But I'm not leaving."

"Yes, and each time you go into Adam's room you send him deeper into depression," Jonathan bluntly told her.

Eleanor made a low, tortured sound of distress, but even so, it caught Jonathan's attention. Long strides quickly took him to her. Sitting beside her on the sofa, he gently took her soft, cold left hand into his large ones, inadvertently covering the wedding band. "Adam is a proud man."

"His father and I raised him that way." Eleanor managed a weak smile, her other hand coming to rest on top of their joined ones. "You helped."

Jonathan nodded. "That I did. He learned to go after and fight for what he wanted in life, but this time he's up against something he can't fight."

"He has to realize we don't think less of him," Kristen said.

"Kristen, he thinks less of himself," Jonathan told the young woman softly. He wished he could make this easier for all of them. "There's never been anything Adam set his mind to do that he couldn't do, and he looked good while he was doing it. He doesn't now, and he's aware of it more than you or I could ever be."

Folding her arms tightly, Kristen stared down at her leopard-print sandals. "It's my fault he left Sausalito. If I hadn't told him I was going to change my plans and spend my spring break with him, he wouldn't have come here."

"Kristen, please don't blame yourself," her mother said. "We all did what we thought best for him, and it's not working."

"I don't want him hurt anymore." Kristen rubbed the heel of her palm across her eyes. "If having that woman is what he wants, then that's what has to be done. Please go bring her back."

"Yes, bring her back," Mrs. Wakefield agreed, finally pulling her hands free from Jonathan's.

Nicole was standing on her Italian slingback heels in seconds. "You can't do that! What's to keep her from leaving Adam or looting the place?" Her slim arm gestured around the antique-filled room. "Some pieces in this room are priceless."

"I value Adam more."

Nicole gasped, a tiny, horrified sound.

"I'm sorry if that came out badly, Nicole. I realize this has been difficult for you as well. You care for him, too, but I feel hiring Ms. Crawford, at least temporarily, may be best at the moment," Mrs. Wakefield reasoned. "As she pointed out, her car doesn't run, so she could hardly leave."

"With the salary you plan to pay her, repairing her car or buying a new one shouldn't be a problem." Unrelenting, arms folded, Nicole remained stiff with indignation and disapproval.

Eleanor nodded. "I agree, and that's why I plan to stay in the cottage. I won't take any chances with Adam."

"I want to stay, too." Kristen crossed to the sofa.

"No, Kristen. Spring break is over tomorrow. You'll return to Stanford, finish your honors thesis, and complete your degree," Mrs. Wakefield said firmly. "Adam and I will be there as planned to see you get your diploma in June."

Kristen bit her lower lip. "I wish you could promise that."

"I promise to try."

For Kristen, whose mother had never broken a promise, that was good enough. "By the time we get through the baccalaureate, then the departmental ceremony afterward, you'll be bored to tears."

"Not a chance. We'll cheer just as loud as when you graduated from high school." Mrs. Wakefield turned to Jonathan. "By the way, how did you get Adam to change his mind?"

"Reasoning," he said evasively. Adam might be upset enough to believe his mother would start incompetency proceedings, but Jonathan knew she wouldn't. Too much had been taken from her son already for her to possibly agree to such a drastic and cruel maneuver. "Now, before she's picked up by a motorist I better go find her and convince her to return."

"You'll do it, Uncle Jon," Kristen said.

"Thanks for the vote of confidence." The light in her black eyes when she looked at him never failed to warm him. He was as proud of her as he was of Adam.

Standing, Jonathan quickly strode from the room. The women followed and watched him get inside his silver luxury sedan and drive away.

"I have a feeling you're going to regret this," Nicole said from beside Eleanor on the wide porch.

Despite the soaring temperature, Eleanor felt chilled and wrapped her arms around her body. "What's one more regret for this family?"

She had made a total mess of things. What if Dr. Wakefield had seriously injured himself? She'd be responsible, wouldn't she? But he looked all right, just angry. In any case, he had his family there to take care of him, which was more than she had.

Wiping the beads of perspiration from her forehead with the flat of her palm, Lilly stopped for a moment to catch her breath. The breeze had died and the heat was oppressive. The thick, sultry air tinged with the smell of stagnant water made drawing in each breath unpleasant.

Hearing a car behind her, Lilly turned and waved frantically for it to stop. To her surprised delight, the big silver luxury car pulled onto the grassy shoulder behind her. She was halfway to the car when the driver's door opened and a man stepped out, tall, broad-shouldered, with streaks of gray at his temple. She immediately recognized him and halted. Fear clawed at her throat. What if he had come after her because Dr. Wakefield had injured himself?

"Ms. Crawford, we didn't get a chance to be introduced earlier." The man extended his large hand. "I'm Dr. Jonathan Delacroix, a close friend of the Wakefields and Adam's godfather."

Ingrained manners made her take the hand although hers was shaking. "He's all right, isn't he?"

"He suffered no ill effects from the fall, if that's what you're asking."

Pulling her hand back, she wrapped her arm once again around the bag, clutching it to her chest. "But he's still angry at me?"

"You. Me. Everyone, I'm afraid," Jonathan answered, his voice sounding tired.

She nodded, feeling only partially relieved. "I didn't mean to make things worse."

"You didn't. In fact, that's why I followed you. To ask you to come back and care for Dr. Wakefield," Jonathan explained.

No matter how much she needed the money or how much she wished she could help, it wouldn't work. He was too angry and she was too afraid of that anger. "He'll be better off with someone else."

"He specifically asked for you."

"He did?" Lilly asked, her big brown eyes widening in disbelief.

Jonathan smiled. He'd been soothing females for thirty-four years professionally and longer nonprofessionally. He'd like to think he was quite good at it. White teeth gleamed. "I'm to bring you back to the estate immediately."

"I don't understand." The furrows in Lilly's forehead deepened.

"I'd be happy to explain everything to you if you'll accompany me back to the house." Jonathan motioned toward his car.

She glanced at his car, then down the road toward hers several yards away. She'd walked enough for one day. She didn't relish walking back to the car in the growing heat if this didn't work out. "Why don't you explain it here?"

A black convertible sports car zoomed recklessly by, causing them to step farther into the weeds away from the road. "My car might be safer and more comfortable."

Lilly studied Dr. Delacroix and said nothing. She didn't know this man with his expensive suit and good looks. But she had lived six long years with a man of similar build, a man who didn't hesitate when they were alone to intimidate and terrorize. The hand that she had shaken was soft and manicured, not rough and callused, but there was strength in it just the same. This man could inflict pain if he chose. Myron had hidden his meanness until it was too late.

"We can talk here."

If Dr. Delacroix thought her refusal strange he didn't comment. "Adam asked for me to get you to return, but he did it under duress. Unknown to his mother, I threatened him with declaring him incompetent if he refused to have help. I'm telling you this because he may take his anger at me out on you."

Lilly swallowed. "H-He's violent?"

"Never. But words can be just as harmful."

She shivered and glanced away. "I know."

Jonathan's shrewd eyes narrowed. "Do you live around here?"

She moistened her lips. "I was just passing through."

"Is there anyplace I could get a reference?" he asked.

Alarm swept through her. Her throat dried even more. "M-Mrs. Wakefield didn't say anything about needing a reference."

"I'm aware of that, but surely you realize she'll have to know something about you," Jonathan said reasonably.

Lilly shifted uneasily. She hadn't realized that at all.

"Is there going to be a problem with the reference?" he pressed, his brow furrowed.

Her gaze slid up to him, then away. "There might be."

Jonathan's voice took on a hard edge: "If you have a police record you won't be able to take care of Adam."

"It isn't that," she blurted, then realized she didn't know what else to say. Instead her gaze centered on the pristine white-shirted chest. Despite the intense heat, he appeared cool and unbothered in his tailored gray double-breasted suit. Perspiration ran in rivulets down her back. Her cotton dress was probably soaked. Nerves or heat, she didn't know. She only knew that she didn't want to admit to the biggest failure in her life.

"Well?" Dr. Delacroix prompted.

She swallowed and tried to think of a plausible explanation. "I recently lost my mother, and since we had no other close family I was traveling to New Orleans to start fresh. I took care of her, so I have no work history," she explained, silently telling herself the lie was necessary for survival.

Jonathan's expression cleared. "Determination in the face of adversity. That's Adam's mantra. He always had a privileged life, but never took it for granted. He worked hard, studied long hours. He was skyrocketing in his career when he was attacked. He thought he ruled his destiny, and then found out how tragically wrong he was."

"What happened to him was terrible, but I don't think he wants anyone's help, especially mine," she said softly.

"He may not want help, but he desperately needs it. At the moment he's feeling alone and desperate. In control of nothing." Jonathan studied Lilly's thin face closely. "I have a feeling you may understand a little of how he feels."

Tensing, she looked at Dr. Delacroix sharply. She didn't want him or anyone else probing into her life. "What if he changes his mind again?"

"As long as he thinks he's in danger of being ruled incompetent, he won't," the doctor told her, slipping his hands into the pockets of his tailored trousers.

"Isn't that rather cruel?" she questioned, unable to keep the distaste from her voice and face.

"Necessary," he corrected. "You saw the condition he and his room were in. He refuses to let anyone clean it or ask for help with any task. That's where you come in. Making sure he takes care of himself."

Indecision had her chewing on her lower lip and unconsciously shaking her head. "What you're asking is not going to be easy."

"We realize that," Jonathan told her. "You'll be in complete charge as far as Adam is concerned. Unknown to him, his mother will stay at her cottage in back of the main house. The couple who take care of the house will return from vacation Monday. However, Adam will remain your responsibility."

She dragged her hand through her hair, encountered the rubber band, and clamped her restless hand around her purse. "How am I to get him to let me clean him and the room?"

Jonathan sighed, withdrawing his hands from his pockets. "I have no idea."

Her mouth gaped.

"All I know is that neither Adam nor his mother or sister can go on this way," Jonathan said tightly. "Those of us who love him just have to be there for him until he can remember the man he was, and pray that his blindness isn't permanent. It won't be easy for any of us, especially Adam."

"He scares me," she said honestly. "I'm afraid I'll do or say the wrong thing and upset him again."

"We all are. We're all groping our way through this. We need your help, Ms. Crawford. Please stay," he asked quietly.

There was something else she needed to know. "You plan to do a reference check on me?"

"I have no choice."

"But I just told you I never worked outside the house."

"Then we'll check character references."

"You can't do that. If . . ." She trailed off, unable to finish the sentence.

" 'If' what? Are you hiding from someone?" Suspicion entered his eyes and voice.

"No," she quickly said, trying with all her might not to look away from Dr. Delacroix's probing stare. "I'm just a private person. I don't like people probing into my life."

"If you want the job, I'll have to." His words left no room for discussion.

Lilly hugged her handbag tighter to her chest. His proposition would solve her immediate problems, but his investigation could also lead Myron to her.

Her stomach churning, she glanced at her car down the road. Every possession she owned, which wasn't much by anyone's standards, was inside. Although no smoke plumes spiraled from the hood, Lord only knew how much the repairs would cost. Repairs she didn't have the money to pay for. She didn't even know where she'd sleep that night.

She turned to Dr. Delacroix and despite the erratic beating of her heart heard herself say, "I give you my word that I'll work hard and do my best to care for Dr. Wakefield."

He shook his head. "That's not good enough."

"Then good-bye." Turning away, she started toward her car.

Chapter Four

"Didn't you find her?"

"I found her," Jonathan answered. He'd dreaded this moment since Lilly had turned her back on him.

"Then where is she?" Eleanor asked, peering around his broad shoulders as if Lilly Crawford might appear.

"I need a drink first." Stepping past an anxious Eleanor onto the marble tile in the foyer, Jonathan headed for the kitchen.

The room was large and airy, with sleek stainless-steel appliances, copper cookware, granite countertops, and white glass-fronted cabinets. Adam couldn't cook worth a damn, but he loved good food and, with the limited number of times he had to enjoy a meal without interruption, wanted the best.

Opening the cabinet, Jonathan couldn't help but remember Adam inspecting every nook and cranny of what he called his investment/retirement house. They'd been like two school kids, nudging each other every chance they got because the realtor couldn't hide the shock from her face that a black man who wasn't an athlete or musician or selling drugs had enough money to pay cash for the $3 million estate if he wanted to.

"Jonathan," Eleanor said in a voice that would not be denied any longer.

"The last time I saw Ms. Crawford she was sitting in her car." Jonathan jerked the slender glass from the shelf. Since he was on call tonight lemonade would have to do instead of the Jack Daniel's he wanted. As far back as he could remember, Eleanor always kept a pitcher of lemonade in the refrigerator in warm weather.

"Why didn't she come back?" Eleanor asked, stepping in front of the refrigerator door Jonathan opened.

Jonathan hated defeat of any kind. He hated worse to see the disappointment in Eleanor's face. He still found it difficult to believe that Lilly Crawford had turned him down. Not many had. "She didn't want me to run a character reference on her."

"I knew it," Nicole said triumphantly, leaning against the island countertop, her hair as shiny and bright as the copper pots overhead.

Eleanor's gaze remained on Jonathan. "Did she say why?"

"Just that she was a private person and didn't like people probing into her life." Jonathan stared pointedly at Eleanor. "Do you mind?"

Eleanor picked up the glass pitcher of lemonade from the refrigerator. "What kind of car was she driving?"

From another woman the question and the withholding of his drink might have seemed incongruent or rude, but he knew better. He'd burned enough midnight oil in med school with Eleanor to know she had a sharp, analytical mind. She had been at the top of her class when she traded a promising career in medicine for marriage. He didn't think she'd regretted her decision for an instant in the years since. Eleanor had always known what she wanted. Now, she wanted what was best for her son and the answers as to why he wasn't getting what he wanted.

Jonathan sighed as he pictured the vehicle and a rumpled Lilly Crawford sitting inside as he had made a point of letting her see him turning around in front of her car. He'd hoped she'd try to stop him. She'd stared straight ahead, sipping clear liquid from a glass jar. "Twelve-year-old Ford, dented, rust spots."

"Then, it would appear that she could use the thousand dollars a week I offered."

"What!" he shouted. "Are you crazy?"

Eleanor sent him a look that had him blushing like an errant child. "Sorry."

The slight upward curve of her lips forgave him. "A thousand dollars, yet she chose to stay in a broken-down car on the side of the road," Eleanor said, her face thoughtful.

"I wouldn't want to do that," Kristen said, her hands jammed in the pockets of her black gabardine pants.

Eleanor glanced at her daughter. "Nor would most people . . . unless the alternative was worse."

"Now, wait a minute, Eleanor. You can't possibly think of hiring her without checking on her." Forgetting how thirsty he was, Jonathan lowered his glass.

"Adam wants her, Jonathan," Eleanor said.

The answer was so simple yet so complex. A mother's love always was. No matter how many times he witnessed it in his practice, it never ceased to amaze him. Perhaps because his mother had been more concerned with the success of her restaurant than her son.

To Eleanor, her family always came first. She was hurting. She couldn't give her child what he needed, so she'd give him what he wanted.

Eleanor loved unconditionally. Jonathan wanted to take her in his arms and remove the burden from her heart and shoulders. The only reason he didn't was that this time he didn't know if it would be more than friendship.

"He'd take anyone to get us to leave," Nicole said in the ensuing silence, coming to stand by them. "You can't hire her. She might be a criminal."

"Do you think she's a criminal or dangerous, Jonathan?" Eleanor asked, taking the glass from his hand and at last pouring the lemonade. Her hand was as steady as the eyes she lifted to his when she finished.

Instead of looking at Eleanor, he studied the cold beads of perspiration forming on the glass. His thoughts returned to Lilly Crawford. She had to be just as hot as he, hotter because she had walked to her car and she didn't have the luxury of air-conditioning. Yet she had turned him down. Stubborn, yes. Frightened, possibly, but dangerous or a criminal . . . "No, I don't think she is," he finally answered.

"Neither do I." Eleanor returned the pitcher to the refrigerator. "Now, do I go get her or will you?"

"I'll go." Jonathan drained the glass in one gulp and handed it to Eleanor. "You're as stubborn as Adam."

"Where do you think he got it from?" Eleanor said, but her voice trembled.

"He'll come through this," Jonathan said, then left.

Nicole glanced from Jonathan's retreating back, to Eleanor. "Mrs. Wake—"

"Please, Nicole," Mrs. Wakefield said, holding up her manicured hand. "I know you mean well, but my mind is made up on this matter."

"You want to trust her because she offered you a ride?" Nicole shook her head in a mixture of disbelief and disgust.

"Initially, yes, but I saw the regret in her face when she came out of Adam's room." Eleanor's arm swept the immaculate kitchen that would make any cook or thief rub her greedy hands together in anticipatory pleasure before finally stopping at the mint-condition hundred-year-old oak pedestal table and four ladder-back chairs in the breakfast nook. "You said it yourself. What person looking for a job, but especially a thief, would pass up a chance to stay here?"

Nicole's lush mouth tightened. "I don't like it."

"I understand that and appreciate your concern. Both Jonathan and I agree that she's not dangerous. If she's a thief, as you suspect, she can't run off without transportation. In the week it takes to earn her first paycheck, I would have had time to be around her more, and if I get any indication that I'm wrong and that she poses the slightest threat to Adam, I'll take immediate measures to get rid of her," Eleanor finished, a hint of steel in her voice.

The frown on Nicole's face shifted into the smile that invariably turned heads wherever she went. "Adam always said you were a lioness where your children were concerned."

"My children are all I have."

"I'd say you were both fortunate," Nicole told her, her voice wistful.

"Adam is lucky to have you," Eleanor said, meaning it. Love and family were worth any sacrifice. "Now, come on and let's get Ms. Crawford's room ready."

The three women were waiting on the front porch when Jonathan pulled up in the Mercedes. Mrs. Wakefield came down the four wooden steps, followed by Kristen and Nicole.

"Thank you, Ms. Crawford, for coming back to care for Adam. Your room is ready."

Nerves still jumpy, Lilly nodded. She couldn't believe it when Dr. Delacroix came back and offered her the job. She'd been suspicious at first, but as he had told her, with just her name he didn't have any means of checking on her. They'd waited for the tow truck in silence. Only when her car was hauled away did panic strike.

Dr. Delacroix must have seen it, because he'd said, "If you are telling the truth, you have nothing to be afraid of. If not . . ."

He hadn't finished; he hadn't needed to. Silently she had gotten into his car. Now, she was walking up the curved staircase again. She could only hope this time the outcome would be different.

"I put you in the room next to Adam." Opening the door, Mrs. Wakefield stepped aside and motioned Lilly to enter.

Beautiful. That was the only word she could think of to describe the bright room. The floral print pillows on the large bed matched the ties in the curtains. The room was almost as spacious as her entire house. "This is my room?" she asked in stunned amazement.

"Yes." Mrs. Wakefield walked around Lilly and opened another door on the far side of the room. "This is the dressing room and bath. You should be very comfortable here. The house staff, Samuel and Odette, take care of the general housekeeping and will be back early Monday morning." She returned to Lilly. "Later I'll show you the cottage where I'm staying, but under no circumstances is Adam to know I'm there."

"Yes, ma'am," she answered, glancing around the room again. She'd never seen so much luxury in one place. "Dr. Delacroix explained everything to me."

"Then we'll go say our good-byes to Adam and leave," Mrs. Wakefield said, then stopped at the door. "I think you should come also."

"Don't you want to be alone?" Lilly asked, trying not to show her nervousness.

"It will be less stressful on all of us if we get everything settled at once."

Without waiting, she left. Kristen immediately followed, as did Jonathan. Nicole stayed, her hazel eyes narrowed on Lilly as if she were back to studying slime that had crawled out of a swamp on its belly.

"If you do anything to harm Adam or his mother, I'll see that you pay for it the rest of your life," Nicole warned coldly.

"I'm not a criminal. I just want a job," Lilly said, barely resisting the temptation to back away from the animosity in the other woman's face.

Kristen reappeared in the doorway. "We're waiting."

With one last meaningful glare, Nicole walked out the door. Wondering why the other woman disliked her so intensely, Lilly slowly followed.

Mrs. Wakefield waited until they were all gathered, then knocked softly on the door. "Adam, Ms. Crawford is here as you requested. We've come to say good-bye, Adam."

Kristen sniffed. "I don't want to leave him."

Eleanor sent her daughter a small smile of support. "I know, but it has to be done."

There was a thump, quickly followed by a curse. Nicole reached for the brass doorknob. Eleanor stuck her arm out in front of the other woman. "He wouldn't want us to see him."

Long seconds passed before the door cracked open. Adam, aviator shades firmly in place, stood in the narrow space no wider than the span of his hand. "Have a safe trip home."

"We will." Eleanor's voice trembled. "I don't suppose you'll change your mind and allow me to stay."

"This is best."

"All right, then give me my good-bye kiss."

Adam tensed, but he didn't move away as Eleanor slowly pushed the door wider, then palmed one of her son's unshaven cheeks and kissed the other. "I love you. Always remember that."

Stepping back, she shoved her knuckled fist into her mouth. Jonathan's arms curved around her. She leaned into his wide chest.

"I'd rather be here with you than studying for finals." Kristen took Eleanor's place and rested her trembling hand on her brother's chest. His hand lifted to briefly clasp hers, then returned to his side.

"You'll ace them as usual. I hate you didn't get a chance to work on your honors thesis. I know how important it is for you."

She swallowed before speaking. "There's still time. I love you."

"Take care, Sis." He stepped back and started to close the door.

"Adam, wait!" Nicole cried, rushing to him. He turned his head around just as she lifted hers to his face. Instead of their lips meeting, the top of his head butted into her chin.

"Ooohhh," Nicole cried, slapping both hands over her mouth.

Adam froze. "What happened?" Silence reigned. "Dammit, what did I do?"

"It's nothing, Adam," Nicole said, her husky voice sounding strange and muffled with Jonathan's handkerchief pressed to her bleeding lower lip.

"Don't treat me like an idiot. I know I did something."

Everyone looked at one another, then away. No one spoke.

Stepping back, Adam slammed the door.

Nicole jumped. Tears glistening in her eyes, she stared at the closed door a long heartbreaking moment, then spun on her heels and ran back down the hall.

It was a good thing Nicole left when she did, Lilly thought, knowing the retreating woman couldn't hear the crash against the wall.

Eleanor Wakefield couldn't sleep. How could she when her children were in so much pain?

With her arms wrapped tightly around her waist, she stared at the light in the third window at the back of the house. Adam's room. He had insisted from the first that the light be kept on. He wanted to be able to see if his sight returned. Eleanor knew the last thing he did before going to sleep and the first thing he did on awakening was hold his hand in front of his eyes. The ritual was a daily torment he put himself through.

If she could, she'd gladly trade places with him. The choice hadn't been hers to make. Head falling forward on her delicate neck, Eleanor pondered the problem that was never far from her mind: was waiting for the hemorrhage to dissolve the right course of action? If they waited too long, the hemorrhage in the back of the eyes could cause permanent retinal detachment and blindness. If they operated now, they might damage the optic nerve and, again, cause permanent blindness. Until a short time ago hemorrhages were removed within two to three weeks, but recent studies had shown that waiting was the wisest and safest course of action.

What to do? Alex and his doctors had chosen to wait, but at what price to her son?

Forcing herself to leave the window, she took a seat on the camelback sofa in the room she had lovingly decorated at Adam's insistence. He'd said the four-room cottage in back of the main house was to be her retreat, a place to do the painting she never seemed to have enough time to do. He'd surprised her on her first visit to Wakefield Manor. She could still see that quick smile of his, the twinkle in his onyx-colored eyes, when he opened the door where a decorator waited.

Adam was the kind of son any parent would be proud of.

Too restless to sit, Eleanor bounded up once again and found herself staring at the back of the house. Light now shone from the window next to Alex's. Lilly Crawford.

Eleanor hoped in this at least she had made the right decision. At the time there hadn't been much choice. As much as it hurt her, she had to come to terms with the fact that instead of her presence comforting her son, it had the opposite effect.

Adam had always been the strong one, the dependable one. Like most young men growing up, he had tested the rules and boundaries, but that was as it should be. He had a good head on his shoulders his father had said. How she wished her husband were still with her to lean on, to guide her.

Randolph Wakefield had been a kind, loving father and husband. Losing him so suddenly five years ago had devastated them all. Now this. If Adam's blindness weren't horrendous enough, the aftermath was tearing their once-close family apart, and she had absolutely no idea how to make it better.

This wasn't drinking or drugs or the influence of unsavory people you could discuss with reason. This was something far more insidious and destructive. She didn't know how to fight, only that she must. Not just for Adam's sake, but for Kristen's.

Eleanor's daughter's life had been shaken enough when her father died of a sudden heart attack while they were playing tennis. She had seen one man she loved and thought invincible succumb; now the big brother she had come to rely on even more since their father's death was struggling to survive.

Kristen had never been as outgoing or as strong as Adam. Eleanor knew that if Adam lost his battle it would have disastrous consequences on her daughter. There had to be a way to save her children from more heartache and pain.

The flash of headlights across the sheer curtain caused Eleanor to frown, then smile. Quickly she went to open the door to admit her late-night visitor.

"Hello, Jonathan."

Jonathan straightened from trying to balance the cardboard box in his hands and ring the lighted doorbell at the same time. "I hope you checked before you opened the door."

Used to his being protective and cautious where she and Kristen were concerned, Eleanor smiled and stood back for him to enter. "Only a few people know I'm here."

Stepping across the threshold onto the hardwood floor, Jonathan stared down at Eleanor's beautiful smiling face, caught as always by her beauty and charm. "Check next time," he said gruffly.

Leaning over, she sniffed appreciatively. "Is that Marie's gumbo?"

Realizing he had lost this particular conversation, Jonathan headed for the kitchen. Besides being independent, Eleanor was headstrong. "Kristen said you hadn't been eating."

The smile slipped from Eleanor's face as she followed. "None of us have."

Setting the cardboard box on the blue-and-white tile counter, he began to take the Styrofoam containers out. "That's going to change. I got Kristen to eat before I took her to the airport by promising I'd get you to eat." He reached into the cabinet and took down a soup bowl trimmed with clusters of ripe blueberries, Eleanor's favorite fruit. "So have a seat."

Eleanor sat, then propped an elbow on the table, her chin on top of her hand, watching Jonathan move around the small kitchen with such ease and economy of motion. No matter how many times she'd seen him, it always amazed her that a big man could move with such grace and elegance. "Thank you for taking her to the airport. She called to let me know she had made it back safely. Tomorrow she's going by my house and have my phone calls forwarded to the cottage."

"She called me, too."

Eleanor wasn't surprised. Kristen would know he was concerned. "Where's your bowl?" she questioned when he set the thick stew in front of her.

"Coming." True to his word, he dished up another bowl of gumbo, removed the foil from still-warm garlic bread, transferred the tossed salad from the plastic container into a clear bowl, then placed napkins and silverware on the table.

Hands on hips, he studied the table, then snapped his fingers and grinned. Reaching back into the box, he brought out a bottle of chilled chardonnay. "I figured we could both use this."

Eleanor lifted her glass. She seldom drank strong liquor, but she loved wines and Jonathan knew the ones she liked best. "You always think of everything."

"I try." Half-filling her glass, he filled his, then set the bottle on the table.

"I thought you were on call?"

"Traded places with Maxwell for Saturday night." Jonathan took his seat. "He has a heavy date."

"You're a bachelor, too. Don't you have plans?"

"You know I tried marriage and it didn't work. Never again." Head downcast, he spread his napkin across his lap instead of looking at her, afraid she'd see the longing he wasn't sure he hid very well at times. Friendship was better than nothing.

"I liked Gloria." Eleanor sipped her wine, then studied Jonathan over the rim of the glass. "I was disappointed it didn't work out between you two."

"She's happy with her podiatrist in Arizona," he said lightly. The marriage had been doomed from the start. He had been unfair to Gloria by asking her to marry him when he loved another woman. What saved him many sleepless nights was that at the time he hadn't known it. He wished his ex-wife well.

"I suppose all marriages can't be as happy as Randolph's and mine." Eleanor's eyes became dreamy. "I considered myself the luckiest woman in the world to have found him."

Uncomfortable with the conversation and ashamed of his jealousy of the man who had been his best friend, Jonathan cut off a thick slice of bread and placed it on her plate. "Enough talk. Eat before the food gets cold."

The first taste was delicious, tempting her taste buds with forgotten pleasure. Eleanor closed her eyes and savored the rich flavors. When she opened them again, Jonathan was staring at her strangely. She laughed self-consciously. "What's the matter?"

Roughly he cleared his throat, then took a bite of gumbo to wash down the knot in his throat. He had to shake his head when it stuck. He reached for his wine and gulped. Thankfully it worked. Now wasn't the time or the place. "Nothing. It's just sometimes I find it hard to believe you have grown children. You look the same as you did when the three of us were in med school at Meharry."

Relaxing, the jittery feeling in her stomach gradually subsiding, Eleanor made a face. "Flatterer. As I remember, you had the silver tongue then also."

"Didn't seem to work with you."

Eleanor's gaze came up sharply, but Jonathan wore his usual teasing smile. "Randolph and I always knew," she said softly. "I miss him still. I wish he was here to help me decide what to do."

"If it's any help, Eleanor, I'm here. I'll always be here for you and the children."

From somewhere she summoned a smile as she reached for his hand. His grasp was strong and steady on top of the hard surface of the table. "Jonathan. I don't know what we would do without you, and I sincerely hope we never have to find out."

"You won't." Ordering himself to let go of her hand, he picked up his spoon. "Finish your meal. I promised Kristen I'd call her tomorrow with a full accounting."

Eleanor dipped her spoon into the bowl, then put it down. "It's difficult to eat when I keep thinking of Adam alone and hurting."

"Not taking care of yourself is not going to help. And what about Kristen?" Jonathan stared at her across the table. "She needs you, too. By not taking care of yourself, you let them both down."

Fury flashed in Eleanor's amber-colored eyes. "You have no right to criticize me."

"Yes, I do. You're all they have. You love them more, but that doesn't negate my love for them or for you."

The anger rushed out of her as quickly as it had come. She leaned back against the high-backed cushioned chair. "You always could make me angrier than anyone else on the planet."

"It's a knack," Jonathan said mildly. Anger, but never the love he craved so desperately.

Eleanor tore off a piece of bread. "Well, don't overdo."

"Wouldn't think of it."

"What do you think of Lilly Crawford?"

Seeing Eleanor finally eating, Jonathan gave serious thought to her question. "I don't know. I wish you'd let me have someone do a check on her. A friend of mine in the police department can trace her through the car registration."

Eleanor took a sip of wine. "You gave her your word and that meant mine. If she were a criminal, she would have thought of that possibility. I'm going to go on instinct and hold off unless she gives us cause." She set her glass aside. "Nicole called as soon as she arrived home from the airport. She reiterated her dislike of Ms. Crawford caring for Adam, but as I explained to her, for the time being that's the way it's going to be."

"I don't think she wants any woman alone with Adam for an extended period of time, as he and Ms. Crawford are bound to be if this works out."

Eleanor raised perfectly arched eyebrows. She wasn't offended by his subtle reference to sex. Adam was very much a man. "But Adam isn't interested in that now."

Jonathan chuckled. "Spoken like a mother. Every man is interested in that, whether he can see or not."

Eleanor felt that hot fluttery feeling again and, for the first time in their relationship, wondered about Jonathan's sex life. She studied Jonathan the way another woman would who might be interested in him as a potential lover, not as a trusted friend of almost forty years.

He was certainly handsome enough, with glossy salt-and-pepper hair at his temples that made him look like the distinguished and successful doctor he was. His unending patience and soft brown eyes had probably comforted countless women in labor. She frowned slightly, remembering his gaze could also be piercing if called for.

The occasion had been shortly after Randolph's death. One of his associates had become pushy in his attention toward her. Jonathan had been in town on one of many trips from Shreveport to check on them and immediately set the man straight with a few terse words. The odious man had never bothered her again. Jonathan wasn't a pushover by any stretch of the imagination.

His broad shoulders and wide chest were strong enough to hold and shelter a woman and her problems, but he also had an ingrained goodness that made the entire package appealing. Why hadn't she noticed before?

"What?" he asked, frowning.

A bit embarrassed, she dipped her spoon into the gumbo. "Woolgathering. Nothing important."

Jonathan wasn't so sure. For one precious moment Eleanor had looked at him the way a woman looks at a man she is interested in. He couldn't have imagined it, but as time passed and she ate her meal, he wasn't so sure. Perhaps he had seen what he had waited almost forty years to see.

For the first time in memory, Lilly had nothing to do. After Dr. Delacroix left to take Nicole and Kristen to the airport, Mrs. Wakefield had shown her the location of the cottage. Once there, Mrs. Wakefield had given Lilly specific instructions regarding the care of her son, then said they'd talk in the morning.

Lilly had returned to find the double stainless-steel refrigerator and freezer and pantry well stocked, as Mrs. Wakefield had indicated they would be. Lilly had prepared Dr. Wakefield's dinner and left it outside his door on the table as Mrs. Wakefield had instructed her to do if he didn't answer. Then she went to her room.

Opening the door to the spacious bedroom done in salmon, slate blue, and yellow, Lilly still found it difficult to believe she was to sleep in the delicate-looking and distinctly feminine room. It was like something out of a dream.

Her fingers trailed down the intricately carved maple headboard that was as tall as she was, the double doors of the mahogany armoire, the pretty bench at the foot of the bed that was covered in the same sunny white-and-yellow fabric as the throw pillows on the bed and on the love seat. Everywhere her eyes touched there was beauty.

When she'd grown tired of looking and touching, she'd unpacked her few clothes and run a bath. She'd felt almost decadent in the white-on-white bathroom and a little impish when she sprinkled in the water some of the bath salts she found on the marble shelf over the immense sunken tub. Sinking into the rose-scented bubbles, she sighed with pleasure, then gasped as the unexpected buoyancy of the water lifted her. She laughed, enjoying the freedom to do so.

She'd played more than she had bathed and enjoyed it, instead of her habit of rushing to finish in case Myron needed her. Getting out, she'd pulled a large white towel from the heated towel rack to dry off. Wealthy people sure knew how to live.

Holding up her faded cotton gown, she could barely distinguish the tiny lilacs on the white background. She glanced at the mound of luxurious bedding. No problems this time distinguishing the plants. Large white hydrangeas were scattered across a ground of luminous yellow on the duvet, shams, and toss pillows. It seemed a shame to wear the old gown.

Grinning, she pulled on the gown and slid beneath the cool cotton sheets to snuggle in comfort. Overhead she caught sight of the detailed scroll around the ceiling of the room and the crystal chandelier. To live here every day, to own all this, had to be the most wonderful thing in the world. For a while, she would enjoy it, too.

The grin slipped from her face as she thought of Dr. Wakefield and the reason she was there. He could no longer see the beautiful house or the well-cared-for grounds. His world was one of darkness.

What if it remained that way?

Scooting down in the bed, Lilly turned over on her side and drew the covers up to her chin. Once she'd thought that her life had to be the most miserable in the world. Today she had learned different.

Mother Crawford had always said if you lived long enough you'd find someone in worse shape. The trick was to keep living.

Leaning over, Lilly cut off the light. Tomorrow she had to be at her best. She no longer thought Dr. Wakefield would harm her physically, but he'd defy her at her every turn. She just had to figure out how to get around him.

Like it or not, they were inexplicably tied to each other, for better or worse. She could only pray she had left the worst behind her in Little Elm.

The next morning she found out how wrong she was.

Chapter Five

"Dr. Wakefield, please unlock the door." Lilly twisted the brass knob again. The unsettling result was the same. "Please, Dr. Wakefield. I have your breakfast and I need to clean the room."

She heard the pleading note in her voice and briefly shut her eyes. A man used to having people jump when he spoke wasn't going to listen to her if she whined. The sad fact was that she was more used to taking orders than she was to giving them.

She glanced down at the untouched tray of food she had left outside his door last night. "You have to eat something or you'll get sick."

Her forehead fell against the solid oak door. "Very good, Lilly. Like he's concerned with getting sick," she muttered to herself.

Using the flat of her hand, she banged against the door. "I have to take care of you. Please."

Silence.

She banged again. "Please, Dr. Wakefield. If I could just come in. I'm supposed to take care of you. Dr. Delacroix and your mother will be calling tonight. What will I tell them?"

More silence. He wasn't going to open the door. All she was going to get was a sore hand. "I'll be back later."

Weariness in every step, Lilly went to the kitchen with the breakfast tray, then returned for the dinner tray. After all the thought she had given to preparing food he wouldn't have to worry about cutting or falling off his fork, he hadn't touched the veal cutlet or green beans.

Shaking her head over the wasted food, she fed it to the garbage disposal. There had to be some way to get him to open his door and listen to reason.

The ringing of the phone made her jump. Cleaning her hands on a dish towel, she slowly crossed the room and picked up the blue wall phone. "Hel— Hello—Wakefield residence."

"Good morning, Lilly. How are things?"

Lilly leaned heavily against the counter. She hadn't expected his mother to call so soon. Last night Lilly had asked Mrs. Wakefield to call her Lilly since she worked for the Wakefields. It might be the shortest job in history.

"Lilly, is everything all right?" Mrs. Wakefield asked anxiously.

She opened her mouth to say, "Yes," but the lie wouldn't come. Keeping her marriage a secret harmed no one. His mother deserved the truth. "He . . . he locked me out," she admitted, sure she was going to be fired.

"I knew my instincts were right."

"Ma'am?"

"If you had said things were fine, I'd have known you were lying," Mrs. Wakefield said bluntly. "Adam wouldn't have succumbed so easily."

Lilly was too overjoyed that she wasn't being fired to be concerned with Mrs. Wakefield's subtle bit of trickery.

"However, I didn't think he'd use his old tricks," Mrs. Wakefield continued, not sounding the least bit disturbed.

"He's done this before?"

"A couple of weeks after he came home from the hospital."

"What did you do?"

"Got an ax and broke his front door in."

Lilly smiled, settling on a padded high-backed stool by the phone. Picking up a pencil, she doodled on the notepad on the counter. She liked and envied Mrs. Wakefield's assurance. "I bet that got his attention."

"It did. You have to take a firm hand with Adam."

Her hand tightened around the pencil. "Dr. Wakefield has a mind of his own."

"I realize that, and unfortunately for you, he thinks he has the upper hand." The sigh that came through the receiver was long and deep. "He's aware what I'd do if that happened."

Lilly sat up straighter. She had to moisten her lips before she spoke: "You want me to take an ax to his door?"

"No. He has to feel he's in control of something. Besides, I don't think force will work this time."

"Then what?"

"I wish I knew. Love and patience certainly haven't. I'll let you try for another day. If you're unable to get him to open up, I'll have to hire someone else. Good-bye."

Slowly Lilly hung up the phone. She didn't want to leave. There was no way she'd find another job that paid as well and offered a place to live. Determination glinted in her eyes.

Adam Wakefield wasn't running her off. She'd run from her last man. Going back to the sink, she flipped the garbage disposal on. She'd figure out something. She had no choice.

Adam paced the floor at the foot of his bed. Five steps forward; five steps back. He was in a foul mood. His beard itched, he needed a bath, and his shirt would probably stand by itself. So would his linen slacks. He'd always been fastidious in his dress and in his person, changing shirts sometimes twice a day. His jaw tightened. How the mighty had fallen. He was afraid the fall wasn't over.

Nothing was working out as he had planned. He hadn't packed enough clean clothes. Worse, he hadn't had a decent bath since he came here. He sat in a couple of inches of water, afraid he'd slip trying to take a bath in the deep, oversize tub and further injure his eyes.

He'd yet to get the hang of adjusting the water temperature in the shower. Unlike the one-knob head shower at his house in Sausalito, this shower had two. Then there was the soap that he'd carefully put in the dish, then knocked out when he reached for it again. Down on hands and knees he'd go until he found it again. He'd chased his last soap!

He paused and scratched the stubbled beard on his face. He'd always been clean-shaven and preferred a regular razor to stay that way. After he'd come out of the hospital, he'd switched to an electric shaver when he kept nicking himself with the razor. It hadn't given him as close a shave, but now he didn't even have that. He'd packed in such a hurry he'd forgotten it, along with half of his other things.

All for nothing. His mother, Kristen, and Nicole had been on the plane. Of course, no one had said anything until it had taken off. Afterward none of them could understand how stupid or betrayed that had made him feel or how angry and worthless it felt to control so little of his life anymore.

He had thought once he reached the estate he'd be in control again. That had been his biggest mistake so far.

He hadn't calculated that he had been here only five times in the last five years, whereas he had lived in his home in Marin County outside San Francisco for six years. Since he was fairly neat, in his mind's eye he already knew the placement of furniture and his possessions there. Here he had to become acclimated with his family and Nicole hovering. In his anger, he had made things worse by barging in and overturning furniture. He should have planned better.

The sudden ringing of the phone startled, then annoyed him. It could only be one of four people. One of the four people he had sent hastily from here yesterday. He could almost detect who the caller was from the persistent ringing of the phone. Nicole. His mother or Kristen might have wished he'd answered the phone, but after eight rings they would have respected his desire for privacy.

Not Nicole.

Her aggressiveness was what had taken her from an unsatisfying career as an accountant to president and CEO of her own temporary agency. That trait was what had attracted him to her in the first place.

In his profession he didn't have time for needy, clingy women. Nicole's assertiveness meant she wouldn't be dependent on him to make her happy, that she understood that there would be many times when his work would make him unavailable. When time permitted, they had enjoyed each other's company in and out of bed. Now he couldn't even give her that.

His mouth flattened as the phone continued to ring. "Let it go, Nicole. Just move on. Please, for both our sakes." Blessedly the phone stopped.

His pacing continued. How he wished he could be left alone. At the same time, he wished he could clutter his mind with so many thoughts that he couldn't think. His laughter was rough and rusty. Perhaps Jonathan hadn't been far off in wanting to declare him incompetent.

His stomach growled. In the midst of the turmoil his life was in, it seemed incongruent that he could be hungry, yet he was. Perhaps he should have eaten. Only the woman would see what a horrendous mess he had made. Food invariably ended up on his shirt or in his lap. He'd lost count of the number of times he had put an empty spoon or fork into his mouth.

He abruptly halted on step three, pivoted, sniffed. He recognized that smell. Fried chicken. An artery clogger if ever there was one. His stomach didn't seem to care, nor his salivary glands. His stomach growled. His mouth watered.

He'd never realized his sense of smell was so acute. If anyone suggested that it was because his other senses were heightened due to his loss of sight, he'd tell him that was a crock. There was nothing scientific to back up such a claim. Still . . . he smelled fried chicken.

She'd knock on his door soon, he was sure. Maybe he'd accept the tray this time. He'd already shown he was in charge by locking her out. Carefully, his hands outstretched, step by humiliating step, he made his way to the door, a straight twenty-one-step path from the foot of his bed.

Time passed. How much he couldn't tell.

Another irritating thing about his blindness was the complete lack of comprehension of the passage of time. The cuckoo clock Nicole had given him a week after he came home from the hospital had driven him crazy. He really had accidentally knocked it off his bedside table and broken it, just as he'd told her. He just wasn't sorry he had.

Becoming annoyed with the woman's tardiness, he pressed his ear against the door. The two-story house was built solid, but he was positive he heard some kind of droning sound. His stomach growled. Where was his dinner?

A thought struck. What if she didn't come back? What if she was downstairs taking it easy, watching the soaps, eating his fried chicken? What if she planned to do nothing, just pocket the money? What was the going rate to take care of a helpless man? Two hundred, three hundred dollars a week? Whatever it was, there was no one in the house to report her if she didn't do her job.

Except him!

Incensed, he jerked open the door. She wasn't getting away with it. "If you don't bring my lunch, you're fired!"

Lilly barely kept from clapping hands together. She did grin and turned over a drumstick in the electric fryer she'd been tending in the hallway. "You're sure you're ready to eat?"

His attention shifted downward. "What are you doing on the floor?"

She scrambled to her feet, almost knocking over the small electric fan positioned on the other side of the skillet to blow the aroma of frying chicken to Adam's room. "Your tray took all the space on the side table and I–I set mine on the floor."

"Well, bring mine inside. Now."

Lilly picked up the tray. "Certainly, Dr. Wakefield." Entering his room, she was prepared for a bigger mess than the day before. She felt a small measure of relief that it wasn't. The chairs and tables were upright; so were the lamps, their bulbs burning, their shades slightly bent. "I'll get the table from the hall and put it by the window. The sun is shining and you can hear the blue jays in the oak trees outside."

His mouth tightened a fraction. He hadn't moved from the door. "No, just put it on the bed. Then you can leave."

"I need to clean up your room." She paused, her hands firmly on the tray.

"Later. Now leave."

Somehow she didn't trust him. "You give me your word."

"Don't question me!" he bit out, but his growling stomach negated the force of his stern order.

Lilly caught back a chuckle. He was human.

His head jerked sharply toward her. "What was that?"

"Nothing, Dr. Wakefield. I'll be back later for the tray and to clean the room." Setting the tray on the rumpled bed, she started from the room, then made a quick detour. "I'll just grab your laundry from the bathroom."

A cursory glance in the room that was bigger than her bath told her she had her work cut out for her. Towels were strewn everywhere. The black tile in the shower could use a good scrub, and so could the tub.

His clothes in her hands, she edged past him. "Meat at twelve, potato salad at three, green beans at six, roll at nine, brow—"

The door closed firmly in her face.

Lilly jerked back, then went down the hall smiling. She had done something right. Gotten Dr. Wakefield to open his door.

Adam caught himself sucking on the chicken bone and tossed it in the direction of his plate. Since he heard a thump instead of a clatter, he set the tray on the floor beside him and felt around on the Persian rug until he found the discarded bone. This time he made sure it reached the tray.

With his back pressed against the footboard of the bed, he sipped his lemonade from the thermos spout. It wasn't one of the reds he would have chosen to complement his meal, but fried chicken wasn't his usual meal, either. However, he had to admit the food was good and so was the lemonade.

Ice cubes clinked as he lowered the thermos. Lots of ice, just the way he liked his beverages. This time he hadn't had to worry about knocking the glass over or ice sliding down into the glass and splashing the liquid up his nose as had happened in the past. Maybe she had possibilities. If she kept out of his way.

"Dr. Wakefield. It's me, Lilly."

Speak of the devil. He found his brownie again and took another generous bite. "I haven't finished."

"Did you have enough?"

Adam grunted. Four drumsticks, potato salad and green beans in little bowls so that he didn't have to chase the food over his plate, and three gooey but delicious brownies. She must be used to feeding truck drivers. "Yes."

"What would you like for dinner? I was thinking chicken-fried steak?"

Apparently she hadn't heard of the dangers of too much cholesterol. He took another bite of his brownie. "Whatever."

Outside the door, Lilly wrung her hands. Maybe she had celebrated too early. Although Mrs. Wakefield had been just as excited and had actually congratulated Lilly on her scheme. "I washed and ironed some of your clothes."

"What?" He scrambled to his feet. "Those shirts were silk and the pants linen."

"Not the ones I washed. I–I checked the labels in the shirts and washed them on Delicate. It's all right."

"Bring one to me now," he ordered. He didn't have any clothes to waste. He wasn't about to ask that traitor Jonathan to bring him more or admit that he wasn't prepared to care for himself. Getting his bearings, Adam went to the door and jerked it open. "Incompetent—"

"Here it is."

He jerked back. "I thought you went to get the shirt."

"I brought it with me. Here it is."

Adam extended his hand, hoping he wouldn't have to grope. He didn't. His fingers closed around soft-cotton material that smelled like sunshine. He barely refrained from lifting the clean shirt to his face. At the moment a too-small shirt was a small price to pay for clean clothes.

"Is it all right?" the woman asked anxiously.

"I suppose," he said, trying to keep the excitement out of his voice.

"I washed your jeans as well." She touched his hand with the denim.

Adam's fingers closed around the pants. "Is this all my laundry?"

"Er—"

"Well?"

He felt the additional weight and pressure of more clothes being added to his pile. He had a pretty good idea what. His cotton briefs. For some reason he felt oddly embarrassed by the situation, as she did. "You can take the tray now."

"You sure you don't want anything else?"

"Positive."

Crossing the room, she started to pick up the tray; then she saw the bed. The sheets were twisted. The geometric black-and-brown comforter hung halfway off the bed. "I'll just straighten up the bed a bit."

"That isn't necessary."

"It's part of my job." She quickly straightened the sheet on one side, then went to the other. "I'll just tuck in this sheet, put your comforter back on, and then I'll be out of your way and you can take a nap." A few more efficient movements and she was finished. "There."

Picking up the tray, she went to the door. As usual, Dr. Wakefield hadn't moved. He certainly guarded his domain. "I'll go start dinner."

This time when the door closed she didn't feel quite so shut out. But she still needed to clean his room.

————

Lilly expected Dr. Wakefield to open the door soon after she knocked with his dinner. What she didn't expect was to see him wearing the same soiled clothes.

"You can put the food on the bed," he instructed.

Unsure of how to delicately suggest he take a bath, Lilly did as instructed. "You said I could clean the room later."

"After I've eaten."

"But—"

"Later," he interrupted.

"Yes, sir." The door shut her out as soon as she stepped past him. Deep in thought, she stared at the closed door. Why hadn't he changed clothes?

She was still puzzled when she went back and found the empty tray outside his door. Somehow she knew if she tried the knob it would be locked.

Sitting on the side of the tub Saturday night, Lilly watched the water gush from the solid brass spout that gleamed like gold. Absently she sprinkled bath salts beneath the spout and watched the bubbles form and rise higher until they threatened to overflow. Time was running out. She had been on the job two days, and she still was no closer to getting Dr. Wakefield or his room cleaned.

Mrs. Wakefield, although pleased that Dr. Wakefield was eating, wanted her son and the room cleaned as well. She informed Lilly that Dr. Delacroix was already making inquiries.

If that weren't enough, the housekeeper and her husband were to return on Monday. If by some remote chance they could take care of Dr. Wakefield's needs, there would be no need for Lilly to remain.

She wanted to stay. The desire now wasn't so much because she had no place else to go but because of a sense of growing accomplishments. It had felt good to see the empty tray, to know that she had accomplished something others hadn't been able to do. Then, too, she had finally figured out why Dr. Wakefield made her uneasy.

She looked at him and saw herself. He was a victim just as she had been and, like her, unwilling to fight back. According to those who loved him, he hadn't been that kind of man in the past. There had to be a way to get him to be the man he used to be.

From all accounts, he had been a neat, clean-shaven man before his blindness. She didn't know if his sloppiness was because he couldn't see himself or because he just didn't care anymore. His mother and Dr. Delacroix were just as puzzled.

Cutting off the water, Lilly slipped off the white terry cloth robe she'd found in the bathroom and stepped into the tub. As soon as she sat down and took her hands from the side of the tub she felt the water lift her. Used to it, she didn't grab for the side of the tub. Instead, she stretched out her legs, leaned back, and reached for her soap, only to knock it out of the holder.

"Gracious, I'll never find—" Her eyes widened. "That's it." Standing, she stepped out of the tub. Without bothering to dry herself, she pulled on her robe, belting it as she went.

She found a ball of twine and a paring knife in the kitchen and raced back to her bathroom. Unwrapping a new bar of soap, she made a hole in the center, then looped the twine through and knotted the ends.

"Please, Lord, let this work."

Before she could let doubts creep in, she went next door and knocked on the door. "Dr. Wakefield. It's me. Please open up. Please."

Adam heard Lilly, then just as quickly dismissed her. He had few pleasures anymore. One of them was listening to baseball games, and he didn't want to be disturbed.

With radio, the great equalizer, every listener was on the same playing field, and the announcer recognized that. With television, the aptly named "boob tube," the announcer's comments were littered with visual expectations. Did you see that? What a great catch. Let's watch a rerun.

"Dr. Wakefield, please. It's important."

His inclination was to continue to ignore her; then he decided to see what had happened. Tonight her soft, southern-accented voice sounded breathless instead of filled with its usual uncertainty. In that, she reminded him of Kristen. Maybe she'd heard something downstairs and it had frightened her. Probably a tree brushing against a window. Kristen certainly hadn't liked being away from the bright lights of the big city her first trip here.

"Dr. Wakefield, please."

"I'm coming." Wishing Monday would hurry so he could send her away, he pushed to his feet and went to the door. He twisted the knob, then cursed under his breath when he realized he had locked it against the same annoying person who continued to annoy him. Unlocking the door, he jerked it open. "What is it?"

"I brought you a present."

"A present?" Had his mother hired an escapee from an insane asylum?

"Here." She grabbed his hand and put the bar of soap in it. "I made it. I was taking a bath and lost my soap in the bubbles and I thought how slippery soap can be. I saw this on television once."

He fingered the soap, then the cord. He honestly didn't know what to say.

"Your tub is bigger than mine, and the first time I got in mine I felt like I was going to float off. I still feel like it sometimes."

He heard the girlish, unself-conscious laughter in her voice, then felt her brush past him. "Where do you think you're going?"

"To run your bath. Now you won't have to worry about finding the soap. While you're bathing, I can change your sheets."

"Come back here!"

"Or do you want me to adjust the water in the shower? I forgot men like showers."

She was talking too fast and confusing him. He wanted her to take her soap and get out of his room. He lifted his arm to fling the soap in her direction, but as his arm came up he gripped it instead. His nose wrinkled at his own odor. He needed a bath.

"Dr. Wakefield?"

"The shower."

A grinning Lilly turned toward the dresser. "I'll get your pajamas."

"I don't wear pajamas."

She stopped midway across the room, then slowly turned to gape at him. His mouth was curved slightly as if he had enjoyed the prospect of shocking her. She cleared her throat. "I'll just take your clean clothes from the foot of the bed and put them on the far right-hand side of the marble vanity."

Without waiting, she went into the bathroom, put his clothes on the counter, then stepped into the immense shower stall. Adjusting the shower-heads away from her, she turned on the water. She laughed as it shot out, glad she didn't have any shoes on when water circled her bare feet.

Stepping out, she dried her feet, then went to the linen closet for fresh towels and bed linen. Placing the fluffy oversize gray towels on the warming rack, she took the maroon-and-gray-striped cotton sheets from the linen closet and left the bathroom.

Dr. Wakefield stood at the foot of the bed, his long-fingered hand clutching the bedpost.

"The shower is waiting for you. I put clean towels on the rack to the left as you leave the shower."

"I . . ." he began, then shoved his free hand through his long hair.

She frowned. In the short space of time she'd known Dr. Wakefield, he'd never been at a loss for words. Then another thought came to her: she had never seen him walk unassisted except for the time he had lunged at her and fallen.

"All this rushing around has made me thirsty. I'm going to the kitchen for a glass of lemonade before I start on the bed. Can I bring you one?"

"No."

"I'll be right back." Crossing the room, she opened the door and closed it with a crisp snap of her wrist.

Adam heard the door close. He toed off his loafers and moved cautiously toward the sound of the running water in the bathroom. She might be annoying, but she definitely had her moments. Shedding his clothes, he located a washcloth, put the loop of soap around his neck, and found his way beneath the warm spray of water.

With a minimum amount of effort, he managed to redirect the stream downward. Closing his eyes, he braced both hands securely against the tiled wall, leaned his head forward, and let the water run over him.

She definitely had her moments.

How had he thought he could do this?

The words hammered through Adam's brain. Head bowed, hands clamped around the edge of the vanity, anger swirled through him. He couldn't remember where his mother had said she had put his toiletries. She had repeated it to him as if he had lost his mind instead of his sight, and in his anger he had blocked out what she had said.

He was as helpless as he was useless.

Two knocks followed by two. "Dr. Wakefield, do you need anything?"

A new pair of eyes, he thought bitterly, anger surging through him again. "Is everything all right?"

"Yes!" he shouted, his head coming up. If he wanted her gone, he'd have to prove to Jonathan and his mother that he could care for himself. There was nothing wrong with his sense of touch or smell.

Unclamping his hands, he slid them atop the cold marble, moving from one oval basin to the other. The heel of his hand hit an object, knocking it over. Glass clinked. He reflexively grabbed for it. More glass clinked and clattered.

The sound of glass shattering on the floor went straight through him. The strong smell of his after-shave filled his nostrils. Liquid tickled his toes.

"Damn!"

"Dr. Wakefield, are you all right?" Lilly cried, knocking on the door again. "Dr. Wakefield?"

"Can't you tell I'm just fine?" he hissed, balling his hands into fists to keep from sweeping the entire mess onto the floor. The main reason he didn't was that he remembered Jonathan's taunt that if he was injured he couldn't take care of himself.

"Well, come on in and clean up this mess," he ordered.

Moistening her dry lips, Lilly slowly opened the door. The sight of Dr. Wakefield with only a towel wrapped carelessly around his waist, water gleaming on his muscled back and shoulders, caused her to pause, her heart to beat a little faster; then she saw the slivers of broken glass scattered around his feet.

"Don't move," she instructed, rushing forward.

"I hadn't planned on it."

Reaching for the wastebasket beneath the counter, she picked up the larger pieces, then used a washcloth to pick up the tiny splinters. She didn't think Dr. Wakefield would wait until she went to the kitchen for a broom and dustpan.

"I'll go get your shoes." Coming to her feet, she rushed back into the bedroom. A quick search in his closet and beside his bed produced a pair of loafers. She guessed he didn't wear slippers, either. Grabbing the shoes, she went back to the bathroom. Seeing the taut way he held himself, she pulled his robe from the hook on the back of the door.

"Here's your robe." Although her hands were trembling, she draped the garment over his shoulders, then hunkered down. "Raise up your right foot."

"Just put them down."

"I might have missed some of the glass," she said quietly.

After a tension-filled moment, Adam lifted his right foot, then his left.

Standing, Lilly rubbed her hands on her thighs. Indecision and a small flicker of fear held her still. She'd seen Myron's body tremble the same way when he raged at her. Afraid the slightest movement on her part would cause him to tear into her, she'd learned to wait until the danger passed.

In the mirror she studied Adam's hunched shoulders, the head turned away from her. Even with the unkempt beard and hair, he was a handsome man. He would have had a lot of women after him. She briefly wondered if Nicole was one of them. Unreasonable as the thought was, she hoped not. Lord knows she wasn't in any position to judge others, but Nicole, although beautiful, appeared cold and suspicious. And that would mean Adam was either like her or so blinded by his love that he didn't see her faults.

Like Lilly had been with Myron. The thought brought her up short.

She hadn't seen beyond Myron's smooth words to the cruel person he really was. All she'd seen was a man she thought she could love forever, a man who in return would love her and give her the children and loving family she'd always wanted.

She'd been wrong and paid dearly for her mistake. Just as Dr. Wakefield was paying for his mistake in not giving his keys to the car thieves. She had a chance to correct her mistake, and at the moment her chance was tied to another man who needed but detested her presence.

Had his blindness made Dr. Wakefield cruel or had he simply hidden his cruelty, as Myron had?

She studied his rigid reflection, wishing she knew the answer. Although his arms were taut, his body rigid, her fear wasn't as strong. The more time passed, the less likelihood there had been of Myron striking out. Like a rattler—if it didn't strike quickly there was always the chance that it would let down its tail and slither off on its belly.

Unless she wanted to face the possibility of Myron finding her and making her go back, she'd better get beyond her fear and do her job. Mrs. Wakefield didn't impress Lilly as the kind of person who bluffed.

She gazed at the heavy cut-glass bottles and tubes with similar shapes scattered on the counter. "What do you want next?"

Startled, Adam's head came up and around. She'd been so quiet he thought she had gone. "I don't like people lurking around."

"I wasn't—yes, sir."

The last two words were so soft, he caught himself leaning toward her. He jerked back. Even over the cloying scent of his after-shave he smelled roses. Maybe he was the one insane. "Put everything in the sink, then leave. That's all for tonight."

"Dr.—"

"Never mind; just leave!"

Lilly jumped, stepped back to leave, then stopped. How many times had she wished for someone to help, to understand? How many times had she been too ashamed and embarrassed to ask for help?

Both of them had been kicked in the teeth by life; maybe together they could fight back. "The bottle of after-shave must have been almost empty, because there wasn't much on the floor, and there's another bottle. Were you planning to shave?"

"Didn't you hear me?"

With trembling hands, Lilly placed the assorted bottles and tubes in the sink, ignoring the menacing voice.

"I've broken plenty of things. So has everyone, but it still gets you when it happens. I never thought of it before, but the cologne sprays and after-shave splashes. Your tube of hair cream is softer than your toothpaste. You ever notice how toothpaste falls off the toothbrush? A lot of times I bet it would be easier to just squirt it in your mouth."

She stole a look at Dr. Wakefield in the mirror. What she saw wasn't reassuring. His face was set, his jaw clenched. The lean muscles of his arms were bunched.

"Your bed is made up and the covers turned back." She slid her hands into the pockets of her robe. "Good night, Dr. Wakefield."

She was at the door of the bathroom when he said, "What's your name?"

"Lilly. Lilly Crawford."

He turned and seemed to stare straight at her. "Well, Lilly Crawford, the next time you disobey my order, you're fired."

She was too stunned to speak.

Turning, he felt in the sink, picked up his toothbrush and the toothpaste dispenser. "And, Lilly?"

Scared, she wondered what else he was going to say. "Y-Yes, sir?"

Putting the bristles beneath the opening, he pushed down on the plunger. A mound of toothpaste rolled out on top of the bristles. "Keep your advice to yourself until it's asked for."

Chastised, she left. She didn't hear Adam curse when the naked bristles reached his mouth.

Chapter Six

Adam had a restless night. He wasn't very proud of himself. He hadn't been in a long time. His life had been hell since the carjacking and he had selfishly made everyone else suffer right along with him.

Last night he had reached a new low. He'd never been deliberately cruel, hadn't known he could be. Yet that was exactly what he had been.

Anger had clouded his judgment and he had said things to the woman he shouldn't. She'd tried to help, yet somehow she had made him feel utterly useless. Like a spiteful child, he had struck back.

Initially, her thin, unsteady voice had meant nothing to him, but as his anger cooled and he had time to think he recalled another voice that was just as unsteady and unsure, Kristen's. He'd heard the same uncertainty in his sister's voice too many times to count. Beautiful, talented, shy, and unassuming, she reached to the deepest part of him when no one else could.

He owed Lilly an apology, owed his entire family and Nicole one. The jury was still out on Jonathan, but that didn't mean Adam had changed his mind about being left alone.

He'd regain his sight soon. They just had to give him space until he did.

Two brief knocks, followed by two more.

He stopped pacing in front of his bedroom door. She hadn't called his name and inexplicably he missed the breathless, hesitant catch in the soft drawl of her voice. Texas, he'd bet. She must be angry with him.

Good. It was better if she remained pissed and out of his way. An apology from him would be an open invitation for her to start giving him advice again.

Opening the door, he stepped aside. "You know where to place the tray."

"Yes, sir."

Silently she passed back by him. The only reason he knew was the hint of roses. Without thought, he leaned into the smell. Then he realized what he was doing and swung the door shut.

Over her shoulder Lilly glanced back at the slammed door, then continued down the stairs to the kitchen for her own breakfast. She detested cold eggs and usually waited until she returned from Dr. Wakefield's room before cooking hers. This morning there had been no need. He didn't want to talk to her any more than she wanted to be in his presence or be reminded of what had happened last night.

Picking up the stoneware plate, she took a seat in the breakfast nook in one of the ladder-back chairs facing the curtainless arched window. Absently munching on a strip of bacon, she watched two squirrels chase each other across the green lawn, then spring onto the trunk of an oak tree and disappear into the leafy foliage.

Beyond the trees she could see pink azaleas in full bloom beneath a cloudless pale blue sky. The day would be perfect.

But not for her. Her appetite gone, she dropped the bacon back on the plate and leaned back in her chair.

She had been so proud of herself, so hopeful that Dr. Wakefield had finally begun to accept her. She'd been wrong. Last night he had made that painfully clear.

"Keep your advice to yourself until it's asked for."

The harshly spoken words still had the ability to make her flinch. They were too much of a reminder of how Myron had treated her, what he might have said to her. Only, with him, she would have been too afraid to voice her opinion. From the mess she had made of things, maybe she should have dealt the same way with Dr. Wakefield.

She hadn't, and now she wasn't sure how to proceed or even if she would have the chance. Mrs. Wakefield had been very clear; if Lilly couldn't do the job she'd have to hire someone who could.

Then where would she go?

She'd have money coming to her, but she wasn't sure how much, since she wasn't sure if Mrs. Wakefield planned to take out taxes. After paying for car repairs, she didn't know what she'd have left . . . if any at all.

Sighing, Lilly picked up her fork and dug into her eggs. She might as well eat while she had the chance. Her meals might become few and far between after leaving. As soon as the eggs settled on her tongue, she frowned and reached for the salt, then the pepper shaker. She was so upset she must have forgotten—

Her head came up; her hand paused. She had prepared Dr. Wakefield's eggs the same way. She was getting up with the salt and pepper shakers when she glanced back at her plate. The salt was indistinguishable, but there was a scattering of the black specks of the pepper.

People usually seasoned to sight just as she had. He wouldn't be able to do it. A simple thing . . . if you could see. Her hand clutched the small glass containers. What would it be like to live in a world of darkness? To be dependent on others?

If she'd been blinded, Myron would have kicked her out or put her in a home just as he had wanted to do to his mother. He hadn't because he didn't want to ruin his good standing in the community and because he just as badly wanted his mother's house and her rental property. Mother Crawford had come up in the Depression and could pinch pennies with the best of them.

Setting the shakers aside, Lilly closed her eyes, felt around on the table for her fork, then proceeded to eat. Two frustrating minutes later, she was on her feet heading for the stairs. If she couldn't last two minutes, how had a man of Dr. Wakefield's stature lasted five weeks?

"Dr. Wakefield. Dr. Wakefield!" she called through the door. "Don't eat the eggs. I left the seasoning out. I'll remake your breakfast if you'll wait. Dr. Wake—"

The door opened. He stood, shades in place, the plate in his hand, a hard frown on his face. "I believe you left something out of the biscuits as well."

"I'm sorry." She swallowed and reached for the plate. He didn't release it. She lifted questioning eyes to his. "I have it."

"Did you do it on purpose?"

"No." She shook her head wildly, then realized he couldn't see. "I . . . I was upset about last night and I wasn't thinking. I didn't realize until I began to eat."

"You're sure it wasn't to teach me a lesson?"

"I wouldn't do anything like that to you or anyone," she said. "I was upset."

He didn't release the plate. "You've been upset before, and this is the first time the food has been unpalatable."

She threw a wild glance at the three perfectly browned biscuits with a bite missing out of one, the scrambled eggs barely touched. "I didn't mean it."

"You meant it, and I got the message." Finally he released the plate and stepped back to close the door.

"Wait!" she yelled, using the flat of her hand to keep the door open. His jaw was clenched, his body taut. "I promise I didn't do it on purpose."

He stopped but didn't say anything, just slanted his head down toward her. Knowing he couldn't see behind his shades didn't lessen his power to intimidate. Lilly could well imagine he had been a formidable man before his accident.

"I have no place else to go if I lose this job," she told him, unsure if she should have admitted how vulnerable she was.

His dark head twisted to one side. "My mother hired a homeless woman?"

She shifted uneasily. "Not exactly. I was passing through on my way to New Orleans. My car broke down near here. She needed someone immediately and I needed a job."

"Serendipity."

"What?"

Two lost souls thrust together. "How much is she paying you?"

Lilly's other hand clamped around the plate. "I think you should ask your mother that."

"I'm asking you." He hadn't stooped so low that he'd fire her if she didn't have enough money to fix her car and leave, preferably getting as far away from him as possible.

"Please, Dr. Wakefield, ask your mother."

The slight tremble in her voice got to him. He wished she didn't remind him so much of Kristen, lost and trying to find her way. "Are you from Texas?"

"H-How did you know?"

"Lucky guess. Now go fix my breakfast."

"Yes, sir."

She was as skittish as a foal, probably had legs just as long from the sound of her running steps. For a brief moment, he recalled nurses and interns scurrying the same way to carry out his orders. They would again.

Thankfully the kitchen had plenty of clean skillets and bowls. Lilly whipped the four eggs, then added the cold, crumbled bacon, chives, green and red peppers, and cheese to make an omelet. Myron had gone to Las Vegas with some of his hunting buddies and come back insisting she learn how to make them for him. For the first time, she was glad he had.

Sliding the steaming omelet onto a clean plate, she then buttered four slices of toast. Rubbing her palms against the sides of her dress, she stared at the tray. At least the chilled fruit was still good.

Picking up the wooden tray, she went upstairs and knocked. "Dr. Wakefield."

The door swung open. "What took you so long?"

"Sorry," she mumbled out of habit. She hadn't been gone over ten minutes. Rushing across the room, she put the tray on the bed, then came back to the door. "Your omelet is at twelve, your toast at six. The fruit is at nine and your juice is to the right of your toast. I'll serve lunch early."

"What's wrong with your car?"

She blinked. "Sir?"

"What is wrong with your car?"

He enunciated each word as if he were talking to a feebleminded person. She flushed and dug her hands into the deep pockets of the white bibbed apron she'd found in the kitchen. "I don't know. The man who drove the tow truck said no one could look at the car until Monday."

"What seemed to be wrong with it?"

Lilly barely kept from hunching her shoulders and squirming. "I don't know very much about cars. It just died, then started smoking like a freight train."

Folding his arms, Adam leaned against the door. "It's irresponsible to operate equipment you know nothing about."

Her head came up at the chastising tone. It was on the tip of her tongue to say something pithy; then she remembered she needed this job. "Yes, sir. Is that all?"

"Yes." He straightened.

She was several steps down the hall when he said, "Call first thing in the morning to see how soon your car will be ready." The door closed.

A chill swept through her. Dr. Wakefield had just given her notice. Her time at Wakefield Manor was running out. She could wait until she was fired or try to figure out a way to ensure that she stayed.

To remain she had to be of some use to him. But how, when he didn't want her help?

With Myron he'd needed her to care for Shayla, to cook and clean, to slake his lust, and, oddly, to dominate. He'd felt power in her weakness.

That wasn't the case with Dr. Wakefield. He wanted nothing from her.

Her spirits sinking, she descended the staircase. There had to be some way to prove to him that he needed her.

"Think, Lilly. Put yourself in his place. What do you want more than anything?"

Freedom! Her brain shouted the word. She'd hated being dependent on a man she loathed for the very food she ate, the roof over her head.

Freedom and independence.

Her hand on the newel cap, she stared back up the stairs. How much stronger was Dr. Wakefield's resentment against her, even though his condition wasn't her fault? She had nothing to do with Myron's meanness, but she'd suffered his wrath just the same.

The difference between the two men, she thought, was that Myron struck out of cruelty, Dr. Wakefield from fear. However, both men put her on the defensive and wanted her to keep her thoughts to herself.

In order to survive with Myron she had let him dictate to her and kept out of his way. If she allowed the same thing to happen with Dr. Wakefield, she might very well end up the homeless person he thought she was.

Like Daniel in the Bible, she had to be brave enough to enter the lion's den and pray that, like him, she came out unscathed.

He shouldn't have come.

Jonathan knew that, but he hadn't been able to convince himself to stay away. Eleanor had sounded so tired and defeated when they had spoken briefly on the phone Saturday night. He'd called her in between one of the four babies he'd delivered. Maxwell had certainly chosen the right night to switch calls. He'd only stay a moment. He just needed to give her something to bring back a hint of the happiness that was usually in her voice.

Reaching across the seat, he picked up the brightly wrapped rectangular package, climbed out of the car, and started up the brick walkway. As always, the red front door surprised him. That she'd chosen such a bright, sassy color amazed all of them and kept him awake at night wondering if beneath her quiet, reserved nature was a passionate woman whose needs matched his own.

The door opened and the object of his desire stood smiling at him. Dressed in a white blouse and black slacks, surrounded by an arched arbor of English ivy, she simply made his heart stop.

"Jonathan, good morning," Eleanor greeted him, wondering why her heart felt odd in her chest. Perhaps it was because of all the pressure in her life lately. "You're out early."

"I wanted to bring you this." Lifting the package, he handed it to her.

Her amber eyes widened, then went from him back to the plum-and-gold paper. "You shouldn't have."

He chuckled, enjoying the delight in her face and eyes. "How do you know if I should or shouldn't until you've opened it?"

Laughing, she sat down on one of the curved stone benches positioned on each side of the door and tore into the present to reveal a paint set. Her slim fingers reverently traced the sable brushes, the pots of oil and watercolors. "Oh, Jonathan, it's perfect."

All the time he'd spent trying to decide how to bring back her laughter was worth it. "I'm glad you like it."

"I do, but I don't have any canvases!" she cried.

"That's the third part of my surprise." He smiled down at her crestfallen expression.

"Third part?"

Unable to resist, he sat down beside her, trying to act natural when their thighs brushed together and the heat of her body mingled with his. "Brunch at Antoine's."

For some unfathomable reason she had trouble getting her thoughts together. "I–I can't leave."

He folded his arms over his wide chest, making him appear more impressive and magnificent. "Why?"

"Adam might need me."

"I need you," he almost blurted. Instead he stood, bringing Eleanor with him. "Lilly is here and you need to eat. I promised Kristen."

The lines of annoyance radiating across her forehead cleared. "I know. We talked this morning. You were a good friend to Randolph and now to us."

Randolph's name pricked something deep and sensitive within Jonathan's soul. He wanted Eleanor to see him as a man, not as the best friend of her dead husband. That she might never do so sent a deep shaft of pain and misery through him. Involuntarily his fingers tightened on her arm; his other hand closed around her free arm, bringing her closer to him.

The hardness that swept across Jonathan's face made Eleanor want to run away and, at the same time, lift her hand to the hard line of his jaw to soothe him. Confused, her hands closed more firmly on the paint set between them.

"Mrs. Wakefield, are you all right?"

Jonathan's and Eleanor's startled gazes jerked sideways. Lilly, her face full of anger, stared at Jonathan.

Dropping one hand, Jonathan said, "Why wouldn't she be?"

Instead of answering, Lilly looked at Mrs. Wakefield. "Are you all right?"

"Why, yes," Eleanor finally answered, trying to smile, but her facial muscles were stiff. Not sure what had just happened between them, but realizing that whatever it was Lilly had picked up on it also, she stepped away from Jonathan and off the porch onto the paved walkway. "Is Adam all right?"

"Yes, ma'am." Lilly's gaze flickered to Dr. Delacroix, then came to rest on Eleanor, whose breathing was rapid and cheeks flushed. Then it hit Lilly. Fear wouldn't cause her cheeks to flush. Desire or embarrassment would. Lilly's own cheeks burned. "I'm sorry. I didn't mean to interrupt."

"You didn't," Jonathan answered, folding his arms and bracing his shoulder against the arbor. "I was just trying to get Eleanor to have brunch with me."

That's not all he was trying to do, Lilly thought. But since she didn't see fear in Mrs. Wakefield's eyes, it was their business. Lilly's business was keeping her job.

"I've been reading in one of Dr. Wakefield's medical books about patients' reactions to sudden blindness, their depression, their fear, how it's important to normalize their life as soon as possible." Moistening her dry lips, Lilly shifted from one tennis-shoe-shod foot to the other. "I looked in the yellow pages and there's a Lighthouse for the Blind in Shreveport. I was thinking maybe they could help."

Eleanor briefly closed her eyes. When they opened they were full of pain. Her voice trembled when she said, "Orientation and Mobility was suggested to Adam to acquaint him with his surroundings when he was released from the hospital. He refused to have the training because he insisted he didn't need it because his vision would return."

Blinking tears from her eyes, she wrapped her arms around her waist. "I went along with him because I didn't want him to think I'd lost faith."

She peered over her shoulder at Jonathan. "I guess I should have listened to you."

Jonathan went to stand by Eleanor, his narrowed gaze on Lilly. "Very astute observation and ingenious on your part." He glanced down at Eleanor. "I guess you were right to hire her. But Lilly points up an important fact. Perhaps we need someone with experience to care for Adam."

Lilly's burgeoning happiness took a nosedive; then she did something totally out of character for her. "I may not be experienced, but I got him to eat and clean up. No one else has been able to do that."

Jonathan lifted a heavy brow at her defensive tone. The gesture was enough to make Lilly remember the influence he had with the Wakefields.

Her voice softened, but the conviction remained. "With the right help, I can do more."

"I'll contact the Lighthouse tomorrow," Eleanor said, excitement in her voice. "Anything else?"

"Maybe you could send for some of his clothes. Washable pants and pullover shirts. It would be nice if there was a table in his room for him to eat on, a way to tell time, books on tape, and one of those battery-operated tape recorders with big control buttons. Puffy paint?"

"Puffy paint?" Eleanor and Jonathan repeated in unison.

"To mark the tags in his clothes and his toilet articles so he can distinguish them." She ordered herself not to fidget under their intense stares. "That's how it was done in the textbook."

"I'll call Kristen and ask her to send his things overnight." Eleanor shook her head. "He said his housekeeper was sending the rest of his things. I'm beginning to wonder since they aren't here."

"Then he'll be happy when they arrive," Lilly said, straight-faced.

Eleanor's lips curved. "Won't he? Thank you for caring, Lilly. Excuse me; I'll go call Kristen." The front door closed behind her.

Lilly turned to go.

"Lilly?" Jonathan called softly.

Clutching the book to her chest, she made herself face him.

"I want what's best for Adam. If that's you, good. If not, then we get someone else. Are we clear?"

"Very," Turning, Lilly started back to the main house, her mind troubled, her steps slow. One hurdle down, one to go.

Odette and Samuel were returning tomorrow.

Eleanor was nervous.

In all the long years of her association with Jonathan, she'd felt many emotions while with him, but nervousness had never been one of them. As she sat beside him while he maneuvered the Mercedes through the surprisingly heavy Sunday traffic at the shopping mall in Shreveport, her thoughts were troubled. She kept her gaze forward.

When she'd gone inside to call Kristen, she'd actually felt relief to be away from Jonathan. If there had been any way of getting out of him taking her shopping for Adam, she would have grabbed at the chance. As it was, she was trapped in the car beside him, unsettled and unsure.

What had happened between them just before Lilly arrived at the cottage?

Hell, Eleanor, she chided herself, as she seemed unable to keep from looking at Jonathan's strong, chiseled profile as he patiently waited for a woman to store the several packages scattered around her feet in the trunk of her car so he could park in her space, *you are not that naive.* There had been a spark of awareness between them. Sudden, sharp, and powerful.

And totally unexpected. It had rattled her, and her stomach had yet to settle.

Obviously it had meant nothing to him. On the drive from Adam's house to the shopping mall thirty minutes away, Jonathan's easygoing demeanor was the same as it always was. He remained the same good old reliable Jonathan she had grown to depend on more and more over the years.

Leaning back against the smooth leather seat, Eleanor was grateful he had chosen to ignore whatever it was that had caused them to react so strongly to each other. No doubt it was due to the stress they both were under. Whatever the reason, it couldn't be allowed to happen again. Adam and Kristen had to be her main concern, her only concern.

Finally the woman got in her car and backed out. Jonathan pulled into the parking space, cut the motor, then unbuckled his seat belt. "I'm glad she wasn't shopping with another woman or we might have been waiting until the mall closed."

"Women are selective. Men just grab," Eleanor said. The instant the words were out of her mouth, Eleanor felt the slow roll in her stomach again and quickly busied herself with her seat belt. "It shouldn't take too long to get the things on Lilly's list; then I want to return."

"What about lunch and your canvases?"

"Maybe another time." Opening the door, Eleanor got out of the car.

Eleanor was a master shopper and she used her skill to quickly purchase the list of items for Adam. But always, always she was aware of Jonathan's presence, the heat from his body, his disturbing gaze. By the time they returned to the car, she was even more on edge and not looking forward in the least to the thirty-minute drive back to Wakefield Manor.

He'd done it now.

Eleanor was skittish and nervous around him, and it was his own fault. She'd jumped each time he had even casually brushed up against her while they were shopping. He hadn't dared try to take her arm as he usually did when they were out.

He had already guessed that the only reason she'd consented to letting him take her shopping instead of driving herself was that she hadn't been able to think of a gracious way out. In all things, Eleanor was a lady. At the moment, the lady wanted nothing to do with him.

All his fault.

He shouldn't have grabbed. It hadn't been the right time. Hell, he didn't know if there would ever be a right time, but at least he'd had her friendship. Now, he wasn't sure if he'd still have that.

Turning into the driveway of Adam's house, he tried to think of something to say to break the silence that had plagued them since they had gotten back into the car, but nothing came. As before, as soon as he braked, she was out of the car. He watched her practically run up the walkway.

Gritting his teeth, he got out and reached in the backseat for the bags. She was waiting for him at the door, her smile overly bright and strained. "Thank you, Jonathan, for taking me shopping. You must have a million things to do on a Sunday. I'll take the packages so you can be on your way."

He stared down into Eleanor's tense face, seeing the narrow line of her compressed lips, the nervous fluttering of the pulse in her neck as she stood in her doorway strategically blocking his entrance. One at a time, he handed her the two bags. "Anytime."

"I'll just go put my purse down and take these straight to Lilly."

Jonathan knew a brush-off when he heard it. "If you need me, call."

"I'll be fine. I shouldn't bother you so much."

His eyes narrowed. It was all he could do not to snarl. "Adam is your son, but he's my godson and I love him, too. Call if either of you need anything."

The bright smile wavered, firmed. "I will. Good-bye."

The door closed with a quiet click. As he walked to his car, Jonathan had the distinct impression that there would be no calls. Eleanor had just shut him out of her life and he had no one to blame but himself.

Eleanor waited until she saw Jonathan drive off before she left the cottage. She wasn't proud of herself. She'd never run from anything or turned her back on a friend before. Today she'd done both.

Nearing the house, she stared up at the window to Adam's room and wondered if she might have to amend her earlier statement. Had she run from the truth that Adam's blindness might be permanent and, in doing so, let him continue to cling to a false hope that was destroying him day by day?

"Mrs. Wakefield."

Eleanor glanced around to see Lilly sitting beneath one of the huge oak trees near the back door to the kitchen. *She's too thin*, Eleanor thought, noticing with a discerning eye the way the wind shaped the cotton dress to Lilly's slender frame. The possibilities were there. Waiting. She just needed a touch of makeup and the right clothes to bring them out, just as the right words were needed to bring Adam out of his shell.

"Is everything all right?" Lilly asked.

"Yes." Eleanor continued across the lawn. "Here are the things you wanted."

Automatically Lilly took the bags. "Would you like to come inside for a cup of coffee?"

"No, thank you. I told Adam I was leaving the house and technically I am, since he gave me the cottage. A minor point, but one that I feel is necessary. So unless something is extremely important, we'll keep in touch by phone," Eleanor said.

"Yes, ma'am."

Eleanor nodded toward one of the bags. "Adam is a big mystery fan. I picked up a couple of books on tape he should enjoy. If you think of anything else, please let me know."

"I will."

"Odette and Samuel should arrive early tomorrow morning. I've left a message on their answering machine to call me tonight no matter how late it is when they arrive home. I'll explain the entire situation to them."

Lilly's fingers dented the paper sack. "You don't think they'll mind me being here, do you?"

"No. From my experience with them, there's not a mean or territorial bone in their bodies. From the first, they've been wonderful to Adam. He trusts them so much they have a household account so they don't have to call him about every little thing they need to ensure the house is cared for."

"How long have they worked for him?"

"Five years. They were here when Adam bought the house. He bought it shortly after his father's death."

"You're widowed?" Lilly asked.

"Yes." Eleanor fingered the diamond ring on her finger. "Randolph and I shared thirty-nine wonderful years together. I miss him still."

"You're one of the lucky couples to have found love," Lilly said, wondering what being loved by a man you loved must feel like.

"Yes, it was. Were you ever married?"

"No." Lilly didn't consider it a lie. Whatever there had been between her and Myron, it certainly hadn't been a marriage.

"Well, I guess I'll get back; I want to call Kristen." She started to leave, then paused. "I wish you could have known Adam before. He was arrogant, but fair. He demanded the best of himself and those who worked with him. He loved life and did everything in his power to ensure that those he cared for were given the best possible care. He had a wicked sense of humor and a mean backhand on the racquetball court."

Lilly had already met the arrogant side of Dr. Wakefield. "Maybe I'll see that side of him one day."

"Yes. Good-bye." This time when Mrs. Wakefield turned away, she kept going.

"Good-bye."

Lilly watched her disappear around a large evergreen shrub. If she didn't know better, she'd think Mrs. Wakefield had more on her mind than her son. Adam's mother had appeared distracted, and although Lilly had known the older woman for only a short time, she didn't think that was usual. Lilly hoped the reason wasn't Dr. Delacroix. Now there was another arrogant man, and if he had his way, she might be looking for another job soon.

She just had to make sure she stayed.

Chapter Seven

Lilly was about to face another hurdle.

Standing in front of the high arched window in the entryway a few minutes before eight Monday morning, Lilly nervously rubbed her hand against the side of her leg. Despite Mrs. Wakefield's growing confidence, Dr. Wakefield's and Dr. Delacroix's warnings had kept Lilly up most of the night.

Mrs. Wakefield might keep her on despite the men's objections, but they could make her life miserable. She wasn't sure she could work where she wasn't wanted. Being subjected to Myron's scorn for six long years was enough for a lifetime. The best thing that could happen was that the men wanted her and approved of her staying. If Samuel and Odette liked her, their support would go a long way in helping her stay.

She had to keep this job and remain off the highway. She'd already called the garage and received the very bad news that the oil pump needed replacing. The bill was already $600, and the man had said it was likely to go up if they found any more problems.

She'd been fuming when she'd hung up the phone. The car had had no oil. Myron had said he'd taken the car in for an oil change three weeks ago. She should have known he was lying. He'd been angry about the car since Mother Crawford had told him that she was giving Lilly her Ford Taurus and putting it in her name.

Myron was an accomplished liar and manipulator. There was no telling what story he might have cooked up to get the police to look for her. He'd be filled with rage at her for leaving, but even more so for her putting him in a bad light in the church and community.

As usual, it would be her fault and not his.

If she could manage to stay for two weeks, surely she'd have enough money to find a job and a place to live. Maybe even in Shreveport. Little Elm was barely a dot and it had a junior college. In a city as large as the one she had passed through there had to be a host of colleges where she could finish her associate degree in business administration.

She'd always be thankful to Mother Crawford for getting Myron to let her attend classes at the junior college while Mother Crawford was at the community center with the other senior citizens. Lilly's mother-in-law had believed in education and in women being able to care for themselves. She'd had to struggle with Myron and his two older brothers after their father died from complications of diabetes. Mother Crawford had learned firsthand what it was to have a low-paying job and hungry children to feed.

When she saw a late-model car turn into the drive, Lilly's heart rate increased. What if they didn't like her? Mrs. Wakefield and Dr. Wakefield had spoken highly of the couple. If they didn't like her, Lilly might be out on her ear today.

Taking a steadying breath, she opened the beveled door and stepped out on the porch just in time to see the big black Buick pass. Tentatively Lilly walked to the edge of the porch by the rattan swing, debating if she should wait or go meet them. A car door slammed, quickly followed by another.

Hands clasped, she waited for the couple to come around the front of the house. When minutes ticked by and they didn't appear, she realized her mistake. They had gone through the side door just as she had the first time she entered the house. Reentering the house, she saw a man and a woman climbing the staircase. The man wore a denim shirt and overalls, the woman a white cotton uniform. His right hand cupped her elbow.

Lilly hurried after them. "Mr. and Mrs. Tucker?"

The couple turned, their brown faces lined with worry.

"Yes, ma'am," the elderly man answered. "I'm Samuel Tucker and this is my wife, Odette. You must be Miss Crawford. Mrs. Wakefield told us about you when we called last night."

"We've been expecting you," Lilly said, then added hopefully, "I was hired to take care of Dr. Wakefield."

Silent tears ran down Odette's plump cheeks. "I still can't believe that terrible thing happened to Dr. Wakefield."

Samuel's long arm circled his wife's shoulders. "Don't start up again. Mrs. Wakefield said we were to act natural."

Odette shook her turban-covered head. "I don't know if I can. The doctor was such a good man. He never did nothing for this to happen to him."

"You got to try, Odette." Samuel looked at Lilly. "Ain't that right, Miss Crawford?"

Lilly didn't know what to say. They were both staring at her as if she were the expert when she was struggling herself. Knowing *what* should be done wasn't the same as knowing how it should be done. She gave them the only truth she knew: "Dr. Wakefield doesn't want to be treated any differently than before."

Dragging a crumpled white handkerchief from her pocket, Odette dried her eyes, then shoved the cloth back inside. From the rumpled appearance of the handkerchief, it had been used many times that morning. "If that's what Dr. Wakefield wants, then that's the way it's gonna be. We'll just go on up and pay our respects."

"You can't do that," Lilly blurted.

Both frowned down at her. Samuel spoke first, "You think he wouldn't want to see, I mean . . . I meant . . ." he floundered, glancing at his wife for help. Dragging out her handkerchief again, she wiped away fresh tears.

Seeing the misery on their faces, Lilly admitted her failure. "His room's not clean. He won't let me clean it."

Odette stared at her as if she had lost her mind. "But that man is one of the neatest men I know. Always wants things just so."

"Never seen a man change clothes so many times or take so many baths," Samuel recalled. "He didn't mind hard work, but he'd always come inside afterward to clean up."

"It's different now," Lily told them, searching for the right words much as Samuel had done earlier. "It's like playing blind man's bluff, and you're turned around and around with the blindfold and it's hard to keep your balance and get your bearing. Only Dr. Wakefield can't remove the blindfold."

Odette nodded. "Brother Callahan was the same way when he went blind after that accident. Stays inside now. Never see him at the store or at church anymore, and he used to be an usher you could always depend on."

Lilly didn't say a word, but she couldn't help but wonder if Dr. Wakefield would end up the same way if his sight didn't return. The thought made her feel sick.

"If I had known the doctor wasn't doing well we would have cut our trip short and come back early," Samuel said. "I mentioned that to him last week when he called, but he wouldn't hear of it. Said we deserved the vacation."

So Dr. Wakefield could be kind and considerate, just not to her. "His family cared for him until they hired me. There was nothing more you could have done for him."

"I suppose, but I kinda still wish we had come back. If it hadn't been for Dr. Wakefield we might not have had a fiftieth anniversary." Samuel again curved his arm around his wife's shoulders.

Odette's hand covered his and gently patted it. "I got sugar. Went to three or four doctors and they all thought I was some crazy black woman going through the change." She snorted and shook her head in disgust. "Dr. Wakefield came home when I was at my wits' end, thinking I had cancer. Samuel thought the same. Dr. Wakefield drove us to the emergency room and told the doctor he thought it was my sugar. The blood tests proved he was right. I took great pleasure in sending the lab results to those other quacks."

Lilly tried to reconcile the irate man she knew now with what she was hearing from a woman who had no reason to paint him in a good light. "I understand he was a very well-known doctor."

"I'm alive today because of Dr. Wakefield," Odette said emphatically. "There ain't nothing I wouldn't do for him."

"Same here. Come on, Odette; let's go on up." Samuel grasped his wife's arm, then glanced back at Lilly. "You're coming, Miss Crawford?"

She didn't want to, but from the way they were looking at her, they expected her to accompany them. If she wanted them and Dr. Delacroix to see her as Dr. Wakefield's caregiver, she had to act that way. "Of course."

Lilly's legs felt as if her shoes were made of lead as she followed the Tuckers up the staircase. The kind, caring Dr. Wakefield they knew was gone, and in his place was an angry, unpredictable man who wanted to be left alone. She'd be lucky if he didn't fire her on the spot.

The Tuckers paused in front of their employer's door and turned in unison toward Lilly, who was several steps behind. Since they gave no indication that they were going to knock, Lilly realized they were waiting for her to do so. Apparently they had accepted her as Dr. Wakefield's caregiver and planned on following her lead.

Giving the worried couple a wan smile, Lilly stepped in front of the door and knocked, praying Dr. Wakefield wouldn't ignore them or, worse, open the door and fire her. "Dr. Wakefield? Mr. and Mrs. Tucker are here. They came up to say good morning." Silence.

Dread slithered down her spine. "Dr. Wakefield?"

"Coming."

The gruff voice surprised Lilly. He'd spoken only once through the door. Either he couldn't wait to greet the Tuckers again or he couldn't wait to be rid of her.

The door opened by slow degrees. Dr. Wakefield stood to one side, revealing only a hand-span width of his face and body. He wore what could probably pass for a smile in bad light, one of the shirts Lilly had washed and pressed and the jeans he had on Sunday. His hair was combed, but his beard badly needed shaping. "Hello, Samuel. Odette."

The couple's eyes widened as they took in the changes in the man they hadn't seen since his blindness. Uncertain, they glanced at each other, then back at Dr. Wakefield.

"Morning, Dr. Wakefield," Samuel greeted him, sticking out his hand only to snatch it back in embarrassment.

"Morning, Dr. Wake—" That was as far as Odette got before the tears started again. "I'm sorry." Her voice hitched. "I—I just can't help it."

Adam's fingers on the door frame tightened.

Lilly felt the situation deteriorating and jumped in to help. "Mr. and Mrs. Tucker came up as soon as they arrived," she said, trying to get the conversation going again.

"If we had known how much you needed us, we'd have come back sooner," Samuel said.

"Don't you worry about a thing, Dr. Wakefield. Samuel and I will take care of the place just like we always have."

Adam flinched.

"Why don't we go downstairs and get acquainted?" Lilly suggested.

Odette frowned at her. "Don't you need to stay up here?"

"No!" Adam shouted.

Odette jumped; her weathered face crumpled. She reached for her soggy handkerchief.

"Dr. Wakefield prefers his privacy. Besides, I need to start lunch and wash the bed linen," Lilly said.

"Don't worry about lunch. Dr. Wakefield has always loved my boiled shrimp." Odette beamed, sure of herself in this at least. "Won't be no bother to peel them for him."

Lilly helplessly watched Adam withdraw moment by moment. "How about a jambalaya? That way both of you will be saved the task I always disliked. Is that all right with you, Dr. Wakefield?"

"Yes. Excuse me." His face a rigid mask, he closed the door.

Odette teared up. "I said all the wrong things."

Lilly placed her hand around the trembling shoulder of the older woman. "Showing love and compassion is never wrong. It has to be difficult for you and his family. I didn't know him before, so I have no expectations."

"He was always up when we arrived and in the kitchen, coffee made, waiting for me to cook breakfast while he read the paper or one of his medical journals." Odette's round face saddened. "He was a fine man."

Odette's reference to Dr. Wakefield in the past tense, as if he were dead, disturbed Lilly. "His blindness doesn't make him less of a man. His actions do that."

"But he was a neurosurgeon," Odette reminded her.

"He can't perform neurosurgery, but that doesn't mean his life is over; it means it takes a different direction," Lilly said, thinking of the new direction in her own life. "The first step is regaining his pride and independence."

"How do we help?" Samuel asked.

"By letting him know he's not totally helpless."

"Like letting him peel his shrimp?" Samuel asked slowly.

"If it comes to that," Lilly said, then continued, "But I have a confession to make. I need help myself in fixing the jambalaya."

Odette immediately perked up. "You come with me, child, and I'll show you. We'll have Dr. Wakefield smacking his lips and asking for more." With that, Odette started back downstairs.

Samuel twisted his straw hat in his hands. "Can I speak with you a minute, Miss Crawford?"

"Of course," she told him, trying to keep the fear from her face. "Please call me Lilly."

The older man nodded his gray head. "Thank you for helping my wife."

The tension eased out of her. "I've stood in Odette's shoes," Lilly admitted ruefully. Unfortunately, she probably would be there again.

"All I can say is that I'm glad you're here."

She finally smiled. "So am I." She just hoped she could stay.

He was batting a thousand.

How many more mistakes could he make? How could he have forgotten how emotional Odette was? Perhaps because his housekeeper in San Francisco had been a practical woman whose only concern was that her paycheck be on time. Since she was efficient and trustworthy, kept his house immaculate, was a fairly decent cook, and left him alone after his blindness, they'd gotten along fine.

Odette was a hoverer and worrier. She meant well, but she'd drive both of them crazy within a day. There was no way he could let her care for him. She probably had it in her head to try to pay him back for his help in diagnosing her diabetes. There was no need. Doctors were dedicated to heal, but they weren't infallible. They made mistakes.

He prayed daily that his case wasn't one of those mistakes, that waiting was the right decision, that the new studies on going past the three weeks and allowing the vitreous hemorrhage to dissolve rather than operating and possibly damaging the optic nerve or causing retinal detachment were sound. In the meantime, what did he do about a replacement for Odette?

He had a feeling that if Jonathan had anything to do with hiring a replacement, his choice would probably be a retired nurse who was inflexible, pushy, and a royal pain in the gluteus maximus.

Making his way to the window, Adam turned his face into the soft wind that carried with it the smell of magnolias and roses. There was no way of getting around it. He had to accept the inevitable. As much as it annoyed him, Lilly Crawford would have to stay. Better the devil you knew than the one you didn't know. At least he could control her. He'd just have to make sure it stayed that way.

Lilly could easily see why the Tuckers were so well-liked and respected by the Wakefields and Dr. Delacroix. The elderly couple quickly made Lilly feel accepted. While helping her fix breakfast for Dr. Wakefield, Odette told Lilly about her large family, which included seven children, all boys. The youngest of her fifteen grandchildren was a seven-month-old powerhouse named Cameron, the first male of his generation and spoiled rotten.

This time, hearing about other people's children didn't sadden Lilly. One day she'd have her own. Once again she thanked God that Myron had never gotten her pregnant.

By the time Samuel finished his cup of coffee and left to cut the yard on the riding lawn mower, Odette had almost finished assembling the varied ingredients for the jambalaya. Telling the housekeeper she'd be back shortly, Lilly picked up Dr. Wakefield's breakfast tray, took it to his room, and knocked.

"Dr. Wakefield, your breakfast."

The door swung open immediately. "It's about time."

She opened her mouth to tell him breakfast was just a few minutes later than usual, than snapped her mouth shut. Even before reading it in the textbook, she had figured out that blind people, like most sighted people, had no definite sense of time passing unless they had a clock. In the times she had been in Dr. Wakefield's room, she hadn't seen one.

"Yes, sir." Stepping past him, she set the tray on the bed, then glanced around the room. Beautifully decorated, but layered in dust. The rugs scattered on the floor needed to be spot-cleaned to get the food stains out. She peered closer at something small and black moving on the area rug.

Ants. "My goodness."

"What is it?" he asked, his tone sharp.

Her head came up sharply. "Your . . . your—"

"Spit it out. My food is getting cold."

"Your room needs cleaning."

His full, sensuous lips tightened. "That will be all."

"You have pancakes at twelve. Would you like light, medium, or heavy syrup on them?"

"I can manage."

"Pan sausage at six, sectioned grapefruit in a separate dish at nine. I'll pick up the tray later." This time when she passed, she didn't look back. Downstairs she strolled into the kitchen, proud of herself that she hadn't cowered; then she saw the worry in Odette's heavily lined face.

"What is it?"

"Mrs. Wakefield called while you were upstairs. She wants you to come to the cottage immediately."

She was going to be fired.

There was no other reason Lilly could think of for Mrs. Wakefield wanting to see her. For some reason she must have changed her mind. Hadn't they decided yesterday they'd keep in touch by phone unless something very important came up? She'd classify getting fired as important.

Fighting the stinging moisture in her eyes, Lilly took the paved winding brick walkway through the gardens to the cottage. Scarlet impatiens and pansies led the way. Farther back, clumps of yellow jasmine and honeysuckle scented the air. Warm pinks, hot yellows, mellow blues, brilliant reds stood out in the lush green foliage.

The house came into view when the path straightened. Deep purple tulips lined the walkway to the house. Lilly felt like Little Red Riding Hood going to Grandmother's where the Big Bad Wolf waited. But Little Red Riding Hood had a home to run to. Lilly had nothing and no one.

Pausing, she heard the soft purr of an engine, then saw a black limousine come up the paved drive and stop in front of the cottage. The driver got out and opened the back door. A large gray German shepherd hopped out, then paused. Next came a slender white woman neatly dressed in a tailored navy blue suit and white blouse. Leaning down, she closed her hand over the harness on the animal's back.

The red front door opened before they were halfway up the brick walk.

Eleanor came out of the house and quickly went to meet the woman, her slender hand outstretched. "Mrs. Parker, I'm Eleanor Wakefield. Thank you for coming."

"Hello, Mrs. Wakefield, and thank Jonathan. Good obstetricians are hard to find."

Eleanor barely managed to keep her face impassive at the mention of Jonathan's name. No wonder she'd been able to set up an appointment with a representative of the Lighthouse so quickly. "You're expecting?"

"Yes." The auburn-haired woman beamed. "Three months and counting."

"Congratulations, and it's a good thing I planned on serving tea. This way, and please call me Eleanor."

"I will if you'll call me Harriet, although I've abhorred my first name all of my life."

Eleanor smiled, liking the woman immediately. "Eleanor wouldn't have been my choice, either. The door is directly ahead and up two steps."

"Got it."

As she turned to go up the steps, Eleanor saw Lilly on the other side of the limo, watching them. "Lilly, please come inside and meet Mrs. Parker."

Tension whipped though Lilly. She was about to meet her replacement.

Inside, Lilly's worried gaze immediately went to the visitor sitting on the sofa with a perfectly held and balanced cup of tea in her hands, then dropped to the Seeing Eye dog on the floor beside her feet, his head resting contentedly on his large paws.

"Thank you for coming, Lilly. Harriet Parker, Lilly Crawford, the woman who is caring for my son."

"Pleased to meet you," Harriet said, extending her hand.

Lilly jumped to take the offered hand. "I—yes, ma'am."

Harriet laughed, a bell-like sound. "You don't sound that young and I'm not that old."

At any other time Lilly might have laughed with the woman, but her nerves were stretched too thin. Lilly sat on the edge of the armchair, her back straight.

"Would you like some tea, Lilly?"

"No, thank you." All she wanted to know was how long she had left to work.

Eleanor placed her delicate cup and saucer on the polished cherry table.

"I've asked Mrs. Parker here to help us both understand what is happening to my son and to ask your forgiveness, Lilly."

"Me?" Lilly's eyes rounded.

"Yesterday after you left, I realized I put you in an impossible situation when I asked you to care for Adam," Eleanor admitted. "But, as you pointed out, you have accomplished a great deal with him, and with the proper help you can do much more."

"I believe that's where I come in." Harriet set her cup on the polished table.

Both women watched her smooth movements, and although neither voiced it aloud, they compared them to Adam's awkwardness. "Harriet is a social worker with the Shreveport Lighthouse for the Blind." Picking up a pillow, Eleanor hugged it to her. "I have to believe Adam is going to regain his sight, but he needs help in the meantime."

"He hates being blind," Lilly said softly.

"Would either of you feel differently in his place?" Harriet sat forward, her face serious.

"No." Their answers came in unison.

"Honesty without explanations. We're off to a good start. Let's get something out of the way. I lost my sight seven years ago after an auto accident. I wasn't happy about it. The doctors were stupid and incompetent. I was sure if I could find the right one, he'd fix my eyes. It took long, torturous weeks before I got mad enough to stop feeling sorry for myself and come out fighting.

"What I'm about to say may not be easy to hear, but it's necessary if you're to help Dr. Wakefield. The best scenario is that he regains his sight. The worst is that he doesn't. In the interim, each time he is forced to confront his blindness he's going to strike out until he comes to terms with it and realizes his loss of sight doesn't make him less of a man."

"He studied so long and hard to be a neurosurgeon." Eleanor's voice quivered with strain. "How can you or anyone expect him to give that up without being angry?"

Harriet shook her head of short auburn curls. "I didn't say that. Anger is good. Directed in the right way, it can accomplish a great deal. From what

Jonathan and you have told me, your son's anger is directed at himself and occasionally at those around him. Is that right?"

Eleanor shook her head, her lips pressed tightly together.

"Yes." The answer came from Lilly.

Harriet turned toward her. "Your job will be the toughest, because you'll butt heads with him at every turn. From what I've heard from Jonathan, Dr. Wakefield is a strong, determined man. He's had to be to get to the top of his profession at his age. Now, he'll use those same traits to thwart anyone who might oppose him. It won't be easy. I don't know how tough you are, but to help you will have to be."

Lilly swallowed her fear. "Dr. Wakefield can be intimidating, but I can manage."

Laughter bubbled from Harriet. "Good for you. I don't envy you your job. You'll have to push him and he'll push back. I'm married to a doctor, and they can be as arrogant as they come."

Lilly caught a flash of light as Harriet picked up her cup and took a sip of tea. A huge diamond ring glinted on her ring finger. Lilly had a band Myron later told her he'd gotten from the pawnshop for fifteen dollars. He'd said more than once that he'd paid too much. She'd left it on his kitchen table.

"Your wedding ring is beautiful."

"And ostentatious. Did I mention doctors are territorial?" Harriet's smile blossomed. "Men are strange creatures, doctors even stranger. The men who attacked Dr. Wakefield not only stole his eyesight, but his identity."

She looked toward both women before continuing. "I don't have to tell you that a neurosurgeon is one of the most esteemed of doctors. In their profession, they operate on the very essence of man. Now Dr. Wakefield finds it difficult, if not impossible, to do simple tasks a four-year-old would run through.

"Being blind isn't easy. Your senses are constantly on alert, your brain working to identify your surroundings. Initially, you may sleep a great deal to rest your brain from all the overload of activity." Placing the cup on the table, she lifted both hands palms out. Her nails were neatly polished a delicate pink.

"The pads of your fingertips become your eyes. You can see the window behind me. I feel the warmth of sunshine on my neck, but if it were dark I wouldn't be able to do that. With the aid of my cane and the sound wave bouncing back from tapping the area around me, I'd know there was a solid object ahead of me, approximately how far away it was. But not until I touched it could I identify it."

"How long did it take you to learn that?" Eleanor asked, her tea forgotten.

"Six long, arduous months. But it depends how much time and effort you're willing to put into the process."

"Adam will be seeing by then," Mrs. Wakefield said, but her voice lacked conviction.

"In the meantime, how much quality of life is he having now?" Harriet asked.

"He's miserable," Lilly found herself answering once again. "He wants to be independent so badly and can't."

"He can't because he refuses to learn or because no one has shown him how?" Harriet asked, her question hanging in the air.

"That's probably my fault, because I didn't want to push the issue. I didn't want him to think I had lost hope," Eleanor confessed.

"That's understandable, but what about now? Shouldn't the idea at least be presented to him?"

"Lilly and Jonathan think so," Eleanor said slowly. "I just don't know. He's so angry and defiant. He doesn't want any of his family near him."

"Then you'll have to either defy him or get someone else to broach the subject with him or teach him without him knowing he's being taught. But I warn you, trying to teach a person who doesn't want to learn anything is next to impossible. I know; I've tried."

Eleanor glanced at Lilly. Although the older woman didn't say anything, the speculation was clear on her face.

"But if you get past the denial and the anger, you can open up a whole new world for him. There are optical scanners that can read print, all sorts of devices that will allow him to gain independence. Orientation and Mobility classes can teach him how to get around independently." Reaching into the bag, she pulled out a bright orange pocket folder and held it toward Eleanor. "Here's some information you both might find handy on devices and programs."

"Thank you." Eleanor briefly opened the folder, then passed it to Lilly, who hesitated only for a moment before taking it.

"I've probably given you more questions than answers, but each case is different. Just like some people prefer a cane and others a guide dog."

"He's beautiful," Lilly said, her slim arms wrapped around the folder.

Harriet patted the dog's head affectionately. "Thanks, and I heartily agree. He's quite undeserving of the name my husband insisted we call him."

"What name?" Eleanor asked.

"Killer." At the mention of his name, the dog lifted his head and stared at his mistress. "Lloyd wanted any would-be attacker to know beforehand what he might be getting tangled up with."

"That sounds sensible," Eleanor said.

"In case either of you are wondering, I met Lloyd two years after I lost my sight. He says he never worked so hard in his life to get a date." She laughed again, free and guileless.

Lilly listened to the sound and again wondered why she, with sight, hadn't chosen as well.

Lifting her fingertips to the face of her watch, Harriet stood. Killer rose with her. "I'm sorry to rush off, but I have another appointment at ten."

"Thank you for coming." Eleanor came to her feet.

"My pleasure. I haven't ridden in a limousine since my wedding. Don't hesitate to call if you'd like to talk. It's going to take tough love for Dr. Wakefield's wake-up call. He may curse you now, but he'll sing your praises later. Good-bye."

Both women walked Harriet to the waiting limousine, then watched it drive away.

"What do you think?" Eleanor asked.

Lilly answered honestly. "He'd be happier if he were more independent, but he's going to fight me."

Eleanor's gaze was probing and direct. "Underneath all that rage and self-pity is the proud, determined man I raised. Help me; help him."

"Does that mean you aren't going to fire me even if he or Dr. Delacroix asks you to?"

"Do you think I'd have asked you to meet Harriet if I was considering that alternative?"

Lilly felt fear and relief at the same time. "No."

Eleanor extended her hand. "Good. Then we're in this together for the long haul, no matter what."

Lilly stared at the brilliant colors surrounding her, the cloudless blue sky, and the colorful flowers and immediately thought of the black abyss Adam lived in. She lifted her hand. "No matter what."

Chapter Eight

She was a fraud. Dr. Wakefield knew it; she knew it.

The folder in her lap, Lilly sat on the stone bench beneath the lacy canopy of a lantern tree. Dumb luck had allowed her to make some inroads with Dr. Wakefield, but if Harriet Parker was right, and Lilly had every reason to believe she was, a good amount of cunning and skill would be needed to effect a change in Dr. Wakefield. Two things Lilly didn't have.

She was setting herself up for failure if she tried to do more than care for Dr. Wakefield's basic needs. Why had she told Mrs. Wakefield she'd try?

Because you're crazy, she thought, then closed her eyes and leaned her head against the coarse bark of the tree trunk. If only it were that simple. She couldn't forget the first time she saw Dr. Wakefield. Lost and lonely, defeated and defiant, and so very frightened.

She knew what it was to be lost and lonely, defeated and frightened. She was learning defiance. In some ways, Dr. Wakefield was her counterpart. Perhaps in helping him face his demons, she could learn to face hers.

Clutching the folder to her chest, she rose and went inside the house. There was a phone call she had to make.

Upstairs in her bedroom, Lilly stared at the white telephone on her nightstand. Fear almost consumed her. *Just make the call,* she ordered herself, but she made no move to do so. It wasn't as if Myron could trace the call. She was in control of her life now, and it was time she started acting like it.

Without further hesitation, she snatched up the phone and dialed. The drawling voice on the other end answered on the third ring, "Good morning. The law office of Kenneth Powell. Can I help you?"

Lilly licked her dry lips. "This is Lilly Crawford. Mr. Powell asked me to call him this morning."

"May I ask what this is in regard to, Mrs. Crawford?"

"To find out if my—my husband was served with divorce papers yet."

"Please hold. I'll see if Mr. Powell is available."

Lilly mumbled, "Yes." Eyes closed, she silently prayed, *Please let it be all right. Please le—*

"Mrs. Crawford."

Her eyelids flew upward. "Yes."

"Your husband was served the papers this morning."

"Thank God." Her trembling legs were unable to support her any longer. She sagged down on the bed.

"He also almost got himself arrested."

"What?"

"According to the officer who served the papers, Mr. Crawford became confrontational toward him after reading you had cited mental cruelty in your petition," Mr. Powell explained. "The only reason he wasn't taken in was because he appeared so distraught to the officer. Your husband kept saying how he'd lost his mother and now the woman he loved."

"He never loved me," Lilly hissed, coming to her feet.

"He filed a missing persons report on you when you didn't come home Thursday evening. Friday night, your church held an all-night prayer vigil for your safe return."

Lilly was stunned, then realized she shouldn't have been. Myron always seemed to beat her. No matter what she did, it was never good enough. "He won again."

"This isn't a popularity contest, Mrs. Crawford."

"Yes, it is," she said quietly. She didn't try to explain to her lawyer that she'd been trying to get the people of Little Elm to respect her for as long as she could remember. For a while she had succeeded, but now . . .

"He seems to think you ran off with a man."

Lilly couldn't think of an answer to that outrageous lie, so she said nothing.

Myron was playing his role of the forsaken husband for all it was worth. She'd probably be stoned if she went back to Little Elm.

"Where are you calling from?" Mr. Powell asked in the lengthening silence.

She frowned. Was there a hint of distrust in his voice? "You believe him, don't you?"

"You're my client," he answered.

"That's not what I asked you."

"According to the officer I spoke with a short while ago, there were tears in Mr. Crawford's eyes when he came to the police station Thursday night. The officer understood how hard it was on him to be hit with the divorce papers while at work."

Lilly sat on the bed again. The worst possible way for Myron to find out was on his job. It would be all over the plant in a matter of hours that she'd filed for divorce, but Myron would keep the reason to himself. To save face, he'd do everything in his power to tarnish her reputation. It wouldn't matter that for the past six years there had not been one whisper of gossip about her, that she'd been a faithful member of the church, a faithful wife, a caring daughter-in-law.

Instead they'd remember who her mother was and, with Myron there to play the deserted, wronged husband, Lilly's reputation would be irrevocably ruined.

She'd lost again. She'd never felt so alone in her entire life.

"I remember the bruise on your face the day you came to make an appointment."

The statement caught her off guard and had her palming her left cheek. "You do?"

"Your husband has a volatile temper. It's a matter of record after his near-confrontation with the officer who served the papers."

Hope flittered through her. "Then . . . then you do believe me?"

"If I didn't, I wouldn't have taken your case. Are you in New Orleans?"

"I never made it," she said. "My car broke down, but I got a job outside Shreveport."

"Good. Give me the phone number. I'll keep you posted on how things progress. Since there's no community property, we're probably looking at forty-five to sixty days."

"I only want my freedom," Lilly said, then gave him the phone number. "I'll be in touch."

Lilly hung up the phone, trembling not with fear this time but with fury. Myron had destroyed her dreams; now he wanted to destroy the reputation she'd tried so hard to build. This time she'd fight. He'd taken the last thing from her.

Picking up the folder, she started reading through it again. She could do this for one simple reason. She had no choice.

Pick your battles.

Mother Crawford had always maintained that people who were smart chose when to walk and when and if they took a stand. Lilly could only hope that she had chosen the right time because, before another day came, she was going to clean Dr. Wakefield's room.

"Where do you want your dining table?"

"What?" Adam asked, guarding the entrance to his room Tuesday afternoon.

"Your dining table," Lilly explained. If they were going to normalize his routine as Mrs. Parker had suggested, he needed to eat at a table, and not on the bed or floor. "It's about the height and width of a card table, except this one is inlaid and has scalloped sides. By the balcony would be nice so you can catch the breeze and hear the birds singing."

Adam's face turned mutinous. "I don't want any more furniture in here."

Lilly wasn't surprised by his answer. She hadn't expected him to like anything else getting in his way, but she had also thought of a way of getting around any objections. "Your mother sent it. I'm sure she's going to ask about it when she calls tonight or tomorrow."

"She's going to call?"

"Wouldn't you in her place? Where should I put it?"

Adam started to step back, then paused. Furrows raced across his forehead. "How heavy is the thing? Do you need to get Samuel?"

Surprised by his concern, Lilly blinked. "No. It's not very heavy."

"How heavy is not very?" he pressed.

"I've lifted grocery sacks that were heavier," she told him truthfully. "Now where would you like for me to put it?"

"There's an upholstered side chair by the door leading to the balcony."

"Good choice."

Placing the table in front of the chair, she left his room to get his tray. She set it on the table. "Roast turkey sandwich at twelve. Potato salad at six. Green salad at nine. Iced tea. I put your stereo control on the tray to your far left. The stereo is about forty-five degrees to the left of your table. Enjoy your lunch. Oh, yes, Odette said to leave room for dinner tonight. Chicken breasts stuffed with cornbread dressing."

Adam closed the door. Carefully he made his way to the table, circled it, then sat down. Using his hands, he ran them across the sides of the table, then moved inward to find his napkin and flatware. He picked up his sandwich, bit, and chewed.

He was halfway through his meal before realizing his neck and back weren't stiff from hunching over his plate and his butt didn't hurt. He took another bite and leaned back in his chair without worrying about balancing the tray or spilling food. Maybe he'd call his mother tonight to tell her he appreciated her trusting him enough to go home and thank her for the table.

"I saw ants this morning in your room," Lilly informed Dr. Wakefield the moment she picked up his dinner tray. She'd briefly spoken with Harriet by phone that morning, and the social worker had been very specific on being firm and consistent with Dr. Wakefield.

Folding his arms, Adam leisurely crossed his long legs at the ankles. He leaned back in his leather chair, more relaxed than she'd ever seen him. Stuffed probably. For the first time he hadn't stood guard over the door. He was probably too full to move after eating two huge stuffed chicken breasts, a tossed green salad, four corn-bread muffins, and a huge chunk of German chocolate cake.

"There are no ants in here."

His smug assurance, sitting there all clean in clothes she had washed and ironed, his belly full, irritated her no end. She and Odette worked hard to fix his meals. Men!

Dishes rattled as she plopped the tray back on the table. Grabbing his hand, she drew it toward the floor.

Immediately he stiffened and tried to pull away. "What are you doing?"

"Proving I'm no liar."

He snatched his hand away. "Are you crazy or just sadistic?"

"You may want to live in an ant-infested room and I might consider letting you if I didn't have to come in here."

"That's what you're paid to do," he snapped. She aggravated him no end.

"I'm also paid to clean this room and it's not getting done." She tried a new tact. "First ants, then roaches. I remember when I was in elementary school and one crawled into Deloris' ear when she was in bed sleep—"

"There are no roaches in here!" he shouted.

More accustomed to his loud outbursts, she didn't move a muscle. "Yet."

"Well, clean the damn room." He waited for her to say something to aggravate him again, but nothing came. Neither had she gone out the door. He always knew when she came and went. The scent of roses trailed in her wake.

His head twisted to one side. "Say something. You're still there. I hear you breathing."

"You cursed me. I won't have that anymore."

"What?" She could easily give him a headache.

"You cursed me," she repeated, her voice trembling.

The hurt tone got to him if nothing else did. "I did not curse you."

The silence that came this time was longer; then he heard her footsteps and the opening of the door. "I haven't dismissed you yet."

The door banged shut. He was out of the chair before he knew it. He reached the door in seven steps instead of ten and jerked it open. "Come back here, Lilly." Faintly he heard the thump of feet running down the stairs.

He took another step toward the sound, then caught himself. He became disoriented too easily to leave the room. What if he fell down the stairs and injured himself worse?

Frantically he turned, his heart thumping loudly in his chest. The rhythm only abated when he was inside his room again with the door closed. She could go to the moon for all he cared. Save him the trouble of firing her.

Taking his seat, he leaned back in his chair, found the controls, and switched on the stereo, listening to an aria from the opera *Madame Butterfly*. Unconsciously he also listened for the sound of his door opening.

Lilly got as far as the garden on the north side of the house. Adam's room was on the south side. Her temper spent, she sat on a stone bench amid blooming azaleas and daffodils. She'd never been able to stay angry at people for long. That's how Myron had gotten by with so much. He didn't have to make excuses for his behavior; she made them for him.

She should have washed his favorite shirt. Should have fried the chicken crispier. Should have kept the house cleaner. She should have been better, smarter, prettier. Her best was never good enough. She'd bowed down without a word. She'd tried so hard not to be her mother's daughter that she'd let him take her self-respect and grind it beneath his feet.

Holding her head up, she closed her eyes and let her face meet the sun. Taking a deep breath, she let the clean air clear her head. She'd started out trying to persuade Dr. Wakefield to let her clean his room and ended up doing what she had always wanted and never had the courage to do, stand up to Myron.

Her head hung between her shoulders. She'd snuck off like a thief from Myron. The words she wanted to hurl at him burned her throat like acid. She detested him for what he had done to her and herself for letting him do it. He'd stolen her dreams and she had silently let him. She'd stayed for Rafe and Mother Crawford, but she'd never had the courage to stand up to Myron. Instead, she had let him make her life a living hell.

But she had a chance now, and she wasn't going to let anyone stand in her way . . . and that included Dr. Wakefield.

The knock caught Adam by surprise. He knew it was Lilly. He recognized the tentative two taps, pause, two taps. He thought if she returned, she'd storm back in the same way she'd stormed out. Too bad he couldn't tell her to storm right back out. "Come in."

"I've come for your tray." The door closed quietly. "What do you want for breakfast?"

"I detest women who sulk."

"How about oatmeal?"

He hated oatmeal, and since Lilly had never mentioned the ghastly cereal or cooked it for him before, she probably knew it. Reminding himself that the devil he knew was better, he said, "All right. I apologize if I offended your sensibilities."

"Now you're making fun of me."

From her affronted tone he could well imagine her frowning at him. For the first time he wondered what she looked like. "I wasn't making fun of you. I was thinking of what I've come to, discussing so trivial a subject as ants."

"You won't think that if they bite you."

"I guess not."

"I'll just get the tray and say good night if there is nothing else you need." The door opened again.

His head lifted from the back of the chair. "You're going to leave me alone again, with ants crawling everywhere? What if I'm allergic to them?"

"Are you?"

"I haven't been bitten since I was a child, but I could have developed toxins."

"Speak English."

"Become allergic to the bites. So . . . please clean up this room."

"All right," she said, trying to sound put out but silently overjoyed. She'd done it! "I don't want you swelling up like Herbert after his bee sting. His face was so tight and red he looked like a baked sweet potato before you stick a fork into it and let the air out."

"Lilly, you do have a way with words."

Adam's words lingering in her thoughts, Lilly left to get the cleaning supplies. She had no idea if he had complimented her or insulted her. Probably insulted her. She did talk more around him, but it was so he wouldn't feel so disconnected with his surroundings and could "picture" what was going on around him. She was still developing that steel in her backbone.

An hour later, Lilly surveyed Adam's clean room with pleasure. The air smelled faintly of lemon furniture polish and pine cleaner. Every surface, including the hardwood oak floor, gleamed. Not a particle of food remained on the area rugs.

"I hope you're finished," Adam said from his chair, scratching his beard-covered face. "The racket from the vacuum cleaner is aggravating."

"So are ant bites." Lilly picked up the bucket containing her supplies with one hand and the vacuum cleaner with the other. "Is your beard itching?"

Adam immediately stopped scratching. "No."

"Rafe tried to grow one once but gave it up because he said it itched like a bear. You're sure you don't want to shave it off?"

It briefly ran through Adam's mind to ask who Rafe was; then he decided against it. "Positive. Now, how about an omelet for breakfast?"

The UPS truck and Samuel and Odette arrived the same time Wednesday morning. UPS had tried Monday and Tuesday but hadn't been able to find the house. They probably would have still been looking if Eleanor hadn't called Tuesday afternoon to see why the delivery hadn't been made. Now that it was here Lilly could only shake her head at the three large cardboard boxes on the porch. "His sister must have sent all of his clothes."

Samuel picked up a box before answering. "Doubt it. Dr. Wakefield had a lot of clothes."

Odette grinned, showing an overbite. "He's a good-looking man and he knows how to dress. Caused a stir wherever he went. The time he took me to the emergency room, I had so many nurses in my room you couldn't move." She picked up a box and ignored Samuel's narrowed eyes. "Whenever he was here, I didn't have any trouble getting extra help cleaning up the place."

Intrigued and remembering the muscles delineating his back, Lilly flushed and picked up the third box. "You don't say."

"You women put those back down. I can take these up myself," Samuel told them.

"Women aren't helpless," Odette said and entered the house.

"Stubborn woman," Samuel mumbled and followed.

Slowly Lilly trailed behind them. There had been annoyance in Samuel's voice, but concern and love as well. Two things Lilly had never known from a man and no longer particularly cared if she ever did.

Her current concern was more pressing: how to get Dr. Wakefield to accept the clothes without becoming angry. Lilly might have sounded confident to his mother, but she wasn't so sure as she climbed the stairs.

As she expected, Odette and Samuel set their boxes down across from the doorway, leaving room for her box . . . and for her to knock. Despite her trepidation, Lilly placed her box in front of Dr. Wakefield's door and did just that.

"Dr. Wakefield. Dr. Wakefield." Trying not to show her concern when there was no answer, she knocked again. "Dr. Wakefield. Dr. Wakefield."

The door jerked open. "I'm not deaf, although you could make a man wish he were. My breakfast won't get that cold."

Lilly's eyes widened. He stood in the doorway, his jeans unsnapped, a white towel around his neck. Moisture beaded on his muscular chest. Obviously he had been in the shower.

"I . . ." her voice croaked. She swallowed. Except in magazines, she'd never seen a more perfectly sculpted body. And even scowling with his shades on, he was a strikingly handsome man.

"Well, bring it in," he ordered, standing back.

Lilly bent to pick up the box, then straightened. "It's not your breakfast. There was a UPS delivery. Three boxes. Odette and Samuel helped me bring them up."

"Odette's here?" he said, quickly shoving the door partially closed.

Lilly frowned. What had gotten into him?

Behind her, Odette laughed. "I've seen a man's naked chest before, Dr. Wakefield."

"You should have said you weren't alone sooner. Let me get a shirt." The door snapped shut.

Lilly barely repressed a sigh. Would there ever be a day when Dr. Wakefield didn't reprimand her about something?

The door opened again. Dr. Wakefield had on a shirt, unevenly buttoned. "What's in them?"

"Let us put them down and get them opened first," Lilly answered. Samuel already had his pocketknife out slicing through the mailing tape. Lilly went behind him, pulling back the top and inspecting the contents. "Clothes."

"Clothes," Dr. Wakefield repeated slowly.

"Enough so that I won't have to wash for a long time. I'll come back later to put everything up," she told him.

"I'll help," Odette quickly offered.

"If you don't mind, I'd rather you cook me a peach cobbler instead," Adam said, slowly turning toward the direction the housekeeper's voice had come from.

Odette's flagging smile brightened. "Loaded with peaches and lots of crust, just the way you like it."

"As I recall, Samuel likes his cobbler the same way."

Pleased that Adam remembered, the older man nodded his gray head. "You have a good memory, Dr. Wakefield."

"I won't keep you then," Adam said mildly.

Realizing they had been dismissed even if the older couple didn't, Lilly said, "All right. The boxes are directly in front of your five-drawer dresser. The first box is short-sleeved knit shirts; the second box is jeans and slacks; the third box is suits with shirts and ties. The clothes in the first two boxes are pretty much mix-and-match in earth tones. The closet is about fifteen feet away to the left of the dresser. Your omelet will be served in thirty minutes."

Long after the door closed, Adam remained where he was. He knew who was responsible for the clothes. Making his way to the phone at his bedside, he picked up the receiver and punched in 0 for operator assistance. For the first time, he didn't feel as much animosity in explaining why he needed her to dial the number for him.

The answer came on the third ring. "Hello."

"Hello, Mother."

"Adam? What is it? Are you all right?"

The flurry of questions and love behind them caused him to tighten his hand briefly on the receiver, then briefly tuck his head in shame. He certainly hadn't acted like a loving son in the past weeks. "I'm fine. I just wanted to thank you for the table and the clothes. They arrived this morning."

"You aren't upset with me?" she asked, surprise obvious in her voice.

Adam felt worse. "I should be the one asking that question."

"I love you, Adam."

To his mother love meant everything. "I know leaving me here wasn't easy. Thank you for giving me the time and space."

"Oh, Adam," her voice wavered, hitched.

Adam fought the sudden lump in his own throat. "Don't cry. I'm going to come through this. It'll be all right."

"Of course you are."

He knew one certain thing that would cheer her up. "Kristen's graduation is coming up, and we have to be there, don't we?"

"Yes, we do," Eleanor agreed, her voice stronger.

"Good-bye, and thanks again."

"Good-bye, Adam." Eleanor hung up the phone, guilt battling with happiness in her heart. Not once since the accident had Adam called her. Now, the first time he had, it was because of her subterfuge.

Folding her arms, Eleanor leaned her back against the cabinet in the kitchen where she had been preparing a cup of coffee. She believed in honesty. She hadn't been honest with Adam, certainly not with Jonathan. Both incidents troubled her. With Adam, she had made the only decision possible. With Jonathan, she wasn't so sure.

Picking up the carafe, she poured coffee into a mug and sipped. In college she had quickly learned to take her coffee black and strong. Sugar and cream diluted the caffeine kick she needed to stay awake and alert to study.

Of its own volition, her mind returned to Jonathan. She'd met him her first year in med school. He'd never been dismissive of her as a woman studying to be a doctor, as some of the other male students had been. He'd been fun-loving, the complete opposite of serious Randolph.

Her coffee forgotten, Eleanor stared out the window. She hadn't a choice when Randolph was taken away from her. She had with Jonathan, and she couldn't help wondering if she had made the right decision.

She missed Jonathan's calming presence, his ability to make her laugh and not take herself too seriously. At any other time, she'd be on the phone telling him about Adam's call, sharing her happiness with him. She'd never realized how much he'd insinuated himself in her life, how much she looked forward to sharing with him, being with him.

But Sunday had changed things somehow. Until she was sure of how to handle the subtle shift in their friendship, she wasn't going to see him.

Of course he'd called, but she'd always told him she was too busy to talk. Taking the coffee with her into the living room, she looked around the beautiful, immaculate room. She's never been less busy in her life. In San Francisco she had a full calendar. Here she moped and worried.

Not anymore. Returning to the kitchen, she poured out her coffee and rinsed the cup. She should be celebrating, not moping in the cottage. And that was exactly what she was going to do.

Chapter Nine

Adam's progress was slow. More than one curse word had slipped past his lips as he'd unpacked the box of shirts. *How could one man have this many clothes?* he asked himself, then grimaced.

If he recalled correctly, he had four closets full. He liked to look nice and had always had the money to buy what he wanted.

A knock sounded on his door. He recognized it as Lilly's. He picked up another shirt before answering, "Come in." He didn't know why, only that it was important that she was aware that he didn't need help.

"A ham-and-cheese omelet at twelve, hash browns at six." The tray rattled slightly as she set it on the table. "You're doing a good job of unpacking."

Somehow her words bothered him. "You didn't think I could?"

"What I thought was that rich people didn't do much of that sort of thing." Her voice and the faint hint of roses moved closer, then away. "When you're finished, ring downstairs and I'll remove the boxes."

Adam listened to the door closing, then moved the empty box out of the way. He reached into the second box, picked up a pair of what felt like khaki pants, and put them into the fourth drawer with a growing sense of accomplishment. Lilly hadn't tried to help or pat him on the head for completing a task a four-year-old could do. Instead, she'd acted as if she'd expected him to unpack by himself. And that was exactly what he was going to do.

Downstairs Lilly entered an empty kitchen. She didn't discover the reason until she looked out the window. Odette and Eleanor sat on the same stone bench Lilly favored, the bushel of purple hull peas Odette had brought that morning between them. Grabbing a bowl from beneath the cabinet, Lilly went to join them.

Mrs. Wakefield glanced up as soon as Lilly stepped out of the house. "Good morning, Lilly. How's Adam?"

Lilly didn't have to look at Odette to know she was waiting for the answer almost as much. It hadn't taken Lilly long to learn the jovial housekeeper was a worrier and protective of those she cared about. Dr. Wakefield was counted in that number. "He was almost finished unpacking the box of shirts."

"You don't think he needs help?" Eleanor asked, tiny lines radiating across her forehead.

Lilly was sure Odette was the cause of Eleanor's concern. "I don't think a man of Dr. Wakefield's intelligence needs help in unpacking a box."

"But he's blind," Odette blurted, then flickered a worried glance at Mrs. Wakefield.

To Eleanor's credit, she didn't flinch at the blunt statement. She simply waited for Lilly's reply.

"Being blind doesn't make him helpless or suddenly less intelligent," Lilly said gently, grateful for the literature Harriet had left for her to read. "More important, he hates being treated as if he were."

"Lilly's right." Eleanor picked up another pea pod and snapped the top. "Even as a child, Adam was self-sufficient and detested me helping him dress or tie his shoes. He's probably hated me hovering."

"He knows you love him," Lilly told her.

"Yes, he said so a little while ago when he called. I have you to thank for that." Eleanor's smile was warm. "He should have been thanking you for the clothes and table."

Lilly shook her head. "He was ready to toss the table back until I said you'd sent it."

"He was a willful child."

"Who grew into a willful adult," Lilly said. The older women laughed and Lilly with them. Then she plucked a handful of peas from the bushel basket and sank gracefully to the ground.

Watching her, Odette shook her head. "If I got down there you'd never get me back up."

Lilly smiled and crossed her legs beneath the full hem of her skirt. "It remains to be seen if I need help."

"You won't," Odette said with a shake of her head. "I've seen you go up and down those stairs enough to know. The extra cleaning women I hire dread those stairs."

"I don't." Lilly shelled a pod and reached for another. "They add to the beauty and charm of this place. It wouldn't be the same otherwise."

"You see the beauty; others see the work. Samuel and I have been here for over thirty years. Dr. Wakefield is the third owner." She paused, a pod in her hand. "When the previous owner's wife heard he was being transferred and they had to move, she cried for a week. Samuel and I were a bit worried that the new owner might not want to keep us. You could have knocked me over with a feather when Dr. Wakefield and Dr. Delacroix showed up."

Eleanor's hands stilled. "Adam and Jonathan were out for a drive when he saw the FOR SALE sign in the front yard. Adam immediately decided he wanted the house. He calls it his investment/retirement house." Pain flickered in her amber-colored eyes. "Now it's his refuge."

"There's nothing wrong with a refuge." Lilly glanced around the immaculate grounds. "Most people want a place to go during bad times. I can't imagine one more perfect than this."

"But a refuge can become a cage. I don't want that for Adam," Eleanor said, her lips compressed tightly together.

"It won't. You said yourself that he called this morning. Has he done that before?"

"No," she admitted quietly.

Lilly nodded her satisfaction. "He's slowly getting there. You just have to keep believing and have faith."

"I know. It's just . . ." Eleanor's eyes misted.

Leaning over, Lilly placed her hand gently on top of the other woman's. "Walking by faith is never easy. Especially when it's being tested day after day. All I can say is that giving up is not the answer." With all the upheaval in her life, that was the one truth Lilly was sure of.

Eleanor's lips gently curved upward. "I'm glad your car broke down."

"I never thought I'd say so, but so am I."

"What's this about your car breaking down?" Odette wanted to know.

Lilly told her the entire story and, although Eleanor hadn't asked, told about the recent death of her "mother," as Lilly affectionately called Mother Crawford because that was the name she had grown up hearing. She finished by telling them of her intention of driving to New Orleans to start a new life.

"You got any more family?" Odette asked.

Lily thought briefly of her stepson, Rafe, then shook her head. He had been more like a little brother than a son. "No. I'm all alone."

"Not anymore," Odette said firmly.

Lilly hadn't expected to feel the warmth the housekeeper's words gave her or the sudden stinging in her throat. "Thank you, Odette."

"Did you give Adam the tapes yet?" Eleanor wanted to know.

"No. I can't think of a way to get him to listen to them. As sure as I'm sitting here, if I just gave them to him he'd stick them in the closet and not listen to them, although I know he has to be bored in that room all day."

Odette's hands paused over the half-filled bowl of peas. "He never slept past eight, and after breakfast he'd be out with Samuel in the yard, on that computer, or doing something else. He never stayed in his room."

"He had two offices, one in San Francisco and one in Sausalito near his home. He was always on the go."

The three women paused and pondered.

"You ladies sure look nice resting there. Morning, Miss Lilly, Mrs. Wakefield. Wish I could just sit around under a big tree and rest all day." Tipping his hat, Samuel smiled broadly and walked past them and entered the kitchen's back door.

"Men," all three women said simultaneously, then laughed out loud.

"But Lord, what would we do without them?" Odette asked.

"We wouldn't have to cook and clean, that's for sure," Lilly responded.

"But we also wouldn't have the love and companionship," Eleanor pointed out.

"Amen," Odette said.

Lilly remained quiet, then became aware that the two women were staring at her. She searched her mind for anything to say and could think of nothing good to say about men.

The back kitchen door opened and Samuel came out with a red thermos in his hand. "Don't either of you try to bring those empty boxes back downstairs. I'll get them when I come back."

Odette harrumphed. "That man thinks I'm helpless."

"Jonathan is the same way," Eleanor said; then she and Odette looked at each other and grinned. Eleanor turned to Lilly. "I think Samuel just helped solve your problem."

Pride was an awesome thing. It could defeat, challenge, inspire. At the moment Adam freely admitted that while unpacking the three boxes he had experienced all three emotions.

With a last, final pat against the suits hanging in his closet, he closed the door. Trying to get the three suits on hangers had nudged him close to defeat. Finally he had sat on the floor. Getting the crease straight and aligned in the pants had been long and tedious but satisfying.

He'd unpacked all three boxes by himself. He wasn't helpless.

Turning, he went to his chair and sat down in front of his tray on the table. The omelet was stone cold. So was the rest of his food.

He'd spent enough nights in hospitals to have more than a nodding acquaintance with cold food; that's why he detested it so much and enjoyed his food at the correct temperature and well prepared.

He leaned back against the chair. Of course, he could always call the kitchen. If Lilly wasn't there, Odette probably was. A smile touched his face. She was probably busy cooking his cobbler. The smile vanished. He wished he'd told her he wanted it for lunch.

He straightened at the knock on his door. Lilly.

Rising, he stepped around the table and went to answer the door. "My breakfast is cold."

"I can take care of that if you can help me with this."

"What?"

"The battery won't snap in my tape recorder. I could go back down and see if Odette could help, if you're busy."

His hand flexed on the door. Sometimes he wondered about the woman. What the hell did she expect him to do?

"Here, I'll show you."

Before he could protest, she lifted one of his hands and curled it around one end of the recorder. The other hand she placed on top, then slowly moved his fingers over a round, solid rise. The battery.

"When I pop one in the other pops out. My finger is getting sore. I want to hear this book on tape while I clean up."

The pad of his thumb slowly raked over the battery.

"You're probably thinking I shouldn't own this, either, since I can't operate it, but I'm trying to learn. And before you ask about my car, it won't be ready for another week. They had to order parts."

The relief he felt that she was staying was as disturbing as it was surprising. "What's wrong with your car?"

The sigh was long-suffering. Her warm breath gently brushed across his face. "I think it would be easier to tell you what's right with it. An oil pump that has gone out is the major problem. At least at the moment."

"Are you sure? Some mechanics try to get over on women."

"Dr. Delacroix called them, so I guess I can trust them."

"Still, have Jonathan call the garage and speak to the mechanic for you."

"He doesn't have time."

"Don't you ever get tired of arguing?" he snapped.

"I'm sorry."

The tightness went out of his voice. "I didn't mean to snap," he told her, recalling the last incident when he'd upset her and she'd run away. "Let's get this fixed. What kind of tape is—"

"The killer was in the cave. Erin knew it just as surely as she knew she was next to die. The only question that remained was how long she had left to live."

"You fixed it!" Lilly cried.

"It's a book on tape?" Adam questioned.

"Yes. I like listening to them sometimes, although I'm going to have to pass on this particular one. I thought the tape was straight fiction. Mystery is all right when I'm with someone; otherwise I'll be looking over my shoulder and getting nothing done or up all night checking under the bed."

"That's childish."

"All right, then you listen to it and, if you don't get scared, I'll bring you a bowl of peach cobbler as soon as it's done."

Adam's hands itched for the tape. Mysteries were his favorites. He enjoyed pitting himself against the protagonist, trying to solve the crime first. Trying to keep the excitement out of his voice, he said, "Add a couple of scoops of vanilla ice cream and you have yourself a deal."

"Shake." Lilly's hand touched his. The handshake was brief.

"I'll go to my room and get the rest of the tapes. The recorder is one of those five-button, big old-fashioned ones. Button one is RECORD, two is REWIND, three FAST FORWARD, four PLAY, five STOP. Got it?"

"Just bring the rest of the tapes," he ordered.

"Be right back."

While she was gone, he returned to the chair. He'd had an antique like this in high school. While taking some college courses his senior year and auditing others, he'd used the tape recorder extensively. It was better than taking notes and more reliable than asking for the notes of his classmates. His fingers felt the indentations in the buttons. He could do this.

"Here are the rest of the tapes. I'm putting the case on your table. There are twelve in all. Thirteen hours and twenty-five minutes of nail-biting listening. Remember button two will rewind."

"I remember."

"I'll be back with a hot breakfast. If you jump when I knock there'll be no ice cream." There was laughter in her voice. "I'm putting you on your honor."

He hit the REWIND button and heard the whir of the tape. "Just tell Odette to remember I like lots of crust."

"Like you said, I remember."

Adam didn't flinch when Lilly brought him another breakfast tray. He did show his annoyance at the interruption and shushed her. Lilly barely kept from shuddering as the narrator gave the gruesome details of carnage left by the unseen forces of evil. Unfazed, Dr. Wakefield forked his waffle into his mouth.

"Save room for cobbler," she said and opened the door.

"And the ice cream."

Lilly closed the door on a recorded scream. She might not have been untruthful about her reaction to murder mysteries after all. Her hand on the railing, she went to the kitchen and straight to the upright freezer. There wasn't a doubt in her mind that Dr. Wakefield would win the bet. She couldn't be happier.

However, a few minutes later she closed the stainless-steel door with a frown on her face. "There's no ice cream."

Odette glanced up from rolling out the crust for the cobbler. "Like I told you, I'm a diabetic, and that's the one food I can't resist, so I don't keep it anyplace I can be tempted."

Lilly walked over to her. "I promised Dr. Wakefield ice cream."

"I can send Samuel into town." Odette laid down the rolling pin.

"No, he was trying to finish cleaning out the azaleas beds. I'll go see if Mrs. Wakefield can go." Outside, Lilly quickly took the path to the cottage and knocked.

Eleanor frowned on opening the door and seeing Lilly. "Lilly, what is it?"

Lilly quickly explained the situation. "Samuel is cleaning out the azalea bed, and Dr. Wakefield is expecting his ice cream. I thought I'd ask you."

"Of course. Come on in; I'll get my keys." Eleanor returned shortly with her purse. "Is there anything else?"

"There might be one thing. Has he always worn a beard?"

"No, just since the accident. Why?"

"He's always scratching at it," Lilly told her. "I think it bothers him. When I cleaned up his room, there was after-shave lotion, but no shaving equipment."

"I thought he had just decided not to bother with shaving. He always preferred a razor, but after his blindness he kept nicking himself. I seem to have missed something else." Eleanor's words were as forlorn as her face.

"Because you're too close to him. Everything is new to me, and I notice things you might not," Lilly consoled her. "Dr. Wakefield certainly isn't talkative about what he wants, except to be left alone."

"From what you've said, that has changed."

"Some, but he still has a long way to go."

"At least he's on the road. I'll be back as soon as I can. I'll pick up a razor while I'm there."

"The woman was dead. Her car had stopped and she had hitchhiked with a kind-faced man who turned out to be a serial killer. The boyfriend waiting for her at

the restaurant would never see her again. The killer had made sure of that."

Adam's fingers fumbled as he hit the STOP button. He rolled his shoulders to get the tension out. That story was fiction. The author had a vivid and grisly imagination. There was no reason to think the same thing would happen to Lilly when she left. He himself had been chosen at random because of the car he'd driven. The two addicts who attacked him wanted to sell the car to a chop shop—they'd needed the money for their drug habit. They hadn't gotten away with it, but he was living in a world of darkness nevertheless. Even their being caught and jailed didn't change that.

He hit the PLAY button and settled back. Fiction was not reality.

Adam thought he was doing fine until a hunter in the story accidentally stumbled upon the woman's remains. By the time Forensics made a positive identification and the boyfriend had been notified, Adam felt the tension seep back into his body.

Lilly would probably be just as gullible to offer a ride to a baby-faced hitchhiker. Kristen had. When Adam had found out, he'd read her the riot act; then his mother and Jonathan had raked her over the coals as well. Kristen had promised never to do anything so dangerous again. Young women alone were too vulnerable.

Adam hit the STOP button. Was Lilly young? He thought so, then wondered why. It didn't take long to recall the shy, hesitant tone of her voice, the quickness with which the angles of her voice would shift, the briskness of her steps. Plus he never remembered her being winded when she reached his room after climbing the stairs. Together these things pointed to a young, agile woman.

Getting up, Adam went to the phone. In less than a minute Jonathan was on the phone. "Glad you decided to speak to me again."

"Don't make me sorry," Adam quipped, realizing how much he had missed hearing the other man's voice.

Jonathan chuckled. "Straight to the point. I'm taking *Lady Lost* out this weekend. Want to join me?"

Lady Lost was Jonathan's thirty-foot speedboat. She handled like a dream. "A criminal name for such a sweet boat."

"Better than *Paradise*," Jonathan retorted, then added, "but we both know why you named her that."

Before Nicole, there had been a steady progression of women in Adam's life. He'd enjoyed making love as the boat gently rode the waves. Like his vision, those days might be gone forever.

"Look, I called about something else," Adam said, his voice impatient.

"I'm listening."

"I want you to call the garage and check on Lilly's car. Make sure she's not being taken."

"Pardon me while I shake the phone."

Jonathan's droll sense of humor could be funny or irritating. At the moment, Adam wanted to shake *him*. "Just do it. She plans on driving to New Orleans after she leaves here. I just want to make sure she gets there."

"You two seem to be getting along."

"She's irritating as hell, but she means well," Adam said.

"In that case, I'll call the garage."

"Thanks."

"Anything else you need?"

"Yes, but you can't give it to me." Quietly he hung up the phone.

Something was wrong. Lilly looked at the barely touched meat loaf on the plate for dinner. He hadn't eaten lunch, either. "You want something else?"

"No."

Lilly bit her lip. She didn't know what had happened to send him into this depression, unless it was the tapes. But Mrs. Wakefield had said he'd enjoyed listening to them in the past. So there had to be another reason, but what?

Her spirits plummeted. It wasn't likely he was going to tell her. "Odette is going to be disappointed. She enjoyed preparing meals."

"I'm not hungry." Slouched in the leather chair, he still wore his robe. His arms rested loosely on the armrest; his long legs were stretched out in front of him.

"You haven't been hungry for a couple of days now," she ventured.

"I'd like to rest now."

All he did was rest. Today he hadn't gotten out of bed until dinner. "Would you like me to turn the radio on?"

"No."

"Are you sure there's nothing else I can get you?"

"I'm sure."

"I'll check on you before I go to bed."

"Don't bother. I'll be asleep and won't hear the door."

Meaning he didn't plan on answering the door. "I'll see you in the morning."

His hands tightened on the armrests. "No doubt."

Leaving, Lilly went back downstairs. Odette and Samuel waited in the kitchen. It was almost six and they usually were gone by now, but both were concerned by the depression Dr. Wakefield had been experiencing since last Friday.

"Maybe if I fixed some more gumbo?" Odette said, looking at the barely touched meat loaf on the tray.

"He wouldn't eat it." Lilly scraped the food into the sink.

Behind her the phone rang. They all knew who it was.

Setting down the plate, Lilly reluctantly answered the phone. She had been hoping to have better news. "Hello, Mrs. Wakefield. There's no change. . . . Yes, I'll call in the morning." Hanging up, she went back to the sink, pressing her hands against the countertop.

"What happened? One minute he was gobbling food like there was no tomorrow, and now for the past two days he's barely touched his meals."

"He's got to eat," Samuel said, his dark brows furrowed in concern.

"Yes," Lilly said and faced the worried couple. "But I have no idea how to get him to do so."

She wasn't home.

The disappointment was sharp and deep when there was no answer to Jonathan's repeated knock on Eleanor's door. His broad shoulders slumped. He thought he finally had a reason to ensure that Eleanor face him and talk with him. This afternoon when Harriet had come for her appointment, she'd told him the talking clock Eleanor had ordered was in. He'd jumped at the chance to deliver it, sure that this time she couldn't evade him or put him off. No matter how things had deteriorated between them, she was too well-mannered not to answer her door.

And now she wasn't home.

Heaving a sigh, he went back to his car and took the circular drive that passed the main house. He might as well leave the clock and go home. There was no reason to wait. It was safe to assume that if Eleanor saw his car in her driveway, she'd leave.

Getting out, he saw the groundskeeper, Samuel, digging in the flower bed and waved. Adam couldn't have gotten anyone better to care for his home. Walking up the wooden steps and across the wide white porch, Jonathan rang the door chime.

A few minutes later the door opened. Lilly, dressed in a simple cotton dress that appeared freshly washed and ironed, stood in the doorway. Her hand remained on the doorknob.

Weariness flashed in her brown eyes. "Good afternoon, Dr. Delacroix."

Jonathan lifted a heavy brow. His opinion of the rightness of Lilly Crawford was another matter. "Good afternoon, Ms. Crawford."

"Please come in." She stepped back.

Jonathan noticed the reluctance in her movement and decided to ignore it. Once he was over the threshold, his gaze went to the staircase and beyond. "Is Adam upstairs?"

"Yes. Are you going up?"

"Not today. Do you know where Mrs. Wakefield is?"

"Yes."

He waited for her to elaborate. Nothing. Apparently she had picked up on the undercurrents between him and Eleanor and wasn't happy about it. He got the distinct impression that she was trying to protect Eleanor.

"Where is she?"

"She went for a walk."

"On the grounds?"

"Yes."

Jonathan worked to keep the annoyance from his face. The house sat on five acres. "Do you know when she'll return?"

"No, sir."

Was there satisfaction in her answer? Studying the slight upward curve of her lips, he decided there probably was. "Please give this to her. It's the talking clock you wanted for Adam."

Lilly had the clock in her hand in seconds. She looked from him to the cardboard casing. He could almost feel her anticipation. "I'm sure she won't mind," Jonathan said.

Opening the box, Lilly took out the fat, triangular object. "Now he won't feel so lost."

Although the words were mere whispers, Jonathan heard them. "You really care," he said in astonishment.

Her head jerked up; weariness was back, but so was a brief flash of anger. "Why does that surprise you?"

"Because Eleanor hired you out of desperation and I got the distinct impression that you took the job for the same reason," he said bluntly.

"But that doesn't mean I don't care about another person's pain and suffering."

"Adam can't have made caring for him easy," he returned.

Lilly's eyes narrowed. "Do you treat your difficult patients with less care?"

"No."

"Yet you expect me to." Her words were a statement, not a question. Before he could answer, her chin lifted. "If you're sure you don't want to see Dr. Wakefield, I have to get back."

He'd been dismissed. Expertly. He opened the front door. "Adam called me about your car."

"He called? When?"

He frowned at the excitement in her voice. "Three days ago."

"What did you say to him? Did you threaten to have him declared incompetent again?" she asked, anger sweeping across her expressive features.

"Of course not. Why would you suggest such a thing?"

"He's almost stopped eating," she told him, biting her lower lip. "We don't know what to do."

Jonathan's eyes narrowed. "Why didn't she call me?"

"She—"

Jonathan didn't wait for an answer. Hurrying past Lilly, he hit the stairs at a fast clip. "Fix some soup and bring it up."

Lilly didn't question him, just went to prepare the food.

The knock was brisk and brief before the bedroom door opened. "Adam, what the hell are you trying to do to yourself?"

Slouched in his chair, Adam lifted one heavy brow. "Come with more threats, Jonathan?"

"I've come to knock some sense into your thick skull."

"Go on. I can't see it coming."

"You certainly are a bastard today. Having a good time feeling sorry for yourself, aren't you?"

"I don't know anyone who has more of a right."

"People love you, Adam."

"They pity me. Just like you do."

Adam suddenly found himself dragged up. He came out of his lethargy enough to shove at Jonathan's wide chest and found it immovable.

"I don't want to hear that crap. Hell, I admit life threw you a hard curve, but you still have hope; you still have life," Jonathan said tightly.

"Being blind! What kind of life is that?" Adam snarled.

"It's what you make of it, Adam. Last night I had to tell a husband his wife was dead and that he'd have to raise their twin girls by himself. A blood clot, a stupid blood clot. She was only twenty-four years old. She'd been laughing and planning to take her daughters home and spoil them. What do you want to bet she'd trade places with you in a heartbeat to be able to hold her children, hear their laughter, feel her husband's arm around her?"

The misery in Jonathan's voice penetrated Adam's own anguish. He'd lost his own share of patients. "I'm sorry."

Jonathan released the lapels of Adam's robe. "No matter how many times it happens, it still tears you up inside."

"Sit down."

"How do you know I'm not sitting down?"

"By the angle of your voice," Adam answered. "Now sit and tell me about her."

Lilly stood at the door with the tray in her hands, tears forming in her eyes and running down her cheeks as she listened to Dr. Delacroix. Mother Crawford always said each person always thought his heartache was the worst until he heard someone else's.

"You did all you could to prevent this from happening. I'm sure of that, Jonathan."

"Knowing that doesn't make it easier. Life is precious. Wasting it angers the hell out of me," Jonathan answered tightly.

Adam rubbed his neck where the collar of the robe had bitten into the skin. "I noticed."

Lilly knocked on the partially opened door and entered. "I brought you some soup, Dr. Wakefield."

"Is there a sandwich with it?" he asked.

"No, but if you give me five minutes there will be."

"Bring one for Jonathan. You haven't eaten today, have you?"

"No."

Lilly mouthed, *Thank you*, to Dr. Delacroix and hurried back downstairs. When she returned, Adam's dining table was between the two men. Placing the pita bread ham sandwiches in front of them, she told Dr. Wakefield the position, pleased that before she left he picked up his sandwich and took a hefty bite. Whatever the crisis had been, it was over.

Lilly was waiting for Dr. Delacroix when he came downstairs. There was no sense beating around the bush. "Thank you. I–I didn't know what to do. I guess you were right about my experience."

"I was wrong. You have something infinitely better. Empathy. I thank you for that. Good night." He was almost to his car when the door behind him opened. He glanced over his shoulder.

"I forgot to ask how much the talking clock cost?"

He surprised her by answering without hesitation. "Sixteen seventy-eight. Tax and shipping included."

Lilly studied the well-dressed man whose very size made her wary. He obviously cared about the Wakefields. She'd been judged unfairly too many times in the past not to feel a little guilty about doing the same to Dr. Delacroix.

"By the way, Mrs. Wakefield returned while you were upstairs with Dr. Wakefield. I told her you had gotten him to eat. She's at the cottage."

Jonathan studied Lilly a long time before a slow smile spread across his handsome face. "Thank you. I think I'll drop by."

"I thought you might."

Chapter Ten

"Why didn't you call about Adam?" Jonathan hurled the words without preamble when Eleanor opened the door.

Her fingers clutched the doorknob. She'd known before opening the door that he was angry. She'd seen that side of him too many times in the past not to recognize what the set jaw, the narrowed gaze, the tense shoulders meant. She just hadn't correctly calculated the degree of his anger.

However, even if she had, after Lilly called a few minutes earlier with news of how he had gotten Adam to eat, Eleanor would have opened the door in any case. He'd gotten through to Adam when they were all floundering. She owed him that courtesy.

"Why?" he repeated.

Her accelerated heartbeat, the strange fluttering in her stomach, were the reasons she hadn't called, reasons she couldn't possibly share with him. "I didn't want to worry you."

His handsome face harshened. "That's a crock, Eleanor. I love him, too, and you damn well know it. Now why didn't you call?"

Eleanor felt the pounding in her head that had been a slow tapping for the past three days become the loud clang of an angry anvil. Her fingertips massaged her throbbing temples. She would have faced the devil himself if she thought it would help Adam, but she hadn't been able to call an old friend because his mere presence sent her heart skipping in her chest.

She moistened her dry lips before she spoke. "Thank you for helping, but do you think we could discuss this later?"

Jonathan's shrewd brown eyes narrowed. "What's the matter? You have a headache?"

"Yes. So, if you don't mind . . ."

"I do mind," he said and brushed past her into the house.

Incensed, Eleanor whirled around. "What do you think you're doing?"

Jonathan kept walking. Fuming, Eleanor closed the front door and followed. When she entered the kitchen he was bent over looking inside the refrigerator.

"What are you doing?"

Straightening, he shut the door. "You're not eating again."

She'd had enough of his interference, of her acting like a simpering fool. "You'll have to forgive me if I forgot to eat when my son wasn't eating."

"Would starving yourself help Adam? Would going blind help?"

Her head snapped back. "You've gone too far."

"I haven't gone far enough." He began opening cabinets, then turned to face her. "Did you stock food after you decided to stay?"

Beside a few staples, she hadn't. "The main house has everything I need."

"Then why aren't they here? Why aren't you taking care of yourself?"

She couldn't answer. The pounding became worse. Her hands went back to her temples. "Jonathan, please. I really don't feel well."

"Be glad I can see that or you'd see just how upset I am," he said, advancing on her. Unsure of his mood, she cringed. Despite the anger in his face, the hand that closed around her forearm was gentle. "Come on."

Eleanor tried unsuccessfully to pry his unrelenting fingers loose. "Stop. What are you doing?"

"Making sure you eat. You need more than a sandwich."

"I'm not Adam!"

He stopped and stared down at her, his brown eyes blazing. "In some ways you're as blind as he is." He started toward the door again.

Eleanor didn't say anything. She didn't think he meant physical blindness, but she didn't want to discuss it.

Opening the passenger side of his car, he helped her in, then went around and climbed inside. Instead of starting the car, his hands flexed on the steering wheel. His face looked hard, remote, but there was something else there that pulled at Eleanor. "Are you all right?"

He looked at her, his gaze piercing ice. "Would you care if I wasn't?"

The question was like a slap to her face. The hurt was overwhelming. "How can you say anything so cruel to me?"

"Is it any crueler of you to shut me out of your life, out of Adam's life, as if neither of you matter to me?"

Eleanor tucked her head. He was right, yet there was no way she could explain. Even now, she wanted to lay her head on his shoulder, have him comfort her the way he used to, but fear of how far she'd take that comfort held her immobile.

"Eleanor," he said quietly, and no power on earth could have kept her from raising her head. What she saw in his dark eyes was a misery equal to her own. "I missed you."

Tears pricked her eyes; emotion knotted her throat. "I missed you, too."

His sad smile almost broke her heart. "We've been friends too long to let anything come between us. What do you say we forget this week happened and start over?"

He was giving both of them an out. She'd been wrong. He had picked up on the currents between them. Thankfully both of them realized to act upon them might ruin their friendship. A risk neither was willing to take. "After we eat, I'd like to pick up a couple of canvases."

His hand briefly covered hers. "I'd like nothing better."

Lilly tidied the room and turned down Adam's bed. She felt the time was right for another nudge. Kneeling beside the leather chair he sat in, she said, "I've brought you something. Listen."

"Seven-thirteen P.M." said an animated female voice.

He jerked upright. "What?"

"It's a talking clock. Give me your hands."

Slowly he extended his hands and she wrapped his long fingers around the squat, fat, triangular shape. "You can set the time for automatic or manual."

The three control buttons on top were the size and shape of the keys on his computer keyboard. Adam thought of the cuckoo clock that had driven him crazy and asked, "Which one is for the manual control?"

"The second one. Here." She moved his index finger to the indented button and pushed.

"Seven-thirteen P.M."

Adam clicked the button again. Again it noted the time in its electronic voice. A frown worked its way across his forehead. "Where did this come from?"

Lilly crossed her long legs under her. She'd already decided what to say. "I asked your mother to get it for me. Dr. Delacroix dropped it off tonight."

"Why?"

"The clock will help me keep my job."

"How?"

She almost smiled. Dr. Wakefield certainly didn't take anything at face value. "By letting you know that I'm doing my duties in a timely manner."

His fingers closed around the bulky shape and he hefted the clock. "I thought you were low on funds."

"I am, but I consider the clock a necessity. If I don't keep this job, I won't be able to get my car out of the shop."

"You do realize that this may work against you?"

"How?"

"Now I'll really be able to tell if you're loafing." Sitting back, he pushed the MANUAL button.

Lilly rolled her eyes. No one but Dr. Wakefield would say such a thing.

The itching beard woke Adam up. Scowling, he sat up in bed, his fingernails raking through the stubble. It was all her fault. He'd been doing just fine—well, almost just fine—until she had started talking about some guy's itching beard. She was strange. At times she was a motormouth; other times she was strangely silent.

Knowing the scratching only made the itching worse, he got out of bed and went to the bathroom to splash cool water on his face. He caught himself scratching in the bathroom and returned to bed. Frowning, he wondering what time it was, then almost smiled as he made his way to his clock and punched the button.

"Two-o-five A.M."

Setting the clock down, Adam picked up the phone and punched in the first two buttons. If he had to be up, then so did she.

A sleepy Lilly answered on the second ring, her voice husky with sleep. "Hello."

For some perverse reason Adam enjoyed the fact that he had awakened her. "My beard is itching."

"What?"

"My beard is itching and you have to do something about it," he told her, his hand going back to his face.

"It's the middle of the night."

"Two-o-five A.M., to be precise," he answered, satisfaction in his voice. "You must have a razor of some type. Bring it." He hung up the phone and went to the sink in the bathroom.

Dressed in his bathrobe and jeans, his arms folded across his chest, his legs crossed at the ankles, Adam leaned back against the marble vanity. His chin was thrust out and he looked immensely pleased with himself when Lilly entered the bathroom.

"I have the razor."

"Good." With surprising agility, he hooked his bare foot around a stainless-steel stool to pull it from beneath the vanity, then sat down on the soft padded leather seat. "I'm ready."

"What?"

"I want you to shave me."

Her eyes widened. "I've never shaved anyone before."

"I've never let a woman shave me before, so I'd say we're even."

"You're sure about this?"

"I'd like to get some sleep before the next century." Pushing his shades back firmly on his nose, he lifted his chin.

"Remember, this was your idea." Her hand unsteady, she turned on the hot water, then draped a towel around his neck. Wetting a hand towel, she wrung out most of the moisture and wrapped it around his face.

"You're standing wrong. You'll have to get behind me or between my legs."

"What!" she shrieked.

"Don't go woman on me. Come on; this thing is itching."

Not sure what he meant, she debated her choices. If she got behind him and had to lean his head back it would be even with her breasts. She was already shaking her head as she took a tentative step between his legs. Thank heaven she had taken time to put on her robe. With trembling hands, she removed the towel from his face, rewet it, then pressed it to his beard.

"Umm," he sighed, refolding his arms and relaxing against the vanity.

Her hand shook a little more. She tried not to think where his head would be if she had stepped behind him. "You're all right?"

"Yes. Use short, even strokes and I'll remain that way."

Removing the towel, she squirted the foaming white shaving cream into the palm of her hand, then quickly spread it over his face, around his mouth, beneath his nose.

"Here goes." The first swipe of the razor on his face sounded as if she were scraping sand paper, but hair, not skin, came off. Pleased, she repeated the motion, gaining confidence with each stroke.

Five minutes later, she straightened. "Finished. You can wash your face again. The sink is to your right. Your after-shave is next to the right of that."

Getting up, Adam wrinkled his nose, then rubbed his hand over his face. "Don't you ever get tired of badgering me?"

"Helping you," she said before she thought, then tensed as uneasiness swept through her.

"So you say." Slowly he stood and faced the sink. "Good night. I can finish from here."

Her relief was immense, but she wasn't home free yet. "Then I'll leave you with this for the future." Lifting his hand, she put a small black leather pouch in it. "Everything is marked with raised letters. Shaving cream is SC, moisturizer is M, face cream, although I'm not sure what you need it for, is FC."

"Marked?"

"Puff paint."

He twisted the soft leather case in his hands, then turned his head toward her. "You had this ready, didn't you?"

A lie was useless. "Yes."

"Then why didn't you just give it to me?"

It was now or never. "You don't take suggestions very well."

His long fingers flexed on the case. "The tape recorder was for me all along, wasn't it?"

She took a leap of faith and answered, "Yes."

"You tricked me."

Although there was no heat in the words, her nervousness increased. "I only did it to help."

He turned his back to her and faced the sink. "That will be all."

Feeling miserable, she turned to leave. "Good night, Dr. Wakefield."

"Lilly."

She stiffened. She was almost afraid to turn. "Yes?"

"Thank you."

Relief and happiness flooded her. The wide smile on her face carried over to her voice: "You're welcome."

"What time do you bring my tray for breakfast?"

"Eight."

"Don't be late."

At exactly eight the next morning, Lilly knocked on Dr. Wakefield's door. "Dr. Wake—"

The door opened, and Dr. Wakefield stood in the doorway. "Come in. I'm starving."

It took a few seconds for Lilly to get past how the yellow Polo shirt delineated the muscles in his wide chest, the clean smell of his spicy after-shave. Odette had been right: Dr. Wakefield was a good-looking man.

"Lilly?"

"Potato pancakes at twelve, link sausages at six, hash browns at nine." She placed the tray on the table and waited, hoping this time he'd come to the table while she was still in the room. He didn't. She tried another tack: "It's a gorgeous day outside. Would you like to take a walk later on?"

The pleasant expression on his face vanished. "No."

"You need exercise."

"Don't tell me what I need," he snapped.

Lilly saw all her hard-earned progress fading away. "I'm sorry. I just thought you'd like to get some fresh air."

"Why do you think the balcony windows are open?"

She shifted from one foot to the other. "Can Samuel drive me into town this morning to get my car?"

He took a step toward her. "You're sure it's fixed?"

"The mechanic said it was. He said it was ready yesterday, but he had to wait for an inspection." Lilly frowned. "He acted as if I knew what he was talking about."

"I had Jonathan check out your car."

"He told me. Why?"

"To make sure you reach New Orleans safely." Stepping back, he opened the door wider. "My breakfast is getting cold."

Dismissed, she started from the room, then stopped when she was even with him. "Thank you for helping."

She was out the door when he called her. "Lilly?"

"You aren't going to fire me now that my car is fixed, are you?" she asked, her voice shaky.

His mouth flattened. "Don't pick up any hitchhikers on your way back." The door closed.

"What has gotten into him?" she muttered, then started down the hallway. She stopped abruptly and stared back at the closed door. He'd been attacked when he'd stopped.

She continued down the stairs. Despite Dr. Wakefield's animosity and gruffness at times, he'd done what Myron never had thought to do, worry about her safety and ensure that she had a safe car to drive.

Shreveport, Louisiana, with its old red-brick buildings and streets in the downtown area, reminded Lilly a little of Little Elm. But there the similarities ended. In Little Elm there were no freeways to get lost on, no riverboats a short distance away to lure modern-day gamblers, no giant malls or billboards everywhere you looked.

And although Texas and Louisiana connected, there was a laziness about Shreveport that she hadn't found in Little Elm. It was easily distinguishable in the slow, almost thoughtful way people talked and moved. There was an open friendliness, with men tipping their caps and hats and women nodding and smiling.

Perhaps, she reasoned, that was because there she had been prejudged. In

Shreveport, she was an employee of an important doctor, not the daughter of a woman who went through men like Kleenex.

"You need to go anyplace else, Miss Lilly?" Samuel asked, walking with Lilly to her car.

He'd already taken her to the bank to cash the check Mrs. Wakefield had given her. Her hands had trembled as the teller counted $1,500 into her hand. She'd almost cried when she had to pay $900.63 to the mechanic.

"No. I've spent enough money for today."

"Yes'm." He opened her car door. "But I always figure it's better to have it to spend than not have it."

Pausing, she looked back up at his lined leathery face. "You're right. Thanks for reminding me."

"You follow me closely now. The freeway can be tricky."

She pulled the door closed, then rolled down the window. "That's how I got lost."

"Not this time. Dr. Wakefield called down to the kitchen and told Odette to tell me to see you got back safely."

"He did?"

"Yes'm. Dr. Wakefield takes care of his own, always has. You follow close now." With that last warning, he went to his car.

Lilly started the car. The engine ignited immediately and she pulled out behind Samuel's black Buick. The scent of strawberries filled the air. Lilly sniffed, noticing the high shine in the faded dashboard, the windshield free of the carcasses of bugs. They'd detailed the car. Then she noticed something else.

Cool air gushed from the vents and bathed her face. The air-conditioning worked for the first time in five years. Rolling up the windows, she eased to a stop behind Samuel. Maybe, just maybe, things were turning in her favor.

As soon as Lilly walked into the kitchen, Odette looked up and rushed toward her. "Is he all right?" Lilly asked anxiously.

"Dr. Wakefield's fine, but some man's been calling you since you left."

She tried to swallow the dread clawing at her throat and couldn't. "Did–did he give a name?"

"Kenneth Powell."

Lilly sagged in relief. The phone rang again.

Odette's and Lilly's gaze met; then Lilly rushed to the phone. "Hello."

"Mrs. Crawford?"

"Mr. Powell, what is it?" she asked, recognizing the Southern drawl in his voice immediately.

"We got trouble. Your husband has decided to contest the divorce and the grounds of your petition."

Lilly glanced at Odette's watchful face. "I'll call back." Hanging up the phone, she started out of the kitchen.

"You remember, child, if you got troubles you got folks who care about you," the older woman said.

Nodding, Lilly rushed out of the kitchen. In her room she quickly called her lawyer's office. "This is Lilly Crawford. Tell me again."

"I met with your husband and his lawyer this morning. He's willing to give you the divorce if you'll agree to remove the original language in your petition. If you do, the divorce will automatically go through in about thirty days."

"If I don't?" Myron wouldn't do anything unless it was for his benefit.

"This possibly could drag on for months," he answered simply.

"Change to what?"

" 'Irreconcilable differences.' His lawyer pointed out your husband has his reputation to consider."

Rage swept through her. "He should have thought of his reputation before he hit me, treated me like dirt."

"What is your answer?"

"No," she said tightly. She knew she was being unreasonable, but she wasn't giving in to Myron ever again. For the first time in her life, she had the means and the courage to stand up for herself. Pure stubbornness or not, she had no intention of backing down.

"The burden of proof will be on us, and that will take investigation, which will take money."

Why did it always come down to money? "How much?"

"Five hundred dollars to begin with. I'll place it in an open account and draw out of that as needed."

Briefly she squeezed her eyes shut. "I'll wire the money this afternoon."

"You must have gotten a pretty good job," he said.

"Yes, I did. Anything else?"

"No."

"Good-bye, Mr. Powell."

"Where is she?" Adam asked, the phone clutched in his hand. It was past one.

"She had to go back into town, Dr. Wakefield," Odette told him. "She said she had business to take care of."

"What kind of business?"

"I'm not sure. She just asked what the address was here and left."

"Tell her I want to see her as soon as she returns."

Adam hung up the phone and went to the window. He'd been on edge since Lilly left that morning. He shouldn't have snapped at her, but he had enough of people trying to get him out of his room. He was comfortable here. He knew where everything was, and it was safe.

But what if she had kept going? Samuel had reluctantly admitted he'd taken her to the bank and she'd cashed her paycheck.

Where the hell was she?

"Dr. Wakefield," came the soft voice followed by two knocks.

Lilly. He whirled. "Come in."

"You wanted—"

"Where have you been?" Silence. "Well?"

"I had some business to take care of. I told Odette."

He heard the shakiness in her voice. "What's the matter?"

"I . . . nothing. Odette said you wanted to wait for your lunch. Are you ready now?"

"Come here." He thought she wasn't going to comply until he felt her presence, smelled the fragrance of roses. "Are you crying?"

"No."

Not willing to take her word, he lifted his hand and unerringly found her face. Her skin was smooth beneath his fingertips. "You aren't going to tell me what's going on, are you?"

"No." Her voice trembled.

"Are you in trouble with the police?"

"No."

He sighed in exasperation. "Can you say any other word?"

"Sorry."

His hand fell. "Lilly, you could definitely drive me insane."

The deep grooves running across his forehead clearly said he was annoyed, but he had also gone out of his way to help her and ensure that she was safe. "I appreciate you looking after me. My mother—" She bit back the words *in-law,* quickly correcting the mistake she'd almost made. "My mother was the only one who ever did that before."

"What about your father?"

"Left when I was a baby."

"That must have been hard," he said, hearing the flat inflection of her voice. "My father was busy, but he was a big part of my life."

"Your mother told me he was a wonderful man."

"He was. He had a thriving practice, but he was there when it counted. My father, Jonathan, and Mother were in medical school together."

"Your mother?"

"Top of her class until she decided to marry my father and drop out."

"She gave up her career for him?"

He shook his head. "People used to say that all the time, but Mother always said she hadn't given up anything, that she'd gained and she never regretted her decision for a moment." His face saddened. "Losing him was hard on her."

"But she has you and your sister, and memories linger."

"Yes, they do."

Lilly realized that they were having a conversation like two normal people, not adversaries. "I was going to fix chicken salad for lunch. You want me to bring you a tray?"

"Thanks, and while we eat you can tell me about what they did to your car."

Her mouth opened, then closed. "You want us to have lunch together?"

"Isn't that what I just said?"

"If I do, you aren't going to be perturbed with me if I don't know everything, are you?"

Heavy eyebrows lifted over his shades. "I promise to try."

"Good enough."

Dr. Wakefield kept his word. They talked more than they ate. Lilly wasn't sure if that was because he was still nervous about eating in front of people or because he simply wasn't hungry. Having carried his usually empty plates back to the kitchen, she felt it was more of the former.

Telling him she had to help Odette with supper and that she'd pick up his tray later, she left. She knew she had been right when she went back and only fragments of the potato chips and bits of bread remained.

Lying in bed that night, she stared up at the ceiling of the moonlit room. Life was a mystery. You never knew if misery or happiness was waiting around the corner. You just had to be ready. She hadn't been ready today when her lawyer called. She'd almost crumpled. Dr. Wakefield didn't know it, but he had helped her not to. His intervention was all the more profound when she knew he was fighting his own misery, his own demons.

She vowed again to help him fight and win his battle, if possible, just as he had helped her today.

The day was beautiful. Blue skies stretched forever, swept by a gentle easterly wind. Lilly breathed in the fresh-scented air and stepped off the back porch. It was quiet and peaceful here and filled with a calm beauty.

Immediately her thoughts went to Dr. Wakefield shut in his room. Not wanting a repeat of last week she hadn't dared mention going out again. However, if he wouldn't go out, she'd take the outside inside to him.

Seeing Samuel pruning, she walked over to him. "Samuel, would it be all right if I cut some flowers for Dr. Wakefield's room?"

Stopping, he rubbed the sleeve of his long-sleeved shirt across his perspiration-dampened forehead. "Yes'm."

"Good. Which ones do you suggest?"

"The roses, lilies, and tulips might make a nice arrangement." He nodded toward the front of the property. "The doctor and I had talked about adding a couple more beds of flowers to the front yard. Maybe some hydrangeas or tulips in all colors of the rainbow in a winding trail along the fence line. Guess it'll have to wait now."

"Why?"

"He's bl—" Samuel stopped himself and looked away.

Lilly realized he hadn't meant the words spitefully. Dr. Wakefield was more than an employer to Samuel. He was a respected friend. "I thought we agreed not to treat him any differently?" she said.

"He can't walk the grounds with me, tell me how wide or how far from the fence he wants the beds," Samuel said logically.

Before answering, Lilly glanced around the beautiful yard. It was the first week of May. Color was everywhere, drawing one's eyes and soothing the senses. She couldn't name all the flowers and trees, but some she knew: daffodils, pansies, geraniums, azaleas, dogwood, and redbud trees.

"Odette says you've been here over thirty years. How much of this design is your idea?"

"Most of it," he said, then caught her meaning, already shaking his head. "But I never do anything without discussing it with the owner first."

"Has Dr. Wakefield ever not liked anything you suggested?"

"No," Samuel said slowly. "But there's always a first time."

"Why don't we go see?"

Adam felt restless, bored, and trapped. He'd tried to listen to the new tape Lilly had given him that morning, but the dull monotone of the person reading the book almost made him want to commit murder. The baseball games also had ceased to amuse and entertain.

"Dr. Wakefield."

Adam whirled from the balcony and started toward his door, unconsciously anticipating matching wits with Lilly. "What are you going to badger me about this time?"

"We can come back," Samuel said hesitantly.

"Samuel?" Adam said, surprise in his voice. "I thought you were Lilly."

"I'm here," she said. "I brought you a surprise and Samuel came along to talk with you."

He smelled the fragrance. "Flowers."

"Red and yellow roses, creamy magnolia and gardenia blossoms. Your room will smell wonderful," she said, going past him. "I brought you two vases. One to go to the far right of your nightstand. The other in the middle of the vanity. Samuel, why don't you tell Dr. Wakefield your ideas for the flower beds in the front?"

"I, er . . ." Samuel faltered.

"Dr. Wakefield, Samuel said you had thought of increasing the beauty of Wakefield Manor with additional seasonal flower beds along the fence line," Lilly intervened.

Adam had wanted to develop a flower garden showcase similar to those he had seen in Europe, but that had been before his blindness. "That will have to wait."

"Yes, sir. Whenever you're ready," Samuel quickly said.

"What did you want to plant?" Lilly asked, coming to stand by Adam.

"Geraniums, irises, pansies, tulips, camellias."

"That's what Samuel thought. How far back and how wide did you want the beds?" she questioned.

Adam sighed impatiently and ran his hand over his head. "I don't know."

"Would it be as far back at this room? Would the bed be as wide as yours?" she asked.

"I'm not sure." She was rapidly pushing him into snapping at her again.

"Samuel, what do you think?" Lilly asked. "I'm sure Dr. Wakefield values your opinion."

"I've always been very pleased with Samuel's work, unlike some people," Adam said before Samuel could answer, hoping she'd get the point.

"Thank you, Dr. Wakefield. Hearing you say that means a lot," Samuel said.

"I'm lucky to have you," Adam said, meaning it. He never had to worry about Wakefield Manor or unnecessary withdrawals against the household account.

Encouraged, Samuel said, "Maybe the beds in the front could be a couple hundred feet back, twice the length of the hall, and half as wide as that wide bed you sleep in. I could border everything with monkey grass if we just did the tulips. The camellias as a backdrop for daffodils, snapdragons, and begonias for March and April. Then in the summer I could switch to begonias, impatiens, and snapdragons."

"That sounds beautiful," Lilly said.

Adam thought so, too, but he'd planned on having an active part in the planning of the garden. Even with Samuel's helpful hints, he couldn't judge distance. He wanted to "see" the placement. "It'll wait for a few months."

"Yes, sir." The disappointment in the elderly man's voice was evident.

"Thanks for coming up," Adam told him.

"No bother. I was just trying to tame those red-tipped photenias on the east side of the yard," the gardener said. "They're over six feet and blooming. We had a mild winter and the yard did well."

"Samuel, why don't you write down what you plan and we'll discuss it?" Adam offered, suddenly anxious to make amends for his earlier abruptness.

"Yes, sir. I'll do that."

"In the meantime, have you given any thought to taming the acres at the back of the house?" Adam asked, wanting to give the man something.

"I have. It'll be kinda like little clearings of flowers so you never know what you're gonna find, short mixed with tall plants and flowers. There'll be paths wide enough for two people, so you could walk and enjoy them. No sense having flowers if you can't enjoy them," Samuel mused. "Be nice to bunch delphiniums, roses, daylilies, and variegated irises in long, curved borders. It'll take muscles, time, and money, but it'll be worth it."

Thoughtfully Adam rubbed his chin. "An iris-lined pond in a quiet nook with a series of waterfalls would add serenity to the gardens."

"Yes, sir, it would." Samuel's voice sounded eager already.

"Then get started right away. By this time next year I'll be able to see what progress you've made."

Samuel waited a second too long before he replied, "Yes, sir." Lilly knew it the instant she saw the harshness in Adam's face replace the speculation.

Outside the door, she and Samuel were quiet as they walked a few feet down the hall. "I'm sorry. I thought taking an interest in what was going on around the house would be good for him."

"Not your fault. It was mine." Samuel gripped his straw hat in his hands. "He kinda threw me off when he said he'd see the gardens. Mrs. Wakefield said the doctors weren't sure."

"He hasn't given up hope."

"A man's gotta have hope, Miss Lilly." Nodding, he went down the hallway.

Sighing, Lilly went to Dr. Wakefield's room and knocked.

"What is it now, Lilly?"

She opened the door. He stood in the exact place they had left him, his chin thrust forward belligerently, his shoulders thrown back. He was freshly shaven, wearing a melon-colored Polo shirt and stonewashed jeans. He looked fit and handsome. "You could always come outside and walk the grounds."

His lips tightened. "A waste of Samuel's time and mine."

"He doesn't mind."

"I do."

The last days had been calm. She'd almost forgotten how temperamental Dr. Wakefield could be. But at least she now realized he would never harm her. She walked to him, close enough to see her reflection in his shades when he turned toward her. "You enjoying the new tapes?"

"Not especially."

"Why?" she asked, trying to figure out where this particular mood had come from.

"The woman's voice is irritating."

Glancing around for the tape recorder, Lilly walked over and hit the PLAY button. In seconds she understood and hit STOP. "I bet Edgar Gunn wanted to commit murder," she said, referring to the author.

Adam's lips twitched.

Seeing it, she came to a quick decision. "I was planning on going into town this afternoon. Why don't I pick up the book and read it to you?"

He shrugged. "You couldn't do any worse."

"Dr. Wakefield, you are too kind."

What had seemed like a good idea to Lilly hours earlier no longer seemed that way.

"Are you going to read or stand there?" Adam asked sharply.

"In biblical times, didn't royalty throw people who didn't please them to the lions?" she asked, only half-teasing.

Adam's mouth twitched. "The only lions around here are the stone ones by the pool."

"I guess I'm safe then." Picking up a footstool that had been pushed against the wall, she placed it near Adam's feet, sat down in front of his chair, and opened the book. "Do you want me to start at the beginning?"

He frowned. "You're on the floor?"

"Footstool. I'll put it back," she quickly told him. "Mother Crawford always liked me to sit close so she could catch the words faster."

"Interesting way of phrasing." Folding his arms, he leaned back in his chair. "All right, scare me."

She did, using the inflections of her voice to show the different characters and the terror. She might have read longer, but she yawned.

"What time it is?" Adam asked.

"Twelve-thirty," Lilly answered around another yawn.

"Go to bed," Adam instructed. "We'll continue tomorrow."

Fighting another yawn, Lilly replaced the footstool. "Good night, Dr. Wakefield."

"Will you be able to sleep?" he asked.

"If you hear footsteps thundering down the hall coming this way, it will be me," she told him with a laugh.

"Maybe you should read *Silent Prey* after lunch?" he suggested.

"I don't mind an hour after lunch, but mystery stories are best just before bed." She opened the door.

"Leave it ajar if you want."

The offer surprised and delighted her. "I think I will. No sense being like Julia in *Silent Prey* and fumbling with a doorknob while the killer is coming."

"You're scaring yourself."

"It's all right this time."

"Why?"

"Because I have you to protect me," she answered simply and left.

Adam sat in his chair, thinking of what Lilly had said and totally unaware of the pleased expression on his face.

Chapter Eleven

Despite reading *Silent Prey*, Lilly had no difficulty sleeping that night or the next. She began to look forward to the times she and Adam had together after lunch and at night before bed. From his reaction, he enjoyed their times together as well. In a week, she had finished one book and started on *The Being*.

Samuel interrupted one afternoon a week later. His hat in his hand, he came in and perched on the edge of an armchair. "I drew up the plans for the back, and I thought you might like to hear them. But if you don't mind, I'd just like to wait until next summer and you can walk the grounds with me. There's a couple of places that the lily pond might go, but I wanna be sure. Is it all right to wait?"

"Next summer would be fine," Adam said flatly.

Samuel pushed to his feet. "I better get back to work."

"He's a good man," Lilly commented after the gardener had gone.

"Did you put him up to this?" Adam asked, his voice like chips of jagged ice.

Lilly's eyes widened. "No."

Adam came to his feet. "Wasn't that another ploy to give the poor old depressed doctor a way to be useful, to give him hope?"

"No."

"I don't believe you. He'd never come up here on his own."

"Why would you say such a thing? He admires and respects you."

Adam whirled, his fists clenched. "He pities me and it probably sickens him to see me this way, just as it sickens me to have him see me."

Suddenly a scream, a real one, ripped through the house. It was chilling and full of pain and fear.

Lilly and Adam froze.

"Help! Help!" Samuel's frantic yell boomed through the house.

Lilly flung open Adam's door and raced down the hallway toward the stairs.

"What is it? What happened?" yelled Adam from behind her.

She never paused. "I don't know!"

Lilly hit the stairs running. She didn't stop until she barreled into the kitchen. On the floor flat on her back Odette moaned and whimpered. Samuel, her hand clutched in his, knelt by her side. A few feet away were scattered mixing bowls and an overturned step stool.

"Lord, help me!" she cried.

The plea spurned Lilly into action. Rushing across the room, she knelt on the other side of the housekeeper and took her free hand. "Lie still, Odette. Where do you hurt?"

Tears streamed down the woman's face. "Oh, God, all over. I hope I didn't break my hip like Sister Jackson."

Lilly's frightened gaze flew up to Samuel.

"Hush that nonsense," he chided, his voice unsteady. "You just got the wind knocked out of you. You should have waited for me to put up the mixing bowl, woman."

"I hurt, Samuel. I hurt!" she cried, a stream of tears rolling down her face. "Go get Dr. Wakefield."

"Odet—"

"I want Dr. Wakefield!" she cried, cutting off her husband. "He'll know what to do."

Samuel's callused hand tightened on his wife's for a second; then he nodded and lifted his head. "Go get Dr. Wakefield."

Lilly looked from husband to wife; their eyes were pleading for her to do as they asked. "He may not come."

"He'll come." Odette drew in a deep breath. "Just go tell him. He'll come for me."

"He'll come," Samuel confirmed.

"Maybe we should just call an ambulance," Lilly suggested, trying to remain calm.

"Oh, my Lord! I want Dr. Wakefield," Odette sobbed.

"Hush that crying, woman, or you'll get your pressure up. Miss Lilly is gonna go get him, and I bet you he'll say you're just fine."

Odette closed her eyes, tears leaking from beneath the lids. "I want Dr. Wakefield."

"I'll go get him." Lowering Odette's hand gently to the floor, Lilly dashed out of the room.

"What's happening? Someone answer me!" yelled Adam.

Lilly heard Dr. Wakefield's voice the moment she rounded the corner of the hallway leading to the stairs. It appeared she wouldn't have to go get Dr. Wakefield. He was coming to them. Or so she thought until she reached the base of the stairs and saw him, both hands clutched around the newel cap.

Cautiously he stuck one foot out only to withdraw it. Even from the foot of the stairs, she could see the fear in his face. The reason that he never wanted to leave his room was suddenly answered.

"Odette fell off the folding step stool, and she's asking for you," Lilly explained, continuing up the stairs.

Adam jerked back. "Me?"

Praying she was doing the right thing, Lilly came up beside him and took his free hand so that he was between her and the stair railing. "You. She's frightened. She became worse when I mentioned calling the ambulance. Samuel is concerned about her blood pressure."

"I—I can't."

"Dr. Wakefield!" Samuel's voice called from below.

"They need your help."

His face furious, Adam turned on her. "I can't even help myself."

"Then help someone else. Forget yourself and go help Odette. Calm her enough so I can call the ambulance."

"It's not—"

"Nothing is easy. I know. Now come on and take my arm. You lead off."

For a moment she didn't think he would do it; then he took her arm, drew a deep breath, and stuck a foot out.

"We're coming!" Lilly yelled, praying Dr. Wakefield wouldn't give up. He didn't. Lilly prayed each step, giving out a progress report as they went.

As soon as they entered the kitchen, Odette cried, "I knew you'd come. I just knew it."

"Odette. I–I don't know how much help I can be."

"I've been here praying, and I know you can help," Odette told him.

Adam didn't move.

"You are going to help her, aren't you, Dr. Wakefield?" Samuel asked, his leathery brown face showing fear for the first time.

Adam lifted his hands. Hands that he couldn't see.

To be needed. He was a doctor. A surgeon. Once he had been on his way to being the best in his field.

"Please," Lilly whispered. "Please."

"Take me to her side."

Lilly complied, leading him to Odette and then stopping so he could kneel by the fallen woman. He was barely settled before Odette reached out and tightly grasped his hand.

Adam folded his other hand over hers. Slowly he moved his fingers to her pulse. Satisfied with what his fingertips told him, he ran his hand up her arm to her face. Cool. Not sweaty. "Do you hurt anywhere?"

"My back. My head. My sit-down. My legs."

"Let's start at the head and go down." His hand went to her head and felt the cloth. "Wearing your turban?"

"I washed my hair and didn't have time to press it out." Despite the situation, she sounded chagrined.

"As I recall, you always looked rather stately in your turban." His hand gently slipped the covering off and checked her head for lumps. "Do you recall hitting your head?"

"No, but it happened fast. That's how Sister Jackson broke her hip." She sniffled.

Adam's examination moved to her shoulder. "I think we can rule that out. Hip fractures are very painful, and every movement would be uncomfortable. I'm not hearing the hitch in your voice."

Odette closed her eyes. "Thank the Lord."

"Let's see about the rest of you. Here we go. Neck. Right arm. Left arm." His fingertips followed the map his words described. "Lilly, let me know if she shows any signs of pain."

Adam waited, listening to Lilly's calm voice reporting Odette's reactions. "Move the leg that doesn't hurt first. Start with the toes, then ankle, knee, hip."

Odette had no difficulty with the left leg. She got as far as her ankle on the right leg before she cried out.

"Stop," Adam ordered. "Help me to where her leg is," he told Lilly. She did as instructed and he immediately felt the warmth, the slight distension. Without waiting for assistance, he found the left ankle, compared. "You injured your right ankle, Odette. I can't tell how badly, but Lilly was right in wanting to call the ambulance."

Samuel was already getting up to call.

"Notify Dr. Brown, too, Samuel. Lilly, get two quart bags and fill them with crushed ice. Then, see if you can find a couple of ten-pound bags of sugar or flour to hold them in place. I don't want her ankle to move more than necessary. That should be good enough until the paramedics get here and splint it."

Samuel came back to his wife's side. "The ambulance is on the way and I called your doctor. Thank you, Dr. Wakefield."

Adam nodded. "Lilly, you better go wait by the road. This place is not the easiest to find."

"I'll go," offered Samuel.

"Stay with Odette," Lilly told him.

"And I'll stay here and let Odette hold my hand," Adam said, giving the woman's hand a gentle squeeze. "Now, what have those rambunctious grandchildren of yours been up to lately?"

It seemed forever instead of the ten minutes it took for the ambulance to come. Lilly waved them down. The ambulance stopped even with her. A young black woman jumped out.

"Hi. Where's the person needing help?"

"Up at the house," Lilly answered.

"Hop in."

"Thank you." Lilly scrambled inside.

"She fell off a kitchen stool?" the female attendant asked.

"Yes. Dr. Wakefield thinks she did something to her ankle."

"A doctor has already seen her?" asked the burly male ambulance driver.

Unconsciously Lilly shifted closer to the door. The man had a surly bulldog look about him that reminded her too much of Myron. "He lives there. He told us to call the ambulance."

"Lucky for her," the woman said.

The ambulance came to a halt directly in front of the steps. The wail of the siren faded, but the red light continued to flash. Piling out of the vehicle, the attendants went to the back for their case.

"Lilly, what happened? Is Adam all right?" Eleanor cried, running from around the side of the house.

"He's fine. Odette fell and he had us call the ambulance."

"Adam?" Surprise flashed across her face.

"Which way?" asked the male attendant, his broad face unsmiling.

"This way." Lilly led them to the kitchen, then stepped aside.

"I think I'm about to be replaced." Adam came to his feet, reaching out his hand. "Lilly."

"Coming, Dr. Wakefield."

The male attendant stopped, the emergency case banging against his leg. "He's the doctor who told you to call?"

"Yes," Lilly answered.

"You got to be kidding. That guy is blind," the male attendant said, his voice filled with derision. "I'm sick and tired of all these false runs. This is the fourth one today."

"My son is a prominent neurosurgeon," Eleanor declared. "If he said to call an ambulance there was reason."

"Mother?" Frowning, Adam turned toward her voice. "When did you get here?"

"I—" Eleanor hesitated. "We'll talk about it later, once Odette is taken care of."

The male attendant turned to go. "This is a wash. I'm not taking the advice of a blind man."

"Samuel?" Odette whimpered in pain and fear.

Samuel came to his feet. "I called the ambulance and I'm telling you you'd better take my wife in, and you had better do it to the best of your ability, as limited as it seems to be. I already called my wife's doctor and he's expecting her and we're going in that ambulance."

"It's your money to waste," the surly man said.

"John," the female attendant hissed in warning.

"I'll go get the cart," John said and left.

"Take me to my room," Adam ordered, his voice tight and strained.

"I'm sor—"

"Now," Adam said, cutting Lilly off.

"Come on." She hooked his hand through her arm and led him out of the room.

"Adam—"

"Not now, Mother."

Her hands clamped together, Eleanor stepped aside and let them pass.

Lilly glanced around as the sound of the gurney rolling over the hardwood floor faded into silence when it reached the area rugs. His lip curled, the attendant stared at them. Lilly mouthed, *bully* and led Adam up the stairs.

Eleanor was so angry she was trembling. Too angry to stand still, she paced the length of the counter in Adam's kitchen, the telephone gripped in her hand.

"Eleanor, what is it?"

"Jonathan, I'm so angry I could spit."

"Then spit and tell me how I can help," he told her.

His calm, reassuring voice almost made her smile until she thought of Adam's face, the look of defeat, when he left the kitchen. Quickly she told Jonathan what had happened, ending with, "Please check on Odette and get me the name of that attendant. He hasn't heard the last of this."

"I'll call the ER to see who is on duty and check on Odette. As soon as I can, I'll leave here and go over there personally," he told her. "And leave the attendant to me."

Eleanor heard the tightness in Jonathan's voice, and oddly, it eased some of her anger. He was the first person she had called when the hospital notified her that Adam had been hurt. He'd chartered a plane and been there in four hours as calm and reassuring as he was now.

"How did Adam take you being there?"

"Not very well," she admitted. Jonathan always seemed to know the things she didn't have to speak. "Perhaps I should have gone as he requested."

"Adam loves you, Eleanor. He's not angry at you, but at the situation."

"I know, but it's just so hard." Tears welled up in her eyes. "Why?"

"Would knowing the answer make any difference? Would it make this any easier on any of us?"

"No," she answered softly. She forgot at times that she wasn't the only one suffering. "I'll let you get back to your patients."

"I'll be out after I leave the hospital."

"You don't have to do that. It's a long drive."

"I'll see you around seven. Good-bye."

Eleanor hung up the phone feeling better. She wasn't alone. As long as she had Jonathan she wasn't alone.

Going to the foot of the stairs, she stared up. If only Adam had someone who would stand by his side no matter what he said or did. To let him know that he mattered. Nicole certainly wasn't that person. She was an intelligent, beautiful, ambitious woman. She'd tried, but she hadn't been able to stick. Few women could have when nothing was being given in return. It took unconditional love and understanding to keep caring for someone without expecting anything in return. Eleanor had been aware of that when she walked away from a medical career and married Randolph. He'd shown his love in countless small ways: notes on her pillows, impromptu rendezvous, midnight suppers. But she'd always been aware his career came first.

Not an easy lesson, but one she had learned as any wife of a doctor must learn. Illness was seldom convenient, to the patient, to the physician's family, to the attending physician. But if the bond was strong enough, the love and the marriage would survive.

Adam needed someone. Eleanor just wished she knew who.

"Please leave."

Lilly heard the words, saw the humiliation and defeat in Adam's face, felt tears prick her eyes. She knew what it was to feel the same way. "You need to eat."

"I need to be left alone."

For the first time, something inside her didn't go still and quiet at his raised voice. She'd seen him with Odette and now understood what a wonderful and caring doctor he must have been. "That ambulance attendant was wrong."

Adam's shoulders jerked. "He was right. How could I help someone when I can't even help myself?"

Without thinking, she caught his arm when he would have moved away from her. "You did help. You calmed Odette, reassured her enough so she didn't get hysterical about going to the hospital in the ambulance. That's more than her husband or I could do."

"You said it. She was hysterical. She's probably fine."

"You didn't think that when you examined her."

His laugh was bitter. "A blind doctor. No wonder the attendant was incredulous." He pulled his arm free. "Go, Lilly. Please."

She watched him feel his way across the room. "You have to eat."

Finding the chair, Adam sat down and turned his head.

She was used to him shutting her out, but this time it was different. He had been defiant in the past, but this time there was defeat in the slump of his shoulders, the bowed head.

"You have to eat," she repeated, barely getting the words past the lump in her throat. "I'll go fix you a tray."

Leaving the room, she started down the stairs and saw Mrs. Wakefield. The older woman met her halfway.

She searched Lilly's face, then slapped the flat of her hand on the banister. "I wish I could get my hands on that ignorant man."

"Me, too," Lilly said, anger creeping into her voice. "He had no right to talk to Dr. Wakefield that way."

For a long time Eleanor studied the usually quiet Lilly, who was now almost as angry as she was. The few occasions that Lilly had called or come to the cottage had been brief. Eleanor had gotten the distinct impression that at times Lilly was afraid of her own shadow. It didn't take much thought on

Eleanor's part to figure out the reason, but now she was upset on Adam's behalf.

"Thank you, Lilly, for caring."

Lilly flushed and clasped her hands in front of her. "He was so gentle and caring with Odette. He calmed her down and made her relax. He must have been a wonderful doctor."

"He was. That's why this is so senseless and painful for all of us."

"But he can still get better, can't he?" Lilly questioned.

"I pray so, Lilly," Eleanor said, her gaze going up the stairs. "I don't suppose it would be a good idea to go up and talk to him."

Lilly saw the heartache in the older woman's face and felt helpless. "He doesn't want to see anyone."

Eleanor nodded and wrapped her arms around her waist. "Do you have any children, Lilly?"

The question caught her off guard. She had wanted Shayla and Rafe to be hers, but they never had been. "No."

"It's one of the most rewarding experiences you can have. You want them to be happy, to be loved. You'd give anything for that, pray for that to happen." Once again she stared up the stairs. "A mother should be able to help her children."

If there was one thing Lilly understood, it was the need to be needed, to know you made a difference in someone's life. She also understood how it felt to fail. Acting on instinct, she tentatively touched Eleanor's shoulder. "I was just going to fix Dr. Wakefield dinner. Would you like to help?"

"He used to love my stuffed pork chops."

"Then stuffed pork chops it is." Gently but firmly she led Eleanor to the kitchen.

The step stool was still overturned, the stainless-steel mixing bowls scattered over the tile floor. Quickly Lilly crossed the room to pick up the step stool and put it in the closet.

When Lilly turned, Eleanor had already picked up the bowls and placed them in the sink. Somehow Lilly wasn't surprised. Eleanor Wakefield wasn't a pampered woman or one who sat around waiting for others to do for her. "Do you think Dr. Delacroix could find out how Odette is doing?"

"I've already called," Eleanor said, turning on the faucet in the sink to wash the bowls. "He's going to check on her and come by later."

Lilly opened the freezer door, took out a package of pork chops, and went to the microwave to defrost them. "Then we better fix extra."

Uneasily Lilly stood outside Adam's door. It had been two hours since Odette had been taken to the hospital. Lilly thought she'd have news of the house-keeper's condition by now. She didn't.

Dr. Delacroix had called to say there had been a pileup on the freeway and the emergency room was in chaos. Eleanor had returned to the cottage after extracting a promise from Lilly that she would call her after she left Adam's room.

Propping the tray between her body and the door, she knocked. She didn't expect an answer, and she didn't get one. "Dr. Wakefield, I have your supper tray." Opening the door, she stepped inside the dark room. The light from the hallway only penetrated a few feet. The room had never before been in complete darkness since she arrived.

She shivered and flicked on the light. She saw him immediately.

He sat in the wingback leather chair. His long legs sprawled in front of him, his wrists limply hanging over the arm of the chair, his dark head thrown back as if he were staring at the ceiling.

Closing the door, she set the tray on the table. "Stuffed pork chops. Your mother helped. She said they used to be one of your favorites."

He didn't move.

She swallowed. "We still haven't heard how Odette is doing. Dr. Delacroix went to the hospital, but there was a pileup on the interstate and the emergency room is a madhouse."

Silence.

She removed the silver dome from the tray. "Meat at twelve, steamed broccoli at six. Apple pie at nine in a dessert plate."

"Take it back."

"Dr.—"

"Just leave me alone. Please."

Lilly replaced the lid, but she couldn't make herself pick up the tray. Instead she pulled up another chair near his.

He straightened. "What are you doing?"

"Staying." Crossing the room, she flicked off the light switch, then felt her way back to the chair and sat down. "I didn't put Samuel up to talking to you today. I admit to doing it the first time, though. He wanted to show you he had faith you'd plan the garden together."

"A blind doctor and gardener. How interesting."

"You can't let what that man said bother you. I know about people like him who try to make others feel small so they can feel superior. My husband was just like him."

"Your husband?" He shifted toward her. "You never mentioned a husband."

Shame and embarrassment swept through her as it always did when she thought of her marriage. "I filed for divorce."

"Why?"

"He hit me," she whispered. "I–I made excuses every time it happened. Mother Crawford wasn't my mother; she was my mother-in-law and the kindest, sweetest person I ever knew. After—after she died I packed up and left while he was at work. I was on my way to New Orleans when my car broke down. That's why I went back to town the day I got my car out of the shop. Myron is going to fight the divorce. I had to send my lawyer more money." She felt Adam's fingertips brush her arm, then slide down until his fingers entwined with hers. There was strength in his hand, a quiet gentleness. "I bet before you lost your sight you wouldn't have let anyone question your judgment."

His hand jerked. Afraid he'd pull away, her hand twisted and clasped his. "You lost your sight because of the greed and cruelty of others. Don't let anyone else take more. Please."

"Don't waste your tears on me, Lilly."

"I'm not," she said, brushing the moisture away.

"I was an arrogant bastard. I thought I made my own destiny. I was a fool." His thumb grazed the top of her hand. "My stupidity was just as much the cause of my losing my sight as their greed."

"How can you say that? You don't know they wouldn't have attacked you anyway."

"No, I don't. But in my arrogance, I thought I was invincible. I had just finished a marathon surgery. Over seven hours. I was high on my own power."

"That doesn't excuse them," she said. "Myron always said it was my fault that he yelled. He said he hit me because I questioned him. That was an excuse, not a reason. I realize that now." Her hand tightened. "It took me years to realize I might not have control, but I had choices. That was the turning point for me."

"You were right to leave."

"I know that now." She swallowed. "I'm never going back."

"No, you won't."

The sound of the phone ringing startled both of them. Whoever called had dialed Dr. Wakefield's private extension.

"Take a message. I don't want to talk with anyone."

"What if it's your mother?"

"Tell her I'll call her tomorrow."

Realizing there wasn't any point in arguing with him, Lilly rose and went to answer the phone. "Ouch."

"What happened?"

"I walked into the foot of the bed."

"Turn on the light before you break your neck!" Adam snapped.

"Yes, sir." Lilly turned on the lamp on the nightstand, then snatched up the phone on the fifth ring. "Hello. . . .

"Oh, my goodness. Wait a minute," she said, her fingers clamped tight on the phone. "It's Odette's oldest son, Samuel Junior. Odette had a fracture and he wants to thank you."

"Are you sure?"

"Come talk to him yourself," Lilly said, experiencing a strange mixture of feelings, sadness that Odette was injured but relief that Dr. Wakefield had been right.

With smooth movements that were so different from hers, Dr. Wakefield walked to the bedside table and took the phone. "This is Dr. Wakefield. She's resting comfortably? . . . I see. Put her on.

"Odette, stop fussing. Considering your diabetes and hypertension, I think spending the night in the hospital is a wise decision." Adam's lip twitched. "I don't think your doctor needs to call and discuss the management of your care with me, but I appreciate the confidence. Let me speak with Samuel.

"Samuel, take as long as you need off with Odette. I can tell she's going

to be a difficult patient. . . . You're welcome. Good night. Thanks for calling."
He hung up the phone, a smile growing on his face "I'm suddenly hungry."

"It won't take but a minute to heat up your dinner."

"This time I don't mind cold food, but you could do something else for me."

"What?"

"Call Mother's number and let her know."

Eleanor was looking out the cottage window for Jonathan when he pulled up. Opening the door, she rushed out. By the time he had gotten out of the car, she was standing there, a broad smile on her face. "Odette and her family called Adam. He called me. Isn't that wonderful?"

It was all he could do not to graze his knuckles down her cheek. "I was there when they called."

She made a face. "I might have known."

"They were hesitant to call since it was late, but I convinced them that Adam might like hearing he was right."

She hooked her arm through his and led him back inside. "Thank you, Jonathan."

"You might also be interested in knowing that even without a formal complaint filed by Samuel, the female attendant had already spoken to her superiors."

Eleanor's temper flared again. "Good for her, but it doesn't end there."

Jonathan palmed her cheeks. Immediately she stilled. "Let me take care of it. In the meantime, I smell something delicious."

Eleanor laughed despite her accelerated heartbeat, her nervous stomach. "Jonathan, do you ever think of more than food?"

Brown eyes glowed. "Frequently."

The smile froze on Eleanor's face. Her nipples actually tingled.

Slowly Jonathan's hands slid from her face, leaving in their wake heated flesh and a growing desire to feel his hands again. "But sometimes a man has to take what he can get."

"Pork chops," she managed.

"It's a start," Jonathan said.

Eleanor stared into his intent gaze and felt as if she were on a precipice and the dirt was crumbling beneath her feet. One wrong move and she'd go over the edge. "I'll fix your plate."

Jonathan watched Eleanor hurry away and almost smiled. Soon. Very soon she'd be rushing toward him and into his arms.

Hands in his pockets, he followed her into the kitchen.

A sound woke Lilly up. Lifting her head from the pillow, she listened. Music. A piano.

Reaching over, she turned on the light. She frowned, then threw back the covers and went into the hallway. It was definitely a piano, and the sound was coming from downstairs. It couldn't be.

She turned the light on in the hall and swiftly ran down the steps, the volume of the music and her surety growing with each running step. She burst into the living room with her chest heaving.

Trembling fingers clicked on the light switch. Adam sat at the piano. His fingers danced over the keys with a precision that brought the bright sheen of tears to her eyes. She brushed them away and sat in the nearest chair.

Suddenly he stopped. His dark head twisted to one side. "Lilly?"

She swallowed the lump in her throat and found her voice: "I didn't mean to interrupt."

He turned and Lilly's breath caught. On his handsome face he wore a teasing smile she'd never seen before. "You didn't."

"You play beautifully."

"Thanks. I haven't played in years."

"I always wanted to, but we never had the money," she said wistfully, glad the old pain and anger were no longer there.

"Come here. I'll teach you."

Her shoulders snapped back. "What?"

"You don't think I could do it?" He folded his arms across his chest in an obvious challenge.

"I didn't say that," she hastened to reassure him.

He scooted over and patted the wooden bench beside him. "Then come and sit down."

Uneasiness moved through her. "Maybe we should wait for morning?"

"Why? We're both up. Neither one of us has to get up early, so why wait?"

In the face of such logic, she didn't have an answer. "All right." Her bare feet were silent as she crossed to him. She slipped onto the bench beside Adam. The instant she did, she realized her mistake. The coolness of the cherry wood bench and the heat of his muscled body against hers jolted her nervous system. "Oh."

"What's the matter?"

"I, er . . . nothing."

"Give me your hands," he requested, holding his out.

She didn't want to. Even now she remembered the softness of his and the roughness of her own.

"Lilly?"

She stuck out hands that shook. "Don't be disappointed if I don't learn very easily."

He took her hands in his. "Why would you say that?"

She opened her mouth to say, "Because Myron always said so," then said instead, "It's the middle of the night and my brain isn't functioning at top level."

He smiled and the sight did strange things to her insides. "Mine is. This is easy. I'll play the melody and you play the chords."

"What—what song are we going to play?" she asked, extremely conscious of him in a way that she had never been of Myron.

"Beethoven's 'Moonlight Sonata.' "

"What?" She tried to snatch her hands back.

Laughing, he held them firmly in his. "Lilly, I promise you can do this. You just have to trust me."

The laughter and his words caused a warm rush of feelings inside. "I trust you. It's me I don't trust."

"Then allow me to prove how mistaken you are." Taking her fingers, he placed them on the keys, three notes for each hand. "Now, when I pause you simply strike the keys. The melody is slow, a bit haunting, but the chord gives the music power. Ready?"

Lilly stared at his long, elegant fingers on the white keys, and said a little prayer that she wouldn't shake his emerging confidence. "Ready."

The movement of his fingers, the beauty of the piece, almost caught her off guard the first time he paused. The second time she was ready. She struck the notes and listened as Adam played on.

She was playing Beethoven. The music was as beautiful and as haunting as Adam had said. Laughter, free and easy, drifted from her mouth. "I'm doing it. I'm doing it."

His laughter joined in. He finished with a flourish. "Told you. Now, what else shall we play?"

Since most of the songs she knew were spirituals, she chose those, singing along with the music. She had a strong, clear voice and soon became more caught up in the words than what her fingers were playing. There were tears in her eyes when the last note of "How Great Thou Art" softly ebbed away.

"You have a beautiful voice," Adam said.

Lilly sniffed, rubbing the back of her hand over her eyes. "Thank you, but it was your playing."

"Seems we make a good team," he said quietly.

All of a sudden, she became aware once again of their thighs touching, of her being in her nightgown with nothing underneath. While playing and singing, one or both of them had scooted closer. Heat flushed her cheeks.

"This team member is getting sleepy." She stood. "I think I'll go up."

"I'll go with you." Closing the lid, he slid off the bench.

Automatically she stepped beside him and let him take her arm. They stopped at the bottom of the stairs. "You get to lead again."

"Does this mean you're not going to badger me anymore?"

"Help," she corrected.

"Oh, yes. I forgot."

Smiling, they went up the steps.

Chapter Twelve

Adam was restless. Not the kind of restless that had kept him on edge since his blindness, but restless with the anticipation of getting the day started. Standing in front of Lilly's bedroom door, he contemplated for the umpteenth time that morning whether he should wake her. It had been after two when they had come upstairs for the second time last night. That was a scant five hours ago.

Folding his arms, he leaned against her door. Thanks to Lilly, he didn't have to live in a black void wondering about the passage of time. However, now it presented another problem. Since he was well aware of the early hour, should he wake her?

The unavoidable truth was that he missed her. He'd thoroughly enjoyed playing the piano by himself, but her shy, hesitant presence had increased his enjoyment.

She had faith in him yesterday after Odette's accident. She never doubted. Neither had Samuel and Odette. Despite his blindness, they had trusted his judgment. The male attendant had seen a blind man and prejudged him without looking for himself to see if Odette was injured. He'd judged Adam as Adam had judged himself, worthless and of no value to anyone.

But they both had been wrong. In giving reassurance to Odette, Adam knew he had received much more.

He thought of returning to his room and letting Lilly sleep, but the thought quickly disappeared and he gave in to temptation. He rationalized his decision by thinking there was no schedule to follow. Smiling, he raised his hand and knocked. The day was theirs to do as they pleased.

Lilly snuggled deeper into the pillow, but the persistent sound continued. Finally the sound penetrated. Knocking. Someone was at the door.

She jerked upright in bed. Throwing back the lightweight comforter, she scrambled out of bed, grabbing her robe from the foot of the bed as she passed. Opening the door, she was shocked to see Dr. Wakefield, arms folded, leaning against the doorjamb. "Dr. Wakefield!"

"Good morning."

"Is everything all right?" Her gaze ran over him silently. He certainly looked fit and well. He had on a turquoise Polo shirt and a pair of snug-fitting jeans that encased his long, muscular legs. Lilly shivered and pulled the lapels of the cotton robe closer together.

He tucked his head sheepishly. "I'm hungry."

Relief swept through her. She should have known. "Give me ten minutes. I'll come to your door and knock."

"Thanks."

Closing the door, Lilly quickly got the clothes she always laid out the night before and went to the bathroom to bathe and dress. In less than the time allotted she knocked on his door.

The door opened before she lowered her hand to her side. He stepped into the hallway. "You're right on time."

She smiled as he took her arm. "I may regret getting you that clock."

"That's a distinct possibility."

At the stairs, she paused and allowed him to find the railing with his left hand and take the lead going downstairs. She remained silent until they reached the bottom of the stairs. He might act casual, but his fingers had tightly gripped her arm on the way down.

"What would you like for breakfast?" she asked when they entered the kitchen.

"Surprise me."

"Since you're hungry, how about a quick omelet? You can beat the eggs."

His steps hesitated. "We might have a small omelet."

"You didn't doubt me on the piano; I don't doubt you whisking eggs."

She paused by the curved end of the kitchen counter. "Stool or the breakfast table?"

"Since you're going to make me work for my breakfast, the stool."

She took his hand and placed it on the padded seat. "Watch it when you slide on. The cabinet has gotten my knees a couple of times."

"As I recall, it's jumped out at me a time or two." Sitting, he placed his hand on the sparkling countertop. "Ready to work for my breakfast."

Lilly hoped she was doing the right thing. Finding a bowl, she cracked six eggs, picked up the whisk, and took everything to Adam. "Eggs can be slippery little devils, so I always start slow."

Silently Adam took the bowl and whisk. Lilly made herself move away and not watch. "Bacon or sausage?"

"Doesn't matter."

Lilly heard the tightness in his voice and opened the refrigerator. "Why don't I fix both?" Removing the meat, she reached for a knife and heard the scraping of the whisk against the side of the bowl. She glanced around to see Adam's stiff movements. But he was trying.

"Together, we'll have breakfast in no time. Remember, we're a team."

"I don't think you'll ever let me forget," Adam said, his lower lip tucked between his teeth in concentration, stirring instead of whisking, but Lilly couldn't have been prouder.

Eleanor walked briskly along the path from the cottage toward the main house. She needed a cup of coffee and had used the last of hers yesterday morning. She made a face. After seeing Adam, she was going grocery shopping. She didn't want a repeat of Jonathan checking out her food supply. Even as the thought annoyed her, she felt a little thrill of delight that he cared enough to check.

She was going up the steps to the kitchen when the sound of laughter caused her to go stock-still. Then she closed her eyes and gave thanks. She'd despaired of ever hearing Adam's carefree laughter again.

"Good morning, Adam, Lilly," she greeted them, opening the screen door and coming inside.

"Good morning, Mother," Adam said.

"Good morning, Eleanor. Have a seat. I'll get you a cup of coffee, and thanks to Adam, there's plenty of French toast and fixin's for an omelet."

Eleanor glanced at the smug expression on her son's face. "Explain."

"I had to work for my breakfast. I did the eggs," Adam told her. "I did a pretty good job, if I do say so."

Pulling out a chair, she sat down at the round table across from her son. "I can't wait to taste for myself."

Lilly set a cup of black coffee by Eleanor. "Here's your coffee. Black."

Eleanor sipped her coffee and studied her son's happy expression. "I like that smile on your face."

Pushing the plate away, he leaned forward and placed his arms on the table. "I put you and Kristen through a lot. Thanks for hanging in there."

"What else would your family do?"

"Here's your breakfast," Lilly said, setting the plate in front of the other woman and handing her flatware and a sunny yellow napkin.

"Looks good." Eleanor forked a bite of the omelet in her mouth. "Ummm, delicious. Can I come back every morning?"

"You aren't moving back into the house?" Adam asked, pausing with his cup of coffee in his hands.

She laid her fork aside and came to a quick decision. "I rather like the cottage. Besides, you and Lilly can do whatever you've planned without having to worry about entertaining me."

His brows bunched. He took a sip of coffee, then replaced the mug on the table. "I haven't thought much past this morning."

"If you'd like, you could get a handle on your mail. You have two boxes like the kind copying paper comes in that are crammed full. I had Kristen ship them to me last week. I went through it and discarded the junk mail, but you still have a lot of correspondence. Working together, Lilly and I could start going through it." Arms folded, Eleanor leaned across the table. "Your accountant's been taking care of most of your business, but you know your father always insisted that we know where our money was being spent."

Adam nodded. "Lilly, if you'll help me navigate to my study I'll contact my accountant first; then I have a couple of calls to place and then we can go through the mail."

Sitting behind the desk in his study, Adam listened to the phone ring in Kristen's apartment. Aware that his sister wasn't a morning person, he patiently waited for her to wake up enough to recognize the ringing of the phone and answer it. Her first class wasn't until nine. It was barely seven on the Coast.

"Hello."

Her soft, East Coast–accented voice sounded husky and gravelly from sleep. "Wake up, sleepyhead, and talk to your big brother."

"Adam! Oh, Adam." All sleepiness left Kristen's voice, to be replaced by ringing excitement. "It's so good to hear your voice. I was hoping you'd call so I could tell you how proud of you I am."

He leaned back in the leather chair, the corners of his mouth tilted upward in a reluctant smile. "I guess Mother called you."

"Last night. You know how she is."

They both were aware that their mother had followed a predictable pattern, bragging on her children. Just as they were both aware that in the weeks following his accident his behavior had been appalling rather than heroic, but neither brought it up. "So how are the studies going?"

"They're about to get better."

He accepted her cryptic statement. She had worried and suffered right along with him. "Everything is going to be all right. Mother, Jonathan, and I will be there to see you graduate next month."

"I'm counting on it. I've missed you, big brother."

"The same goes here."

"Then why don't I come down for the weekend?"

"No way. I distinctly remember the last weeks of undergrad school. Papers coming out of the wazoo. Stay and study."

"Spoilsport."

He chuckled. "You'll thank me when exam time comes."

"It's good hearing you laugh again."

"It feels good. Now, go study."

"Bye, Adam. I love you."

"I love you, too. Bye."

He hung up the phone, dreading the next call. But there was no way around it. Getting the operator on the line again, Adam placed a call to Nicole at her office in downtown San Francisco.

Despite it being early, he knew that unless she had a business appointment, she'd be there. She believed that good work ethics and responsibility started at the top.

"Nicole Ashe." The tone was polished and smooth as silk. It fit perfectly the image that Nicole always wanted to project.

"Hello, Nicole."

"Adam?" Surprise quickly gave way to unbridled delight. "Oh, Adam, honey. It's wonderful hearing your voice. When are you coming back?"

His fingers drummed on the desk blotter. "Not for a while."

"Why not?"

He never realized until then how much it annoyed him for Nicole to question him. Usually he ignored her. "I enjoy being here."

"How can you say that? I'm here. Your friends are here." Her tone became petulant.

"I made them as uncomfortable as they made me." His fingers stopped their drumming motion and closed into a tight fist.

"What about me?" she asked, her voice deepening to a suggestive husky purr. "Don't you miss me? Don't you want to be with me?"

"Nicole," he said and sat forward in his seat, dreading what was coming next. "I don't want to hurt you, but you know it can never be as it was between us."

"Yes, it can if you'll only let it."

He hated the plaintive note in her voice. "We both know better. Cut your losses and move on."

"It's her, isn't it?"

His fingers touched a pen on his desk. He picked it up. "Her who?"

"That Lilly person."

He drummed the pen on the desk, wondering how he could quickly end the call without hurting Nicole's feelings. "Lilly has nothing to do with my decision."

"Yes, she does." Nicole's voice cooled. "Since you didn't want to speak with me, I called Kristen. She's kept me informed about the woman your mother hired."

"She helped me."

"For a thousand dollars a week, I should hope so."

His shoulders snapped back in shock. "What?"

"Didn't you know?"

He clutched the pen. He felt betrayed, used, and it came through in his voice: "No. No, I didn't."

"I'm sorry if this sounds harsh, but she did it for the money. If you're staying for her, you have no reason to."

"Yes, why else would she or anyone put up with a blind man?" Bitterness tinged each word.

"I didn't mean it that way," she hastened to reassure him.

"Good-bye, Nicole."

"No, Adam, wait. Let me expl—"

Adam carefully placed the receiver in the cradle instead of slamming it as he wanted. Anger churned through him, at himself, at Lilly. She'd been paid an exorbitant amount to care for him. He recalled her pleading the first time she came to his room. She wanted to stay for the money, not because she felt anything for him. She'd been doing a job, nothing more.

The phone rang again and he ignored it. He didn't want to speak to Nicole again, and he was positive it was her. He wasn't sure why the amount of Lilly's salary bothered him, but it did.

"Dr. Wakefield, Nicole Ashe is on the phone," Lilly said as she entered the study.

Adam lifted his head and turned in the direction her voice had come from. "How much did my mother pay you, Lilly?"

"What?"

He rose and planted both hands on the desk. "How much did my mother pay you to care for a hopelessly depressed blind man?"

The words lashed out at her. Finally she understood. "That's why Ms. Ashe sounded so upset on the phone. She told you."

Adam's lips thinned with anger. "No wonder you were so anxious to stay. No wonder no matter what I did or said you always came back. You would have taken care of the devil for that kind of money."

There was no use denying his words. He had spoken the truth. "I was desperate, yes, but I also wanted to help you."

"Spare me the humanitarianism. The longer you stayed, the more you earned. I was a meal ticket." His laugh was bitter. "To think I thought . . ." His voice trailed off, his head lowered.

"Dr. Wake—"

His head came up sharply. "You're fired."

"What?" Her eyes widened with shock.

"Get your things and get out. I want you gone within the hour. You hear me? Get out!"

She wouldn't cry. Lilly told herself that, but it didn't stop the silent tears flowing down her cheeks. Her fault again for believing, for letting her guard slip even a tiny bit. She had only herself to blame for the ache in her chest.

She shouldn't have let herself care about him as a person. Men weren't to be trusted. They played with your emotions. Shutting the suitcase, she dragged it from the bed and left her bedroom. She met an anxious-appearing Eleanor on the stairs.

"Lilly, Nicole called. She said Adam became upset when she mentioned your salary."

"He fired me."

Eleanor's eyes widened and she came to Lilly and placed her hand on her trembling arm. "He's upset. He'll calm down once he's had time to think this through."

"He doesn't want me here." That admission hurt. Hurt badly.

"Yes, he does. He's just too upset now to realize it," Eleanor said. "I had no idea he'd be so upset about your salary."

Lilly worked her shoulders. "It doesn't matter. I'll be going. Thank you for trusting me to take care of Dr. Wakefield."

"Lilly—"

"I'm not staying. I won't be treated like this again. Myron was enough."

"Myron?"

There was no reason not to tell her. "I lied. I was married. I filed for divorce and left my abusive husband the day my car broke down. I left there with no firm job prospects, few clothes, and very little money. That's why I didn't want to have a reference check. I didn't want him to find me." She spoke past the stinging in her throat. "Mother Crawford wasn't my mother;

she was my mother-in-law. She and my stepson, Rafe, were the only good thing to come out of my marriage. When I left Myron, I promised myself that I'd never be subjected to that kind of treatment again. I deserve better."

"Lilly, I'm sorry."

"Not your fault. Good-bye, Eleanor. Please tell Dr. Delacroix good-bye for me." The lump in her throat threatening to choke her, she stepped around Eleanor and quickly went down the stairs.

Eleanor went down the stairs behind Lilly, but her destination was the study. His shoulders bent, his head resting in the palms of his hands, Adam sat behind his desk. The sight tore through Eleanor, but she refused to let his dejected appearance dissuade her. "What did you say to her?"

"Not now, Mother." His voice was tired.

"Yes, now. Lilly came here afraid of her own shadow and I just learned why, an abusive husband, but she stayed and stuck it out to help you. She almost didn't take the job because Jonathan wanted a reference check. Even with the offer of a thousand dollars a week, she chose to sit in a broken-down car. That took fear and courage."

"But she took the job, didn't she? The money was too good to turn down."

"It might have been initially for the money, but I saw the look on her face when she came from your room the first time. She cared and she's shown me she cares time and time again. I stayed in the cottage to ensure that I wasn't mistaken about her. Do you think for one instant that if I thought she was only here for the money I wouldn't have hired someone else?"

Adam rocked back in his chair. "Just proves she's a good actress. She annoyed me."

"And by doing so she got you to forget that you were blind and act instead of react. After she got you to eat and get cleaned up, I would have let her stay in any case. In fact, I told her as much. She had a job, regardless. But she kept trying to think of ways to help you. Everything from the tapes to the clothes was her idea. Not mine. And you just kicked her in the teeth!"

Slowly his head came up. "I didn't know."

"And you didn't ask. You just struck out the same way you've been doing since your blindness. I've been disappointed, even hurt, by your actions, but I've never been ashamed of you until this moment."

He flinched at the cutting remark but knew it was deserved. "Mother, I'm sorry."

"I'm not the one you should be apologizing to." Eleanor wasn't in a forgiving frame of mind.

For an endless moment, Adam sat there; then he stood and hurried around the desk and straight into the Chippendale armchair.

"Damn!" He and the chair both toppled.

"Adam!" Eleanor rushed to him, then hesitated. In the past he had never wanted help.

"Mother, could you please help me up and show me to the garage?" He reached out his hand to her. "I think it's time I became the man you raised me to be."

Brushing tears from her eyes, Lilly opened the door of her car, tossed her suitcase on the front seat, and slid in beside it, chastising herself as she did so. She had no reason to cry. She had money in her pocket; her car was running. She had nothing to cry about. It had just been a job.

And she had come to care about Dr. Wakefield more than she should.

Tears fell harder. Clutching the steering wheel, she leaned her head against it and cried.

"I thought I told you not to waste tears on me."

Stunned, she jerked her head up to see Adam standing beside the open door of the car she had forgotten to close. "How . . ." she began, then saw the answer to how he had found his way to the garage. Eleanor stood a short distance away. "Go back inside, Dr. Wakefield."

"Ordering me around again." It was more of a statement than a question.

"I never ordered you around," Lilly told him, wishing she didn't recall when that had been a joke between them. "Please move so I can close the door."

He moved closer. Reaching out, he touched her shoulder, then slid his hand down to grasp her hand and tug. "Come on; let's go back into the house."

"No, I'm leaving."

"I'm sorry, Lilly. Sorrier than you'll ever know."

"Some hurts can't be mended with words."

His breath hissed in sharply. His mouth tightened. "I'd never abuse you like he did."

"You hurt me," she said softly, her voice thick with unshed tears. "Don't you think I know how it feels to be used? How it feels not to be wanted for yourself? Myron did that to me for six years."

Anger shot through Adam. "I'm not that slime of a husband."

"Then you think I'm a user like he was?"

"Never. You've got to believe me." Adam raked his hand over his head in growing frustration. "Oh, hel—heck, Lilly. Never that. Never that."

"Do you have any idea how you made me feel?" she asked, her words so quiet he had to bend his head to hear them. Then he wished he hadn't.

She sounded defeated, lost. Guilt ate at him. His only defense was the truth, a truth that would leave him as defenseless as she.

"Do you think I wasn't hurt? No matter how much I pushed you away, you always came back. No one ever did that, except my family. Besides Jonathan, you're the only person who never caved in or acted differently. You never treated me as if my blindness diminished my intelligence." He paused and drew in a deep breath. "I thought it was more than a job. I thought you . . . hell, I thought you cared about me like I care about you."

He cared.

His words rushed though her like a healing balm. He cared. He'd cursed, but it was out of frustration, not hatred or disrespect.

"Please stay," he continued, his hand gripping hers tightly. "You haven't finished reading *The Third Degree*. I doubt if Mother will read it to me, as upset as she is with me."

The joy spiraling within Lilly took a nosedive. "That's what you want me for, to read, cook, and clean?"

"No. I could hire someone to do that," Adam told her. "I want you for what no amount of money can buy. As a true friend. Please stay."

Lilly sniffed and brushed the last lingering tears from her eyes. A true friend. She'd only had one in her entire life. "On one condition?"

"Name it."

"You teach me to really play the piano."

"It's a deal."

———

Eleanor was waiting for them when they emerged from the garage arm in arm. "I'll just go to the cottage and get the mail."

"You can't carry that much by yourself," Adam protested. "I'll go with you."

Both women traded worried glances. Lilly spoke first. "The path is smooth, but I don't think you should carry a big box."

"I didn't intend to. Mother probably has a handled shopping bag or two that we can use."

Eleanor glanced at Lilly for guidance. Getting Adam out of the house and down the steps to the garage had been awkward for both of them. The winding path to the cottage was twice that distance.

Adam, his jaw clenched, spoke into the growing silence: "I'm not helpless."

"We never thought you were," Lilly said, praying she was making the right decision. The worst thing they could do was discourage Adam's emerging confidence with their own fears. "While you two are getting the mail, I'll take my things back upstairs."

"Come on, Mother," Adam said, reaching for his mother's arm and feeling her tremble. He leaned over and whispered, "Think of this as helping me take my first baby steps. I might have fallen, but I got up and I learned."

"You certainly did," Eleanor said, her voice steadier. "Lilly, we'll be back in a little bit."

Lilly watched them trying to find a rhythm to their steps and knew they were going to be all right when Adam bumped into his mother and almost fell. Instead of reacting with embarrassment or anger, he had laughed. He wasn't afraid of trying and failing. He'd come a long ways from the angry, frightened man she'd met when she arrived.

And she'd helped. No one could take that away from her. She was good at something.

Grabbing her suitcase, Lilly went inside. She was passing the telephone stand in the hallway when the phone rang. Pausing, she picked up the receiver. "Wakefield residence." The line clicked dead.

Shrugging, she hung up the phone and continued upstairs to her room. Deciding unpacking could wait, she came back downstairs and went to the kitchen and started to finish cleaning up. She wanted all the household duties out of the way so she could help Adam if he needed her. She'd just finished when the phone rang again. "Wakefield residence."

There was no answer, but she could tell there was someone on the line. Myron? Her stomach knotted in fear. "Who's there?"

"I want to speak to Adam."

Nicole. Lilly recognized the silky voice and the bad attitude immediately. "Why do you dislike me?"

"I asked to speak with Adam."

Lilly's fingers flexed on the phone. Nicole had the same demanding way about her that Myron had. "Unless you answer my question, you aren't going to."

Nicole's quick intake of breath echoed through the phone. "Why, you. You're just the hired help!"

"If I were just that, I wouldn't bother you so much," Lilly said, sure she was right.

"Don't give yourself more importance than you have," Nicole said tartly. "Adam admires sophisticated, beautiful women. Even blind, you can't possibly think he'd want you."

"You're jealous," Lilly said, the unbelievable thought taking root in her brain and sprouting like a dandelion after a hard spring rain. She laughed at the absurdity of it and the undeniable pleasure it gave her.

"I'd be a fool to be jealous of you!"

"You won't get an argument from me," Lilly said. "Those things you think so highly of don't mean squat to Adam now, and although you may not be aware of it yet, he's a better man for it. Surface means nothing to him, and that's what worries you, isn't it, Nicole? You're all show."

"How dare you speak to me that way. Wait until I tell Eleanor and Adam."

"After you hurt Adam, do you think either of them will want to speak with you? You tried to paint me in a poor light, not once thinking of how it might make Adam feel. You might be beautiful and sophisticated, as you said, but you're selfish and unsure of yourself with Adam."

"You—"

"Instead of calling me names, Nicole, your time would be better served trying to think of a way to apologize to Adam and his mother for causing trouble. They're nice enough to forgive you and think you acted out of love and concern for him." Lilly's tone cooled. "I know better. I've known someone just like you who gave everyone the impression of being kind and generous but who was actually mean and spiteful. I'll tell Adam you called." She hung up the phone, feeling proud of herself until she felt a presence behind her and turned.

"Dr. Delacroix!" Her heart threatened to beat out of her chest.

This time it wasn't his build that intimidated her but the sharpness in his brown eyes. "What was that all about?"

Nervously Lilly rubbed her hand against the side of her leg. She and Dr. Delacroix were on better terms now, but she was well aware she had no right to speak to Nicole that way. "Nicole and I had a difference of opinion."

His long legs carried him too quickly from the doorway to within a few feet of her. "What about?"

"I think you should ask Eleanor."

"I would if she were here."

So that was the reason for Nicole's repeated phone calls, Lilly thought. She hadn't been able to reach Eleanor at the cottage, so she had called the main house. Lilly glanced at the back kitchen door. "She and Adam went to her cottage. They're probably on their way back. You could take the path and meet them."

Instead of taking the hint, he said, "If Nicole did something to upset Adam or Eleanor, I want to know and I want to know now."

Lilly started to step back from him as he advanced purposefully toward her again; then she stopped. He wasn't Myron. He wouldn't abuse others to make himself feel important. She'd seen the tender way he stared at Eleanor, the love in his eyes for Adam.

"All right, I'll tell you. But I'll do it while I marinate the roast for dinner."

"Whatever it takes."

In clear, concise words she related what had happened after Adam spoke with Nicole on the phone. Lilly ended by saying, "Instead of hurting me as she intended, she hurt Adam."

"You're right about one thing," Jonathan said from where he leaned negligently against the counter, his legs crossed at the ankles, his arms folded.

Lilly glanced over her shoulder as she bent to place the marinated meat inside the refrigerator. "What?"

"She's jealous."

Lilly flushed and turned toward the refrigerator. "I–I didn't mean it the way it probably sounded." Closing the door, she went back to clean up the countertop and busily began putting away the spices for the marinade. For the first time in a long time, she wished that her hands weren't callused and worn, her face so angular, her clothes faded.

"Then you wouldn't care that Adam and Nicole had a very close relationship before his blindness?"

There was no mistaking his meaning. Her hands shook as she picked up the plastic wrap and placed it back in the cabinet. "I'm just the hired help."

Strong, gentle hands closed around her shoulders and turned her toward him. Jonathan stared deep into Lilly's sad wide eyes. "Take some advice from a man who's been there. Lying to yourself only makes it harder."

Her heart boomed in her chest, but not from fear. "I don't know what you're talking about."

Jonathan's face filled with despair. "I'm afraid you do. Soon you'll have to stop and admit it to yourself, and then, Lilly, you'll learn what true heartache really is."

The door behind them slammed.

Chapter Thirteen

Jonathan glanced over his shoulder and saw Eleanor and Adam with two handled bags in his hands. The look of shock on Eleanor's face caused Jonathan to drop his hands and quickly step away from Lilly. As soon as he'd moved, he realized his mistake. He'd acted as if he'd been caught in an indiscretion.

Lilly, not sensing the undercurrents, went to them and took Adam's arm. "Dr. Delacroix is here to see you and Eleanor, Adam."

"It must be Wednesday," Adam said, allowing Lilly to lead him farther into the room.

"Yes," Jonathan said, his gaze going behind Adam to Eleanor, who remained unmoved. "I didn't get a chance to take *Lady Lost* out last weekend; I thought I'd take her for a run on my day off."

"You have a horse?" Lilly asked.

"A speedboat," Adam said, wistfulness in his voice. "But she can't beat mine."

Jonathan cut his eyes to him. "You'll never let me forget that race. You want to come with me?"

Adam shook his head. He might have climbed a hill or two. He wasn't ready for a mountain. "Maybe another time."

"How about you, Eleanor?" Jonathan asked, his gaze going back to Eleanor. She wouldn't meet his eyes.

"I have to help Adam," she said quietly.

"Lilly can do that, Mother." Adam held up the bags. "This will keep us busy for most of the day. Go on. You need to get out."

"Maybe Lilly would like to go in my place," Eleanor said, aware of the brief spark of jealousy she had felt when she saw Jonathan staring down into Lilly's eyes, his hands on her shoulders. She fought hard to dispel it.

Lilly shook her head. "I've never been on a boat before. I'm not sure I'd like it."

"Looks like it's you and me, Eleanor," Jonathan said.

Eleanor tried to tell herself she hadn't heard the possessive note in Jonathan's voice and, if she had, that she shouldn't feel pleased. There was nothing between him and Lilly. Jonathan didn't practice duplicity. He wouldn't pay court to two women at the same time. The instant the thought materialized, Eleanor stiffened. She was teetering on the edge of that cliff again. "Perhaps some other time, Jonathan. I planned to go see Odette today."

"I'll drive you," Jonathan offered. "I called before I left. She was being discharged this morning."

Adam smiled. "I bet Dr. Brown is thrilled."

Jonathan had to smile with him. "I've never seen him so harried. Last night he was ready to pull out the few strands of hair left on his head."

"Odette is strong-willed," Adam said.

"Just like another woman I know," Jonathan said, his gaze back on Eleanor.

"Please give her my best," Lilly said. "Eleanor, could you please take her some flowers from me? If it's all right, I'll repay you when you get back."

"That's a marvelous idea, Lilly," Adam said. "Pick up an arrangement from me, too."

Eleanor, who was trying to think of a gracious excuse to go in later by herself, felt trapped. From the pleased look on Jonathan's face, he was well aware of her predicament. "Of course."

"We better get going." Jonathan crossed the room and lightly took Eleanor's arm. "It'll take time for Eleanor to pick out the right flowers."

She arched a brow. "I am not that indecisive."

"Never said you were, but you have always known what you wanted and you've never settled for less."

"I've never seen the sense in settling when you can have what you want," she said with asperity.

"I couldn't agree more."

Eleanor felt her stomach roll as he stared down at her, felt the unexpected heat generated from their close proximity, the exciting feel of his hand on her bare forearm, the brief flare of the heat in his dark eyes.

A woman wouldn't have to settle with Jonathan.

She quickly banished the unsettling thought from her mind. Jonathan was just a friend.

Jonathan had seen the quick flare of interest in Eleanor's eyes. He hid the knowledge in his heart. Walking beside her to her cottage through the quiet garden, he felt again the rightness of his love for this woman who loved so strongly. His patience was slowly being rewarded. He realized that he had to let her come to him.

Walking up the steps, she opened the door to her cottage. "It won't take but a moment to change."

Jonathan watched the nervous flutter of pulse in the base of her throat and wanted to press his lips against it to soothe her. Her eyes were wide, wary, watchful. She expected him to pounce. Now that he knew she was awakening to her feelings for him, he could wait.

"I'll just sit here on the porch. It isn't often I get a chance to do that."

The relief in her eyes was instantaneous. "Of course."

Jonathan sat down and draped his arms on the back of the wooden bench, trying to calm the desire churning through his body. Soon, very soon, Eleanor would be his and he could give free rein to all the ways he wanted to love her.

In thirty-nine years of wanting he'd had a lot of time to fantasize.

Her back pressed against the door, Eleanor tried to calm her racing heart. Her palms were actually damp. Annoyed with herself, she pushed away from the door and went into her bedroom to change. She'd never been frazzled. There wasn't a time in her life she hadn't known what she wanted or how to get it.

Reaching into the closet, she took out a white sheath and laid it on the bed. When Mary and Alfred Delouth's only child chose to follow in her father's and grandfather's footsteps into medicine, no one doubted she'd carry on the family tradition. She had the brains, the guts, and the drive. She finished high school at fifteen, with twenty-five acceptance letters to the most prestigious universities in the country and enough scholarship money for ten students.

Then, in her second year in medical school, she'd looked up into the brownest eyes she'd ever seen and fallen head over heels in love with Randolph Wakefield, a senior medical student. Thankfully, he had felt the same way.

Pulling off her blouse and skirt, she reached for the linen dress. Poor, sweet Randolph hadn't known what hit him. She could have returned to medical school after Adam's birth. But after she held him in her arms, looked into his bright eyes, she had realized that medicine was no longer where her heart lay. Her family was.

She'd always known what she wanted and how to get it.

Her lipstick poised, she stared at her reflection in the mirror and critically assessed herself. She wore her fifty-nine years well, thanks to a good metabolism and good genes. High cheekbones were still distinguishable; the skin on her face and beneath her neck was smooth and firm.

Her eyebrows might be shaped professionally, but everything else was as God had given her. Proof of that was the faint streaks of gray hair at her temples, which she refused to dye. Her gaze dipped to her reasonably firm breasts, then lower to her waist. She frowned on seeing the faint rounded outline.

And reality hit.

Capping the lipstick with an irritated flick of her wrist, she picked up her bag. She wasn't twenty, with legs as long as a gazelle's and a figure that turned heads. It had been so long since she had paid any attention to how men viewed her that she had probably read too much into the way Jonathan had looked at her. Perhaps she should cut back on her estrogen dosage.

He stood up when she stepped onto the porch. The sun shone over his broad shoulders, silhouetting him. Her breath snagged. There was no denying that Jonathan was a formidable man.

"That didn't take long." His big hand lifted to rest on the small of her back as they went down the walk.

His hand felt like a brand upon her skin. She said the first thing that came into her scattered mind: "Randolph hated to be kept waiting."

"But seeing you, I bet he didn't mind," Jonathan said easily, leading her past two giant stone urns of impatiens and moss roses.

She flushed at the compliment and sucked in her stomach. "He said he didn't."

"For the right woman, a man would wait a lifetime. I know I would." Jonathan opened the door to the Mercedes.

The words were spoken with such quiet passion that Eleanor felt them all the way to her soul. She and Randolph had shared passion and so very much love and happiness. She missed him, but she also realized how blessed they both had been. "I had my one great love, Jonathan. I pray you find yours." She slid inside the car.

Jonathan closed the door and slowly walked around to climb inside. He commended himself on not slamming either of their doors, then speaking in a normal tone when he asked Eleanor if she had a special florist shop in mind. He glanced over when she didn't answer.

"Eleanor?"

She lifted her head and tears shimmered in her amber eyes. His gut clenched.

"What is it?" he asked, afraid he knew the answer.

She sniffed and reached for a tissue in the tiny black purse that couldn't have held much else. "I just felt sad for a moment, that's all."

"Randolph?" he asked, hating himself for the jealousy and unable to do anything about it.

"I . . . no. I just felt sad." She gave him a watery smile. "I should be tap-dancing on the ceiling. Adam is coming back to us."

The pad of his thumb, the only safe way of touching her, brushed the tears away from her smooth cheek. "The past weeks haven't been easy. All the tension has finally caught up with you."

"I suppose." She sniffed one last time and reached for her seat belt. "We better get going. If I tear up again you have permission to shake some sense into me."

"How about if I kiss some sense into you?"

She jumped and whirled around to face him. "What?"

There was such affront in her eyes that he had to laugh. The sound got tangled in his throat when her eyes strayed to his mouth with open speculation. He started the car. It was that or grab Eleanor and satisfy both of their curiosities. "I use a florist by my office. We'll try there first."

Odette and Samuel Tucker had lived in their neat frame house since the first day of their marriage fifty years ago. They'd raised their seven sons, welcomed their wives, and doted on their fifteen grandchildren. In their opinion, God had blessed them.

"Thank you, Eleanor and Dr. Delacroix. These flowers are beautiful," Odette said, her eyes going once again to the two bouquets of roses and mixed cut flowers that sat in the living room amid family portraits and her collection of black angels.

"We all wanted to wish you a speedy recovery."

"She will if she stops trying to tell the doctor what to do," Samuel said from a straight-back chair pulled up to the couch on which Odette reclined.

"He wants me to stay off work for six weeks. What kind of nonsense is that?" she asked, obviously incensed and with no intention of listening.

"Considering your medical history. I think it's a wise decision." Jonathan eyed her distended ankle propped up on two pillows. "They won't be able to put the cast on until the swelling goes down. Getting around Adam's house on those hardwood floors and rugs might be unstable with a cast on. The stairs are certainly out."

"Told you." Samuel nodded emphatically.

Worry swept across Odette's face. "I'm not used to idleness. Besides, I need to get back to work."

"Odette, if it's your salary you're concerned about, please don't worry. It'll continue. And don't worry about Adam. Thanks to your faith in him, he was in the kitchen this morning eating breakfast and laughing with Lilly," Eleanor told her.

Odette's eyes brightened. "You don't say?"

"I do say." Eleanor smiled. "You made him remember the wonderful doctor he was."

"Praise the Lord," Odette said, with a nod of her turban-covered head. "Not that I don't trust the Lord, but I was wondering why I had this accident. The Lord certainly works in mysterious ways. Dr. Wakefield helped me get the help I needed with my diabetes. My falling down helped him the same way."

"Odette, you mentioned last night you haven't been able to spend much time with your grandson. After the cast is put on and you're up and about, you could spend more time with him if you didn't go back to work," Jonathan suggested. It was no secret that Odette doted on her latest grandchild.

"He's such a honey. This morning he had a little bit of my biscuit and smacked his lips."

"If Dorothea sees you feeding Cameron solid food, she'll have a fit."

Odette harrumphed and crossed her arms. "Won't hurt him none. Just look at his daddy and uncles. You sure Lilly and Dr. Wakefield can get along by themselves?"

"Positive," Eleanor said, recalling their laughter.

"Well, then, I guess I stay here and worry this old man."

"Old?" Samuel pushed to his feet with an agility that belied his seventy-one years. "I better go get your medicine before I become too feeble to move."

Odette just smiled.

Eleanor watched the interaction between Odette and Samuel. Their love for each other showed clearly with every word, every gesture, every glance. They were among the lucky people who were blessed to find that one person in all the universe who made their life complete. Jonathan hadn't been that fortunate. That was the reason she had cried, the thought that he might never find such happiness. He had so much love to offer.

"Here you go," Samuel said, handing Odette her medicine and holding the glass of water until she had put the pills in her mouth.

"You make an excellent caregiver, Samuel," Jonathan said.

"It ain't hard when you care about the person." He took the glass. "Even if they are as stubborn as a mule."

"I couldn't agree more," Jonathan said. He and Samuel completely ignored the outraged expressions of the women.

Adam had come to a decision. It hadn't been an easy one to make. His hands outstretched, he bent from the waist and "patted" the air on the way to his desk in the study. He felt the solid walnut wood, then followed the smooth edge of his desk until he could sit in his Chippendale swivel-tilt chair.

The feeling of accomplishment he'd felt when he helped Odette three days ago was slowly ebbing away. Each time he had to wait for Lilly or his mother to take him farther than the living room, it chipped away at his self-esteem bit by bit.

Yesterday he'd tried to find his way by himself to the kitchen and had tripped on a bench against the wall in the hallway. Thankfully, when he'd fallen he hit his head on the padded seat and not the exposed wood on the arms or on the hardwood floor, but the incident had frightened him and caused him to pull back.

For the rest of the day he'd gone no farther than his room and his study by himself. Fear was creeping over him again. He could feel it. If he didn't get a handle on it and gain some real independence, he'd revert back to the way he had been.

He couldn't have that. He'd hated his life and had begun to hate others.

Reaching out, he picked up the phone and punched in the first two numbers. The phone would ring on every phone in the house except his private line in his bedroom.

"Yes, Dr. Wakefield?"

Somehow her voice always reached through his fear. He eased back in his seat. "Lilly, could you please come to my study?"

"Yes. Do you need me to bring you anything?"

He had to smile. She continuously tried to fatten him up. "No, just you."

There was a slight pause, then, "I'll be right there."

Hanging up, he tried to figure out if he had imagined that breathless catch in her voice and why it pleased him to think he had not.

"Yes, sir?"

The pleasure of moments ago evaporated. He frowned. "From now on call me Adam."

"But—"

"We can argue about this, but I'll win, and there's another matter I want to discuss with you," he said.

The spark of annoyance Lilly felt at Dr. Wakefield's imperious tone was short-lived. That was who he was. She perched on the end of a chair. "What matter?"

"I want you to understand that I appreciate everything you've done for me, but I need more." The fingers on his right hand fiddled with a gold pen.

Since she was reasonably sure he wasn't working his way up to firing her, she asked, "In what way?"

"I'm tired of depending on you and Mother to get me where I need to go, tired of bumping into furniture, tired of fanning the air," he finished, his voice tight.

"If you took Orientation and Mobility classes you'd be able to go where you want without our help," she suggested, holding her breath for his reaction.

He rocked forward in his chair. "How did you know about that?"

She barely kept from squirming. "Your mother was able to get a social worker by the name of Harriet Parker to come out and talk with us about the best ways to help you. One of the things she mentioned was Orientation and Mobility classes."

"Could you please call Mother and ask her for the phone number?" Picking up the phone, he set it closer to her, then shoved the gold pen and a pad toward her.

Breathing a sigh of relief, she stood. "Of course." In seconds she had Eleanor on the phone and the information. "Do you want me to dial it for you so you can speak to Harriet?"

"Thank you." No one but Lilly seemed to understand his need to do as much for himself as possible. He thought the reason was probably because they were both fighting to turn their lives around.

"Mrs. Parker, please hold. Eleanor Wakefield's son, Dr. Wakefield, would like to speak with you."

Adam's fingers circled the phone, feeling the lingering heat of Lilly's hand and its calming influence. She never doubted him. "Mrs. Parker, thank you for taking my call. I'd like to inquire about taking O&M classes." There was a long pause. "Tomorrow at one here would be fine."

Lilly tapped his shoulder and whispered in his ear, "You need to send a car for her."

The warm breath against his ear caused his mind to race in an entirely different direction. "What?"

"She has a guide dog."

Adam nodded his understanding. She hadn't described the social worker as blind but had let him know just the same. "I'll send a car for you. . . . All right. I'll expect you and Mr. Dillion at one. Good-bye."

"I better go find the tea service," Lilly said when Adam hung up the phone. "Do you think finger sandwiches and lemon cookies will be all right to serve? Maybe I better ask Eleanor."

"Whatever you prepare will be fine, Lilly." Adam's mind was on trying to figure out why his body had reacted so oddly to the breath of a woman. His body hadn't wanted sex since his accident. Nicole could testify to that.

"I don't think Odette would agree with you," Lilly said, worry in her voice. "I'm going to call your mother. I don't want you embarrassed."

Adam came out of his musings. "Lilly, you're making too much of this."

"You can't tell me you haven't always served your guests the best."

He had, but that was before. Then he realized that, to Lilly, before was no different from now. "Perhaps you should ask Mother."

"I will."

They hadn't discussed the menu with Adam, but judging from the compliments of his two guests, they had done well. His mother sat beside him, serving and keeping the conversation flowing. Lilly, off to the left, was quieter. He'd asked her to sit, but she'd refused.

"You have a beautiful estate, Dr. Wakefield," Harriet said.

Caught off guard by the comment, Adam was unable to hide his astonishment. "Th-Thank you."

Laughter erupted, followed by a voice aged by whiskey and smoke: "He's too polite to ask how you know, Harriet."

Adam frowned in the direction the voice had come from, directly across from him. Since Brent Dillion's hands were the size of dinner plates, Adam thought he was probably bigger and broader than Jonathan. There the resemblance ended. The man had none of Jonathan's smooth manners or tact.

Adam was beginning to wonder if Harriet had been right in her high praise of the O&M instructor. "I don't think that comment was necessary, Mr. Dillion."

"I disagree and so will Harriet. Blindness demands two things: honesty and trust. Without them, you're heading for trouble," he said. "And call me Brent."

"Brent's right, Dr. Wakefield. I may not agree with his methods, but he gets the job done," Harriet said. "As for how I knew, he described the grounds to me as he drove in. The echo in the room, the feel of the tapestry chair I'm in also helped."

"How long did it take you to learn that?" Adam asked, leaning forward.

"Weeks, perhaps months, but as I explained to your mother, it depends on how much effort the person is willing to put into it," she told him.

"I'll be seeing by then." Adam firmly crossed his arms and sat back on the sofa.

Brent Dillion's gaze narrowed on Eleanor as the cup rattled in the saucer in her hand. "In the meantime, you want to get around by yourself, is that right?" Brent asked.

"Yes." Adam had no idea why the man irritated him.

"You don't like me, do you?"

Eleanor opened her mouth, but Brent held up his hand.

"No."

"I can imagine. I'm big, bold, brash, and worse, I can see."

Unfolding his arms, Adam surged to his feet. He felt Lilly touch his arm and caught himself in time to keep from jerking away. "I didn't invite you here to insult me."

"Ladies, can you please excuse us for a bit?" Brent asked. "Doc and I have some talking to do. Go on. Don't come back unless you hear something breaking."

"Very funny," Adam said, clearly not amused.

"Yeah, I'm a riot." Brent sat back down. "Since the ladies have left I'm sitting, so you might as well take a load off."

Adam sat. "I heard them leave and since the angle of your voice changed, I'm aware you're sitting."

"Do you know how many people in the world couldn't have made that deduction? Sighted people depend too much on their eyes and forget their other senses. They let their sight distract them. Doc, I'm proud of you."

His expression one of bored indifference, Adam said, "Yes, I can tell by your voice."

Rough laughter rumbled. "I guess you can tell why I've gone through two wives and countless meaningful relationships. You have a special lady?"

"No." The word was clipped and didn't invite conversation.

"This is good tea. You sure you don't want any? No? Well, where was I? Oh, yes. Dating for the visually impaired." He took a loud sip of tea. "I have unsighted buddies on my golf team who get more ladies than I do. At first they were hesitant to approach a woman, but they soon got over it. Now they listen to what and how it's said instead of looking at face and body measurements."

"They play golf and they're blind?" Intrigued in spite of himself, Adam unfolded his arms.

"Yep. I have to sight the ball, tell the direction, but they do the rest by themselves." Brent placed his cup on the table. "The only things an unsighted person can't do are drive and read."

Adam's hands flexed. "Lilly says there is a computer program that can read print."

"Sure is. Various programs run from about two-fifty to over a thousand bucks; then you have to figure in the optical scanner and if you need to upgrade your computer. Shouldn't be hard for a stepper like you."

"That's condescending."

"Yeah, maybe, but I see you sitting there, rich and successful, looking down your nose at me, angry at me because an uncouth guy like me can see and you can't. Well, let me tell you about what pisses me off," Brent said, his voice taking on a hard edge. "It's a single working mother whose out-of-control diabetes takes her sight, a hardworking steelworker who forgot to flip his helmet down when he fired up the blowtorch and now can't support his three children. You don't know how fortunate you are, Doc."

Adam felt the anger sweeping through him. "I was a neurosurgeon. It takes skill, courage, and finesse to incise into the brain. You have to know where and how to approach the lesion, especially if it's in a delicate or eloquent area. And you sure as hell better know what you're looking for and what to do when you get in there. Do you possibly have any idea how long it took to learn?"

"No, Doc, but I got a feeling you're going to tell me," Brent said mildly.

"I studied sixteen years after high school. Only two-thirds of the doctors that go into medicine finish. That number is cut in half for neurosurgeons. Intelligence is rarely the problem. What gets you is the emotional stress. The long hours. At a little over two thousand, we're probably the smallest of the surgical specialties. I was on my way to being the best. Now, I can't cut into a damn piece of meat without making a mess." His hand fisted the front of the Polo shirt he wore. "I'm reduced to wearing these because I have trouble buttoning a damn shirt correctly."

"And you have the money to buy as much meat or as many of those shirts as you want. You won't get any sympathy from me," Brent shot back.

Adam's head snapped back. "I wasn't asking for any."

"The hell you weren't. Your blindness was a bump in the road to you; for some it's careening off a cliff. You can still pay the rent and live large. Your children aren't going hungry; the wolf isn't at your door. You don't have to worry about what do you do when the people who've always depended on you can't." Brent ticked off each word with biting precision. "*That* takes your pride."

"That's where you're wrong," Adam said just as heatedly. "Money has never been the measure of what my family and I feel for each other. I know about lost pride. I've been so far down I didn't think I'd ever get up again, but I have. To you, because I have money, that makes my blindness livable. I'd give away every cent to be able to see again." He came to his feet, his chest heaving with anger. "That's not an option. I have to start where I am and go from here. I plan to stay up and stay a man. With or without your help. Good-bye and thanks for coming." He retook his seat. "Please see yourself out."

"Do you still want to work with me?"

"Do *you* want to work with *me*?" Adam countered. He could tolerate the obnoxious, outspoken man; he couldn't tolerate being lost.

"The way I see it, we can only go up from here. My hand is directly in front of you if you want to shake it."

Adam came to his feet and reached out. A large hand firmly enclosed his. "By the way, I was ticked that you could see. How did you know?"

"Occupational hazard and your body language," Brent explained, withdrawing his hand. "If I eat a quick lunch, I can fit you in between two and three Monday, Wednesday, and Friday."

"Can't we increase the hours?" He wanted to learn as much as possible as soon as possible.

"Not unless we clone me. I came out here as a favor to Harriet. I'm squeezing you in as it is."

The man and woman, Adam thought. "I'd like to offer financial assistance to the young mother and the steelworker."

The unexpected slap to his back almost toppled Adam. "You've got heart, Doc. Sally is now a court reporter and Simon is the top salesman for his insurance company."

"Was that little story a prod or test or motivation?" Adam asked, irritation creeping back into his voice.

"All three. I don't have time for temperamental, stuck-up, snooty people. Too many others need my time," Brent said.

"If you're as good as you are arrogant, you must be amazing."

"I am, Doc; believe me, I am. Now, let's go take a look at your computer to see how quickly we can have you searching the Web."

Lilly was all thumbs. She couldn't seem to concentrate on the piano keys. No matter how much she tried to block out the pressure of Adam's thigh against hers, she couldn't. If she scooted over, he'd invariably reach over to guide her hands and their bodies would connect again.

His touching her hands only increased her nervousness. She'd started putting Vaseline on them at night and wearing her church gloves to soften them, but she couldn't tell any difference. They remained callused and rough from six years of keeping her house spotless. Adam's hands, like his mother's and Nicole's, were smooth, the nails short and rounded. Lilly had searched for a nail file in one of the seven bathrooms and hadn't found one yet.

Her thoughts elsewhere, she hit D instead of C, B when it should have been A. Finally she drew back her trembling hands and folded them in her lap. She'd humiliated herself enough for one night. "I guess I'm tired. Why don't we stop for tonight?"

"What's the matter? You've been tense all afternoon."

"I guess I was worried about you and that man. I thought you were going to fight."

She had paced the entire time. It had surprised her to see them walk into the kitchen together, unharmed and talking cordially.

"Try again. There has to be more to it."

She fidgeted. "There isn't, Adam."

"That's the first time you've called me by my first name," he said gently.

She swallowed and tucked her head. Like a child, she had practiced so she wouldn't stumble over it and reveal how being near him made her feel strange and excited at once. "I–I should go upstairs."

Before she could move, he took her hands in his. "Talk to me. Is it something I've done or said? Did Nicole call again?"

"No."

"Your lawyer?"

"No."

"Lilly, we aren't going to go through the one-word answers again, are we?"

She glanced up. He wore a teasing smile on his face. Despite herself, her heart skipped a beat.

"Your pulse is racing."

"I–I must be coming down with some kind of bug," she said, skirting around the truth.

"Why didn't you say something sooner?" Rising, he pulled her to her feet. "Let's get you upstairs and to bed. Don't you dare get out of that bed tomorrow. I should have thought of this sooner. You need help. Odette won't be back for five more weeks. I'll have Mother call an agency tomorrow."

The consequences of her duplicity were quick and unsettling. "I'll be fine. There's no need to call the agency."

He must have heard the frantic note in her voice, because he stopped halfway out of the room. "You don't think I'd hire anyone over you or fire you because you're sick, do you?"

She hadn't. Fear of losing her job no longer kept her awake at night. Her growing feelings for Adam did. She'd thought Myron had killed any possibility of her caring for another man. She'd been wrong.

"I'll be fine after a good night's sleep. Tomorrow I'll call Odette and see when the cleaning crew is scheduled to come."

"We'll see. Now go to bed."

"Good night, Adam." She escaped to her room.

The next morning, Lilly chatted gaily with Adam while she cooked breakfast. She made sure she acted no different. Adam was getting too good at distinguishing her emotions and moods.

Finished, she called Odette and, after chatting for fifteen minutes, learned the crew was due the next day. Happy, Lilly told Adam the information while she was going through his mail with him. Whatever it was that had caused her to forget dreams were highways to unhappiness, she now had it under control. Adam was an employer, nothing more. She had dreamed foolishly before and reaped the bitter consequences. She didn't plan on repeating her mistake.

Brent arrived exactly at two Monday afternoon. Lilly led him into the study and took a seat beside Adam.

"I prefer that my student and I get to know each other alone," Brent said without preamble.

Lilly was already rising. Adam's hand on her arm stopped her. "I'd like her to stay."

Brent rocked back on his booted heels. "Afraid I'll let you walk into a wall or one of these fancy chairs?"

"She stays." Adam was relatively sure that wouldn't happen, but he wanted Lilly there just the same.

Laughter rumbled from a deep chest. "All right, Doc. Let's get to work and see if I can earn that trust of yours."

Adam stood and listened to Brent talk about reference points, naming hallways and corners, landmarks, and positional terminology when all he wanted to do was walk upright like a man. He told him as much.

"Do you let your patients tell you how to diagnose and treat them?"

Adam's tight lips were his answer.

"Thought not. Let's talk about clues, any auditory, tactile, kinesthetic sense that will help you determine location, position, or line of direction. You smell anything?"

"Roses." As soon as the word was out of his mouth he wanted to call it back. He was sure Lilly wouldn't understand, but he wasn't so sure about Brent.

"Roses, huh? Doc, I'd say your kinesthetic memory is working just fine."

"Can we get on with this?" he asked.

"What do you smell, Lilly?" Brent asked, grinning.

"I—er, nothing," she said, a foot away from Adam, and flushed. She wasn't about to admit she smelled Adam's citrus cologne, that she had to catch herself a couple of times to keep from leaning closer to the enticing scent.

Brent grinned. "Imagine that. Two people a foot apart and totally different noses. And might I say, Lilly, that you have a pretty nose."

"Are you going to teach or flirt?" Adam asked, annoyed with Brent. He had no right to flirt with Lilly.

"Teach." With that, Brent began moving through the house. Adam could do nothing but hold on and trust him not to run into a wall.

Chapter Fourteen

The fourth time Brent came, he brought the optical scanner and the read-print program to install on Adam's computer. Adam was awkward in using the arrow keys instead of the mouse, but after a while he was doing fairly well, since the program "told" him when he went wrong.

His confidence that he had overcome all his bumps in the road grew until Brent handed him a cane. To Adam's profound disappointment, he was awkward and off-balance with the black five-foot extension of his arm that came to the middle of his chest.

"Slow down and think, Doc."

"I am," Adam said impatiently, his right hand clenching the rubber grip of the sturdy aluminum cane.

"I understand that you were quite a renowned neurosurgeon," Brent said in a conversational tone.

"Yes," Adam answered, his words clipped as he made his way around the sofa and a chair on his way to his destination, the fireplace.

"Tell me, then, the first time you made an incision, was it as good as the hundredth time?"

"Of course not." Adam barely kept himself from snapping the answer.

"Then how did you learn?" Brent asked mildly.

Finally Adam reached the fireplace and turned toward Brent. "By not giving up, by practicing every chance I got."

"Practice. Ah, yes. Then why on earth did you think the first or second or even the third time you tried to use your cane you would be perfect?"

Adam rubbed the back of his neck. "I don't know; I guess because I was ready to learn."

"Good. That's what I wanted to hear. Learning comes from doing. In this case, by using your cane." Brent glanced at the silent Lilly. "Could you please get me something to drink? I'm as parched as a tick on a dead dog."

"Of course," she said, rising from sitting on the sofa. Her hands had been clamped so tightly together they ached. Every step Adam took, she took with him. Every defeat he experienced, she experienced with him. "What would you like?"

"A margarita, but since I'm on duty, anything fruity, and I'll pretend."

"Would you like something, Dr. Wakefield?" She had decided not to call him Adam when guests were present.

"No."

"I'll be right back."

"Take your time," Brent advised.

Frowning, Lilly said, "All right."

Adam listened to the fading sound of Lilly's shoes on the area rugs, then the hollow sound indicating she was on the hardwood floor in the hallway. "Now that you've gotten rid of Lilly, what's next?"

"Figured you were smart from the first. And to answer your question: what's next is that you begin to learn."

"I thought that's what I was doing already. Was it necessary for her to leave?"

"Yes. Whether you like to admit it or not, she's a distraction. You tense up when she's in the room."

"That's ridiculous. I want her here."

"Exactly, and you have high expectations of yourself when she's looking. You don't want to flounder or fall or bump into furniture. You want to be the self-assured man you've always been. Just like you learned to be that man, you must learn again."

"I told you I'm willing to learn." Brent would try the patience of a saint, and Adam had never been a saint.

"I know what you said, but I'm watching what you're doing and it's piss-poor." Brent crossed to him. "To teach you, I must have your complete concentration. To learn, you must have the same concentration. I don't have it with Lilly here. From the beginning, I told you that I preferred to work without an audience because the student works best that way. It wasn't a whim."

"Here's your drink."

Brent took the glass from Lilly and sipped the fruity concoction of pineapple and orange juice, then handed it back. "Delicious. Dr. Wakefield, are you sure Lilly can't get anything for you?"

Adam arched a brow. He didn't think it was by accident that Brent had addressed him professionally for the first time. He'd wanted to remind Adam that he was the expert here. Not Adam. And as irritating as it might be, Brent was right. Adam had had Jonathan check on the outspoken man, and he was the best. "Lilly."

"Yes?"

He heard her move across the room, smelled the light scent of roses. "Brent feels I'm too macho when you're watching. So I guess you have the rest of the afternoon off. But don't you dare read *The Third Watch* without me."

First came worry that she wouldn't be there if he needed her; then, as what he had said sank in, a smile worked itself across her face. He wouldn't, as he had put it, be macho if he only cared for her professionally. Her heart sang.

"If I did, I'd be too scared to go to sleep tonight. If you gentlemen will excuse me, I have some phone calls to make. I'll be in the kitchen."

As soon as Adam heard the last faint sound of her shoes he said, "Now that she's gone we can start. Or do I get my knuckles rapped?"

"Good one, Doc. I'm strict, but when I turn you loose, I could set you down in the middle of Times Square and you wouldn't hesitate to orientate yourself and find where you need to go."

Adam shook his head and reluctantly grinned. "You certainly don't lack self-confidence."

"Neither do you," Brent said. "Once you have the cane down pat, you might consider a guide dog."

"A guide dog takes too long to train. Besides, when my sight returns, I won't need him."

"Logical, but what if your sight doesn't return?"

Adam's jaw hardened. "It will."

"Then let's get started."

Assured she'd have privacy for a while, Lilly placed a call to her lawyer. His secretary put her through to him immediately. "Hello, Mrs. Crawford."

"Evening, Mr. Powell. How is the investigation going?"

His impatient sigh echoed clearly through the line. "Nothing new. I told you I'd call if there was."

She barely kept from biting her lip or bowing her head. "Yes, but I was hoping he might change his mind about going to court."

"Unfortunately, no."

"You still can't find anyone to testify against him?" she asked, half-sitting on the stool at the counter.

"To everyone I've spoken with, across gender and race lines, Myron Crawford is a kind, generous man who loves his family and never let a friend down."

"What about Rafe?" Her one chance was finding her stepson. He'd suffered more than she had at Myron's hands.

"No luck on locating him. But I'm not sure he'd help our case."

"What do you mean?"

"People here characterize him as a smart but undisciplined and ungrateful troublemaker who left the day of graduation and almost broke his father's and grandmother's hearts," the lawyer told her. "The same people all say Shayla is a sweet young woman who is devoted to her father. By the way, she's going to testify for her father."

Lilly closed her eyes. *There are never those as blind as those who will not see. Myron and Shayla only let you see what benefited them in the long run.* "You couldn't find anyone to testify for me?"

"So far I haven't," the lawyer slowly told her. His tone didn't indicate that he held out much hope that things would change in their favor. "You can always change the reason for your petition for divorce and skip going to court."

Her eyes snapped open. They gleamed with anger. "No! I backed down enough from Myron."

"You may lose."

"But the bottom line is that I wouldn't have backed down and I'll still have my divorce." Too angry to sit, she slid off the stool and began to pace the length of the cord.

"But it'll cost more emotionally and financially. His lawyer is going to come after you, and it won't be nice," he warned.

She suddenly realized that her mother's reputation and what people thought Lilly's was would be the lawyer's key weapons. Her mother might have been loose, but Lilly wasn't. Myron was the only man she'd ever slept with, but no one knew that other than Myron. How long would she have to live under her mother's shadow and shame? "I imagine he will," she finally said.

"You also have to consider that if you lose, you'll have to pay court costs and his lawyer's fee. Hutchinson is a crafty and shrewd devil. It wouldn't surprise me if he's already come up with a figure that's way over the usual amount because his case looks unbeatable," Powell warned. "Whatever the amount, you'd have no recourse but to pay."

She stopped and leaned her head against the base of the curved cabinet at the end of the counter. She'd put back every extra cent she earned. She'd bought nothing that wasn't a necessity. She had more money now than she ever had in her life. Being poor didn't scare her; backing down from Myron again did. "We go to court."

"All right." His tone didn't inspire confidence.

"Good-bye, Mr. Powell." Lilly bowed her head and wrapped her hands around her waist. Would she ever be free?

"Was that your lawyer?"

Lilly spun around sharply. "You move quietly."

He came closer. "And you're being evasive."

How could he know her better than anyone ever had, even Mother Crawford? The thought comforted and frightened her. "Myron is going to fight the grounds of my divorce petition," she said and explained that finding her stepson, Rafe, was her only chance of winning the case. "If I lose I have to pay court costs and his lawyer's fee." She couldn't tell him about her mother's reputation. That was one shame she couldn't bring herself to tell anyone. "I think my lawyer would rather I reword my petition and not go to court."

"Why don't you?"

Her shoulders stiffened. Brown eyes blazed. "Because I couldn't look my-self in the mirror if I did. He cheated me out of six years, almost destroyed my self-respect, stole my dreams. He's not taking anything else."

Adam's hand unerringly reached out to cup her chin. "I'm proud of you." Then his hand was gone, leaving her feeling bereft. "If you need money, any amount of money, let me know. And before you get huffy, consider it a loan."

She had been about to. A man shouldn't be able to read a woman so well. "Thanks for the offer, but I want to do it on my own."

"All right. Just remember, I got your back."

She grinned. "Slang from the eminent Dr. Wakefield?"

"I'm a man of many different talents." He reached for her hand and briefly squeezed it before releasing it and turning toward the door leading out of the kitchen. "Let's go for a walk so I can practice and show off to Brent."

Lilly walked beside him. "I think you like him."

Adam paused and stepped around the settee against the wall in the hall. "Why would I like an arrogant, overbearing, opinionated man?"

"Maybe because he reminds you of someone very close to you?" Lilly said, going through the front door Adam opened for her.

"Why, Lilly, I thought you liked Jonathan."

Laughing, they went down the front steps together.

Brent proved to be as good as he prophesied. After three weeks, Adam could go through the main rooms of the house without help or difficulty. Reference points and landmarks, those initially irritating terms, enabled him to move freely, avoid objects, and find what he wanted. To celebrate he invited Jonathan to dinner.

Lilly wanted the occasion to be a memorable one. She pored over recipe books and checked twice with Odette and Eleanor about Adam's favorite foods before settling on honey-glazed ham as the main course. The slices would be big enough for Adam to find and cut without difficulty, and there was little likelihood of the meat falling off his fork. She chose baby asparagus and roasted red bliss potatoes for the same reason.

Dessert had to be special. No matter how much Adam teased her about her high-cholesterol, calorie-laden cooking, he usually asked for seconds and often thirds.

Grinning, Lilly sat back in her chair at the table in the breakfast nook, listening to the faint strains of music. Beethoven again. Adam usually played after lunch. Twice a week, on Tuesday and Friday, she'd join him then or after supper for her lessons. She was still learning to "sight" her keys. Adam was patient but firm. He intended her to learn to play the piano. She understood it was his way of saying he was sorry, but it was also to give her confidence.

Lilly went back to flipping through the cookbooks. Odette had at least a dozen and had admitted ruefully to Lilly when she called that she didn't use any of them. She cooked from scratch. The more Lilly flipped, the more she realized she wasn't going to find the answer for a dessert. She didn't want a mishap. Perhaps she should take Odette's rule and cook from scratch a dessert she was familiar with.

Her hand clutched the hardbound book. There was only one that she considered fancy enough to fit the occasion. The dessert she wanted to prepare had been taught to her by Mother Crawford and handed down through four generations of Crawford women, although Lilly didn't consider herself a Crawford woman. The last time she had cooked the pie had been at Myron's insistence two weeks before Mother Crawford's death. Just thinking of Myron angered her.

Closing the book, Lilly went outside. Still restless, she started walking. The sight of the rosebushes in bloom stopped her. They were Mother Crawford's favorite. The kind woman had given Lilly more love than anyone else before or since. Thinking back, she recalled what Mother Crawford had said when she was teaching Lilly the recipe.

"This is given to only one Crawford woman in each generation to hand down to the next. It's an honor and a trust. You make sure you know who you're giving it to." Then she had looked Lilly straight in the eye and said, "I never taught anyone else this and I don't aim to. Crawford or no, I would have picked you."

At the time Lilly hadn't thought anything of her words except her happiness that Mother Crawford had that much trust in her and that, for once, she wasn't standing in line behind Carol, Myron's first wife.

Mother Crawford had given the family recipe to her, Lilly. She had loved her and had faith in her. Turning, Lilly went back to the kitchen. She knew what she wanted to prepare for dessert, a family recipe based on love and trust.

"Show time."

Adam opened the door to his bedroom and walked into the hall. Lilly had offered to accompany him to dinner, but he wanted to do it by himself. It wasn't pride that ruled his decision but his increasing need to regain as much of his independence as possible. He wore a white shirt, a gray silk tie, and a herringbone two-button suit for the occasion. Now all he had to do was get downstairs.

From experience, he knew navigating the hallway wouldn't be much of a problem. He'd practiced numerous times by himself without a mishap. With the cane repeatedly making an arch above the floor, he made his way to the top of the stairs. Here things would get a little trickier, but nothing, Brent had assured Adam, he couldn't handle. He'd gone up and down several times, but never without Brent being there to guide and warn him.

"Pretend I'm there," Brent had said.

Adam anchored the cane to the back of the first step and moved up diagonally with it, then drew in a fortifying breath and stepped into nothingness. As always, his heart rate increased; his palms dampened.

When his foot settled on the stair beside his cane, he breathed a sigh of relief, then immediately repeated the process. Brent had warned Adam of the fear that could paralyze a person. That was one lesson Adam already knew.

"How long have you been there?"

"Just since the last few stairs," his mother said, stepping to the right side of him at the bottom of the stairs. "Do you want to take my arm?"

"Thanks." His hand closed around her upper forearm. "Has Jonathan made it yet?"

"You know I make it a practice never to be late for surgery or a meal," Jonathan said, his voice followed by his distinctive laughter coming from directly in front of Adam. "Thanks for the invitation."

"Thanks for hanging in there," Adam said, stopping at his mother's slight pause. From the number of steps and the direction they had taken he knew they were in front of the sofa in the living room.

"When you love someone you have no choice," Jonathan said softly.

Adam felt the sudden tension in his mother and wondered about the cause; then his puzzlement cleared. She was probably worried about him and his first dinner party since his blindness. Reaching over, he touched her arm in reassurance.

"We're having before-dinner drinks in here," Eleanor said, her voice slightly husky. "Lilly should be here shortly."

"What would you like to drink, Adam?" Jonathan asked.

"Nothing, thank you," Adam said. He was about to ask about Lilly when he heard her footsteps. "I was wondering where you were."

"Just checking on dinner one last time," Lilly said, hoping Eleanor didn't comment that instead of her shirtwaist dress she was wearing a white blouse and the navy blue skirt to her suit. She'd put her hair up in a chignon and wore the small pearl earrings she'd gotten when she worked at JC Penney.

"You look lovely tonight, Lilly," Eleanor said.

"Thanks," Lilly said, pleased. Eleanor always looked good, as she did now in a pink floral silk dress.

"What did you fix tonight that is going to shoot my cholesterol level sky high?" Adam teased, reaching out his hand.

Immediately she took it, used to the little jolt she felt. Brent had called the contact anchoring; she just called it titillating. "Honey-glazed ham and a special dessert."

"Jonathan, if you'll escort Mother, we can go in. Lilly will sit on my right."

"I can't—"

"For once, don't argue." In one smooth motion, he took her arm and went to the dining room.

Lilly, afraid of balking and throwing him off-balance, helplessly followed. She didn't say anything until he released her to step behind her chair and pull it out smoothly. Fleetingly she wondered how long he had practiced the simple task to make it seem so effortless.

Not for anything would she ruin his triumph. "I'll sit for a moment, but then I have to get up and serve."

Adam released her chair once she was seated; then he took his own seat. "We'll manage."

"I have an idea," Eleanor said. "I'll put everything on the serving cart and bring it in."

"Excellent idea. I'll help," said Jonathan.

"No," Eleanor said, waving him back into his seat. "Please stay seated."

"I'll go." Lilly was already pushing back her chair.

"Keep her here, Adam," Eleanor admonished. "She's been working all day cooking and polishing silverware. Lilly, you didn't want any help then, but let me do this."

Lilly realized his mother needed to help make the evening a success. "Thank you. I have the serving dishes already set out."

Eleanor hurried to the kitchen.

Lilly watched Jonathan watch Eleanor leave. "Jonathan, the sangria is in the refrigerator. Could you get it, please, and fill the glasses?"

"I'm on it." Standing, he followed Eleanor into the kitchen.

Eleanor removed the ham from the roasting pan and placed it on the platter, careful not to disturb the garnish of parsley. She was thankful she had finished when Jonathan strolled in. Her palms actually dampened. No matter how much she tried, she couldn't stop thinking of the kiss he'd playfully mentioned. "I can manage."

"Lilly sent me for the sangria."

"Oh," she said and turned away to reach for the sautéed baby asparagus. She transferred them into a chafing dish and noticed Jonathan was still there. Her questioning gaze went from him to the glass pitcher of iced punch in his hands.

Jonathan nodded toward the living room and the sound of laughter. "I thought it might be easier for Lilly to get more comfortable if it was just she and Adam there for a few minutes."

Eleanor's nerves settled. "I'm glad you and she seem to be getting along."

He shrugged broad shoulders beneath the tailored gray suit coat, then came over to lean against the cabinet, one hand beneath the glass pitcher he held. "We discovered we have a common goal."

Eleanor didn't have to ask what the common goal was. She did need to seek reassurance in another matter. "It's going to be all right, isn't it, Jonathan?"

He hesitated, then set the pitcher down and came to her to take her shoulders in his big hands. "If you're asking if Adam's sight will return, I can't give you any guarantees. If you're asking if he's becoming more and more like the man we knew, the answer is yes. But if you're asking if he doesn't regain his sight, will he shut us out again, I honestly don't know."

"You could have lied."

Slowly he shook his head. "I'll never lie to you, Eleanor. About anything." Dropping his hands, he stepped back and picked up the pitcher. "You sure you don't need any help?"

She started to say yes and then realized before "it" happened she would have thought nothing of Jonathan helping. "After you serve Lilly and Adam, if I'm not out, you can come back and help."

"Will do. By the way, you start on the painting for my office yet?"

She responded to the twinkling in his dark eyes. "I have."

"I don't suppose you're going to tell me what subject you decided on?"

"I always said you were a very perceptive man, Jonathan."

He stood smiling at her for a few moments longer, then strolled from the room.

Watching his long, graceful strides, Eleanor felt a calming of her spirit. No matter how erratic her emotions ran in regard to Jonathan, she'd be forever grateful that he was an important and needed part of her and her children's life.

To Lilly's delight, dinner went smoothly. Adam was initially hesitant to tackle cutting his ham, but once he had the first bite in his mouth, the tension visibly drained out of him. For Lilly, it had taken longer. She knew how much this dinner meant to Adam. If it didn't go well, he might not try again.

"Lilly," Jonathan said, "I see what Adam meant."

"This dessert is decadent," Eleanor said, taking another bite of pie loaded with pineapple, walnuts, and pecans.

"Told you," Adam said with satisfaction, digging into his second slice of pineapple praline pie.

Lilly had a wide grin on her face that was getting bigger by the second. "Thank you. It's a recipe that has been handed down through four generations."

"Your family's?" Eleanor asked.

The smile on Lilly's face wavered. "My mother wasn't much on cooking.

Mother Crawford taught me. She was the one good thing that came out of my marriage. She was eighty-one years old when she died and probably never regretted a thing she did."

"Very few people can probably say that," Adam said with feeling. "She sounds like she was a wonderful woman."

"She was." The memories, tempered by time, were not as painful. "I'll always remember her and be glad we met."

"From the way you speak of her, she must have felt the same way about you." Adam sipped his drink. "I can't imagine she shared her recipe with many people."

"I was the only one," Lilly admitted proudly.

"Then be thankful for the time you had together," Eleanor said softly.

"I am, despite how things turned out otherwise." Lilly folded her hands in her lap. "I'll never regret she was a part of my life."

"I'm glad she entrusted you with the recipe. I need a dessert for the monthly potluck dinner the day after tomorrow at the office. Do you think you could cook me a pie like this one?" Jonathan laid his fork on his empty plate. "Of course, I'd pay you and buy the ingredients. My staff teases me all the time about trying to fake them out by putting whatever I get from the deli in a bowl from home. This would shut them up for good."

"I've tasted your cooking," Adam teased. "They should be thankful."

"That's what I've tried to tell them, but they aren't listening." He turned to Lilly. "So, how about making me a hit with my staff?"

"I don't know," Lilly said, a bit uneasy. She'd never cooked for anyone outside the family before Adam.

"Go on, Lilly. Stick it to him," Adam said with a laugh.

"For a pie like this, I'll pay."

"You really want me to bake you a pie?" Lilly asked, her eyes wide.

Jonathan leaned over to pull his wallet from his hip pocket. "I'll pay you tonight if you'd like. How much?"

A bit embarrassed, she held up her hand as Jonathan opened his wallet. "Please. I don't want any money."

"You're sure?"

"Positive, but the ingredients will come from the kitch—"

"And are on the house," Eleanor said, cutting Lilly off.

Jonathan shoved his wallet back in his pocket. "Then I can pick up the pie tomorrow night?"

Lilly glanced first at Adam, then at Eleanor. Both appeared to approve. "Will around six-thirty be all right?"

Jonathan grinned. "Isn't that dinnertime?"

Everyone at the table laughed.

The next night Jonathan came for dinner, and when he left he had Lilly's pie safely in a pie carrier. Adam had harassed him by saying that he planned to call his office the next day to see if the whole pie arrived. Jonathan had accepted the good-natured teasing with his usual smile.

Lilly watched the clock all Friday morning. She figured the potluck luncheon would probably start around eleven and go until one. What if they didn't like her pie? Occasionally, even a favorite recipe failed.

When the phone in the kitchen rang a little after twelve, she sprang to pick up the receiver. "Hello?"

"Lilly, this is Jonathan."

"They didn't like my pie," she said, feeling her stomach knot.

"*Like* is hardly the word."

"Oh." She slumped against the kitchen counter.

"They went crazy over it. Of course, then I had to admit I didn't cook it." He chuckled.

"They did?" She brightened immediately.

"They did. That's the reason I called. Two other people in my office want to order a pie. So how much and when can you deliver them?"

"What?" Her spine straightened as she came away from the counter.

"How much and when can you deliver them?" he repeated, then shushed someone. "Excuse me; you probably heard them asking over my shoulder about this afternoon. I told them that's too soon."

"I'm not sure about a price," Lilly finally managed.

"I realize this is sort of sudden. Think about it and call me back. The number is five-five-five five-five-five-four. Just tell the receptionist—who, incidentally, wants a pie—who you are and she'll get me to the phone. Good-bye."

"Good-bye." Dazed, Lilly hung up the phone. Then, as the full impact of the call hit her, she went racing to Adam in the living room. He was playing another of those intricate melodies he loved, but he stopped when she was barely inside the room.

His dark head lifted and he turned toward her. "Lilly, what's the matter?"

By now she was used to him recognizing her footsteps. "I didn't mean to disturb you, but I need to ask you a question."

Swinging all the way around on the piano bench, he said, "Shoot."

Twisting her hands, she continued toward him until she was less than three feet in front of him. "Dr. Delacroix call—"

"I thought you agreed to call him Jonathan after dinner the other night?"

"I did, but I guess in the excitement I forgot," she explained.

"I can hear it in your voice."

Despite her quandary, she smiled. "You're getting good at that."

He shrugged and crossed his arms over his chest. "What's up with Jonathan?"

"Two people in his office want to buy my pies and he wants to know how much I'd charge."

"Congratulations. It seems you're about to become an entrepreneur."

"I don't think it will come to that, but I don't want to disappoint the people who work for Dr. De— Jonathan. But I have no idea how much to charge; besides, I have a job."

Adam unfolded his arms and scooted over. "Come here, Lilly."

She hesitated only a moment, then sat beside him.

"Thanks. I was getting a crick in my neck."

"Sorry."

"Take that word out of your vocabulary."

He felt her tense beside him, then relax. "I'm trying."

"Good." He reached out. Automatically she placed her hand in his. "Take all the time you need. Thankfully, I'm becoming pretty self-sufficient, so you can make and deliver your pies whenever it's convenient for you. Your car is running and Jonathan's office isn't that difficult to locate. As for price, gourmet pies can sell for as much as fifty to seventy-five dollars."

"Fifty to seventy-five dollars!" she shrieked.

Adam chuckled. "Guess I shocked you. But invariably the more people pay for something, the more valuable they deem it."

"But–but," Lilly stammered. "I couldn't charge that much. I'm not a gourmet cook."

"By whose standards?" Adam asked, his thumb lazily stroking the back of her hand. "Exclusivity is another food selling point. Where else are they going to get an original dessert that has been handed down for four generations?"

The way he said it sounded reasonable, but his thumb stroking her hand was scattering her thoughts. "I–I don't know."

"I do," Adam said with supreme male confidence. "However, since you're still hesitant, compromise and charge Jonathan's staff members a special rate of twenty-five dollars. Jonathan will gain points. They'll think they've gotten a bargain, and you'll have sold your pies at a good price. It's a win-win situation."

"You're sure?"

"Yes." He tugged her to her feet. "Go over there to the phone and call Jonathan and take the orders."

"What if no one wants a pie at that price? Twenty-five dollars would buy five pies at the local Piggly-Wiggly back home."

"Not gourmet pies, it wouldn't, and they'll want it. If it's one thing I've learned about people in the South, it's that they like good food and are willing to pay for it. Now stop dithering and call."

Hesitant but unable to think of a good argument not to, Lilly went to the phone on the end table and dialed. As Jonathan had predicted, the receptionist's cheery voice became excited when Lilly identified herself. Conversely, the woman's excitement caused Lilly's doubts to increase.

"Lilly, I hope you've called with an answer that isn't going to make my staff unhappy. You now have five orders," Jonathan told her.

"Five?" Lilly squeaked.

"And I wouldn't be surprised if the number went up. If I wasn't watching my cholesterol, I'd order another one myself," he told her. "So what do I tell them?"

Lilly glanced back at Adam. As if aware of her stare, he said, "You can do this. Stop doubting yourself. You reached the turning point when you left Little Elm. Remember?"

"After thinking about it, I decided that since they are your employees the cost will be twenty-five dollars and I can deliver them Monday afternoon."

"Hold on."

Lilly placed her hand over the mouthpiece. "He's asking them."

She had barely gotten the words out before Jonathan was back on the line. "You have four sales and my heartfelt thanks."

"If the other person changed their mind becau—"

"I certainly hope you weren't going to lower your price when you've already given my staff a discount," Jonathan said.

"I—Yes, I was," she admitted.

"Don't. Restaurant prices don't fluctuate for the customer and neither should yours."

"You are so much like Adam," she said, unaware of the smile on her lips.

"Thanks for the compliment. Gotta run. Bye."

"Bye." She hung up the phone.

"What was that about Jonathan being like me?"

Crossing the room, Lilly retook her seat beside Adam, a smile playing around her lips as she retold him what Jonathan had said.

"Some people expect to buy a Mercedes for the price of a Chevrolet. You get what you pay for."

"If I'm going to have those pies ready, I better go to the grocery store. I'll let Eleanor know I'm leaving."

"That won't be necessary. I'm going with you."

"W-What?" She surged to her feet. "You can't!"

Adam rose with her. "And why not?"

"It's that Chevrolet you were speaking about a few minutes ago," she told him with obvious worry in her voice.

The corners of his mouth twitched. "I've ridden in Chevrolets before."

"I was speaking figuratively. My car is a worn-out, faded twelve-year-old Ford Taurus. The velour seats are worn, the dashboard faded, the floor mats threadbare. It's nothing like you're used to."

"Those things won't matter to me," he said quietly.

"Oh, Adam, I didn't mean it that way!" she cried, but both knew she did.

"Caring too much about personal possessions is what got me where I am. The car will be fine. Unless you'd rather I not go with you?"

"Now who's talking nonsense? I'll go get my purse and the car keys." She paused at the doorway. "You need anything from your room?"

"My baseball cap. I can't remember where I tossed it."

"I'll find it, and I'll be back in two minutes."

Upstairs she quickly got her things and Adam's cap from the top of his armoire where she had placed it while cleaning, and then she hurried back downstairs. Adam was waiting at the foot of the stairs for her. "Let me call Eleanor to see if she needs anything."

After speaking with Eleanor a few minutes, Lilly had another potential passenger. She placed her hand over the mouthpiece, wondering why she hadn't expected this to happen. "Eleanor wants to go with us. I told her we're going in my car and she said it didn't matter."

Adam popped his baseball cap on his head. "Tell her I have dibs on the front seat."

Lilly removed her hand and spoke into the mouthpiece: "We'll meet you at the garage. Adam says he has dibs on the front seat."

Chapter Fifteen

Adam and his mother climbed inside Lilly's car and buckled their seat belts as if they were seated on supple leather instead of slick velour seats. The Ford was clean, if a bit faded. Adam's willingness to leave the grounds for the first time since he arrived was all that really mattered.

"Here." Lilly handed Adam a pen and a notepad as soon as she finished buckling her seat belt. "I didn't have time to write down what I needed. I always forget if I don't have it written down."

Adam's fingers trembled, then firmed. "Don't say anything if you can't read my writing."

In the rearview mirror Lilly watched the worry fade from Eleanor's face. "Doctors are notorious for their bad handwriting, but if I can't read it, I figure your mother can."

"Your father's handwriting was nearly illegible and I had no problems," Eleanor said.

"What are you writing?" Lilly asked Adam, putting the car into gear and backing out of the garage.

" 'Book.' You finished *The Perfect Alibi*. Maybe there's a decent book section in the grocery store."

"If not, we can run by the bookstore after we finish grocery shopping. There's nothing that will spoil," Lilly told him.

"We'll see," Adam said carefully.

Adam had nearly changed his mind by the time Lilly parked at the grocery store. What if he wasn't ready? Instead of letting fear rule him, he pushed it aside, unbuckled his seat belt, and got out. He took Lilly's arm, but he was well aware that his mother was on the other side of him.

Inside the store, Lilly obtained a cart, placed his hands on the handle, then slowly steered it through the store. To the casual observer he was a man wearing sunglasses and a cap, pushing a cart. If the observer looked more closely, he'd see the cane and the upward tilt of Adam's head that he practiced daily to bring back into correct alignment.

Ten minutes into shopping, Lilly walked up to his right. "Eleanor is going to take the cart and get in line while we go check out the books."

Fear came again, but before it could take root and grow, Adam reached out. He located Lilly's arm, and positioned his hand just above her elbow. He tried to relax his grip but knew he wasn't succeeding. "Sorry."

"A very smart man once told me to take that word out of my vocabulary."

"Did you listen?"

"I'm trying."

"In that case, let's go find that book."

She started walking. His heart boomed. His throat dried as she led him through the store. He was a blind man in a maze with only the touch of her arm to guide him, trusting her not to let him walk into anything. Immediately he realized how different and scary this was away from his house. He just as immediately realized he trusted her. His fingers relaxed.

"We're almost there, Adam."

"See anything remotely interesting?" he asked when they stopped.

"A couple. I'll read the blurb and you can tell me which one you'd like." Lilly plucked a few books from the rack. Adam thought the second one about a murder in a casino had possibilities.

"*Double or Nothing* it is." Lilly took his arm and joined Eleanor, who was in line to check out. Lilly gave her the keys to her car. "You two can wait in the car. This shouldn't take long."

"Mama, why is that woman leading that man around?" asked a high-pitched voice.

"Hush, Michelle."

The three of them froze. Lilly's and Eleanor's gaze went to Adam, unsure of what to expect. "Adam, I'm tired. Why don't we go to the car?" Eleanor said, reaching for his arm.

"I'm not. I'll push the cart and you go on to the car." His jaw tight, his hands gripped the handle.

Lilly's throat ached. She could do nothing, say nothing, to help. So she gave him the support the only way she could. She stepped beside him and placed her hand briefly next to his.

He didn't say anything on the way back to the house. Once there he excused himself and went straight to his room.

"Do you think one of us should go up?" Eleanor asked, staring up after her son.

Lilly placed her hand on the newel post and watched Adam until he was out of sight. "Let's wait until dinner."

Lilly took a deep breath and knocked. Adam hadn't come back downstairs since they returned from the grocery store.

"Adam." Becoming concerned when he didn't answer, she knocked again. "Adam, dinner is ready."

"I'm not—"

Her hand already on the knob twisted. He wasn't hiding in his room if she could help it.

The door swung open. She gasped and slammed it shut, her cheeks burning.

The door opened. She pivoted sharply and squeezed her eyes shut. Her breathing was out of kilter. She could still see him naked, the breadth of his shoulders, the muscled hardness of his chest, the tapered waist and long legs.

"I–I'm sorry. I didn't know you weren't dressed."

"Obviously."

"I–I'll wait downstairs." She started easing away, forgot about the table, and bumped into it. Down she went.

"Lilly! Watch out!" Realizing what had happened, he knelt and reached out his hand to help her up. His fingers pressed something soft and resilient. Her sharp intake of breath told him what it was.

"Sorry." His hand shifted farther to left of her breast and closed around her upper forearm. "You all right?"

"Are you dressed?"

"Your eyes closed?" he asked, laughter lurking just under the surface of his voice.

"Of course they are!"

"I thought you'd been married?"

"That's not the same and you know it."

"I suppose you're right. Open your eyes. I have my robe on."

One eye opened, then the other. Her gaze didn't drop below midchest. The robe hung loosely on his shoulders. A smattering of dark chest hair ran in a dramatic V to his waist. Her head snapped up. He was grinning. And her behind hurt.

"Glad you find this funny."

"Why didn't you wait to come in?"

"I thought you were upset by what that little girl said and you were going to tell me you weren't coming downstairs for dinner," she told him truthfully.

"And you weren't going to let me sulk, is that it?"

Although she wasn't sure of his mood, she was sure of her answer. "No. You've come too far. I figure we both have. You don't let me backslide. I'm not letting you, either."

"We're a team, huh?"

"We certainly are."

His head lowered for a second, then lifted. "I almost did; then I started thinking. I've made strides in the past weeks. Good ones. My blindness doesn't impose limits on me. I do. Asking for help doesn't mean you're helpless."

"About time you figured that out," Lilly said. A pat on the back was the last thing he needed. "Now, if you'll help me up, I'll go tell Eleanor you're on your way."

Standing, he smoothly brought her up with him. "Maybe you're the one who should be eating more."

"I'm fine," she said, wishing he'd close his robe, wishing he didn't smell so good. He must have just stepped from the shower. She groaned. The last thing she needed to be thinking of was Adam naked beneath the spray of water.

"You're hurt?" he asked.

"No." She swallowed. "I better go."

"Thanks for caring." Raising her hand, he kissed her palm. "I'll be downstairs as soon as I dress."

The door closed with Lilly's hand still in midair. Closing her eyes, she leaned against the wall, Jonathan's words that day in the kitchen coming back to her. She'd done the unthinkable with the impossible, but if she could she wouldn't change a thing. Adam needed her, and being needed was almost as good as being loved. She told herself that all the way downstairs, but when Adam came into the dining room she knew she lied and just as surely knew that being needed was all she'd ever have.

Lilly strolled from the mailbox with a carryall full of mail. Since the day after Odette's accident, Adam had filled out a request that all his mail be forwarded from his home in Sausalito. She bet the mailman on the route was sorry. She didn't see how one person could get so much mail. Magazines, circulars, newspapers. Eleanor had told her one afternoon when they were going through his mail together that the amount was less than half of what he had received when he was practicing.

Opening the front door, she continued to the study, where Adam would be waiting. More than likely he'd be on the computer. He was becoming very adept at finding information. Day by day, bit by bit, he pushed back the walls that had once bound him.

"Mail's in."

Without turning from the computer, he said, "What's there today?"

Putting the canvas bag on his desk, she began lifting out the letters. "Medical journals, a garden magazine, circulars." She stopped and stared down at the thick, six-by-six book in a hand that had suddenly became unsteady.

"That all?"

"The catalog from Shreveport Junior College," she said quietly.

He spun around in the chair. "When is registration for the summer session?"

"I don't know about this, Adam. Maybe I should wait?"

"Your business is growing. You have steady customers. You need to know how to ensure your business will be successful, and finishing your degree will enable you to do that." His tone broached no argument.

"I'm still a small business."

He held out his hand. "It might take me longer for the scanner to input the information onto the computer to read to me, but I'll find out eventually, so you might as well tell me."

"All right." She'd met few people more stubborn than he. She opened the book. "June first."

"Next week. Perfect. The fact that you're going to college is bound to weigh heavily in your favor when you go to court."

"Immoral people go to college, too."

Standing, he came around the desk without the aid of the cane. "True, but you'll have Mother and me as character witnesses."

"What?"

"We talked it over. When you go back for your hearing, you won't go alone."

The tears pricked her eyes and flowed down her cheek. "Th-Tha—" She couldn't get the words out.

"Lilly." He pulled her into his arms. She went readily, her head resting over the strong beat of his heart. "You aren't alone anymore. There are people who care about you."

She tried to stem the flow of tears, but the more she tried, the more they flowed.

"Don't be afraid. He won't hurt you. I promise."

She shook her head. She wasn't crying over Myron; her heartache was for what could never be. Pushing away, she wiped the tears away. "I didn't mean to cry all over you."

"Any time."

She laid the catalog aside. "I'll look over the catalog later. Let's get through your mail." She reached in the bag and pulled out a letter. "It's from Kristen."

"It must be her invitation. The other night on the phone she said it was in the mail." Without asking, Lilly handed the letter to him. He opened the invitation as he rounded the desk. The pads of his fingertips traced the raised letters; then he placed it on the scanner. "Come on. Come on," Adam coaxed. "Maybe I should have let—"

The computer cut him off and read Kristen's invitation and her note on the inside indicating that she was graduating with distinction and honors. Adam let out a loud yell.

"I take it that's good," Lilly teased.

"You need a 4-point grade average to graduate with distinction. Stanford doesn't have cum laude. To graduate with honors requires the undergrad to write a thesis that resulted in a major research paper," Adam explained with unabashed pride.

"She's so young. I can understand why you're so proud of her!" Lilly exclaimed.

"Don't let that beautiful face and quiet manner fool you. She's brilliant. It might take her a long time to decide what she wants, but once she does there's no stopping her. You remind me of her a lot."

Adam picked up the phone and dialed. "Mother, I want you to hear something."

Lilly half-listened this time as the optical scanner read the invitation once again. Her mind was stuck back on Adam's reference to her reminding him of his sister. They were nothing alike. Lilly heard Eleanor's unladylike shout. Her and Adam's love for each other was so evident. Briefly Lilly wondered what it must have been like to grow up secure in knowing you were loved and wanted.

Adam replaced the receiver. "Mother is on her way."

"I heard," Lilly said. "She's the kind of mother every child should have."

"Mother Crawford sounds as if she was the same way."

Lilly didn't even think of correcting him. It wasn't Minnie Crawford's fault that Myron hadn't been the kind of son she could be proud of. "Yes, she was."

Eleanor arrived at the house breathless. She read the invitation, then listened as the computer did the same. The voice on the computer had barely faded before Adam had the operator on the line to place a call to Kristen.

"Trying to show your big brother up?" he teased when she was on the line. "I'm proud of you, Sis. Hold on. Here's Mother."

Eleanor took the phone. "I'm so proud I could walk all the way to California for your graduation." She laughed. "I guess if I did I would be too tired to be at my best for the commencement ceremony at the stadium, then later at the art department. We'll come in Saturday morning." She nodded. "I'll make arrangements as soon as I get off the phone."

Adam tapped his mother on the arm. "Hold on, Kristen. Adam is trying to tell me something."

"You can fly back today if she needs you. Lilly and I can come up later."

Lilly, who had been standing quietly to the side, blinked. She started to tell them she couldn't go, but Eleanor was already speaking, "I can fly back today if you need me to help with anything. Your last exam isn't until Wednesday. . . . I see. I'll stay here and we'll all fly up together then. I'd love to have a dinner party Saturday night. Perhaps you can invite Eric. . . . Wonderful. I'll call you later today when the plans are firmed up. Love you. Bye."

Eleanor hung up and turned to Adam. "She did it, Adam."

"She certainly did. In grand style." He folded his arms. "She hadn't mentioned Eric lately. I guess they're still dating."

Eleanor smiled. "Why is it that big brothers never like their younger sisters' dates?"

"Because we have reasons," he came back, but he was smiling, too.

"I–I can't go with you," Lilly finally managed, still standing in front of his desk.

Adam twirled in his chair toward her. "And why not?"

"I–I'm just the hired help," she said, using Nicole's words and hating them just as much now as she had then.

His mouth tightened. "After all we've been through together, you think that's all we are to each other?"

Lilly sent a worried glance toward Eleanor. Her blank expression told her nothing.

"What happened to us being a team? You aren't going to let me go off without you to test Brent's bragging, are you?"

"I—"

"No arguing. You're going," Adam cut her off. "Isn't that right, Mother?"

"I quite agree," Eleanor said firmly. "You've helped make this possible."

Lilly looked at Eleanor, always fashionably and neatly dressed as she was now in a white poplin shirt and floral print sarong skirt, then thought of the equally impressive Nicole and Kristen. "I have nothing to wear."

Laughing, Adam shook his head. "Just like a woman."

"A sensible woman," Eleanor said. She'd wanted to take Lilly in hand for weeks and now had the perfect opportunity. "If you want, I could help you decide on a few outfits. Perhaps a new style for your hair."

Lilly's hands went to her ponytailed hair. She hadn't been inside a beauty salon in over three months. "I'd appreciate it."

"You may not after you finish," Adam said.

Lilly frowned. "Why?"

"Mother makes an expedition of shopping, searching for the right dress in the right color. Father used to say turning Mother loose in a clothing store was like turning a child loose in a candy store. She'll sample everything before coming to a decision."

Eleanor lifted a regal shoulder. "What can I say? I'm fussy about what I wear, and I want quality, style, and endurance. It often takes time to find all three."

"You always look wonderful."

"Thank you, Lilly. We'll get started immediately after breakfast in the morning," Eleanor said.

"Better eat a good breakfast and wear comfortable shoes." Adam sat back and folded his arms.

"It couldn't be that bad," Lilly said.

"You'll see," was all Adam said.

Jonathan sat behind his desk on the eighth floor of the medical building and enjoyed a rare leisure moment. This morning they were running ahead of schedule. He'd never believed in overbooking, but the moments when he could relax in his office were few and far between. He wanted time to listen to his patients and time for them to listen to him.

For that reason, each exam room was painted a pale pastel except for the wall facing the exam table, which was covered in floral silk wallpaper. Fluid watercolor paintings hung on the wall. On the ceiling directly over the table were landscapes of sweeping vistas, mountain waterfalls, endless oceans for the patient to focus on.

Giving the best care couldn't be rushed. He demanded nothing less from his staff or from himself. His patients had to know that when he was there with them, they had Jonathan's undivided attention.

The diplomas on the wall behind him attested that he had spent years studying to be the best. He worked long hours, but he didn't mind. He had a lovely big house, beautifully furnished thanks to his ex-wife, but nothing and no one to share it with. Not even a goldfish.

He had achieved professional success but was still working on his personal life. Unlike his mother, he thought the possibility of being loved was well worth the risk involved. His mother had stopped believing when he was nine and her world shattered.

After all the years Jonathan could still vividly remember his mother begging his father to stay, desperately unpacking his clothes as quickly as he packed them. Finally he'd walked out of the four-bedroom brick house his mother had loved so well, and kept meticulously clean, with only the clothes on his back. He'd gotten inside his shiny new Cadillac Jonathan had never ridden in. Inside the car was a young black woman half his father's age. Jonathan's mother had screamed at the woman and called her a whore and a home wrecker.

His father had retaliated by yelling back that Sophia gave him what a man needed. He'd gotten in the white Eldorado and driven off, taking with him Jonathan's mother's heart.

Tears running down her cheeks, she had looked at Jonathan and told him things about his father's affair that no child should have to hear. She promised to make his father sorry he had walked out on her. She had made good that promise, and Jonathan had paid right along with his father by growing up in a house without love, without warmth.

The intercom buzzed and Jonathan immediately hit the speaker. "Yes?"

"Kristen Wakefield on line two."

"Thanks." Eagerly he reached for the phone. Yes, loving far outweighed the risks involved. "I was wondering when I'd hear from you."

"Your invitation should be waiting for you when you get home," she said excitedly.

"Mother and Adam received theirs this morning and called. I'll have you know I'm graduating with honors and distinction."

Some of the happiness faded. Eleanor hadn't called. Before now they had always shared Kristen's triumphs and tribulations. "Doesn't surprise me. I always knew you had it in you to succeed at whatever you went after."

"Passing the courses was easy. It's life that throws you for a loop."

He picked up on the sudden tension in her voice. "What's the matter?"

"It's Eric. I've been dating him off and on for a few months. You met him when you came up when Adam was in the hospital."

Jonathan remembered a thin, light-skinned, well-dressed young man with gray eyes who had watched and never smiled. "The political science major who transferred to Stanford this semester?"

"That's right. He's graduating, too, and has a job with a very prestigious firm in New York. He wants me to go."

Jonathan's eyes blazed. He jerked forward. "You aren't talking about living together, are you?"

She laughed. "No, Uncle Jon. Just finding a job there. There are some wonderful museums in New York. With my art history major and honors thesis being published, I stand a very good chance of being hired."

"New York can be an unfriendly city," he told her.

"I'll be fine. Eric's family is near. They live in the Hamptons."

The Hamptons meant money, but money, in Jonathan's opinion, didn't mean character. It did mean Eric wasn't after Kristen's money. He sighed. It was an undeniable fact that most men wanted intimacy before marriage, but those same men wanted their daughters to postpone intimacy until after marriage. They knew sex had nothing to do with love and commitment, just hormones.

"I thought you were going to work at the art museum in New Orleans?" he said.

"I was, but now I'm not sure. I could apply at the Museum of Modern Art in New York just as well. My adviser knows the director there and doesn't think I'll have a problem." Her voice softened. "I really like Eric. He's not like all the other men I've dated. He doesn't grab or want to know what my family is into. He likes me for myself."

If all the man had to offer was restraint, although admirable, it wasn't a basis for a long-term relationship. "Give yourself time, Kristen. You're only twenty."

"But life's not promised." Her voice quieted. "I thought Daddy would be here forever."

Randolph's death had hit Kristen the hardest. She had been Daddy's little girl, and Randolph had doted on her. "He loved and he was loved. You can't ask for much better."

"I have to go. Eric should be arriving shortly. A group of us are going sailing on his boat."

Kristen blocked all attempts to talk about her father's death. Jonathan had mentioned the possibility of professional help to Eleanor, but she hadn't wanted to pursue the matter. Jonathan had disagreed. You couldn't heal and move on until you allowed the grieving process to run its course. So far Kristen hadn't.

"All right. I'll see you at commencement."

"Eric is coming to a dinner Mother is having for me Saturday night before baccalaureate, so you'll get to meet him."

Jonathan wasn't sure he was invited, so all he said was, "Bye, Kristen, and be careful."

"Bye, Uncle Jon. I will."

Troubled, Jonathan hung up the phone. Kristen was looking for something, had been looking since the death of her father. He just hoped she didn't look in the wrong place.

"Dr. Delacroix, you have a phone call," the receptionist's cheerful voice announced over the exam room intercom.

Jonathan paused in his exam of the extended abdomen of Mrs. Garza. This was her first pregnancy. She was five months and expecting twins. He tried not to let himself think of the young mother with twins he had lost, but it was difficult not to. He wouldn't lose this time.

"Dr. Delacroix?"

"Take a message."

"It's Mrs. Wakefield."

Jonathan's splayed fingers paused and he glanced at his patient. Mrs. Garza's brown eyes watched his every movement. His staff was trained to notify him immediately if any member of the Wakefield family called. However, if it were an emergency, Eleanor would have said so.

He smiled at his patient in reassurance and spoke over his shoulder: "Please tell Mrs. Wakefield I'll call back in five minutes."

To Mrs. Garza, he said, "You want to see if you can hear their heartbeats?"

Her eyes widened and brightened. "Does a duck waddle?"

Laughing, he pulled the fetal Doppler from his head, placed it over her head, then positioned the bell on her bulging abdomen. When tears glistened in her eyes and rolled down her cheeks, he knew he had made the right decision.

He didn't doubt that the death of his postpartum patient was discussed among his expectant mothers, and that doubts they had never thought of probably had begun to creep insidiously into their minds. They craved reassurance that they and their babies were doing well, would continue to do well. It was his responsibility to give it to them.

Simply, Mrs. Garza had needed him more than Eleanor. A fact he was afraid would always be true.

Six minutes later, Jonathan went to his office and punched in Eleanor's number. He didn't bother sitting. Their conversations lately, when they had them, were brief.

"Hello."

"Hello, Eleanor. Sorry. I had a patient on the table," Jonathan explained.

"Is everything all right?" Eleanor asked.

"So far. She's expecting twins and this is her first pregnancy."

"Adam told me about the young patient you lost, Jonathan," Eleanor said. "I hope you're not second-guessing yourself."

He eased onto the corner of his desk. How well she knew him. "Not anymore. Kristen called."

"I knew she would. That's why I'm calling. I need to know if you want to fly back with us on the chartered plane Saturday or do you want to make your own plans?"

He usually stayed with Eleanor when he went to San Francisco. He'd done so when Randolph was alive, and that had never changed. "I can make my own arrangements," he said, his voice tight.

"Jonathan, I'm aware you can make the arrangements. I asked if you want to go with us," she replied crisply. "Lilly is going, too."

He relaxed a bit. "Adam's idea, I bet."

"Yes, but I agree totally with the decision," Eleanor said. "She's marvelous with him. They have fun together."

"Ouch. Nicole is not going to like hearing that."

"Her problem. Do you want to fly out with us? We leave on June tenth and return on the twelfth. Kristen is coming back with us. Are those dates agreeable?"

He didn't bother flipping though his calendar. He'd already made arrangements to be out those days. Stanford's late graduation worked in his favor in getting the time off. "You have another passenger." He decided to push a bit. "Will it be a problem for me to stay at your place?"

"No," she answered, but her voice sounded unsteady.

"Good. Just let me know what time to show up at the airport and I'll be there. How's the progress on my painting?" he asked casually. "My bare wall is crying to be covered."

"I'm working on it."

"Care to change your mind and give me a hint?"

"No." There was the old laughter in her voice. "Good-bye, Jonathan."

"Good-bye, Eleanor." Jonathan hung up the phone. He wondered what Eleanor would do if he showed up in her room at home in San Francisco and claimed he had been sleepwalking.

Brain him with a lamp probably. But what if she didn't?

Pondering the possibilities and his options, he went to see his next patient. He was tired of waiting for Eleanor, but the lady showed no indication that he was even a blip on her screen.

Come hell or high water, in San Francisco that was going to change.

Chapter Sixteen

Early the next morning, Lilly learned what Adam meant. By eight-thirty her head was hanging over the shampoo bowl. Eleanor said you should look your best when shopping for clothes. An off hair day could ruin the look of a great outfit. When Lilly had asked whether taking clothes off and on wouldn't ruin her hairstyle, Eleanor had shaken her head. She'd shopped enough to be able to pick out what looked best on sight.

Afterward they went from boutique to boutique, where Eleanor discarded what Lilly thought were beautiful suits or dresses without her trying on a single one. Eleanor hadn't liked the cut, the hang, the color. Lilly began to wonder if they'd find anything.

They'd called Adam around lunch. He was happily eating the turkey salad Lilly had left in the refrigerator.

It was now close to two and Lilly's mouth watered just thinking of the salad, but she said nothing. If Eleanor thought enough of her to take time to help her find a suit, she certainly wasn't going to complain about being a little hungry.

She cut a glance at Eleanor, her brows bunched, as she discarded one outfit after another in boutique number seven. Catching a look at some of the discreet price tags, Lilly was glad Eleanor hadn't found anything.

"If we don't find anything suitable here, we'll stop for—" Eleanor inhaled sharply and lifted a suit the color of washed sand from the racks. "Lilly, I think our search is over."

The three-piece pantsuit was gorgeous. Lilly didn't want to like it, because she knew she couldn't afford it. She'd tried to tell Eleanor at the first boutique, but she'd simply talked over her.

"How much is it?" Lilly whispered. The saleswomen, as Eleanor had requested, had let them browse, but Lilly still didn't want them to know all she could possibly do was browse and embarrass Eleanor if she came to the shop again.

"Lilly, let's try it on first."

"Would you like a dressing room?" The saleswoman appeared out of seemingly nowhere.

"Yes," Eleanor said.

"Certainly. This way."

Lilly wanted to hang back, but Eleanor took her by the arm and followed the young saleslady into a dressing room that looked more like a full-size room with its floor-to-ceiling mirrors on three sides, a raised platform, and silk-covered walls in a soft white. Beside a comfortable-looking overstuffed chair was a small table with a crystal bowl of potpourri and a fat scented candle.

"Just press the call button if you need any assistance." Smiling, the clerk left, closing the white door behind her.

Lilly dived for the price tag. Her eyes bugged. "I can't afford this!"

"Lilly, you don't even know if you're going to like it," Eleanor reasoned, hanging the suit up, then taking Lilly's purse from her. "It may fit terrible. Just try it on."

Since that sounded reasonable, Lilly unbuttoned her suit jacket and stepped out of her skirt. She was still adamant about the outfit until Eleanor had her step on the platform and face the mirror. All Lilly could do was stare.

The long-sleeved sand tweed cardigan over a matching sheer camisole with cream straight-legged trousers looked heavenly. Lilly had to admit she looked good in it. Eleanor certainly knew clothes. She'd been right about the suit, just as she had been right to kindly suggest that Lilly have her hair done in soft curls that framed her face.

"I'll be back."

Lilly nodded, then looked at the price tag again and sighed. It hadn't miraculously changed. Eight hundred and ninety-nine dollars.

"Put these on."

In the mirror Lilly saw Eleanor and the saleslady with more jewelry spilling from her hands. Deciding protest was useless at the moment, Lilly put on a snake-embossed leather belt in metallic wheat, a multistrand topaz-colored crystal necklace, and matching ear clips.

"Sensational. I knew it!" Eleanor exclaimed.

The saleswoman nodded in agreement. "You have a good eye. Miss, the sand color, in the bamboo weave, looks good on you."

"Thank you," Lilly managed. She did look good and she wanted to cry.

"We don't need to see the other accessories."

"Ring if you need me," the woman said and left.

"All you need now is a pair of high-heeled sandals and a bag. Mission accomplished," Eleanor said, smiling. Then the smile faded. "I wish Adam could see you."

Lilly's heart clutched. "He'll see one day."

Eleanor nodded her head and smiled. "Of course he will. Get dressed and we'll go back to the house. I'll wait outside."

"I'll be right out." Lilly dressed, then joined Eleanor, who was quietly speaking with the saleslady.

"Lilly, why didn't you bring your suit out with you?"

The saleslady stepped around the counter. "I'll be happy to get it for her."

"There's no need," Lilly said, stopping the woman. "I've changed my mind."

"But, Lilly—"

"Please, Eleanor. I'd like to go now." She glanced at her watch. "It's almost three. I didn't think we'd be gone this long."

"Adam is fine. The old Adam might not have called me, but the new Adam would have."

Lilly knew Eleanor was right but didn't see the sense of wasting more time looking at clothes she couldn't afford. "I'd still like to go back."

"You're sure?"

"Yes."

Eleanor's shoulders slumped. She turned to the saleslady. "Please put those things on hold we were discussing earlier, and I'll come back tomorrow and pick them up."

The woman perked up. "Certainly, Mrs. Wakefield."

"Eleanor," Lilly said. "You wouldn't go behind my back and buy those things for me, would you?"

"Certainly not. I don't believe in subterfuge. Let's go home."

Outside in Eleanor's car, Lilly couldn't help but remember Eleanor did indeed practice subterfuge and did it very well.

"How many trips will it take to get all of the packages out of the car?" Adam asked as he met Lilly and Eleanor coming into the house as he was leaving the kitchen with a glass of iced tea.

"None, I'm afraid," Eleanor said.

"That's a first," Adam said.

Lilly glanced from mother to son. "It's my fault. I'm afraid the dresses were a little bit out of my price range."

Adam frowned. "I told Mother to get what you wanted."

"That's very generous of you, Adam, but I want to pay for my own clothes." Lilly moistened her dry lips. "We didn't get a chance to go to the shopping mall. I thought maybe I could go in tomorrow and look, if you don't mind."

"Of course I don't mind, but I'm still having trouble believing Mother came home empty-handed."

"Surprised me, too," Eleanor said.

Lilly felt miserable for some reason. "All right, if you must know, your mother did find the most wonderful outfit I could have imagined. But it was too expensive and, before you offer again, the answer is no."

"What color was it? What did it look like?" he asked as he sat beside Lilly on the sofa in the living room.

Because descriptions were so important to him, she let herself indulge in describing the outfit. "It was a three-piece pantsuit. The collarless waist-length long-sleeved cardigan had a matching sheer camisole the color of sand, and it had straight-legged cream-colored trousers."

"It looked fabulous on her and she looked sensational in it. The color highlighted her dark brown eyes and warm honey skin," Eleanor said.

Adam twisted his head to one side. "I wondered what color your eyes were."

Lilly's heart skipped a beat, then thudded in her chest. Her mouth opened, but nothing came out.

Eleanor had no such trouble. "The color combination was perfect. I found just the right accessories. Belt, necklace, earclips to bring everything together. All she needed was shoes and a bag, and I hasten to bet I could have found them by the end of the day."

"Call the store, Mother, and have them hold the outfit for Lilly."

"No, you can't," she said as Adam's mother got up. "Please. I'm sure I can find a dress or suit at the mall that will do just as nicely."

"It's almost the end of May. Summer merchandise has been picked over for graduations, weddings, you name it." Eleanor lifted one regal brow. "Chya, the salesperson, told me they received the suit you tried on three weeks ago, but due to the narrow cut of the jacket sleeves, no one had been able to wear it until you."

"I can't afford it."

"How much did it—"

"Adam," Lilly said, cutting him off. "I'm not letting you or your mother buy me the pantsuit."

He leveled his dark shades at her for a long time. "Actually, knowing how stubborn and independent you are, I was thinking more of helping you earn the money."

Lilly didn't understand, but Eleanor did. "Fifty pies should allow her to have a clear profit margin and get shoes and a bag."

"I seem to remember you remarking the other day how good business was," Adam said.

"It is, but I have no intention of spending that kind of money on a suit that I'll only wear once." She rose. "This discussion is over. I'm sure I'll find a dress at the mall. I'm going upstairs to change. Thanks for taking me shopping, Eleanor. Sorry if it was a waste of your time."

"It wasn't. Besides, your hair looks lovely."

"You got your hair styled?" Adam stood and reached out to explore.

Lilly averted her head. "Just curly. I'd better go up and change so I can start on dinner."

Adam listened to Lilly's running steps on the stairs. "I never would have thought that of her."

"What?" Eleanor said, coming to stand by her son.

"That she was too perfect to touch."

"That's not Lilly and you know it. She's probably just nervous and anxious about finding a dress." She hooked her arm though his. "Can I get you anything before I go to the cottage? I need to work on Jonathan's painting."

"No, thanks. I think I'll go work on the computer with the voice recognition program."

"Did you get it to read the book I bought?"

"I didn't try. Lilly does a better job."

Eleanor lifted a regal brow. "Does she now?"

"Yes. I'll see you at dinner." Kissing her on the cheek, Adam headed for his study, unaware of his mother's speculative gaze.

Adam booted up the computer and got into the software program but not much else. He couldn't forget Lilly pulling away from him. She'd never done that before. Her action surprised and bothered him.

He would have expected that from Nicole. She never wanted to be less than perfect. Picking her up for a date, he was always aware that she didn't like to be mussed. He hadn't minded because he'd liked having a beautiful, elegant woman on his arm. How shallow he had been.

Adam reared back in his chair. Perhaps that's what Lilly aspired to be. He hoped not. He much preferred the woman who sat on the foot stool by his chair and read with such empathy and depth.

"Adam, dinner is ready."

"I'll be there in a minute." Moving his right hand to the arrow keys, he shut down the computer, located his cane, and went into dinner. But he soon discovered he had no appetite.

"Please excuse me. I think I'd like to take a walk."

"If you'll wait until I clear the table, I'll go with you," Lilly said.

"No. Stay."

Lilly watched him leave alone. That was another of the routines they had together, a walk after dinner. Then they'd come back and clean up the kitchen. Last night she had talked him into drying the plates.

"You think he's all right?" she asked, staring after him.

"I thought so earlier, but now I'm not so sure." Eleanor answered.

Lilly turned sharply toward her. "What do you mean?"

Eleanor's eyes narrowed. "He reached out to you today and you rejected him. Why?"

"I didn't . . ." Her voice trailed away; her head lowered. That's exactly what she had done.

"Adam is at a vulnerable point in his life now. You, more than most people, understand that." Eleanor stood and began clearing the table. "I'll take care of this if you have something else you need to take care of."

Lilly's head came up. She understood completely. "He may not want to talk with me."

Eleanor's smile was gentle. "Thank goodness that never stopped you before."

Rising, Lilly went outside. It was a moonless night. As soon as she was ten feet from the porch, she was in total darkness. "Adam, where are you? Adam?"

She walked farther down the path toward the front gate. "If you make me break my neck, who'll fix you those high-calorie meals you secretly love? Adam?" She heard the desperation in her voice and didn't care. "Adam, please answer me."

"You walked by me. I'm on the porch."

She whirled, squinting her eyes and going back up the steps, then peered into the darkness. She didn't see him sitting in the swing until she was almost on him. "Why didn't you answer sooner?"

"I didn't think you wanted to be bothered."

"Oh, Adam." She sat down heavily beside him.

He put the swing in motion. For a long time there was just silence and the two of them in a world by themselves.

"The stars are out. They fill the sky. No moon. You can feel the breeze, smell the mixed scents of the flowers. It's peaceful here. Mother Crawford would have loved Wakefield Manor."

He didn't say anything, just kept the swing moving.

She leaned back in the seat. There was no way around this, so she might as well get it over with.

"The first time I saw your mother and Kristen they looked perfect. Then

Nicole walked out of the house and she looked perfect. Hair, skin, teeth, perfect." She looked at him. "You look perfect."

The swing stopped.

"It's natural to you, the way you move, dress, act." She sighed. "If I had gone into that boutique by myself, not one of those women would have paid me any attention. They couldn't do enough for Eleanor."

"I'm not perfect, Lilly."

"This has nothing to do with sight. My hair is coarse. Do you know I started wearing gloves and Vaseline each night to try and help my hands become softer? Your hands are softer than mine, your hair a better grade, your clothes fit better, your—"

He laughed and grabbed her hand, holding it tight when she would have pulled away. When she started to get up, his hand curved around her shoulder. "I'm not perfect and neither is Mother or Kristen or Nicole. We all have flaws. I probably have more than all three of them put together. I hate this darkness, but it's taught me that what's on the inside is much more valuable than what's on the outside." His thumb grazed across the calluses on her hand.

"You used these hands to help me in countless ways. Perhaps soft hands couldn't have done that. You are who you are, Lilly, and, to me, a wonderful, caring woman. You can't ask any more of yourself, and others shouldn't."

His words touched her heart and soothed the jagged places in her soul. "You didn't eat much dinner. If you come inside I'll fix you a plate."

"You're always trying to fatten me up."

"You have to eat."

"I'd rather sit here for a while."

Disappointed and trying to tell herself she understood, she swallowed and said, "I'll leave you alone."

His thumb brushed across the top of her hand. "I meant with you unless you have something else to do."

"No. No, I don't." Nothing was more important than being with Adam.

He settled back, setting the swing into motion, his hand still holding hers.

Lilly relaxed against the rattan back of the swing. Their bodies touched from shoulder to knee and she gave no thought to moving away and thought the night was just about perfect.

————

Eleanor wasn't a nosy or interfering mother. She kept telling herself this as she cleared the table, loaded the dishwasher, and put the leftovers in the refrigerator. But it was hard not to go outside and see what was happening. Obviously, Lilly had found Adam, but what had happened afterward?

Eleanor debated briefly whether she should take the circuitous route to her house to find out the answer to her question, then decided against it. She cut off the overhead light in the kitchen, leaving only the recessed light over the sink on. Lilly and Adam seemed to do well without her interference; she'd just have to contain her curiosity. Opening the back door, she went down the back steps and took the well-lit path to the cottage. Going inside, she went to her room to change into a smock. She needed to finish Jonathan's painting.

Standing in front of the watercolor of his boat, *Lady Lost,* she frowned. When she started the painting she had thought it was perfect. Now, she wasn't so sure. Perhaps she should have chosen flowers, she thought, then shook her head. Jonathan needed a stronger image, and the *Lady Lost* riding the crest of a wind-tossed sea was that image. At the helm, legs spread, his big, strong hands gripping the helm, stood Jonathan.

Eleanor dipped her sable brush into the paint. Perhaps painting him would help her stop wanting him.

Lilly was at the mall the next morning when it opened. With a map of the stores clutched in her hand, she started at one end and worked her way to the other. Some of the stores only required a cursory glance to know what they carried was too girlish or garish. By midafternoon, she had tried on more dresses than she had previously in her life. Although a few had possibilities, none of them brought the sparkle to her eyes that the suit in the boutique had.

Sitting on a bench, her purse in her lap, she admitted that she wanted to look good, for herself, for Adam, for his family. She wanted to make Nicole's eyes pop. That wouldn't happen in a dress from JC Penney. Adam's world was one of the senses. He wouldn't be turned on by a midprice polyester knit. Not that she wanted to turn him on, she quickly told herself.

She admitted she was lying to herself when she thought of the perfume she had spritzed on earlier at Foley's. But her money was for her to start a new life. She couldn't stay with Adam forever. Odette would return and where would that leave Lilly? Adam was gaining his independence more and more each day.

She had to be ready financially, if not emotionally, when she had to leave. The orders were growing for her pies, and selling them had increased her savings. Squandering the money on a dress seemed wasteful. She'd always been sensible and frugal.

A young couple strolled past her, arm in arm, hugging and stealing kisses. Lilly's mind went to Adam, the feel of his taut thigh against her, his elegant fingers on her arm. She absorbed him through tactile senses as much as he did her. Long after she left, she'd have memories.

Standing, she headed out of the mall with determined steps. Occasionally you had to throw caution to the wind. If she saved the money and Myron's lawyer got his hands on it, she'd kick herself. She was buying that pantsuit.

If she could find the shop.

Luckily she remembered the name, but she had to stop and ask directions three times before she pulled up in front of Loretta Blum's. The name was written in gold script on the awning leading past neatly trimmed shrubs and on the half-glass door. Inside, Lilly went immediately to the rack where the suit had hung. It wasn't there.

"May I help you?"

Lilly glanced around at a different woman from the one who had helped her the day before. She swallowed. "I was in here yesterday and there was a three-piece suit in washed sand with straight trousers."

The young blonde's face fell. "That's sold. Perhaps I could help you find something else."

"Sold?" Lilly repeated numbly. "But–but it was just here."

"I'm sorry. A messenger picked it up this morning."

"I see." Shoulders slumped, she started from the store.

"You could look at some of the other fashions," the woman offered hopefully.

Lilly kept walking. "No, thank you."

Disappointed, she climbed into the car and drove home. It didn't help her mood that she became lost on the freeway again. She arrived home after three that afternoon, tired and irritable.

Walking up on the porch, she saw Brent and Adam rounding the corner of the house. She waited until they reached the steps. "Hello."

"Hi," Adam greeted her, a smile on his perspiration-dampened face. "I was beginning to worry about you. You find a dress?"

"No."

"You can go back tomorrow," he told her, coming up the steps to stand by her. Behind him, Brent nodded his approval of his student.

"I don't think so." Lilly barely kept from sighing. "Either of you want anything to drink?"

"I'll take a rain check, Lilly," Brent said. "See you one last time before you go to your sister's graduation," he said to Adam, opening the door to his beat-up green Volkswagen. "I don't want you making me look bad." Getting in the car, he drove off.

Taking her arm, Adam started inside the house. "Now, tell me about this shopping expedition."

"There's nothing to tell."

"I think there is." He led her to the breakfast nook and pulled out a chair. "You wearing a new perfume?"

Her eyes rounded. "I—I just sprayed a bit on at a store."

"I like the other one better."

Lilly sank heavily into her chair. Her one luxury. She'd liked the crystal bath salts she'd found in her bathroom so much that she had bought some for herself.

"You want lemonade or iced tea?"

She was up in an instant. "I can—"

"So can I." He was already moving toward the glass-fronted cabinet. "Lemonade or tea?"

She tried to think of which pitcher was closer to the front. "Lemonade."

He reached the cabinet, opened the door, then reached inside. "Dishes. Glasses in the other one, right?"

"Right." Yesterday, when she and Eleanor had gone shopping, she'd left his plate, glass, and utensils on the table.

He took down one glass, then another. Clutching them to his chest, he went to the refrigerator. Locating the glass brace in the ice dispenser, he pushed. The motor whirred. Ice cubes clinked in the glass. He did the same with the next glass. Opening the refrigerator, he set one glass on the shelf and felt until he came to a round pitcher. Filling one glass with lemonade, he took it to the table, then returned and repeated the process.

Lilly had her hands clamped together as he slid triumphantly onto the seat beside her. "You've been practicing."

"While you were gone. I may need to get another motor for the ice maker." His hand shook a little as he lifted his glass and drank. "It was Brent's idea to put lemonade in the fat, round pitcher and tea in the skinny one. Now drink."

Bossy, she thought, but drank deeply. "The best lemonade I've ever tasted."

He smiled and relaxed more in his chair. "Then you'll tell me why you didn't sound too happy when you came home?"

She leaned on the table and wrapped her hands around the tall glass. She could evade the question, but why bother? She told him everything. "The Bible says 'Pride goeth before a fall.' "

"I believe it also says 'Seek and you shall find.' " He set his glass aside. "If you're up to it, I'd like to hear the ending of *The Third Hour*."

"Sure."

"Tell me about your drive into town," he requested as they climbed the stairs together.

Lilly was happy to oblige. She loved the riverboats with their tall masts and the throngs of people there taking a chance with the roll of the dice or the pull of the lever. Life was the same way. You never knew what lay ahead. She had taken a wrong turn and it turned out to be the best thing that could have happened to her.

Adam paused in front of her door.

"I'll get the book and be right out." She opened the door and came to a dead stop. Her breath hissed out. She spun toward a smiling Adam. "It's the suit!"

"Do you think I wouldn't let you have your heart's desire?" he said, his hand lifting to touch her cheek.

Without giving herself time to think, she hugged him. Immediately his arms came around her. She felt the shock of her body pressed to his all the way to her toes. Wonderful and exciting. Because she wanted to keep holding him, because she was just realizing what her heart's desire was, and it was not a pantsuit, she stepped back. "Adam, thank you."

His arms drifted from around her waist with obvious reluctance. "Mother had the saleslady put it back. A special-delivery messenger brought it out while you were in town."

"I'll pay you back; I promise."

"We'll talk about it later. Aren't you going over there and ooh and aah?" he asked, still smiling.

His hand in hers, she went to the suit on the bed. "It's beautiful," she said.

"I bet you'll be beautiful in it," he said.

She squeezed his hand, her heart shattering. She'd never be beautiful. "I'll get *The Third Night*."

A tug of his hand stopped her. His free hand cupped her cheek. "Never let anyone define who you are, Lilly. Promise me?"

With his hand on her face, she actually felt beautiful, so it wasn't difficult to say, "I promise." The hard part would come when he wasn't there to reassure her.

This was it, Lilly thought, and got out of her car. Her hand fluttered briefly to her hair; then she started toward the administration building of Shreveport Junior College. Each step closer, her nervousness increased. All around her, students of various ages and races hurried from place to place.

"Application, transcript, Social Security card, driver's license, or some form of photo ID," the woman behind the elongated table asked without even looking up.

Silently Lilly handed the woman the manila folder in her hand. Thankfully, when she'd left Myron, she'd taken her college transcript and other important papers. She'd already checked with her lawyer and learned there was no way Myron could trace her from her Social Security card.

Finally, the woman at the table looked up. In her hand was Lilly's driver's license. "Texas driver's license. You have to be a resident a year not to pay out-of-state fees."

"Yes, ma'am. I know I have to pay the out-of-state fees." Another chunk out of her savings.

The young black woman placed Lilly's application beside her keyboard and typed in the requested courses. "Business two-o-one on Monday through Friday from eleven to one and Marketing two-ten on Tuesday and Thursday from two to four." She glanced up. "Both courses are available. Is that what you want?"

"Yes, ma'am."

Nodding, the woman hit PRINT, and in a matter of seconds a sheet of paper rolled from the printer. Reaching over, she tore off the perforated sheet and handed it to Lilly. "Go to the business office and pay for the courses. You can go to the bookstore for your books today or later. I'd advise today."

The sheet safely tucked in her folder, Lilly went to the admission office and got in another line. Her fingers hesitated as she counted out the money for the courses and again when she paid for her books.

Sliding across the seat in the car, she placed her hand on her books. She had done it. She'd taken another step toward her freedom, and Adam had helped her. He was as good for her as she was for him.

When she arrived home after one, she knew she had been right. He'd waited to eat with her. Nothing could have pleased her more as they devoured roast beef sandwiches and coleslaw while they discussed the day together.

She went to sleep that night and dreamed of endless possibilities.

Monday morning Lilly took her seat in the front of her business class, her number-two pencil sharpened and ready. By the time one o'clock arrived, she had pages of notes, her hand was tired from writing, and her brain felt as if it were on overload.

She left campus without much enthusiasm to return. She had always been an average student. She wasn't sure if she was cut out to take accelerated courses in the summer.

"How did it go?" Adam asked the moment she sat down in the swing beside him. Since he usually didn't sit outside, she had to assume he had been waiting for her. The idea warmed and shamed her.

She bit her lip before answering. "It might be a bit more difficult than I thought. Maybe I should wait until regular classes."

He twisted toward her. "What happened?"

She explained and ended by saying, "I can't keep up."

"You can't keep up because you're so busy writing that you can't process the information," he told her. "I had the same problem. What you need is a tape recorder." He stood and reached for her hand. "We'll go into town and get one."

Adam hadn't been to town since their shopping expedition to the grocery store.

"I can use the other one," Lilly said.

He was already heading back inside the house. "Too bulky. Besides, you don't have any blank tapes." He stopped at the phone in the hallway and dialed. "Mother, Lilly and I are going into town. . . . All right, bye." He hung up and took her arm. "Let's go."

She didn't budge. "Eleanor coming?"

"No, she's working on Jonathan's painting. Stop stalling."

She started toward the door. "The only reason I'm letting you get away with this is on the outside possibility that you might be right, plus there's a drive-in hamburger place on the way."

Adam shuddered. "Your cholesterol level is probably three-ninety."

Lilly opened the door of her car she had left in the driveway. "Does that mean you don't want one or the French fries or a thick strawberry shake I'm going to order?"

Breaking down his cane, Adam got inside the car. "No. I don't." He waited until he heard the squeak in the door. "I want a chocolate shake."

Lilly grinned and closed his door.

They found a tape recorder Lilly could hold in the palm of her hand. She blinked when she saw the price of the tapes, but she went to the register anyway with them and the tape recorder. She was relatively sure that if she didn't get them they would show up much as her dress had.

The hamburger was greasy and delicious; so were the French fries and shakes. To make up for their gluttony, they went for a long walk when they arrived back at the house. Dinner was a salad with low-calorie dressing.

While Adam kept her company and measured out the nuts for the pies, she rolled out the piecrusts for the ten pies for the ladies' auxiliary at Memorial Hospital. Word of mouth was bringing in a steady flow of orders. Her life would be wonderful if she didn't have the divorce hanging over her head.

Her hand paused as she crimped the edges of the piecrusts. She had to gain her freedom, and she had to expose Myron for what he was. She had a chance for a better life and she was taking it.

The next day when she went to class, she found Adam had been right. With her mind on what the instructor said and not on getting it down on paper, she was able to absorb the information better. When she told Adam over a late lunch, his comment was, "Told you we made a good team."

She went to sleep wishing that were true.

Chapter Seventeen

Lilly had never flown before. Of course, she'd seen the private jets on television and wasn't that surprised to see the flight attendant or that the inside of the cabin resembled a small living room. Adam, Eleanor, and Jonathan insisted it was no big deal, and Lilly wanted to believe them until the Gulfstream started down the runway, then lifted skyward. Her newly manicured nails dug into the armrests. She pressed her head against the back of the seat, flattening her freshly done curls.

Lilly inhaled sharply; Adam's hand was suddenly there. She clutched it thankfully and prayed her stomach she had left on the ground would catch up with her.

"It's all right, Lilly. We're just climbing to get altitude," Adam reassured her. "Pretty soon, we'll level off and you won't feel like you've been shot out of a cannon."

"I–I just wasn't expecting it."

"You'll soon be an old pro at this," he said, then added, "Are your eyes open or shut?"

"Shut."

He laughed. "Well, take a deep breath and open them. We're flying into a sunrise, and there's nothing like those vivid colors."

Lilly partially opened one eye, then the other, and looked out the window by her shoulder. Brilliant shades of blue and purple filled the horizon. "Oh, Adam, it's breathtaking!"

"See, flying does have its advantages. This is worth missing classes Monday."

"My instructors didn't mind my leaving the two tape recorders to tape the classes just like you said," she agreed. "I just hope I do well on the tests next week."

"You will. I'll help you study," he told her. "Now, how about a glass of wine to celebrate your first flight?"

"Are you going to have one, too?"

"A gentleman never lets a lady drink alone."

Across from them, Eleanor listened to Lilly's and Adam's easy banter. She had once been the same way with Jonathan. Now, she stared down at a decorating magazine. It was a shield. She wasn't proud of it, but she hadn't been proud in a long time.

"You thinking of redoing your house in San Francisco?"

She glanced up and was caught by brilliant brown eyes. She quickly glanced back at the magazine. "No."

"I see." Jonathan settled back in his seat. Indeed he did see. He and Eleanor had flown together many times in the past. She might bring a magazine, but she never got around to opening it. They had too much to talk about.

He settled back in his seat and listened to Lilly talk quietly to Adam. Eleanor could ignore him all she wanted for now, but tonight . . . tonight that would definitely change.

San Francisco International Airport resembled a shopping mall to Lilly. Stores lined the wide corridors as far as she could see. The only difference was the luggage people carried with them.

She probably would have gotten a crick in her neck except that she forgot about the shops and the people when Adam hesitated. She edged closer. "I've never seen so many rushing people in one place. I'm glad I'm not here by myself."

"So am I," he admitted quietly.

Outside, a limousine waited. The driver loaded the luggage and they were off again. It was Lilly's first limousine ride, and her eyes widened at the spaciousness inside, the TV, and the wet bar. "I have to say it again."

"Say what?" Eleanor asked.

"Rich people sure know how to live," Lilly said, then, thinking they might be offended added, "They also know how to love."

"We certainly do," Jonathan said.

"I couldn't agree more," Adam said, sitting hip to shoulder beside Lilly, her hand in his.

Lilly's heart beat faster.

Eleanor swallowed.

The residential neighborhood was very exclusive. All the homes were located behind an ivy-covered ten-foot stone wall. Lilly edged forward on her seat as the limousine turned into a stone entrance and the black wrought-iron gates slowly opened. The car pulled through and followed the tree-lined curve.

As the driveway straightened there stood a French château nestled in a veritable forest. The immaculate grounds were as well tended as those at Wakefield Manor.

Kristen, wearing navy pants and a cream-colored blouse, ran out of the double front door. Directly behind her was Nicole in a hot pink double-breasted jacket and matching skirt that stopped midway on her long legs. Lilly didn't know why the sight of the other woman annoyed her but was immensely happy she had gone back to Foley's and purchased black linen slacks and a crisp white blouse for the trip and another dress for the baccalaureate services.

"Adam!" Kristen exclaimed, throwing her arms exuberantly around him as soon as he emerged from the limousine and straightened. "I missed you."

He hugged her to him. "Same here."

"I–I was afraid you wouldn't make it."

Stepping back, he playfully pulled her long, straight hair. "Not for anything would I have missed tomorrow. You're my annoying little sister."

"Hello, Adam."

Adam tensed, then turned toward the silken honeyed voice. "Hello, Nicole. I didn't know you were going to be here."

"Kristen invited me over. I hope you don't mind?"

"No. This is an important time for Kristen," he said politely. "I'm glad you could come."

"Why don't we all go inside?" Eleanor said. She had spoken only briefly to Nicole since the day Adam had fired, then rehired Lilly. Eleanor didn't think Adam had spoken to Nicole at all. From the way Kristen kept glancing between the two, she wasn't aware that their relationship had changed.

"Good idea," Jonathan said finally. "I'll help the driver with the luggage, then settle up with him."

"That's already taken care of, Jonathan," Eleanor said.

"Then I'll just help with the luggage," he said.

"Carl can get them," she said, referring to the butler.

"I'll just help."

For some ungodly reason Jonathan's answer annoyed the hell out of Eleanor. "Suit yourself." She started toward the house.

"You bet I will," Jonathan said under his breath and went to help the driver pull suitcases from the trunk.

"Lilly," Adam said, and Lilly moved to his side. Leaning over, she whispered in his ear, reacclimating him. Nodding, he extended his cane, and they started toward the house. Kristen walked beside Adam.

Nicole noted the tableau and her lush red mouth tightened.

Jonathan looked from Nicole to Lilly and his lips twitched. Should be an interesting weekend.

The high arched entryway led to an immense living room with pale golden walls, designer furniture, and thick off-white carpeting. Lilly and Adam sat by each other on the cream-colored silk sofa. Kristen was on Adam's other side. Across from them, Eleanor and Nicole were seated in the matching love seat.

"How was the trip?" Kristen asked, one long leg pulled under her.

"Fine," Adam said, a glass of white wine in his hand. "We'll make a flyer out of Lilly yet."

"Don't bet on it." Lilly rubbed her stomach and sipped her iced tea.

Nicole, seated across from them, barely kept from snarling. "Adam, some friends are going to Dino's tonight. You want to go?"

"Thanks, but count me out. The flight wore me out."

"You want to lie down?" Lilly asked, her hand on his shoulder.

"I'm fine."

Reassured, Lilly settled back in her seat. When she bent to set her glass down, she stared straight into the open animosity on Nicole's beautiful face. Lilly tensed. She'd almost forgotten how it felt to be disliked so intensely. "I'll go help Jonathan with the luggage."

"Carl can help," Adam said.

"I'll just check and make sure. Excuse me." Lilly rose before Adam could stop her and left the room.

"I wasn't aware that she was coming," Nicole said tightly, her fingers gripping the stem of the wineglass in agitation.

"I invited her," Adam said.

"We both invited her," Eleanor added, her tone crisp.

"Isn't it a little unusual for the hired help to accompany her employer on a family trip?" Nicole set her glass on the round glass-topped table with a sharp clink.

Adam's face hardened. "I'm not concerned with what's unusual or not. Lilly is a big part of the reason I'm here."

"Of course," Nicole quickly placated him, but her eyes were glacial.

Lilly opened the front door just as Jonathan was about to open it. "Here. Let me help."

He handed her Eleanor's Louis Vuitton overnight case. "Get too hot in there for you?"

She wrinkled her nose. There was no sense in pretending. "You might say that."

"No pain, no glory." He set two large suitcases inside the entryway, then reached for the other three.

"Some of us aren't as good at fighting for what we want." Her gaze centered on Nicole snuggled up against Adam.

Jonathan closed the door and followed the direction of Lilly's gaze. Eleanor glanced at him, then away.

"It's not strength as much as finding out how badly you want it and what you're willing to go through to get it. Once you decide that, the rest is easy."

Lilly shook her head. Some wars were impossible to win. "No offense, but I think you're wrong."

"None taken."

"Dr. Delacroix, I'll take those bags," Carl said, picking up some of Eleanor's luggage. "I'm sorry I wasn't here. I was giving instructions to the cook for tonight's dinner."

"No problem, Carl. This is Mrs. Crawford, Adam's assistant."

"Hello, Carl," Lilly greeted him.

The middle-aged man nodded. "Mrs. Crawford. Your room is next to Dr. Wakefield's. You're on the same wing, Dr. Delacroix, in the last room."

Jonathan didn't say anything but followed the butler to his new room assignment, at the farthest possible distance from Eleanor's room. A few minutes later he met Lilly in the hallway as she came out of her room. Together they joined the others downstairs.

"Mission accomplished," Jonathan said as he walked into the living room.

"Was your room all right, Lilly?" Adam asked, glancing over his shoulder in the direction Jonathan's voice had come from.

"It's beautiful," she said, suddenly feeling awkward again. "I think I'll go upstairs and unpack."

"That can wait," Adam said. "Sit down."

Since Nicole had taken her seat, Lilly sat on the tufted hassock near Adam's feet. She glanced up at him. "I feel as if I should have a book in my hand."

Adam smiled. "I'm sure, if you insist, we could find one."

Nicole's eyes narrowed.

"Uncle Jon, what would you like to drink?" Unfolding her leg, Kristen went to the glass serving cart near the sofa.

"Mineral water." He purposefully sat beside Eleanor. Every chance he got he intended to remind her of his presence.

"Here you are." Kristen handed him a heavy cut-crystal glass, then returned to her seat beside Adam.

"Thanks, Kristen." Jonathan casually placed one arm on the back of the love seat and sipped his drink.

Eleanor leaned forward to set her glass on the table, then stood. "I'll go see how Alice is coming with our lunch. Nicole, will you be joining us?"

She snuggled closer to Adam; her pink nails, the exact color of her skirt and jacket, clutched his arm. "I'd love to, thank you."

Lilly stared down at her worn hands. The manicure couldn't take away the calluses or the dryness.

Jonathan set his glass down and pushed to his feet. "Lilly, why don't I show you around?"

She lifted grateful eyes to him. "Thank you."

Eleanor watched them leave through the open French door. The grounds were as well kept as those at Wakefield Manor. There were also lots of private places for a couple who wanted to be alone.

"Mother, are you all right?" Kristen asked.

Eleanor came out of her musing and forced a smile. "Of course. Now, if you'll excuse me." She walked from the room, a strange tightness in her chest.

Lunch was served on the loggia, a covered porch, Lilly learned. She also learned jealousy could steal your appetite and tie your stomach in knots. She barely ate the shrimp on her plate. Nicole's bubbly chatter gave her a headache. She would have gone to her room, but she didn't want to leave Adam.

He wasn't eating, either. He'd said he wasn't hungry. Lilly wasn't sure if that was true or whether he wasn't entirely comfortable eating around Nicole. The woman impressed Lilly as being meticulous and rigid. She certainly sounded like she was that way with her employees.

"My business is really growing, but it's so aggravating trying to hire competent people." She took a sip of wine. "I had to fire a new hire this morning because she was late for her assignment the second day in a row."

"Did she give you an explanation?" Jonathan asked from the foot of the table. Eleanor was at the head.

Nicole waved a negligent hand. Her five-carat diamond-and-sapphire tennis bracelet glinted on her slim wrist. "Something about her car wouldn't start."

Adam's brows bunched. "Then she had a reason."

"An unreliable car translates into an unreliable employee. She should have foreseen the problem the first day she was late and taken measures then for an alternate way of getting to work on time." Her white teeth bit into a shrimp. "I advertise as the best, and that's what I have. If you can't be the best, why bother?"

A quietness settled over the table. Nicole glanced around and saw all eyes except Adam's were on her. "Adam, I–I—"

Sitting next to her, he held up his hand. "Since I've spouted the same words, I have no right to be offended by them now."

"You'll get your sight back, and it will be just as it was before." She laid a trembling hand on his arm.

"I'm beginning to wonder if I want it the way it was before," he said quietly. "I wasn't a nice person at times to those working under me."

"You got the job done," Nicole protested, withdrawing her hand.

"Yes, but could there have been a better way?" He frowned down toward the wine in his wineglass.

"You can't be chummy with underlings," Nicole said, and shot Lilly a withering glance. "They try and take advantage of you."

Lilly had had enough. "Excuse me. I need to unpack."

"Certainly," Nicole beamed.

Adam's jaw tightened. Nicole had her claws out today, but he planned to clip them. "I hope you'll be equally as gracious and excuse me."

"Oh, no, Adam, please stay!" Nicole cried.

He absently patted the hand she placed on his arm, then held out his hand. In seconds Lilly was around the table to give him her arm. "Lilly is my invited guest and a friend. Good-bye, Nicole."

Nicole watched them walk away, her hands clenched. Her beeper went off and she jerked it from her waist and read the message. "I have to go." She stood. "I'll see you tomorrow at your baccalaureate, Kristen."

"I'll see you out." Kristen came to her feet.

Jonathan leisurely sipped his drink and wondered how long it would take Eleanor to think of an excuse to leave.

The others had barely left the loggia before Eleanor began clearing the table. "Please help yourself, Jonathan. I want to help get the kitchen cleaned up so Alice can start preparations for the dinner tonight. It's important."

Because Jonathan understood that in that at least she was being honest, he merely inclined his head and lifted his glass. Tonight he wouldn't allow her to run away from him.

———

The dining room was lit by a Venetian glass chandelier over the French oval cherry wood table surrounded by six Louis XVI–style chairs. Baccarat crystal stemware, Bernardaud porcelain dinnerware, and Buccellati sterling silver flatware gleamed. Eleanor had wanted everything to be perfect. This was a celebration for both of her children.

"You've outdone yourself, Eleanor."

She whirled. Jonathan stood a few feet away. He'd changed from the sky blue shirt and lightweight sports jacket to a tailored tan suit that showed his broad shoulders and magnificent build. Why did temptation always look so good?

"You all right?"

"Of course." She glanced back at the table to give her body a chance to calm down. "I was just checking before they come down."

He moved beside her, close enough for her to smell his citrus after-shave each time she inhaled. She had the oddest notion to lick her lips.

"Adam and Kristen are aware of how much you care about them each time they're with you. How could they not be? You're a warm, loving woman."

She turned and looked at him. There was simply no way not to. Even better than her parents, better than Randolph, Jonathan had the uncanny perception of reading her doubts and negating them. In his steady gaze she saw the strength, the love, and the friendship that had been growing between them through the years.

Unconsciously her hand lifted. His enclosed hers almost immediately.

His grasp was strong and infinitely tender. She'd missed the warmth, the reassurance, of his presence, which assured her that whatever problems she faced, she always knew she didn't have to face them alone. "Thank you for always being there."

"I always will."

She'd said those words countless times, heard his reply countless times, yet somehow she felt the difference and, this time, the anticipation in the steady hum of her body.

"Mother, the table is beautiful!" exclaimed Kristen.

Eleanor tried to withdraw her hand, but Jonathan held it firmly. Kristen had seen them holding hands before, yet Eleanor felt the difference in the trembling of her body, in his gaze that had narrowed on her mouth seconds before Kristen entered the room.

"Did you expect any different from your mother?" Jonathan said easily, his arm curving around Kristen's shoulder.

"Not at all, Uncle Jon." Kristen glanced at her watch and frowned. "Eric should be here by now."

"You know traffic on the bridge can be unpredictable," Eleanor said, referring to the Golden Gate Bridge. She'd never seen her daughter so anxious over a man before.

Kristen had changed clothes three times tonight before finally settling on an asymmetrical pine-colored tunic and matching shell of linen and silk faille damask and slim pants in a rayon crepe. Her hair was swept up in a chignon. Emeralds winked in her ears. She looked sophisticated and beautiful and terribly anxious.

Eleanor was glad she was getting a chance to meet Eric again. Their brief encounter the night Adam was injured was a blur. "Dinner will keep if he's a few minutes late."

"But I won't. I'm starved," Adam said.

Eleanor's experienced eyes noted her son's attire and approved. He'd also changed and now wore a black double-breasted blazer. The Spencer knot in his tie was a little crooked, but his smile was perfect. Lilly, wearing the sand-colored outfit from the boutique, stood by his side and looked lovely.

"Do you think we can get Alice to get us something if we beg?" Jonathan asked.

"Don't either of you dare." Eleanor shook her head. "She dotes on both of you, but the kitchen is off-limits. There are canapés and drinks in the living room."

"Come on, Jonathan; let's go hit the food." Adam released Lilly's arm and held out his hand toward his sister. "Kristen, you come, too, and tell me more about Eric so I can decide if I should hire a hit man."

Kristen laughed as expected and extended her arm to Adam as she had seen Lilly do. "He's fabulous, Adam."

Lilly watched Adam, listened to him teasing his sister. "He's come a long way."

"Yes." Eleanor glanced back at the table. "He used to love dinner parties."

"He still does." Lilly came to stand beside Eleanor. "The table is beautiful and so elegant, but what makes it memorable is the people and the love."

"You must have been talking to Jonathan."

Lilly shifted uneasily. Although Jonathan had guessed how she felt about Adam, Lilly wasn't about to talk about it with Eleanor. "A bit. Is there anything I can do?"

"No, thank you. Why don't we join the others?" Deep in thought, Eleanor followed Lilly into the living room. Lilly had definitely been nervous when Eleanor mentioned Jonathan's name. Why? The reason that came circling back to her brain wasn't reassuring.

"Excuse me," Carl said. "Miss Kristen, you have a phone call."

She quickly crossed the room and picked up the extension on the end table in the living room. "Hello. . . . Oh, Eric, we—" The smile on her beautiful face faded. "Of course. I understand. I'll see you tomorrow at commencement." She replaced the receiver. "He's stuck at a surprise party his parents are giving him at the home of a friend of theirs."

Eleanor trampled down her spurt of anger. If there was a surprise party he should have notified Kristen earlier. And why hadn't he at least made the perfunctory offer to invite her?

"Then I get to have you all to myself," Jonathan said, going to her and taking her arm.

"Get in line." Adam unerringly went to Kristen's side.

Her lips shook, then curved into a natural smile. "Let's go in to dinner and see what Alice has prepared."

As they were being seated at the table, the butler quietly removed the extra place setting. Kristen blinked rapidly, then turned her head away. Eleanor and Jonathan shared a look. Tomorrow, they wanted some answers from Eric Fawnsworth.

Adam stepped out of the limousine, then held out his hand for Lilly. Her firm, warm hand, as always, was reassuring. He'd thought he was ready for this, but he felt ice in the pit of his stomach just as he had the first time he held a scalpel in his hand.

Stanford Stadium was the site of the commencement ceremony with over 5,000 undergraduate and graduate students. The ceremony was elective, but

Kristen had wanted to attend. Despite the anticipated crush of people, Adam had wanted to be there to support her.

"Although it's an hour before the ceremony, people are already gathering," Lilly said, her voice as anxious as he felt.

"It's going to get worse before it gets better. Let's go." He started out before fear had a chance to grab him, knowing full well Lilly would take over. His mother had gone ahead with Kristen to help her with her cap and gown. Jonathan had followed an hour later to save them seats.

"Adam! Adam! Wait up!" yelled a male voice.

Adam stopped; his heart, which had been beating double time, picked up the beat. His hand flexed on Lilly's arm.

"Adam. I thought that was you. When did you get into town?"

Behind his glasses Adam closed his eyes and tried to recall the voice. He couldn't. He felt adrift again.

"We arrived yesterday. I'm Lilly Crawford, Dr. Wakefield's assistant." Lilly held out her hand to the gangly young man. He switched his attention from Adam to her.

"Sorry. I'm Dr. Harold Sparks." His grip was strong and steady. "I got so excited to see—" His voice stopped abruptly. "Damn."

As suddenly as Adam's insecurity had come, it was gone. His friends were just as unsure of themselves as he was. The ones who weren't his friends didn't matter. Harold, a vascular surgeon, and a Yankee with the occasional disposition of a warthog was a friend.

"Wish I had a tape recorder. The nurses in ICU would never believe you apologized." Adam held out his free hand. "Good to see you, too."

"I left several messages for you," Dr. Sparks said. "Your housekeeper said you were out of town for an indefinite period."

"I was. Sorry I didn't get your messages. I came back for Kristen's graduation," Adam explained. He felt the brush of people going by him, Lilly's subtle tug. "I think we might be holding up traffic."

"Ah, right," Dr. Sparks said, and fell into step beside Adam as they continued toward the stadium's entrance. "My cousin's daughter is graduating today."

Lilly paused. "The bleachers. Step."

Adam stepped up, waited for Lilly to come along beside him. He didn't need vision to know Sparks' sharp eyes were glued to them.

"I don't see Jonathan yet," Lilly told him. "He said he'd be on the fifty-yard line on the side facing the podium on the field."

Adam didn't particularly look forward to wandering the stadium. "Sparks, you remember Dr. Jonathan Delacroix, don't you?"

"Sure. You brought him to the hospital a number of times."

"We're meeting him here," Adam told him. "Do you think you could help us find him? He should be on the fifty-yard line."

"I'm on it." Dr. Sparks glanced around the crowded stadium that was steadily filling with people. "You wait here and I'll be back."

"Thank you," Adam said.

Lilly moved out of the steady flow of traffic onto one of the aisles. "We can sit here. As tall as your friend is, he shouldn't have any trouble finding Dr. Delacroix in this crowd." She waited until Adam sat; then she sat beside him.

"Jonathan probably has his eyes peeled for us. He worries almost as much as Mother does." Adam tucked his feet back as far as they would go to keep the aisle clear.

"I'd say that was a good thing," Lilly said, then twisted sideways to let a couple with two small children pass.

"I'd say you were right."

No sooner were the words out of his mouth than Sparks reappeared. "He's down in front. I'll take you to him."

"I can find it," Lilly said. "We don't want to keep you."

He stared at Adam. "There's enough room for one more. If you don't mind, I'd like to sit with you."

Adam didn't hesitate. "I don't mind."

As they waited for Eleanor to join them and the commencement ceremonies to begin, several other acquaintances recognized Adam and came by to say hello. When awkwardness occurred, Adam, Lilly, or Jonathan helped smooth over the moment.

Eleanor joined the group and imperceptibly hesitated when Jonathan scooted over for her to sit between him and Adam; then she edged by him and took her seat. This was no time to go hormonal. Adam was laughing with his friends, and her daughter was about to take top honors at her college graduation.

When she saw Nicole coming toward them and sighed, she felt more than saw Jonathan's gaze on her. "What?" he asked.

"You'll see," she whispered.

"Hello, everyone," Nicole said. "I was afraid I wouldn't find you in this madhouse. It's a good thing Kristen told me where you'd be sitting." The wattage of her smile increased. "I hope someone saved me a seat."

The two men in the bleachers below and one behind them quickly scooted over, as did Dr. Sparks next to Lilly. Eleanor could see why.

Nicole had pulled out all the stops. She was absolutely striking in a papaya silk jacket over a short apricot skirt that revealed a wealth of long legs. As she passed by them, Eleanor caught a whiff of the seductive and expensive perfume she wore. For Adam, who experienced through his senses, it was an all-out assault.

Nicole stopped in front of Lilly. "Do you mind?"

Lilly moved.

Sitting, Nicole crossed her legs. Nylon whispered. "I promised Kristen I'd be here."

"I'm sure she appreciates it," Adam said, his voice tight.

A robust man with a black cap and gold tassels with three gold stripes on each sleeve of his robe stepped up to the microphone on the raised covered platform on the stadium floor. A hush fell over the 30,000 people in attendance.

Lilly had never felt so lonely in her life.

Eleanor didn't like what she saw. She was a lioness where her children were concerned, and she could tell that Eric Fawnsworth wasn't right for her daughter as Kristen practically dragged him to where they waited outside the stadium. The baccalaureate ceremonies were over, and now each department would have their own commencement, where the diplomas would be handed out.

"Mother, you remember Eric, don't you?" Kristen's eyes glowed with happiness.

"Of course," Eleanor said easily, extending her hand.

The hand that closed around hers was baby soft, the handshake limp. "Hello, Mrs. Wakefield. Please accept my apologies again for not being able to attend your dinner party last night. If it hadn't been my parents, I would have left."

Smooth, Eleanor thought, but something about the eyes bothered her. "I quite understand." She turned to Jonathan. "This is Dr. Jonathan Delacroix, a family friend."

"Dr. Delacroix."

"Eric."

Eleanor's disquiet increased at Jonathan's clipped greeting. He was usually a warm, friendly person.

Kristen glanced around. "Where's Adam?"

"He and Lilly went to the Cummings Art Building to wait for us," Eleanor said. "Since the commencement program is set to start in thirty minutes, we better get over there ourselves."

"My ceremony is on the other side of campus. See you, Kris." With an absent brush of his lips against her cheek, Eric faded into the crowd, his long black robe flapping.

Kristen stared longingly after him.

Jonathan and Eleanor traded worried looks.

Since there were only twenty-five students receiving degrees in the Department of Art and Art History and the ceremonies took place in front of the building under the lofty branches of a 200-year-old oak tree, there was more of a family atmosphere than at the stadium. Lilly might have enjoyed it more if Nicole hadn't plastered herself to Adam again and ignored Lilly.

Adam had tried a couple of times to include Lilly in their conversation, but she wasn't as talkative as Nicole or as knowledgeable and soon found herself with nothing to say. By the time the program was over, she was more than ready to leave.

Unfortunately for her, Nicole returned to Eleanor's house with them. She was determined that Adam go with her to a party of a mutual friend. News had spread quickly that Adam had returned. While they were gathered in the living room with drinks, no fewer than five people called saying they wanted him to come.

"Lilly, how about it?" Adam asked, his voice animated.

Seated next to Adam, Lilly could feel Nicole's disapproving glare. "I'm rather tired. I guess I'm still on Central Time. If you don't mind, I think I'll stay and go to bed early."

"You aren't getting sick, are you?" Frowning, he palmed her forehead.

"No." Her voice came out shaky. No matter how many times he touched her, it never failed to send her heart pounding.

"You're more than welcome to come," Nicole said with syrupy sweetness.

Lilly thought fleetingly of changing her mind just to spite the other woman, but she was doing this for Adam. He needed to have his chance to go out without her and succeed. "Thank you, but I'll be fine."

Nicole beamed at Kristen on the love seat next to her. "How about you?"

"I have a date." Standing, she picked up her cap and gown from beside her. "A group of us are celebrating."

"Who's the designated driver?" Jonathan asked.

Kristen walked over and kissed him on his furrowed brow before answering, "A chauffeur in a limousine, courtesy of Mother."

"I thought that would be best." Eleanor stood by the mantel, a glass of untouched white wine in her hand, her expression troubled.

"Is Eric going with you?" Adam asked.

"He's the third stop," Kristen reported with a grin. "We plan to make a night of it and then eat breakfast together, so don't wait up for me." With that she bounded up the stairs.

"I guess I better be going myself." Nicole stood. "I'll be back around eight to pick you up, Adam."

"Thanks."

Kissing him lightly on the cheek, she straightened and smiled triumphantly at Lilly. Carl reached the door just before a jubilant Nicole sashayed through it.

Chapter Eighteen

Nicole picked Adam up at exactly eight. Eleanor walked out with them to Nicole's silver Jaguar. Although Eleanor told herself he needed to get out and visit friends, she worried that something might happen and he'd withdraw again. She had a disquieting feeling that Nicole expected too much of Adam.

"He'll be fine, Eleanor," Jonathan said from by her side.

Eleanor bit her lip and watched the taillights of Nicole's sports car disappear. "Perhaps I should have gone with him."

"No." Jonathan's expression remained unchanged when Eleanor glared at him. "Adam has finally stopped viewing his blindness as a handicap. You have to do the same."

She folded her arms across her chest. "It's difficult."

"Letting go is never easy, but then neither is loving," he said quietly.

In the dim light Eleanor was unable to clearly see Jonathan's expression and for some reason was glad she couldn't. "Let's go back inside."

Jonathan lightly took her elbow, and they returned inside. Lilly met them at the door, her expression as worried as Eleanor's had been. "She'll take care of him, won't she?"

"He'll be fine," Jonathan said, taking Lilly's elbow in his free hand and leading both women to the sofa in the living room. "Nicole is too competitive not to."

"What has that to do with anything?" Lilly asked, perched on the edge of the sofa.

Jonathan poured two glasses of white wine and gave them to the women before answering, "Because she wants to show Adam she can meet his needs as well as you can."

Lilly's cheeks flushed. "I–I—"

Jonathan held up his hands. "I meant professionally, of course."

The words had the opposite effect. "Of course. What possible interest could Adam have in me other than professionally?"

The words were filled with such loneliness that Eleanor said, "Adam is a very astute man. I'd say by now he's aware of how much your friendship has meant."

Lilly stared into her glass of wine. "I suppose. I'm sorry, Jonathan. I'm just worried."

"I wonder if they've arrived yet," Eleanor mused. "I'll just call—"

"You'll do no such thing," Jonathan interrupted and moved the phone on the end table out of Eleanor's reach. "I can see right now that the two of you are going to worry until Adam walks back through that door. He wouldn't want that and neither do I. So it's up to me to see that you don't."

Jonathan took the untouched wine from their unresisting fingers and set the glasses on the table in front of them. "I hear there's a new restaurant on the wharf with lobster that will make you want to slap your mama. What do you say we go check it out?"

Lilly and Eleanor shook their heads. Lilly spoke first. "Adam might call."

"That's right," Eleanor agreed.

Jonathan folded his arms and peered down at them. "Call for what?"

Both women traded blank stares.

"Exactly. There is no possible reason for him to call. Nicole isn't about to abandon him or leave him to fend for himself. Neither is the couple giving the party. They're mutual friends of Adam and Nicole," Jonathan reasoned.

"Still I want to stay." Too restless to sit, Lilly stood. "I think I'll go up and study. There's an exam next week. Good night."

"Good night," Jonathan said, then brought his gaze back to Eleanor. "It's you and me again."

"I—"

"Please," he said, cutting her off before she could make an excuse. "We're leaving tomorrow afternoon and I won't get a chance to go to the restaurant."

There was a twinkle in his eyes so much like the old Jonathan, she was tempted. "If it's such a great place, we may not be able to get a table."

He slid his hands into the pockets of his expertly tailored dove gray slacks. They went beautifully with his black shirt and sports coat. "On the off chance we might go, I made reservations a month ago."

Eleanor's brow arched. "For how many?"

"Five. I thought it would be a great way to cap off the weekend for Adam and Kristen." He shrugged and withdrew his hands from his pockets. "Lilly, too. Make up for my not trusting her at first."

She relaxed. She should have known. Jonathan always thought of others. That was the type of man he was.

"It will be fun, Eleanor. What do you say?"

Yes, it would be. And wasn't she woman enough, disciplined enough, to keep herself under control? "What time is the reservation?"

"Nine."

She came to her feet. "I'll let Lilly know we're leaving and get the keys to the car."

"We won't need the car." He glanced at his Rolex. "A limo should be arriving in ten minutes." At her puzzled frown he continued, "Parking is always a hassle that time of night near the wharf."

"And you didn't want Adam trying to navigate the crowded streets," Eleanor added.

"I was so proud of him today. Both of them." He paused, then added, "Randolph would have been, too."

"Yes, he would have been." She smiled openly. "You helped. You're a good friend, Jonathan."

His expression stilled. "You better hurry."

Eleanor left the room wondering why she had gotten the impression that she had upset Jonathan with her last statement.

Lilly couldn't study or do much of anything except pace the living room. What if she was wrong? What if Adam needed her and she wasn't there? That thought tormented her. She raked her fingers through her hair, then went to the picture window and moved the sheer curtains aside. Nothing.

Her hand fell and she turned away to continue pacing. He'd only been gone a little over an hour. He wouldn't be back so soon.

Then she heard the key in the door and was caught between wanting to know if it was Adam and worried that if it was him, he was not all right. Her dilemma was solved when the door opened and Nicole entered followed by Adam.

Lilly's worried gaze went from Nicole's tightly compressed lips to Adam using his cane. Concern won over discretion. "You're back early."

Adam paused, his head lifting. He was smiling. "I remember Robert's parties as being more fun."

"You didn't enjoy yourself?" she asked, holding her breath as he skirted the footstool and coffee table to take a seat in the armchair.

"Not particularly, so I decided to leave and go to my place and make sure it's still standing." He relaxed in the chair. "I need you to orientate me, if you don't mind."

"No," she quickly assured him. "Eleanor and Jonathan have gone out to dinner. I'll just leave them a note."

"Tell them to pick us up at my place tomorrow!" Adam called after her.

Lilly stopped her headlong flight out of the room and stared at the silent Nicole. From her angry expression, Nicole was aware of Adam's plans for them to spend the night at his house. "Of course. It won't take me long to pack."

"Don't worry about my things except my toiletries and clock," he told her. "There's luggage and clothes at my place."

"I'll hurry." Racing up the stairs, Lilly felt a secret thrill of pleasure that he wanted to be with her.

In her room, she quickly put the small Gucci suitcase Eleanor had lent her on the bed and began dragging clothes from drawers and the closet. She never paused when she heard the knock. There was only one person it could be. "Yes, what is it?"

"Adam and I were involved before his blindness."

Lilly continued folding her slacks. "Yes, I'd figured as much."

Nicole in a form-fitting red dress came farther into the room. For once the outspoken woman appeared subdued. "He was so different then. So much in control."

Lilly finally understood. "He is different, but he's the same man."

"I'm too busy to have to watch out for anyone, or for anyone to depend on." Nicole shook her head of perfectly styled hair. "Tonight at the party, I didn't know how to act or what to do with him."

Lilly whirled sharply. Her voice lashed out in anger and accusation. "You're ashamed of him?"

"No," Nicole denied quickly. "It's just that I'm used to socializing at a party, dancing, not standing around watching to see that Adam doesn't bump into anything and hurt himself."

Her obvious uncertainty diffused some of Lilly's anger toward the other woman. "You just have to acclimate him to his surroundings. Next time—"

"There won't be a next time. It's over between us." Nicole wrapped her slim arms around herself. "Things have been going badly since he lost his sight. Don't think it was because of you."

"I won't." Lilly snapped the suitcase shut and picked it up. "Excuse me; I need to go pack Adam's things."

Nicole stared at Lilly a long time, then unfolded her arms. "I'm glad he has you."

Lilly's eyes widened in shocked amazement.

Nicole shrugged elegant shoulders. "I can be a bitch, but I'm a loyal bitch." She walked to the door. "Finish packing and I'll drop you off. Adam's house is about a mile from mine."

"You weren't planning on returning to the party?"

"The only reason I went there was because of Adam," she admitted, her voice strained.

Lilly studied the polished, beautiful woman a long time. She was hurting. "You really care about him."

"I do, but not enough to care for him the way you do."

Lilly went to Adam's room thinking of what Nicole had said. Despite caring for Adam, she obviously saw him as a burden, a liability. Lilly saw him as a man.

————

Nicole studied Adam as he sat in the chair. If she didn't know better, she'd think he was just lounging with his Gucci wire-rimmed sunglasses on. Tall and athletic, handsome and charming, rich and successful, he had been the epitome of everything she had wanted. His blindness had changed all that.

"Shouldn't be long," she said, coming farther into the room. "It didn't look as if she had much to pack."

"Clothes are not high on her list of priorities," he said.

"I guess it's finally sinking in that it's over between us."

"Nicole—"

She sat on the arm of the sofa across from him. "Don't give me that line about finding someone better."

The corner of his mouth lifted upward. "You never did mince words. I wasn't, but you will."

"Dammit, Adam. We were good together."

"We were safe and superficial," he told her without censure. "There wasn't enough to hold it together after my blindness."

She stared at him. "That's the first time you've said the word."

He shook his dark head. "I must have been a pain in the posterior."

Rising, she went to kneel in front of him and took his hands. "No matter. I wouldn't have left."

"I know." He briefly squeezed her hands. "You're demanding and exacting, but loyal."

"Home training," she quipped, then straightened. "Dad drank, so he was never able to hold down a job for long. Mom liked the nightlife. When they were both home, they fought. I can't remember either of my parents ever coming to school for even one conference, one PTA meeting, one play I was in." She shrugged, wishing the memory still didn't have the power to make her feel as if the fault lay in her, as her parents had shouted every chance they got.

Her hand smoothed the sides of her perfectly styled hair. She was perfect now and they'd never know. She'd made it to the top and that was all that mattered. "I joined every extracurricular activity the school had to stay away from home. Fortunately, it paid off with a scholarship."

Adam knew the story and admired Nicole's perseverance and determination that had garnered her success. But it had not been without a price. She hadn't been back to see her parents since she left home after graduating from high school. Strange how he never noticed before his blindness how lonely and insecure she sounded. "You had a rough time growing up, but you survived."

She retook her seat and crossed long, silky legs. "I learned early to fight for what I wanted."

"This time it wouldn't do any good," he pointed out quietly.

"I know. I've somehow always known I couldn't keep you. Just like I've never been able to keep anyone I cared about. It's easier not caring." Bitterness tinged each word.

"Nicole—"

"No. Don't. I might cry and ruin my image and my makeup."

"Perish the thought," he said, trying to match her mood. "The day you don't look absolutely beautiful is the day the sun falls out of the sky."

"And don't you forget it," Nicole said, her voice steadier and more in control. "Just remember, you didn't dump me. We called it quits together. Right?"

"Right."

"I'm ready." Lilly came into the room with her suitcase in her hands, her eyes for Adam only.

Adam stood and extended his hand. Lilly went to him quickly, a smile on her lips, adoration in her eyes. Nicole turned away and walked to the front door ahead of them. One day she'd find someone who wouldn't leave.

Eleanor quickly read the note that Lilly had left on the table in the living room: "Adam wanted to go to his house. Lilly went to orientate him. Nicole took them."

Jonathan peered down at the sheet of paper in her hands. "I don't think that's the only reason Adam wanted Lilly with him."

"You noticed it, too." Eleanor shook her head. "I don't know if it's dependence, gratitude, or something much more that he feels for her."

"Are you worried?"

She sighed. "Yes. I don't want either of them hurt. Both in their own way have gone through so much misery in the past."

"My Eleanor." He gently pulled her into his arms. "I think they're each exactly what the other needs."

For a brief moment, she stiffened, then relaxed. "I hope so. Love, even when it's real, can hurt."

"I know," he said, despair clear in his deep voice.

She started to pull away and his arms tightened. "Jonathan?"

He set her away from him, but he still held her firmly in his grasp. His eyes were dark and hot.

"Jonathan, what is it?"

"You really want to know?"

There was something in his voice that frightened and delighted her and chased shivers up and down her spine. "Yes."

"I've held this back for more years than I care to remember. I tried to keep this from you, but I can't any longer. My heart won't let me. My soul won't let me." His hand touched her cheek with the lightness of a butterfly's wing. "I love you, Eleanor. Not as a friend, but as a man loves a woman. I've loved you since the moment I first laid eyes on you and I'll love you until the day I die."

Her eyes widened as she stared at him in absolute shock.

"I wanted to tell you so many times, tried to tell you in so many ways." His hand tightened. "I loved Randolph like a brother. I respected the love you two shared because it made you happy, made him happy, even though it tore me up inside. I mourned his death and mourned the loss of you even though I'd never had you because I never thought I would.

"I love you, Eleanor. Every time I've walked away from you has been like tearing a part of me away. I want to hold you, love you, cherish you. I named *Lady Lost* after you because I never thought you'd be mine. And if you don't say something, I may run screaming into the streets."

Her voice trembled as she said, "I thought it was just me. The day at the cottage when Lilly came up unexpectedly. I'd never felt so aware of a man, so needy."

He closed his eyes. "Thank goodness."

Her trembling hands brushed across his lips. She wasn't going to fall off the cliff; she was jumping straight into Jonathan's arms. "Loving you is so easy, it's frightening."

His head turned and he kissed the tips of her fingertips. "Eleanor. Eleanor." He chanted, "I hoped, I prayed, I dreamed of this moment, but nothing in my dreams compares to how I feel now, how the touch of your hand excites me, humbles me."

Tenderly his mouth settled over hers. The kiss was a promise, a prelude. "I want to make love to you."

"Yes." Eleanor moaned; her heart hammered against her ribs.

Picking her up in his arms, he carried her up the stairs and placed her on the bed in his room. "You are so beautiful."

"You make me feel beautiful. I feel all new," she confessed.

He kissed her again, starting at her forehead, then working down to her cheek, the curve of her lips. All the while his fingers were busy with the gold buttons on her suit jacket.

Spreading the jacket, he saw the creamy swell of her breasts above the lacy white froth of her bra. Unable to help himself, he placed his lips there.

Fire shot through Eleanor, but it was quickly followed by unease. Unsteady fingers drew the jacket back together.

"What is it?"

She shook her head, refusing to look at him. Strong, unrelenting fingers lifted her chin. "Eleanor, I love you. If you're having second thoughts, I may want to chew nails, but I'd understand. If you need more—"

She turned her head aside. "It's my stretch marks and I–I haven't been exercising lately."

Jonathan gave thanks that she wasn't looking at him, because she would have seen his incredulous expression and his fighting to keep from smiling. Then he felt like kicking himself for not realizing it himself. Women might desperately want children but not the stretch marks or the thickening of their waistline.

"Eleanor, you could never be anything but beautiful to me. I've loved you forever, wanted you forever. No, you're not the same size you were thirty-nine years ago, and neither am I. You've matured, but . . ." He turned her face back "You're my Eleanor. I didn't fall in love with a great pair of legs, although you do have a great pair, or the sashay of your hips, but come to think of it, I try to watch them every chance I get, or your breasts, but I have imagined my lips on them. I fell in love with a woman whose beautiful spirit on the inside shone just as brightly as her beautiful spirit on the outside, and I've waited years to tell you."

Eleanor quivered. Between her thighs she felt the liquid heat of her desire. She wanted him, and she trusted him. Releasing the jacket, she lay back and opened her arms. "You don't have to wait any longer."

"Eleanor." Her name was a whisper, then a sigh as his lips fitted over hers. His tongue mated with hers, leaving both of them breathless. Lifting his head, he pulled her camisole over her head in one smooth motion.

Not giving her a chance to get nervous again, he kissed her again at the same time he undid the front fastener of her bra. Instantly his hands closed over the round globes, his thumbs grazing against the turgid nipples. His head bent and took one rigid point in his mouth. With teeth and tongue, he suckled and licked.

Beneath him, Eleanor shuddered and moaned. She was incredibly responsive. He'd been right about the passion hidden within her. And he had to have more.

Sitting up, he tore at his clothes, then with only slightly less restraint pulled off the rest of hers. When he finished, his mouth went back to hers. His hand swept down and found her wet and hot. His finger stroked her with the same maddening rhythm as his tongue in her mouth. The twin assaults drove each to the breaking point.

He released her, then lifted himself over her, his eyes glazed with desire. "I love you, Eleanor," he said, then slid into her welcoming warmth. He sighed with the rightness of it, the snug fit of her around him.

"Jonathan."

He moved slowly at first, allowing her body to adjust to his; then he quickened the pace as she moved beneath him, taking him deeper into her body and making her own demands. He eloquently answered each one.

As she cuddled up next to Jonathan, uneasiness crept over Eleanor. "Kristen can't know."

He stiffened and angled his head down. All he saw was the top of her head. "Are you ashamed of what happened between us?"

"Of course not," she answered, hurt that he thought she would be. She lifted her eyes to his. "Never, but she won't understand. She loved her father desperately. You know how lost she was after his death. She won't accept the idea of any man, even a man she admires and loves, courting me."

The anger went out of Jonathan's eyes. He pulled her closer. He couldn't lose her now. He couldn't. His kiss was hard and possessive. "I still can't believe you're actually here with me, that we made love."

Eleanor flushed, but she didn't lower her eyes. "Then perhaps you need a reminder."

"Perhaps I do."

The house was as breathtaking on the outside as Wakefield Manor. The two-story Mediterranean-influenced house with red tile roof and stucco sides gleamed like a multiprism jewel in the floodlights surrounding it. Palm trees lined the driveway.

"You certainly can pick 'em," Lilly said once they were inside the beautifully furnished house. Her gaze wandered from the oak-beamed ceiling to the lighted pool and gazebo that could be seen from the tiled entryway. Cushy upholstered pieces in shades of bone and wheat and African-American paintings created a welcoming atmosphere in the adjoining living room. "Very nice."

"Glad you like it. My room is up the stairs to the left. I have a second office next to it, besides the one downstairs. The guest bedroom is in the other wing. I'll show you."

"Do you want anything before you go up?"

"No." Taking her arm, they mounted the black wrought-iron spiral staircase. He stopped at the first door to the left of the stairs and opened it, then stepped aside. "My housekeeper wasn't expecting me, but she usually keeps things in good shape."

Lilly didn't look inside the room. All her attention was on Adam. She could look at him to her heart's content. Notice the laugh lines radiating from the corners of his eyes, the twin lines that ran across his forehead when he was deep in thought, his sensuous lips. "All I need is a bed."

"You sure?" He frowned. "Maybe I should have waited until morning, but I wanted to spend the night here."

"Adam, I understand," she quickly assured him. He was testing his boundaries, regaining his independence. Knowing he wanted her with him while he did so delighted her beyond measure. "I'm happy you wanted me to come."

He smiled and her heart turned over. "We're a team, remember?"

"I remember. Good night."

Entering her room, she flicked on the light. The room, furnished in earth tones with splashes of green as crisp as a celery stalk, could have been lifted from the pages of an interior design magazine. The deep contrast in their worlds had never been more evident, and soon she'd have to return to hers.

She couldn't get used to flying in chartered jets or riding in limousines or eating on $500 place settings.

Before long, Adam wouldn't need her. Even as the thought filled her heart with happiness, the thought of not seeing him, not being with him, caused an unbearable sadness to course through her. She had to prepare herself for that day, no matter how much the thought broke her heart.

They were young and gifted, talented and wealthy, armed with degrees from an Ivy League college and backed by their influential families. The world lay before them like a bright red marble. All they had to do was reach out and grasp it.

But first they had some partying to do. After four years of studying and hard work they deserved a night on the town. The six Stanford graduates were making it a memorable one, and no city was more beautiful than San Francisco by night.

Kristen had more to celebrate than the rest. The honors and distinction were nice, but as she had told her Uncle Jon, learning came easily for her and if she liked the subject she soaked up the information like a sponge. It was when the books closed that she had trouble.

As she watched Eric slow-dance with one of their friends, the sexually suggestive gyrating movements, now *that* was impossible. He teased her constantly about her prudishness. Yet unlike the other men she had dated, he kept coming back. She took a sip of her wine. Tonight she had planned to finally show him she wasn't prudish. They were going to make love. She hadn't told him yet. She loved him. What woman wouldn't?

He was gorgeous, with eyelashes longer than hers over slumberous gray eyes and a mouth that she loved to kiss. The music stopped. Disappointment went through Kristen as Eric and Sharmane remained on the floor, this time dancing at a fast tempo.

"Kristen, girl, you better watch Sharmane," Candace warned in a hushed whisper, shaking her braid-covered head. "She goes through men like a rat through cheese."

"They're just having fun. Besides they're only dancing," Kristen said. Candace, an economics major from Detroit, tended to be almost as serious as Kristen. That was one of the reasons they got along so well. Her boyfriend, Michael, a pre-med student, was the exact opposite. He was the practical joker of the bunch.

"Humph. If they were horizontal I'd give it another name."

Kristen didn't say anything, but she was glad when Sharmane's date, Howard Beacon, returned from the men's room and pulled Sharmane into his arms. Sharmane plastered her body to the latest man vying for her attention. Candace was right in that respect. Sharmane, who was rich and planned to marry richer, made no secret that she wouldn't buy a pair of shoes without first trying them on. Men like Howard, who was from an old Southern family with banking connections, eagerly got in line.

Eric slid into the booth beside her, smelling of Sharmane's cloying perfume. He leaned over to kiss Kristen. Automatically she pulled back.

His handsome face harshened. "I forgot. Thou shalt not touch." Before she could explain, he picked up his glass and drained the contents. "Waitress. Another."

Concern knitted Kristen's brow. He'd had drinks with dinner and three vodka collins since they arrived at the club. One was usually his limit when they went out. "Perhaps you shouldn't drink anymore."

He turned and stared at her. "It's either that or I tear your clothes off, then take a whip to you before I mount you from behind."

Kristen's eyes widened. Her mouth gaped.

Eric laughed, but it was a hollow sound. He plucked the drink from the waitress's hand and downed half the contents, all the time watching Kristen with cold, narrowed eyes.

Silently Eleanor slipped from Jonathan's arms. On her hands and knees, she tried to find her clothes in the dark. Light flooded the room. She gasped and glanced over her shoulder.

Jonathan stared down at her, a slow sensual grin on his face. Then he threw back the covers and got out of bed, not at all uneasy about his nakedness. "I'm willing to try anything."

Eleanor blinked, then gasped. "Jonathan!"

Chuckling, he squatted beside her. "Just kidding." His hands swept the curve of her back and over her buttocks and squeezed. "Although you are a tempting woman."

Air fluttered out of her lungs. "I–I was looking for my clothes."

His hand swept upward, his eyes never leaving her. "Why didn't you turn on the light?"

Heat followed in the wake of his hand and centered in the core of her womanhood. "I . . . I didn't want to wake you up."

"Proper Eleanor. I like knowing how improper you can be." His voice had dropped to a warm husky purr.

"Jonathan, I have to go. Kristen will be back soon."

His hand paused at the slope of her spine. "And she can't find you here, is that it?"

"Please, Jonathan."

He stared into her eyes for a long time, then lifted his hand and picked the white camisole from the carpet a few inches in front of her. "I guess I can wait until tomorrow night."

"Tomorrow night?" Eleanor repeated.

"Unless you have some objections?"

Eleanor stared at Jonathan, her gaze sweeping over his body, his virile manhood. She licked her lips. "No. No objections at all."

"Good, because I just might have to act improper and change your mind." While Eleanor was trying to decide if she should be indignant at his assurance, he gathered her clothes. "All present and accounted for." He held up a lacy bra. "Since I helped take them off, I feel I should help put them back on."

"I don't think that's a good idea."

He grinned. "You will."

He was dreaming . . . in color.

He was lying on his back in a field of vibrant red and yellow flowers. He heard the drone of bees, the babble of a creek, the neigh of a horse. Contentment lay upon him like a blessing. He blinked, then blinked again at the sun's brightness shining in his eyes. He turned over and the brightness followed. He lifted his hand to block out the irritating light.

Adam roused from sleep slowly and opened his eyes; his right arm lay over his eyes. Despite his blindness he'd continued to dream in colors. A curse or a blessing, he had yet to determine. He moved his arm. The brightness remained.

He didn't move for a long moment, afraid he was still dreaming; then he lifted his hand in front of his face as he had done every morning since his accident and waved his fingers. Shadows swayed.

His breath caught. Afraid to hope, to believe, he did it again. His heart pounded in his chest. The shadow shifted.

"Oh, my God. Lilly! Lilly!"

Sitting up in bed, he waved his hand in front of his face again and again, laughing, unaware tears were coursing down his cheeks. The veil of darkness had lifted from his right eye. Shadows moved in the nebulous of blackness.

"What is it?" Flinging his door wide, Lilly rushed into his room.

"I can see shadows out of my right eye."

"Oh, Adam!" She was across the room in an instant, climbing on the bed with him. "Can you make me out?"

"You're a shape in a fog bank," he said, laughing with unrestrained happiness.

"Oh, my goodness! This means the hemorrhage is clearing."

Laughing, he hugged her to him. "Yes. Yes. Yes."

Laughing just as happily, Lilly hugged him back, then discovered her unbound breasts pressed against the naked wall of his wide chest. She had rushed into his room without a robe. Again. Caught between being embarrassed and enjoying being in his arms, she debated her options for all of two seconds before hugging him harder. She felt the rasp of his beard against her cheek, the strength of his arms holding her, the long fingers splayed on her back.

"I'm going to see again!" he said, boundless delight ringing in each word.

"I'm calling Eleanor and Kristen." Pulling away, Lilly went to the phone and punched in the number.

Adam stood and headed for the shower. "Tell them to pick us up and we can go see Dr. Scott right away."

Lilly dragged her gaze from the ripple of muscles in Adam's back and shot a quick glance at the clock. "It's only seven-fifteen. The doctor won't be in his office."

"Just tell Jonathan. He'll get him there."

Chapter Nineteen

Dr. Louis T. Scott was one of the country's foremost neuro-ophthalmologists, an ophthalmologist who had additional training in neurological diseases. He looked more like an absentminded professor. He barely reached five feet, and no matter what he wore, he always appeared rumpled as he did now, wearing a white lab coat over a white shirt, black bow tie, and dark slacks. His snow-white hair was perpetually spiked over his head, but his eyes were sharply intelligent behind his gold wire-rimmed glasses. He was a patient, thorough man. Too much so in Adam's opinion.

"Well, Louis?" Adam said restlessly.

Dr. Scott lifted his head from studying the back of Adam's eye through a lens light. "There's definitely clearing of the hemorrhage."

"I didn't need you to tell me that. I want to know how long you think it will take for the hemorrhage to completely dissolve so I see again," Adam said.

"You can sit back." Louis moved the refractory light back. He didn't look at Jonathan, who stood to the left of him. "I don't know."

"How can you say that? You must have a clearer picture of the vitreous." Adam waved his hand in front of his face again, then cursed beneath his breath. "Put some Rev-Eyes in. I've gone long enough without seeing."

"You certainly haven't forgotten how to give orders." The elderly man stood and reached for the bottle of eyedrops to reverse the dilation.

"He certainly hasn't," Jonathan said dryly.

"Hold your head back," Dr. Scott ordered and proceeded to put one drop in each eye, then handed Adam a tissue.

"What's next?" Adam dabbed at the excess medicine running down his cheek.

The doctor flicked on the overhead light. "We need to do an optho-ultrasound to be certain, but the iris muscle is functioning in the right eye and I believe the optic nerve is intact."

Adam stilled and closed his eyes. "Thank God."

"Hold on, Adam; I said I think." Folding his arms, Dr. Scott leaned against the counter to Adam's right in the small exam room in the ophthalmology outpatient clinic of the hospital. "Let's get the ultrasound and I can tell more. There's still the question of whether there is retinal detachment due to the hemorrhage," he cautioned.

Adam's hands gripped the arms of the chair. Waiting had been a risk, but so had surgery. Instead of voicing his fear, he asked another question: "Only a couple of techs can perform the test. Is one available?"

The elderly man patted him on the shoulder in reassurance. "Romero is coming in to do the test personally."

Richard Romero was the head of Radiology and a friend. He was also one of the many people Adam had cut from his life. "Thanks for calling him."

"You're one of our own, Adam. We take care of our own. But I don't want you to expect too much from the tests," Scott warned.

"I'm going to see again," Adam said flatly.

The other two men in the room traded worried glances and remained silent.

Lying on the table, Adam couldn't relax. There was too much at stake. The Rev-Eyes had done its job. He now saw vague shapes and shadows out of the right eye. He'd see again. He was sure of it.

"Let me help you sit up." Romero took Adam by the arm and assisted him off the table and to a straight-back chair.

"Well?" Adam asked, aware that his throat was dry, his heart pounding. Romero could read the results while doing the test. "Is there detachment?"

"No," he said quietly.

"I knew it," said Adam. "I knew it."

"Hold on, Adam," Dr. Scott said quietly, too quietly.

Adam whirled toward Dr. Scott, who could read the tests as well as Romero. "What did you see?"

"It's what I can't see." Dr. Scott pulled a stool in front of Adam and straddled it. "I know we agreed to try and let the hemorrhage clear up on its own, because new studies showed there was less risk of permanent damage to the optic nerve or retinal detachment afterward."

"Yes. I know all that." Adam shifted restlessly. "Make your point."

Scott's sigh was long and eloquent. "I think we're pushing it, if we continue to wait. The retina can only take so much. We've gained some good news in that the iris muscle is responsive in the right eye, but we're still in the dark with the left eye."

Adam felt the effects of his words like a heavy weight on his chest. "You– you think the left eye is not going to clear up?"

"I don't know, Adam. But I think we've about used up the time we can safely wait to go in and have a look."

Adam rose, took a step, and realized he wasn't sure where he wanted to go or what he had planned. "I—" He shut his eyes tightly, then opened them. "I won't believe I won't get my vision back."

"Adam—"

"No, Jonathan." Adam held up his hand to stop the words he was sure he didn't want to hear. "I'm going to get my sight back." He stuck out his hand. "Thank you, Louis, for coming so quickly."

His hand was grasped and held. "I want to see you in two weeks. Three at the most."

"By that time, I'll be seeing you," Adam said. He refused to let doubt creep in when his friend released his hand. Firmly he turned to where he had last heard Romero's voice and again extended his hand. "Romero, I owe you one."

Adam heard the squish of the man's shoes on the floor. The sound had come from behind him. Adam waited for the radiologist to come to him as Brent had taught him.

"Glad I could help," Dr. Romero said, shaking Adam's hand. "Take care of yourself, Adam."

"Come on, Jonathan. We have two anxious women waiting outside."

Adam's fingers grasped the fine wool of Jonathan's suit. "Wait until Kristen hears."

Troubled, Jonathan glanced at both doctors. Their faces were grim. "Adam, perhaps you should wait for a couple of weeks."

"I've waited three months, Jonathan." Adam's fingers flexed on Jonathan's arm. "Are we leaving or do I have to find my own way?"

Jonathan moved. Adam never missed a step. Brent had done the same thing many times, in his words training Adam for any eventuality.

Outside the room, the clicking of heels alerted him of the women approaching. "I'm going to see again, Mother."

Eleanor threw herself into his arms and held tight. "Thank God. Thank God."

"That's not exactly what the doctor said, Adam." Jonathan would have given anything not to have Eleanor jerk around and stare at him with fear in her eyes.

"What are you saying?" she asked.

Adam's jaw tightened. "Jonathan is being his pessimistic self, as usual. The hemorrhage is clearing in the right eye."

"Not the left," Jonathan reminded him.

"It will," Adam vowed. "Aren't you going to say something, Lilly?"

Lilly felt as if she had been shown heaven, then hurled into hell. Despair and fear were only two of the many emotions warring within her. "I'm not sure I know what to say."

Adam turned his mutinous face toward Jonathan. "See what you've done?"

Jonathan stared at the crushed expression on Eleanor's face, so totally different from the excitement when she had rushed into his room this morning. "It's not fair if they don't have all the facts."

"Adam, what did Dr. Scott say?" Eleanor asked, her arm slowly withdrawing from around her son's neck.

"He thinks I should have surgery within the next couple of weeks. Three weeks at the most. He's concerned that the hemorrhage will cause scarring if we wait much longer." Defiantly Adam squared his shoulders and lifted his head. "By that time, my vision will have returned, so there's no sense in discussing the matter." He took his mother's arm. "Let's get out of here and go tell Kristen."

Eleanor threw a questioning look at Jonathan. He shook his head. Briefly she closed her eyes and fought the stinging moisture. "Of course. Kristen should be home by now."

"Did you pace the floor and wait for her?" Adam asked as they moved down the carpeted hallway of the outpatient wing of the hospital.

Eleanor was unable to keep from sending a guilty glance back at Jonathan. She flushed.

"I was just teasing, Mother. No need to tense up," Adam told her.

Carl opened the front door by the time the musical chime faded to the last note. They were taking the limo back to the airport as soon as they picked up the luggage and Kristen.

"Thanks, Carl. Where's Kristen?" Eleanor asked as she and Adam entered the house.

The gray-haired man's brow furrowed. "I haven't seen her, Mrs. Wakefield."

"She's not home yet?" Eleanor asked, looking from the obviously uncomfortable-looking butler to the top of the stairs.

"I'm not sure. She has her own key. She could have come in while I was in the back," he told her.

"You haven't heard from her since she left?" Adam asked, worry in his voice.

"I'll go check her room."

Eleanor headed for the stairs, guilt dogging her steps. After she had left Jonathan's room she had gone to her room and taken a long, hot bath. Instead of waiting for Kristen as she had planned, she had fallen asleep in her chaise longue while reading a book and hadn't awakened until Lilly called that morning.

The knock on her daughter's door was brief, almost desperate. If anyth—

"Yes?" Kristen called.

Eleanor sagged with relief. "It's Mother, baby. Can I come in?"

"I'm getting dressed. Give me a minute."

"Is she all right?"

She glanced over her shoulder to see Jonathan; a few feet behind him was Adam, and Lilly was directly behind him. "She's dressing."

"Tell her to hurry." Adam started back down the stairs with Lilly by his side.

Jonathan stared at Eleanor a long moment. "Don't even think it."

She shook her head. It wasn't difficult to know he was aware of her guilt. "Please tell Carl to have Alice prepare breakfast."

"Just remember what I said."

Eleanor opened the door. Kristen was pulling a bulky black sweater over her head. "You'll faint in that once we get off the plane in Shreveport."

"I'll be fine."

Eleanor frowned. Usually after a date or outing Kristen couldn't wait to tell her what had gone on. "Did you have fun?"

Kristen finally turned, but to Eleanor the smile on her daughter's face seemed forced. "Sure."

"You don't sound like it." Eleanor's concern deepened.

"I'm just sad. I'll miss my friends."

"But you'll keep in touch and make new ones," Eleanor assured her, her unease disappearing. Graduation from college was a big step into the unknown. "You've always enjoyed New Orleans."

"I may not be going to New Orleans." Kristen picked up a brush on the dresser and began pulling it through her long, straight hair.

Shock swept across Eleanor's face. "You've already been accepted for a position. You start in August."

Kristen's hand paused. "Eric wants me to get a job in New York. His parents are in the Hamptons. My professor says he could help."

"You've obviously given a great deal of thought to this." Eleanor tried to keep her voice calm. With a mother's instinct she knew Eric was all wrong for her daughter.

"I have. I want to go." Kristen faced her mother.

Her heart sinking, Eleanor studied her daughter closely. "You think you're in love with him, then?"

Kristen's chin lifted. "Yes, and I don't want to lose him."

"Distance shouldn't affect your relationship if you're really in love."

"Did you come up to get me for breakfast?" Kristen replaced the brush on the dresser.

Eleanor realized two things: Kristen's mind was made up, and she hadn't gone to her room when she returned home. Both were disturbing. "Not exactly. Adam wants to tell you himself."

Fear leaped into Kristen's dark eyes. "His eyes aren't getting worse, are they?"

"No." At least Eleanor hoped they weren't.

Kristen was out the door. She hit the stairs running and didn't stop until she was kneeling in front of Adam. "What happened?"

He grinned. "You're a beautiful blur out of my right eye."

"Adam!" she cried, reaching for him.

Laughing, his arms closed around her. She flinched. His hold loosened immediately. "Sorry, I didn't mean to squeeze you so hard."

Her gaze skirted away, then back. "How soon before it clears completely?"

"Dr. Scott isn't sure, but it will," Adam said adamantly.

His sister laughed. "You bet it will. Oh, Adam, this is wonderful. Have you called Nicole yet?"

Beside him, Lilly stiffened.

"No. You might as well know that Nicole and I have decided to call it quits."

Kristen sat back on her heels. "Are you sure?"

"It was over long before now, Kristen," Adam said. "Sometimes it's not meant to be."

"How do you know?" she asked quietly.

Adam heard the doubt in her voice and wondered if she meant generally or was referring to something specific. Before he lost his sight he couldn't have answered. Now he had no problem. "Your heart, your mind, your soul will tell you. All you have to do is listen." He twisted his head to one side. "Is this about Eric?"

"Yes," she said in an excited rush. "If I can get a job at the Museum of Modern Art in New York, and my professor feels that I can, I'm going there instead of New Orleans."

"You're changing plans you've had for the past year for a man you've known only a few months?" Adam asked incredulously.

Kristen impatiently swept her long black hair over her shoulder. "It doesn't take years. Mother knew from the first she wanted Father, and she was the same age."

"You want to marry him?" Eleanor asked, hesitant to point out that at her daughter's age she had been very mature, a sophomore medical student, and as self-assured and opinionated as they came.

Kristen came to her feet. "I didn't say anything about marriage. I'll just go see if Alice is ready to serve."

"I don't like this," Eleanor said as Kristen swept from the room. "I wasn't impressed when I met Eric."

"She's too old to forbid her to see him or move to New York," Jonathan said. "She'd mentioned moving to New York the day she called about her graduation."

Furious, Eleanor whirled on him. "And you didn't tell me?"

Jonathan unflinchingly met the censure in Eleanor's eyes. "Kristen's not the secretive type. I thought she had mentioned it to you."

"Of course, Jonathan. I'm sorry. I should have known." Feeling helpless and not liking it one bit, Eleanor looked back at the empty doorway through which Kristen had disappeared.

"Forget it." Jonathan touched her arm in reassurance. "Why don't I go see what's keeping her? I guess I don't have to tell either of you not to gang up on her or try to push her. You'll only make her more determined to bolt. No matter what, she wants your approval. But if you try to push, she can be as stubborn as either of you ever dared to be."

"What's your opinion of him, Jonathan?" Adam asked, his brows furrowed.

"Not good." This time when he turned away he kept going.

Adam's hand fisted impotently. "Damn. If I could see—"

"It wouldn't change a thing," his mother finished. "She's growing up. We just have to be there for her."

"You're right." He reached out his hand. "Let's go find them."

Lilly stayed where she was on the sofa. There was a distinct ache in the region of her heart, and she was sure it would remain there until the day she died. The pain had begun and spread with each breath ever since Adam's comment on the length of time Kristen had known Eric. A few months. She and Adam had known each other less than that.

She had deluded herself. There was nothing special about Adam's feelings for her. To him she was little more than a glorified companion.

————

Adam was troubled. Lilly hadn't said two words since they left the clinic.

Not that she'd had much of an opportunity. His mother and Jonathan had taken turns drawing Kristen out about her plans, neither approving nor disapproving. It became obvious very quickly that, as she said, her plans had not been finalized. If any of them had anything to say about it, they never would be.

He'd never met Eric, but if Jonathan didn't care for him that was good enough for Adam. But for the moment at least, they didn't have to worry about Kristen. She still planned to return with them to his estate.

His immediate problem was the silent woman sitting next to him.

All during breakfast, Lilly remained quiet. He could understand her rationale not to interfere in a family matter, if that was what it was. He just wished he knew if that was the only reason for her silence.

Although she was mere inches away, he didn't "feel" her. He couldn't explain it any other way except it was almost as if she had shut herself away from him. It scared him. He felt a deep connection with her that he couldn't explain. She'd become an important part of his life. When she was around, even in his darkness she brought a ray of hope. He didn't plan on losing her.

"Lilly, are you finished?"

"W-why. Yes."

He tried to figure out if she had sounded nervous or upset, then decided it didn't matter. He'd find out what was bothering her very shortly.

He came to his feet, shoved his chair beneath the table, then closed his hand on the padded back of her chair. "Please excuse us. We'll be in the gardens. Lilly?"

Her gaze refused to meet those of the others. "Excuse me." Pushing her chair back, she stood and closed trembling fingers around the arm he extended.

Adam spoke when they walked onto the stone patio. "There's a wooden bench by an arbor of bougainvillea. We can sit there."

Lilly knew the place. She and Jonathan had strolled over the entire garden to escape Nicole's possessive behavior. At the time, Lilly had thought she couldn't feel more out of place or hurt. She had been wrong.

"Here we are." Lilly stopped in front of the bench, then glanced at Adam when he made no move to sit.

"Ladies first."

Her breath came in sharply. "Y-You can see?"

"I can feel you looking at me," he answered simply.

She stared at him in openmouthed wonder and embarrassment and immediately thought of all the times she had watched him.

"Please sit down, Lilly."

Head downcast, she sat and folded her hands in her lap.

Sitting close beside her, Adam crossed his long legs, leaned back, and placed his arms on the back of the bench. "What's the matter?"

"Nothing."

"You may as well tell me," he told her. "I'll get it out of you sooner or later."

His self-assurance hit her the wrong way. "Why? Because you're so superior and I'm so stupid?"

"What kind of nonsense is that?" His face furious, he twisted toward her. "You're not stupid, and I don't ever want to hear you refer to yourself that way again. Now tell me what the hell is the matter with you!"

"You don't care, so stop pretending!" she shouted and started to stand.

His hand caught her, and he came to his feet with her. "What has gotten into you? What happened between last night and this morning? Did Nicole call?"

"No, she didn't call. It's you."

"Me?" He frowned, then released her arms. "My blindness never bothered you before."

She pushed against his chest with both hands. He stumbled backward, then quickly righted himself. "Don't you say anything so cruel and asinine. It's what you said."

Adam was lost, and it had nothing to do with his blindness.

He had no idea what he had done or said, but he knew he had better try to figure it out in a hurry. Lilly was spitting mad and she wasn't going easy on him because he couldn't see. Thank goodness.

"Could you give this cruel—unknowingly I might say in my defense—stupid man a clue so he can apologize?"

"It doesn't matter. I'm leaving when we get back."

He was upon her so quickly she didn't have time to move. "No! Talk to me. What did I do? Don't leave me." He pulled her into his arms. "Please."

Stunned, she could do nothing. Then her arms came up around him and held tight. Without being told, she knew that Adam had pleaded for few things in his life. It tore her up to think of him frightened. She was being greedy again, wishing for something that could never be. "I won't leave. I won't leave."

He couldn't tell if it was him trembling or herself. "What did I say?"

She opened her mouth to say, "Nothing," then snapped it shut. Adam was relentless when he wanted something. His single-mindedness was probably what had made him such an exceptional doctor. He'd hound her until she told him. But the truth would expose her.

"I have to know."

She opened her eyes but refused to look at him. "You told Kristen she couldn't possibly give up her plans after knowing Eric for only a few months."

"And?"

Her head fell forward. "We've known each other less than that."

He pushed her from him. His voice and hands gentled. "She hasn't seen him at his worst and helped him to try and be the best. How could you compare them to us?"

"*Us,*" reverberated in her mind over and over. "Us?"

His lips brushed tenderly across her temple. "Our lives aren't what they used to be, but together maybe we can make them what they should be."

"Adam—"

His fingertips touched her lips. "You have a legal matter to get past and I have to get rid of my cane."

"I don't care about the cane," she said, her heart booming in her chest.

"I do." His hand slid to her arm. "They're probably ready by now and waiting on us."

Lilly didn't move. There was another concern they needed to discuss. "I don't want a salary anymore. I have room and board. I use your kitchen for my business; I should be paying you."

"We'll talk about it after your legal expenses are paid. Private investigators aren't cheap."

He was right. Altogether she had spent over fifteen hundred dollars trying to locate Rafe with no success. "I'm thinking of forgetting about finding Rafe."

"Do you want to expose your soon-to-be ex-husband for the creep he is?"

"Yes," she answered immediately.

"Then the investigation will continue and so will your salary."

She shook her head. "But I don't want it anymore."

"I understand and it makes me admire your courage and conviction more, but sadly it takes money to gain your freedom. You've helped me gain mine; now let me help you."

Adam understood her better than anyone else in her life. On tiptoes she kissed his cheek. "Thank you."

"My pleasure."

Chapter Twenty

They had barely gotten inside Wakefield Manor before the phone rang. Kristen ran to pick up the extension in the hall. "Hello." With an audible sigh of disappointment, she turned and held out the phone. "Lilly, it's for you. A Mr. Powell."

"Maybe the investigator found Rafe," Adam suggested.

"Maybe." Lilly didn't think so. None of the phone calls from her lawyer had ever contained good news.

"Come on, Jonathan. Let's get this luggage upstairs." His cane in one hand and a small suitcase in the other, Adam continued toward the stairs. "It's a good thing we went by the cottage to drop your luggage off, Mother. We can make this in one trip instead of five."

"Make that six," Jonathan bantered, following with a large suitcase in each hand and another one beneath his right arm.

"You two should go onstage," Eleanor said, trailing behind.

Handing Lilly the phone, Kristen bounded up the stairs behind them with her laptop. "That's telling them, Mother."

"Hello."

"Mrs. Crawford, I've been trying to reach you since Saturday," came the very perturbed voice of her lawyer.

"I was out of town. What happened?" she asked, watching Adam slowly trudge up the stairs with one hand on the rail, the other clamped around the handle of her borrowed suitcase.

"Your court date has been set. It's July eighth."

Her attention jerked back to the lawyer. "What?"

"Your court date is July eighth," he repeated. "The judge took into consideration your going to college and set the date for the Monday following your final exams."

In three weeks she'd be free of Myron. "Have you been able to find anyone who would testify on my behalf?"

"No."

"Pastor Fowler—"

"Is a character witness for Mr. Crawford. So is half the deacon board and the women's auxiliary."

Lilly leaned against the wall. She had hoped one person might remember her as a kind, giving person, but apparently not if it meant going against Myron. "What time should I be there?"

"Eleven sharp at the courthouse," he instructed. "Whatever you do, don't be late. Wear something conservative. Summer school going all right?"

"Yes. My first test is this week."

"Study hard. We're going to need all the help we can get. Next time you go out of town, let me know."

"I'm sorry. I will."

"Good-bye."

"Good-bye." She replaced the receiver in the cradle. Kent Powell had sounded tired, annoyed, and defeated. He might have given up, but she hadn't. Myron was going to lose.

"Why am I not surprised to find you here?"

Lilly didn't glance up from pouring a can of stewed tomatoes into a bowl that already contained several other ingredients. "Because in a couple of hours it'll be time for dinner. Is Jonathan staying?"

"No. When he called his service one of his mothers had gone into labor. Kristen and Mother both are resting. Or supposed to be. They're both in Kristen's room." Folding his arms, Adam leaned his back against the countertop and stiffed. "Onions."

"For the stuffed bell peppers. We're also having cabbage, candied yams, and corn bread." Setting the can aside, she picked up a wooden spoon. "You aren't tired?"

"I haven't felt this energized in a long time." Lifting his glasses, he looked out the window over the sink. "You can't imagine how good it feels to see light, if only in shadows. When my sight returns, we'll go back to San Francisco and I'll show you around."

Her hand paused. She was at a loss as to what to say. Thankfully, she didn't have to say anything.

"You ever been to the opera or the ballet?"

"No." Little Elm didn't have a theater for live performances.

"You will. The San Francisco Ballet is America's oldest ballet company. And the Dance Theater of Harlem is a Bay Area favorite. There's not a city in the world like San Francisco. It's a visual feast. You're about finished?"

"Yes. You need me to do something?" Picking up a hollowed bell pepper, she spooned the meat mixture into it.

"I was going to read the possible test questions to you if you'd like and help you study for your exam tomorrow." He made a face. "If you don't mind waiting for the computer."

"Thank you. I'd like that."

He nodded. "I'll see you in my study."

Sprinkling croutons on top of the stuffing in the bell peppers, she tried not to think of what would happen if Adam didn't regain his sight.

Jonathan hoped no one in Wakefield Manor looked out their window toward the cottage and saw the headlights of his car. It was almost midnight. Two births had kept him tied up at the hospital until eleven. He didn't like sneaking around, but if it was the only way to have Eleanor he could live with it. She had enough pressure with Kristen's interest in a man they both thought totally unsuitable.

Then there was Adam's unwavering belief that his vision would soon return and his making plans as if it would. On the flight back from San Francisco, nothing would do but for him to call Samuel from the air and remind the gardener to start working on plans for the flower garden in front of the house.

Switching off the motor, Jonathan got out of the car. The front door of the cottage swung open and Eleanor ran to meet him. Opening his arms, he rushed to her and caught her trembling body securely against his.

"I'm here, honey. I'm here."

Her hold was as desperate as her words: "Will he see again?"

There had been no time to talk privately since they'd left the hospital with Adam that morning. "Only God knows."

She shuddered.

Picking her up, he went inside. He kicked the door shut with his foot and sat on the couch, Eleanor still in his arms. "Scott is the best. He does the surgery while looking into the eye with a microscope. Various miniature instruments are placed in the eye through tiny incisions in the sclera. He's performed vitrectomies before, but there's always the risk of retinal detachment. A detachment could require another surgery to repair, and if that fails, the eye will continue to lose sight and blindness will occur."

She whimpered. She knew this better than he, but she needed to face the reality.

"Then there is the complication of cataract from the vitrectomy and the retinal detachment that can occur when you go in to repair the cataract. The way Adam sees it, if his vision clears by itself, he doesn't have to worry about complications."

Jonathan paused and plunged ahead. "If he has the surgery, he runs the risks of complications then and in the months to come. The retina could detach then, five months from now, five years from now, or never. The cataract, if it occurred, would grow slower, but surgery would still be needed and more complications could occur, including detachment. If Adam gets by those possible complications and if the macula, the central retina area, is normal and there are no blind spots, he can return to neurosurgery."

"So, you think the odds aren't in his favor?" Eleanor asked, her voice low and frightened.

Jonathan's large hand reached out and turned her tearstained face to his before he answered. "I never thought you'd be in my arms, but you're here. I never thought I could love so deeply, but I do. No one knows what the future holds. All we can do is pray and trust in a higher power to get us all through this."

Her hand covered his. "I'm glad you're here."

"So am I." His head bent and he covered her lips with his.

Adam had been smiling all Tuesday morning. Hearing the doorbell, he sat forward in his chair and placed both hands on top of his desk. Brent was coming today because they had missed Monday.

Kristen had waited to let the instructor in; then she and her mother were driving into town for lunch and, if he knew them, doing some shopping. Perhaps he should have asked his mother to pick up something for Lilly. She deserved nice things.

"Good evening, Doc. Why the frown?" Brent greeted Adam as he entered the study.

"Just thinking." Just as soon as he got rid of Brent, he'd call his mother on her cell phone.

"Nothing heavy, I hope. Your sister is as beautiful as her mother. How was San Francisco?"

"Thanks, and San Francisco was wonderful, as usual." Adam heard Brent's heavy weight settle in the chair in front of his desk. "In fact, something miraculous happened while I was there. So much so that you won't be needed anymore."

"You're discharging me?" Brent asked incredulously

Adam's face split into a wide grin. "My vision is returning."

"Doc, that's wonderful." He clapped Adam soundly on the back. "How long before your vision returns completely?"

Adam's smile wavered. "We're not sure."

"Doc, you wouldn't be trying to get rid of me beforetime, would you?" Brent questioned, laughter in his deep voice.

"I see no reason for continuing the lessons when my sight is clearing." Why did people refuse to believe he'd regain his sight?

"What do you see?"

Aggravated, Adam clenched his fists. "Shadows."

"Then why didn't you blink or react when I waved my hand in front of your face just now?"

"Because the light is bad in here." Adam shoved up from his desk and walked to the fireplace. "I was going to say I'll miss you."

"Where's your cane?"

"I don't need it."

"You don't want to need it," Brent countered.

"I'll see," Adam said defiantly.

"Tell me what I'm doing."

Adam folded his arms. There was nothing but a blur. He twisted his head to one side without any clearer defining of objects. "I'm not playing some silly game. You can't be this hard up for patients."

"Patients might give up on themselves, but I don't give up on them," he said, unperturbed.

"I'm not giving up. I'm going to see!"

"Adam?"

He switched his attention toward the soft, hesitant voice. His arms dropped to his sides. "Lilly, you're back early. Is everything all right?"

"Professor Higgins let us go early." She had been afraid of this. Adam refused to even entertain the idea that he wouldn't regain his sight. She prayed that he was right, but what if he wasn't? "Maybe you should continue the classes until your sight does come back."

"You, too."

It was crushing to see the disappointment in his face, hear it in his voice. "Me, too. I care about you, just like everyone else." She took a step closer to his belligerent stance. "You don't expect a flat tire, but you carry a spare just in case."

He lifted a heavy brow. "If you had a flat, you wouldn't know how to change the tire."

She placed her hand on his chest. "No, but I'd try. I wouldn't feel lost and helpless like I did when I first came here. You helped teach me."

"Me?"

Her smile was sad. "You had so much taken from you, but you fought back to regain it, moment by moment, day by day. You refused to let life keep you down."

"Oh, Lilly." He held her hand and leaned his forehead forward to touch hers. "I was a mean-tempered, arrogant—"

"At first. Not now," she interrupted.

He sighed. "You see so much in me."

"Just like you do in me."

"Brent?"

"Yo, Doc."

"Drag out the whip." Adam's mouth twisted wryly. "I hope you're aware of what you're putting me through, Lilly."

"I just finished a horrendous pop quiz in marketing because you insisted I finish my degree."

His face intent, Adam grabbed her arms. "How did you do?"

She grinned. "Aced it. Just like the earlier one in business."

His arms circled her, lifted her momentarily off her feet. "That's my girl."

She flushed with pleasure; her heart drummed in her chest; her hands went around his neck. Love flooded her.

"I better get to the kitchen. We had to do a business proposal last week for my marketing class and I did my pies. When the class found out today, I promised to bring a couple to class tomorrow."

"Pies? What pies?" Brent asked, excitement in his voice.

"Don't tell him."

Lilly snatched her hands from around Adam's neck. She'd momentarily forgotten about Brent.

"Come on, Lilly. Doc, have a heart," Brent pleaded.

Adam looped his arm around Lilly's shoulders. "How sweet the sound of an arrogant man begging." He chuckled. "Lilly makes the most decadent pineapple praline pie in the universe. She's developing quite a thriving business selling them. If you're nice to me, I may let her bake you one."

Brent let out a mournful sound. "I'll never get one."

Adam threw back his head and laughed.

He'd be all right, she thought. "I'll be in the kitchen if you need me."

"We do already," Brent said. "Doc misplaced his cane."

"Adam."

Silently Adam went to his desk, bent down, and came up with the cane. "I guess I found it."

"Doc, you really are something."

"Ain't I just," Adam said.

Brent's mouth opened and nothing came out.

"I think you did the impossible, Adam," Lilly said. "Brent is speechless."

"I'm sure it's only temporary. Unfortunately," Adam quipped.

"All right, Laurel and Hardy, that's enough," Brent finally said. "Go bake some pies while I see if Doc has forgotten what he's learned."

"I'm going."

More at ease than she had been on the drive back from her campus, Lilly left. Like Mother Crawford had always said, it was all right to pray to God if you were in a sinking boat, but you'd better not stop bailing water.

Adam was bailing water.

Kristen and Eleanor chose an Italian restaurant. Both loved garlic breadsticks, salad loaded with fresh bacon and croutons, and white and red sauce. They each ordered a different entrée so they could share and handed the waiter the menus.

"I'm glad you came back with us," Eleanor said, trying to feel her way into the conversation.

"Adam needs us, but he's getting better."

"Yes, he is." Eleanor took a sip of red wine, refusing to give in to her fear.

"Is there something between him and Lilly?"

"If you mean romantically, I'm not sure." Eleanor paused as the waiter placed their salads before them. "I am sure his relationship with Nicole is over."

Frowning, Kristen picked up her fork. "But they seemed so perfect together."

"Until Adam's blindness," Eleanor answered. "Whatever they had wasn't strong enough to withstand the strain. True love lasts through good and bad times."

"Like you and Father." Kristen sipped her wine. "You two had that special kind of love that I want to have. You found the one perfect man on earth for you."

Her daughter's words worried her. "Do you think you've found it?"

Kristen shrugged. "Perhaps. This is good salad. Maybe we should take Adam back some."

Eleanor barely kept from sighing. Kristen should have gone into politics instead of art. "The honors thesis you did on how Europe embraced and influenced African-American artists was very good. I can see why the Museum of Modern Art in New York would want you to work for them."

Kristen's head came up. "You wouldn't mind?"

"Yes. I won't lie to you, but I respect you as an adult. You have to make your own decisions."

"New York would be wonderful." Kristen almost sighed. "The best museums in the country are there. Not to mention the best theaters and restaurants. I read someplace that it would take five years to eat at every restaurant there."

"Then you've made up your mind?"

Kristen braced her arms on the table. "Not yet. I'm waiting for the director of the museum to call, and then I have to go up for an interview."

"A formality." Eleanor added pepper to her salad. "He'll hire you. He'd be crazy not to."

Kristen smiled. "I'm glad you're my mother."

"You've made me proud since the day you were born," Eleanor said.

"I've tried," she said softly.

The shadows in her daughter's eyes troubled Eleanor. "You succeeded. No parent was ever prouder. Now eat up so we can see the dessert menu."

Eleanor stood in front of the unfinished canvas, her brush moving with a surety that she had not had in a long time. The reason heated her cheeks and the center of her body. She loved and she was loved. Problems remained, but she had someone to share those problems with.

The delineation of Jonathan's muscled chest and legs needed to be perfect. The sudden squall had caught him unaware. His dark shirt flapped in the wind; his wet jeans were plastered to his legs as lightning flashed in the distance. He pitted his strength against the elements, determined to win, determined to return to *her*.

Eleanor hadn't known that part of the painting when she started, but it was there now. Off in a distance, a light in a cottage glowed. His lover waited.

She finished the last stroke as the doorbell rang. Her heart thumped with anticipation. Setting the brushes to soak, she closed the door to the second bedroom, where she had moved the painting when she returned from San Francisco.

Wiping her hand on a cloth dampened with turpentine, she went to open the door. "Hello."

He pulled her into his arms and kissed her, his hands and mouth greedy for her. "Hello."

Eleanor melted against him. "You'll get paint all over you."

"I'll also get you all over me."

"Oh, Jonathan."

He closed the door, his hand going to the buttons on her smock. "I need you, Eleanor."

"Let me wash up," she said, but she turned her neck to allow him greater access as he began trailing kisses from the curve of her jaw to her throat.

"Not a problem." His hands lifted and began unbuttoning his shirt. "Shall we try the tub or the shower?"

No one had ever called Eleanor slow or stupid. "How about both?"

Only the pale glow of the computer screen shone in Kristen's room. Wearing white silk pajamas, she sat cross-legged in the middle of her bed. She'd been on the computer for the past two hours, sending instant messages to Eric in New York. She needed the darkness.

That was the only way she'd be able to type the words on the computer. She had to. He'd changed, grown colder, but it was her fault. She should have understood she'd lose him if she didn't do what he asked. The night of her graduation he had gotten drunk. Trying to help him up the steps to his apartment, he had fallen, dragging her with him. She'd scraped her back on the steps. Instead of spending the night in his arms, she had been a fifth wheel with her friends. She'd been too ashamed to go home before midnight.

She was ashamed now, but it was better than being alone. Unlike Adam and her mother, she didn't draw people to her. Her friends were few.

She'd lain awake many, many nights contemplating what was in her makeup that eventually repelled people. They'd come, but they'd never stay. There were no kindergarten or high school friends who still kept in touch. She knew that Candace would drift from her as well.

People weren't able to keep loving her. Her father would have, but he had been taken from her. She had to keep Eric. She couldn't lose him, too.

Adam woke up the next morning and immediately waved his hand in front of his face. No change in either eye. Getting out of bed, he went to the balcony, hoping the bright light might pierce the gray in his right eye. Nothing.

Turning away, he went to take a shower. There was always tomorrow. In the bathroom, he squirted toothpaste into his mouth and brushed his teeth, then shaved. He no longer needed to feel the raised lettering. The shape of the bottle, the sprayer, told him if he held after-shave, cologne, or moisturizer.

Back in his room, he pulled on a pair of khaki pants and a Polo shirt. On his dresser was his belt. His tasseled loafers were by the bed. Through necessity, blindness had taught him to be organized. It was either that or spend frustrating moments trying to find where you had carelessly tossed something.

Dressed, he checked the time. Seven-thirteen. There was a stack of medical journals on his desk that he needed to "read." He wanted to be up on everything when he returned to medicine. Picking up his cane, he left his room and went downstairs wondering if he could make a cup of coffee.

Since he didn't know where the ground coffee was kept, it wasn't likely. But there wasn't a doubt in his mind that he could. He continued to his desk and flipped on the computer and waited for it to warm up.

He'd come a long way. He didn't have to be ashamed of his blindness or of his poor behavior. Life had thrown him a hard curve, but life had also prepared him to meet the challenge and survive. He just had to remember. Lilly had helped.

Leaning back in his chair, he tried to picture her in his mind. He knew she was slim and delicate-boned from holding her in his arms. Her head fit just beneath his chin, so she had to be around five-foot-six. He couldn't imagine her wearing heels, as many times as she went up and down the stairs. Her breasts were nicely rounded and would fill the cupping of his hand. All together a very nice combination.

But her face was a blank. He didn't want to ask anyone. He'd wait and see her for himself. After all, it was only a matter of time. Maybe tomorrow.

Later that morning when Lilly came down Adam asked her where the coffee was kept. Immediately she had shown him and, as if it were the most natural thing in the world, then told him he might as well make the coffee.

To his satisfaction he did just that.

Eleanor studied her face in the mirror, trying to see if there was anything that might indicate she had spent a good portion of the night in a man's arms making love. Beside the sparkle in her eyes, she thought there was no change.

Leaving the cottage, she went to the main house to prepare breakfast and help with the housework. With Kristen here, Lilly's workload would increase. Odette wasn't due back for a couple of weeks or longer. She and Cameron were having a ball together. Eleanor had never thought of grandchildren before, but seeing Cameron's sturdy body, the one-toothed grin he bestowed on his grandmother, Eleanor decided she wouldn't mind being a grandmother and spoiling her grandchild.

Adam certainly hadn't been bothered by the possibility of Odette not returning soon. He'd told her to take all the time she needed.

Following the winding path, Eleanor wondered if Kristen might be on to something regarding Adam and Lilly. Eleanor wasn't sure how she felt about a relationship developing between them. As she had told Jonathan, both of their lives were unsettled. They had enough problems on their own. Knocking briefly, she opened the door. "Good morning."

Lilly, standing in front of the griddle on top of the stove, tossed a greeting over her shoulder: "Morning."

"Good morning, Mother." Adam took a plate from the cabinet and held it out for Lilly. She slid four perfectly browned pancakes onto it. "You're just in time."

"I came over to help," Eleanor said.

"Lilly and I have it under control." His cane in one hand, the plate in the other, Adam crossed the room and placed the plate on the table. "Have a seat."

Eleanor did as he requested, noticing the tender way Lilly kept looking at Adam, the way she allowed him to be the man he was. She and Jonathan might not be the only ones with a secret.

Kristen slowly trudged down the stairs. She had a nagging pain at the base of her neck, a reminder of the hours she'd spent on the laptop. She didn't want to think about what she had typed on it, so she pushed it from her mind.

She'd missed breakfast and probably lunch. She didn't feel like eating much anyway.

"Good afternoon, sleepyhead." Her mother's smile was natural and welcoming.

The sight made Kristen feel worse. She plopped on the cushion beside her mother and placed her head on her shoulder, wishing she could crawl into her lap and let her make all the bad stuff go away as she had done so many times when Kristen was a child.

Frowning, Eleanor laid aside the book she had been reading and stared down into her daughter's face. "Everything all right?"

"Why is life so complicated?" Kristen asked.

"To keep it interesting, I suppose." Eleanor's hand swept back strands of hair from her daughter's forehead. "Thinking about your plans for the future?"

She nodded.

"How about a third alternate? Get your master's."

Kristen straightened. "I'm schooled out. I don't know how Adam stood sixteen years of school after college, or Father, either."

"They were doing what they loved."

"I love art with all of its different mediums. I love the way the viewer is just as important to the piece as the artist, but I'm ready to put what I learned into practice."

"Speaking of viewing. How about coming to the cottage and seeing the picture I painted for Jonathan's office? I planned to take it into town today and find a frame."

"That's wonderful." Kristen smiled naturally at her mother. "Why didn't you show it to me yesterday?"

She tweaked her daughter's nose. "Because I just finished last night."

"Has he seen it yet?"

Eleanor's smile wavered. "No."

Kristen bounded up and reached for her mother's hand to pull her up. "Come on. I can't wait to see it."

"It's just a painting. Don't expect too much."

"You're a great artist." Kristin looped her arm with her mother's. "I got my love of art from you."

Pleased, Eleanor's smile broadened as they walked from the room. "Lilly has left for class and Adam is in his study. We'll see if he wants to walk with us."

Kristen paused. "Won't—won't it make him feel bad?"

"I think not telling him would be worse."

They found Adam in his study "reading" the newspaper. "Adam, I finished Jonathan's painting. I'm going to show Kristen; then we're going to go into town to look for a frame. You want to come with us for all or part of the above?"

He waved his left hand. "You two go ahead. I'll see it later."

Eleanor tensed, but all she said was, "I'll take my cell phone with me. Call if you need me."

"I'll be fine." He picked up the talking clock beside his keyboard and activated it.

"Twelve-thirteen."

He set the clock aside. "Lilly should be home in an hour. Take your time."

"You don't like it?"

Eleanor had begun to get nervous. Kristen had been staring at the picture for a good two minutes.

Kristen glanced at the painting, then back at her mother. "It's . . ."

"What?" Eleanor asked, her nervousness increasing.

"Passionate." Her slim hand lifted toward the canvas. "The brush stokes are a subtle mixture of restraint and boldness. There's a fierceness about his face, but the eyes, even in the storm, show tenderness."

Eleanor held her breath, hoping Kristen hadn't seen the white cottage in the distance. Why hadn't she foreseen this? "It's just a painting. Come on; let's go find a frame."

Kristen didn't say anything, but on the drive to Shreveport Eleanor caught her daughter several times watching her with silent speculation.

What had she done? She had to call Jonathan.

Chapter Twenty~One

Jonathan answered Eleanor's frantic summons for help that very night.

After dinner he just happened to drop by Adam's house around seven. He made sure he didn't let his eyes linger on Eleanor any longer than usual or admire the way her pale blue dress curved over her hips. He ordered two pies from Lilly for his office potluck luncheon the next week and wished her well on her finals coming up the same week. Kristen beat him at chess. He discussed the upcoming political elections with Adam.

Shortly after nine, Jonathan said good night. Adam walked him out. Jonathan went home and went to bed. His eyes had popped open two hours later.

His ability to drop off to sleep at will and wake at will had served him well during his career. Babies were notoriously unpredictable. Stretching, he took a shower, dressed, and drove to Eleanor's cottage.

"Jonathan, I don't think you should be here."

She looked absolutely beautiful in a lavender gown with thin straps that showed off her smooth, bare shoulders and the swell of her breasts. "There's no lights on at the house."

"Well, in that case . . ."

He closed the door behind him, taking her in his arms and to bed. Life was good.

———

A week after they returned, Kristen received the call that Eleanor had dreaded. The director of the Museum of Modern Art in New York wanted her to come for an interview. He was very impressed with her honors thesis and the praise from her Stanford professor.

Kristen, usually reserved, had hung up the phone and danced with Eleanor, then Adam. If they were a bit subdued, she didn't appear to notice. Releasing her brother, she'd gone upstairs to call Eric.

"I don't like it," Eleanor said as soon as Kristen was out of hearing range.

"Me neither, but like Jonathan said, showing our disapproval will alienate her."

Kristen came rushing back into the room, her purse strap over her shoulder, her eyes glowing. "I've decided to buy a new suit and get my hair done. If Mother comes with me, will you be all right, Adam?"

"Go ahead."

Adam had walked with them to the door, listening to Kristen's excited voice as they went down the front steps. Minutes later, he heard the car pass and waved. When the sound faded he walked down the steps and into the yard, then turned until he felt the heat of the sun and waved his hand.

No change.

A week had passed and there was no difference in his acuity. He had expected a gradual increase of his vision. It hadn't happened. The question now was, would it improve or was there damage to the macula, the area needed for fine details? If there was, it would make returning to neurosurgery impossible.

Lowering his hand, he went inside and shut the door. Vision change came with age. There were a number of neurosurgeons who had decreased vision. At their national conference last year, there had been an elderly doctor who had vision in only one eye. If the condition was just a refractory problem, glasses and microscopic goggles would allow vision good enough to operate successfully. If the macula or retina was involved, all bets were off. There was no way Adam could incise into the brain, especially if it was a very eloquent area, if he had blind spots caused by retina or macula injury. Partial loss of vision for fine detail would exclude him from the operating room.

Then what?

You could always go into psychiatry! The unsettling thought was enough to make Adam cringe and stiffen his spine. He wasn't giving up.

Eric was going to be surprised.

Kristen was unable to contain her excitement as the cab maneuvered through Manhattan toward his apartment on Park Avenue. She'd purposely led Eric to believe that she was coming the next day. Her mother and Adam had taken her to the airport, and Jonathan had met them there for a hot minute. To her continued relief, Jonathan and her mother had acted no different than they had last week or during the hundreds of times they had been together. There had been no longing looks, no unnecessary touching. It had been foolish to think something was going on between them. Neither would betray her father's memory by sneaking around and having an affair. Her father had been a wonderful man. Although she loved Jonathan, he couldn't take her father's place. No man could.

The cabdriver made one of New York's infamous dives in front of a car. Brakes squeaked. Horns blasted. Hand gestures were made by both parties. Kristen decided she'd rather not watch and looked out the window at the crowded streets and gigantic lighted billboards on the skyscrapers. It was a little after eight, but just as many people would be out at two in the morning. New York teemed with life and excitement, and soon she would be a part of it.

Her interview was tomorrow at ten-fifteen, and when she left she planned to have the job. Just as tonight she planned to show Eric she loved him all the more for waiting until she was ready for intimacy. Her father had wised her up to the hormonal urges of boys while she was still in elementary school. Intimacy should be a commitment, not a stress reliever or a scorecard.

Instead of staying at the Ritz-Carlton, she planned to spend the night with Eric. To keep her family from worrying, she'd called Adam and her mother from JFK Airport to let them know she had made it all right.

As soon as the cab stopped, she paid the driver, collected her bag, and went inside. Eric had given her the access code last night. Stopping briefly at the security checkpoint, she headed for the elevator. The old building might look rather dull on the outside, but on the inside the lobby was spacious and filled with plants and antique furniture. The words *refined* and *stately* came to mind. If she had more time, she'd love to study the paintings on the wall, but now she wanted to see Eric.

The gleaming brass door of the elevator opened, and she stepped into the mirrored enclosure and punched five, then checked her makeup and hair. She smiled to herself. The single-breasted melon-colored suit might appear conservative, but the lacy black underwear beneath was anything but. Eric was going to drool!

Grinning, she stepped off the elevator. Locating his apartment, she set her suitcase on the gently worn carpeted floor and rang the doorbell, her smile ready, her arms open. When he didn't answer, she rang again.

"Eric, please be there. Plea—"

She heard the click of a lock, a deadbolt being slid back. The door opened.

The arms that Kristen had been about to raise stayed at her sides, her jaw slackened as she saw a statuesque woman in a revealing leather bodysuit with cutouts for her rouged nipples. Black stiletto heels and a whip in her hand accessorized the bizarre outfit.

"You're not Star," the woman said.

"I–I . . ." Kristen's gaze went to the door. It was 583-A, but obviously she had made a mistake. "I—"

"Diamond, get your butt back in here and bring Star. I'm not finished."

Kristen's head whipped around. She tried to look beyond the woman in the blond wig and little else. "Eric?"

The frown on the blonde's pretty face cleared. "You're here to take Star's place." She gestured with the handle of the whip. "Your costume in your suitcase? I prefer a backpack myself." Her frown returned when Kristen didn't move. "I don't have all night. I have another appointment at ten. He wants his money's worth. He can't get it up unless you're in leather and talk dirty."

Kristen stared at the handle as if it were a snake.

"What's taking—" Eric stopped when he saw Kristen. He quickly closed his paisley silk robe, but not before she had seen that he was naked beneath. Welts marked his legs.

Kristen felt physically sick. Her hand clutched her stomach.

"What the hell?" he growled. "You aren't supposed to be here until tomorrow."

"I wanted to surprise you," she said, still unable to believe what she was seeing.

The smile that curved his thin mouth was cruel and taunting. His arm curved around the other woman's narrow waist. "I'd say you were the one who was surprised. No matter. Star's late, so you can take her place."

"What?"

Eric's expression hardened. "Grow up, Kris. You think I didn't try to get in your pants because I valued you. Be for real. I like sex and I like it rough. My old man hired a private investigator to keep an eye on me after a little trouble at Cornell the fall semester. That's why I transferred to Stanford. Took a lot of pull on my old man's part to make sure I graduated.

"Since he holds the purse strings until he croaks, I had to toe the line, including finishing college. You were perfect to keep him off my back."

Slowly his words sank in. "You never cared," Kristen whispered.

"You didn't receive honors and distinction for nothing. Me, I barely squeaked by." He bit the woman on the arm, leaving teeth marks. His eyes remained on Kristen.

"You'll pay for that later," Diamond said, rubbing the handle of the whip down his arm.

Despite the revulsion she felt, there was one last question Kristen had to ask: "Why did you invite me?"

"There was always the possibility that I could turn you to the dark side, so to speak." His upper lip curled. "But, on second thought, I don't think you would be worth the effort."

The words were meant to inflict pain. They did, mercilessly so. Yet somehow Kristen found the strength to keep her face expressionless. "For the first time, you're right about me. Now I need to take a bath and forget you ever existed."

Picking up her suitcase, she went downstairs and hailed a cab. At the Ritz-Carlton she registered, went to her suite, stripped, stepped under the spray of hot water, and let the tears fall.

Lilly's life was hectic and getting more so by the day. She couldn't have been more pleased.

Taking care of the house and Adam was no problem, but with going to class and now studying for final exams, running her growing business was beginning to put more pressure on her. Thank goodness her final exams were tomorrow. The only bad thing about it was, five days later she was to appear in court.

She glanced up from the business management textbook in her hand. Adam stood in front of the window in the living room, his face turned toward the darkened night, his hands shoved deep into his pockets. Over the past days he had grown quieter and quieter.

Laying the book aside, Lily went to him. "What's the matter?"

"It's not getting any better."

Her heart clenched. "There's always tomorrow."

"Perhaps not for me."

"Adam, you can't give up." She placed her hand on his shoulder. "Please."

His hand came out of his pocket to glide lightly over her cheek. "Don't mind me. Go back to studying."

Her body trembled. "My head is full. I'd rather take a break and go sit in the swing."

"Mind if I come with you?"

"I insist." Lightly looping her arm through his, she allowed him to lead them outside to the swing. As they sat side by side, hands clasped, Adam set the swing in motion. Neither spoke for a long time.

Lilly broke the silence. "Miracles happen, Adam. It was a miracle that my car stopped near here, but I didn't know it at the time. Don't give up, no matter what."

He squeezed her hand. "I realize how important faith is, Lilly. People think the doctor heals. We don't. We prescribe, incise, but it's a higher power who decides the outcome. I forgot that, and started to depend on myself."

"I used to wonder why God let Myron abuse me. I gave up on Myron, but not on God. You can't, either."

"I used to wonder why me. Why not some other creep? Then I'd wonder what if I had given them the keys? What if the light had been green instead of red? What if some other neurologist had been on call instead of me? You know what I finally decided?"

"What?"

"Even if I knew the reason, I'd still be blind," he said quietly. "It's up to me how I handle it from here."

Jonathan woke up first that morning, then immediately turned to gaze at the woman in the bed beside him. His love for Eleanor still had the power to make him weak. She was all that he had ever wished for. He'd come by late last night and stayed. Noticeably upset about Kristen's trip to New York, she'd gone to sleep in his arms. They hadn't made love, but he had cherished being with her just as much. Love meant caring and sharing in good and bad times.

His mother had been wrong to deny herself love all these years. Even after his father had died, after the woman he'd run off with had deserted him when the judge awarded the restaurant to Jonathan's mother, she had remained bitter. She treated her customers with the Southern hospitality they expected at a four-star restaurant in New Orleans, but she did it out of greed, not graciousness. Nothing he had done or said made the slightest difference in the way she thought. To her, love meant being vulnerable. She'd missed out on so much.

Eleanor stirred in her sleep. The sheet slipped down over her breasts. Desire stirred. He enjoyed watching her, touching her, and he'd finally gotten her out of reaching for her nightgown when they finished making love. He enjoyed their bare skin touching while they were asleep. Last night he had solved the problem by undressing her himself, then holding her until she went to sleep. But there was another enjoyable advantage. At moments like this he didn't have to worry about a nightgown.

In one smooth moment he moved over her, pressed his lips to hers, and gently slid into her moist heat, reveling that even in her sleep she wanted him as he wanted her.

"Jonathan." She breathed his name as her eyelids fluttered open.

He lifted his head and stared down at her. In her eyes he saw all that he had ever wanted or desired. He moved and her eyelids fluttered closed. Her arms went around his shoulders.

"I love you, Eleanor."

"I love you, too."

He took them on a slow ride, letting the pleasure build until her nails dug into his back, her legs locked around his hips. The tempo increased; the thrusts were deep and exquisite. When release came, it was explosive and powerful.

Gathering her to him, Jonathan rolled over in bed, his breathing labored. "I may be getting too old for this."

Her lips brushed across the curve of his jaw. "I hope not."

Chuckling, he came up with her and headed for the shower. "Eleanor, my love, you do keep a man humble."

"It's a knack."

Eleanor hung up the phone and glanced at the clock. Seven-thirty A.M. New York was an hour ahead. Kristen should be in her room. Picking up the phone, Eleanor called Jonathan at his house. He'd left forty minutes ago.

"Hello."

"She still doesn't answer." Even before Jonathan left, Eleanor had tried to call Kristen. She'd continued ever since.

"She probably went downstairs for breakfast." The cordless phone in one hand, Jonathan pulled his navy blue suit from the closet. "She's all right."

Eleanor sat on the edge of the sofa and wished Jonathan were still there. "I suppose. It's just that—"

"She's your baby and your worry." Opening a drawer, he grabbed a clean pair of socks and tossed them on the bed to join the suit and fresh underwear. "She'll call you after the interview."

"I suppose. Have a good day."

"You, too. Love you."

"Love you," Eleanor repeated and hung up the phone.

Rising, she went to the house to see if Adam had heard from Kristen. He hadn't. Not wanting to worry him, she wished Lilly good luck on her final exams that day and went back to the cottage and called again. No answer. Nor did Kristen answer any of the other calls that followed.

Eleanor debated for all of two seconds whether having a nervous mother would detract from Kristen's interview, then reached for the phone. She got a recording at the museum, which didn't open until ten. Her arms folded, she paced the floor and watched the clock.

Kristen had checked out of the hotel that morning without listening to her messages on the off chance that Eric might have called. Just thinking his name made her feel stupid and naive. Her hand holding her stomach, she glanced out the window of the plane as it readied for takeoff to Dallas. There hadn't been a flight to Shreveport until later that afternoon, and she wanted to leave New York.

"Would you like anything to drink?"

"No, thank you." Kristen didn't even glance at the stewardess in first class. She didn't think she could stand to look at another blonde without recalling what a terrible mess she had almost made of her life.

Out of courtesy to the museum's director and respect for her professor, she'd kept the interview. She'd worn a hastily purchased pair of shades and lied that her allergies were the cause of her red, swollen eyes. She had expressed her regret that she had decided against moving to New York, thanked the director for his time, then gone outside and hailed a cab.

"You have about five minutes before you'll have to cut off all electronic equipment," the stewardess advised the businesswoman next to Kristen. The woman had a phone in one manicured hand, the fingers of the other hand flying over her laptop.

Suddenly the words Kristen had typed on the laptop at Eric's urging came hurtling back to her. Embarrassing, lewd words, but she had done it because she thought he loved her. Opening her purse, she pulled out her credit card and reached for the phone.

Adam answered on the second ring. She didn't give him time to ask questions. "I finished the interview. I'm flying to Dallas to visit friends. I'll probably spend the night. I have to hang up now. Bye."

Settling back in the seat, she glanced out the window as the plane backed away from the gate. She was leaving New York, but the shame was going with her.

Adam had planned everything with his mother's help. She'd thrown herself into the preparations once she knew Kristen was fine. When Lilly arrived back from her final exam, he'd purposefully kept her busy in his study until Jonathan had entered. That had been the signal. They'd gone into the dining room together, where his mother had prepared a surprise dinner.

He'd heard Lilly's cry of delight, felt her arms around him, and realized again how much he missed seeing. He'd taken so much for granted in his life. Not anymore.

Seating Lilly to his right at the table, he picked up his wineglass and proposed a toast to the beginning of a career and life for her. Sipping his wine, he came to a decision about his own life.

It remained to be seen if it was the beginning for him or the end.

Unable to sleep, Adam had come downstairs a little after midnight and gone outside. He smelled the rain in the air, listened to the angry thunder, the answering crackle of lightning.

"Adam, are you all right?"

Somehow he wasn't surprised that she was there. Since she'd come into his life she had always been there when he needed her the most.

He held out his hand and she was immediately by his side. "I used to enjoy watching storms. I enjoyed so much that I may never again."

Lilly bit her lower lip; her hand tightened in his. "Adam, you can't give up hope."

"I haven't, but neither can I go on living this way. I called Louis when I went upstairs after dinner. My surgery is scheduled for the day after tomorrow."

"Adam . . ." Fear choked the rest of her words off.

Gently he drew her into his arms. "What have I told you about wasting tears on me?"

She clutched him to her. "I've never met a better man."

Needing to lighten the mood, Adam lifted his head and said, "You didn't think that when we first met."

"Deep down I must have or I wouldn't have stayed."

His hand palmed her cheek. Unbeknownst to him, her eyelids drifted shut. "Maybe I'll be able to go with you for your court hearing."

She bit her lip. "I have to do this on my own, or else I can never be free of him."

"I thought you'd be stubborn about this," he said.

"Some paths you have to walk alone."

"Just so you know at the end of the path I'll be waiting. I'd put off this surgery if I thought you'd let me go with you."

The implication of his words swept through her. Her voice trembled when she asked, "Do you mean that?"

"Do you have to ask?"

"Adam," she said; her arms went around his waist. She felt love and wanted to love. "I wish—"

"Shhh. We'll save all the wishes until you're free and I can see. Now come inside and read me a story. I don't think either of us is going to sleep much tonight."

Kristen checked into a hotel at the airport in Dallas, then checked out around nine. She wanted to be around people who loved her. Unable to get a commercial flight to Shreveport, she rented a car and started driving. She stopped once for gas on the outskirts of town.

As she pulled into the entrance of Adam's house, tension whipped through her again. They'd ask questions about the interview, her trip, Eric. She couldn't tell them. She couldn't.

Leaving the car in one of the two empty bays, she used her key and entered the house through the side door. Thunder drowned out the sound. She was at the stairs when she saw the light shining from beneath the closed door of Adam's study. Quietly she went up the stairs and into her room.

The laptop on the desk in her room was a silent condemnation. Guilt and shame ate at her. Restless, she went back outside as quietly as she had come. She didn't know where she was heading until the path straightened and she saw her mother's cottage.

And her mother and Jonathan in the doorway. Their mouths were pressed passionately together. Jonathan's hands greedily cupped her mother's hips. One of them moaned.

Rage swept through Kristen like the hot blast of a furnace. They were going at it like two animals in heat. "How could you!"

Eleanor jerked away from Jonathan and stared into the enraged face of her daughter a few feet away. "Kristen—"

"I knew something was going on between you."

"Please, let me explain," Eleanor said, reaching out to her daughter. This couldn't be happening.

"How could you defame Father's memory like this, and with his best friend?"

"Your mother and I have nothing to be ashamed of," Jonathan said. "We love each other."

"You love each other so much that you're sneaking off screw—"

"That's enough, Kristen," Jonathan said. "I won't have you talk to your mother that way."

Kristen swept her windblown hair out of her angry face. "How are you going to stop me? Hit me?"

"Jonathan. Kristen. Please," Eleanor pleaded, her tears mixing with the drizzling rain that had started. "You know he'd never hurt you."

"He's hurting me now! You both are!" Tears streamed down Kristen's cheeks. "How can you do something like this? Like a common slut."

Jonathan advanced on Kristen. Eleanor caught his arm. "No."

Kristen didn't flinch. "He couldn't hurt me any more than I already am. I hate you. I hate both of you!" Turning, she ran into the night.

"Kristen." Eleanor started after her.

"Eleanor, wait." Jonathan caught her before she had gone two steps, his strength and determination unshakable.

Eleanor strained against his hold. "Let me go. I have to go after her."

"What about me, Eleanor?" he asked, his voice filled with despair.

She blinked as if she didn't understand him, then turned to look in the direction Kristen had fled. "Kristen!"

"Eleanor." He turned her to face him. "Do you love me?"

"Jon—"

"Do you love me?" The words were quiet and wrenched from his soul.

Eleanor finally stopped fighting and understood the question and the implication behind it. Her heart broke, but there could be only one answer. "My children have to come first."

He stared at her a long time, then released his hold. "Good-bye, Eleanor."

She didn't hear him. She was already running into the rain-swept night. He'd lost her. The pain was crippling. He'd gambled and lost. He wasn't sure he could survive this time.

Chapter Twenty-Two

Kristen burst into the house and headed straight for the one person who could console her. Jonathan and her mother had betrayed her. Not pausing to knock, she opened the study door to see Adam and Lilly sitting on the couch, her head on his shoulder, a closed book in her hands.

Lilly straightened immediately, but not before Kristen had seen Adam's hand in her hair. "What are you doing?" Kristen asked angrily.

"Kristen," Adam straightened up. "When did you get home? How—"

"Apparently I wasn't missed by you or Mother." The look Kristen shot Lilly was accusatory and filled with venom.

Lilly tucked her head and stared down at the closed book in her hand.

"Kristen, what's gotten into you?" Frowning, Adam removed his arm from around Lilly's shoulders.

Jonathan had taken her mother; now Lilly sought to take Adam. Kristen had no intention of losing another person she loved. "I want to see my brother alone."

The book clutched to her chest, Lilly stared at the other woman. "I'll go make some tea. Don't you think it would be best if you changed out of those wet clothes first?"

"You've been out in the rain?" Adam's frown deepened as he came to his feet. "Kristen, what's the matter?"

"Send her away, Adam!" Kristen shouted, her hands gripped by her sides.

Before Adam could comment, Eleanor, drenched, her eyes wide and frightened, came into the room. "Kristen, we have to talk."

Kristen refused to look at her. "I have nothing to say to you."

"What's going on here?" Adam asked.

Kristen finally faced Eleanor. "Are you going to tell him what you've been doing or shall I, Mother?"

Tears mixed with rain ran down Eleanor's cheeks. She reached out to her daughter, but the anger on her face had her lowering her hand. "Kristen, please, try—"

She spun toward her brother. "I just caught her and Jonathan going at it like rabbits," she told him, her voice filled with pain and loathing.

"We were just kissing," Eleanor said.

Kristen jerked around to her mother, her eyes filled with rage. "Would it have stopped at that, Mother? Would it?"

Eleanor hung her head in silent admission. But Kristen hadn't finished.

"He had his hands all over you," Kristen accused. "After all the talk about saving myself for marriage. You acted like a slut."

Eleanor gasped.

"Kristen, that's enough," Adam told her.

But pain and anger ruled Kristen now, and she had no intention of stopping until she had inflicted as much pain on them as she felt they had inflicted on her. This time her anger was directed toward the brother she adored. "You're only saying that because it's obvious you were about to get it on with Lilly."

Adam came around the table and unerringly stopped in front of his sister. "When did you get so foulmouthed and mean-spirited? If Mother was with Jonathan, I'm not going to condemn her. I've learned life is too short not to go after what you want."

His words were like a slap in Kristen's face. She had no one.

"I don't know why I was silly enough to come to you. You always take her side. You two have always been closer. She always loved you best. Father loved me best, and he's gone."

Eleanor's sharp intake of breath cut across the room. "Kristen!"

"Well, I won't stand in the way of either of you. You all can go back to your sordid affairs. I'm leaving!" Whirling, she rushed from the room.

"Kristen."

Eleanor started after her. Adam stopped her.

"Let her go, Mother," Adam said.

"I can't. This is my fault." She tried to pull away, then finally gave up. "It's my fault. What have I done?"

Adam helped her to a chair. Her body seemed to crumple. "Jonathan's a good man."

"I can't lose Kristen." Her hands covered her face. "She hates me."

Adam felt for his mother and sister and for Jonathan. He hadn't thought of the two of them together, but somehow he wasn't surprised, annoyed, or shocked. They both deserved the best, and in his opinion that was exactly what they had found in each other. "She doesn't hate you. She idolized Father. I'll go up and talk to her."

Eleanor's hands came away from her face and reached in desperation for her son's. "You'll make her stay, won't you?"

"I'll try, but sometimes you just have to let go." He turned his head in Lilly's direction. He'd been distracted, but he didn't think she had moved since Kristen began hurling accusations. "Stay with Mother."

"Of course."

Giving his mother a smile of encouragement, he went to Kristen's room and knocked. "Kristen, I'd like to talk to you."

"I don't want to talk to you!" she yelled through the door.

He knocked again. He hadn't thought it would be easy. "Come on, Sis; open the door."

The door opened, but as he went to step in she brushed by him. "Where are you going?"

"What does it look like?"

"I wouldn't know."

Silence stretched for a long moment. "Dammit, Adam. Don't you make me feel sorry for you!" she cried, her voice wavery.

"There's been enough of that. All I want to know is how to make it better." He held out his hand. "We could always talk."

"You can't this time. You don't need me. No one needs me." Her tone was one of absolute misery.

"Kristen, where did you get a crazy idea in your head like that?"

"You have Lilly. Mother has Jonathan," she tossed back flippantly. "I'm superfluous."

"That's ridiculous. We all love you," Adam told her, willing her to understand. "Someday you'll fall in love and you'll understand what I mean. Loving doesn't diminish your capacity to love. It increases it."

"Is that what Lilly has done for you?"

He wasn't sure, but he didn't think he heard sarcasm in her voice. "Yes. I'm not sure how it's all going to work out, but I'm willing to hang in there and trust that it will. Can't you be happy for me?"

"She makes you happy?"

"Very. I can't explain it, except I don't feel blind when I'm with her," he said, feeling the rightness of his words. Lilly had been his salvation. "Perhaps you'll find the same thing with Eric."

He heard the suitcase drop to the floor. "No, I won't. Last night he showed me he didn't want me."

Adam hurt for her and wished he could get his hands on Eric for five minutes. "Do you want to talk about it?"

"No." Her voice hitched. "I was such a fool."

Adam moved closer, the pain in her voice heart-wrenching. Kristen kept too much locked inside. "You're a caring, intelligent, beautiful woman. It's Eric's loss that he couldn't see that. It may sound cruel, but you're better off finding out what kind of man he is now rather than later."

"I really loved him, Adam." Her voice hitched again.

"I wish I could take the pain away, but it will pass. I promise."

"You've never broken a promise yet."

"No, I haven't, and I never will."

Their arms closed around each other at the same time. Her body shook with the force of her tears. Adam held her, brushing her tears away.

"I want you to listen carefully to me. Mother and Father loved each other very much. Neither would have wanted the other to be alone. There's not a better man on the planet than Jonathan. If Father hadn't thought so, he wouldn't have asked him to watch out for us."

She twisted her head away. "I don't want to talk about it."

They might call him stubborn, but he knew Kristen was just as stubborn.

"Then just listen. Mother deserves to be loved. If that man is Jonathan, you have to be willing to let go."

"He can't take Father's place," she said tightly.

"He doesn't want to. Jonathan has always been his own man."

"You didn't see what I saw," Kristen said, then groaned, "I don't seem able to keep from saying the wrong things. Maybe you should let me go."

Adam leaned his head against hers. "We're family and you're staying. You don't have to tiptoe around me any longer, Kristen. And even if I had seen them, I don't think I would condemn them the way you have. You wouldn't, either, if your relationship hadn't ended badly."

His sister was a caring woman. Misery and heartache had caused her to forget, but he knew better than most how much family meant during those times. "Now, come downstairs. You owe Mother and Lilly an apology."

Kristen pulled away. He could imagine her shaking her head of straight black hair. "I don't want to see anyone."

"You're coming," he said firmly. "This family has been through enough. I've caused my share of problems, but whatever happened, we always were assured of each other's love. That hasn't changed."

"I'll come, but I'm not changing my mind about Mother and Jonathan."

Adam squeezed her hand. "One hurdle at a time."

Her head downcast, Eleanor sat huddled on the sofa, her arms wrapped around her. She hadn't reacted at all when Lilly placed a cashmere afghan around her shoulders or dried her hair with a towel from the downstairs bathroom.

"Mother," Adam said from beside his sister.

Eleanor's head came up; her shoulders straightened. The afghan slid unnoticed from her shoulders as she came to her feet. "Kristen, I'm sorry. Please. I won't see Jonathan again."

"Mo—"

"I promise," she said, cutting Adam off. "I love you. I won't let anything come between us."

Kristen blinked back the tears in her eyes. Her chest felt as if it had a tight band around it. "I don't want to see Unc—him for a while."

"You won't." Eleanor closed her heart to the misery sweeping through her.

Her children had always come first, but it had never hurt before. "You won't."

"Why don't you both get out of those wet clothes?" Lilly suggested. "Eleanor, I'll get the bedroom across the hall from Kristen's ready for you."

Uncertain, Eleanor looked at Kristen. "Is that all right with you?"

The tears that had welled in her daughter's eyes spilled over. "Mother, I'm so sorry. I didn't mean those things I said. I didn't. It's just—"

Eleanor pulled her daughter into her arms. "It's all right. It's all right, Kristen."

Kristen lifted her head from her mother's shoulder and stared at Lilly. "Please, forgive me, but I wouldn't blame you if you didn't."

"Don't worry about it." Lilly smiled although her heart was breaking at the misery and heartache in Eleanor's and Kristen's faces. Jonathan had to be hurting, too. All because they were in love. Love shouldn't hurt, but Lilly was coming to realize that it did. She had waited most of her life, and her waiting would continue. Adam could never be hers no matter how much she wished otherwise.

Kristen sniffed. "Thank you."

Adam curved his arms around his mother and sister. "I'd planned to tell you in the morning, but I think now is as good a time as any. My vitrectomy is scheduled for the day after tomorrow."

Shock quickly replaced by apprehension rippled across the women's faces. "Are you sure, Adam?" Eleanor asked.

"I'm tired of my life being in limbo." His mouth firmed. "One way or the other, I want to know. I've already called and chartered the plane."

"If you hadn't stopped me from leaving, I never would have forgiven myself!" Kristen cried.

Eleanor switched her attention to her younger child. "There's no reason for you to leave."

"If you're lying, I'll leave and I'll never come back. I swear," Kristen warned, her gaze steady.

"I've never lied to you." Seeing her daughter begin to tremble, Eleanor took charge. "Come on; let's get out of these wet clothes. Maybe you can let me have a gown and Lilly can bring some hot tea."

"I'll bring it right up," Lilly said, escaping to the kitchen. Love was supposed to heal, not tear families apart.

"You're all right?"

Startled, Lilly jerked around. Adam moved toward her with all the surety of a sighted person and just as silently. Contrary to popular belief, people who were blind didn't tap their canes on the floor unless they were using the echo of the sound to locate solid objects. "You shouldn't worry about me. It's your family and Jonathan who are miserable."

He stopped in front of her and brushed his knuckles down her cheek. "I worry about all the people I care about."

For a few heavenly seconds she closed her eyes and savored his brief touch, which left her legs weak and shaky. "You're a good man, Adam."

His smile was slow and easy and caused her heart to pound wildly in her chest. "I know a lot of people who might not agree with you."

"I know a lot who would." Because she wanted to reach out and touch him and yield to the sweet melting need she felt for him, she picked up the teapot instead and placed it on the tray. She wouldn't make the lies Myron said about her true. "I'd better take this upstairs."

"All right." He started from the room. "I'll be waiting in my room."

"Kristen might not approve."

"I'm not giving you up." He disappeared around the corner.

Lilly's hands shook as she lifted the tray. *If only* . . . she thought and shook her head. She had a lot to be thankful for. Wishing for more was greedy, but when she was with Adam she felt like being greedy and grabbing with both hands. Readying the tea, she took it upstairs and knocked.

"Come in!" Kristen called.

Lilly opened the door to see Eleanor sitting behind Kristen on the white iron queen-size bed brushing her daughter's hair. Mounds of colorful throw pillows were on the bed behind them. Both women wore white bathrobes.

Lilly set the tray on the top of the turned-back-down bedspread. "Let me know if you need anything."

"We won't," Kristen said, staring at Lilly intently. "Adam came in to say good night. I imagine he's waiting for you."

"Yes." Lilly felt a blush heat her cheeks.

"Good night, Lilly." Despite Eleanor's drawn features and red-rimmed eyes, she managed to smile.

"Good night."

Lilly went to Adam's room and knocked. She had years of loneliness ahead of her; she was grabbing every bit of pleasure she could.

"Come in."

He was sitting in his chair, the book in his lap. "I was beginning to wonder if you were coming."

Crossing the room, she took the book from his lap and sat facing him on the leather footstool by the side of his chair. "I'm here. Now where did we leave off?"

Long after Lilly had returned to her room and gone to bed, she lay awake. The Wakefields were a close-knit family, perhaps too close to allow anyone else in. She didn't have any illusions about Adam's feelings for her. He depended on her, but he didn't love her. She wasn't sophisticated, beautiful, wealthy, or cultured. She'd never traveled farther than 300 miles from her birthplace until she'd gone to California. He'd settled for her because she was comfortable. He was at ease around her. He might tell himself it went deeper than that, but she knew better. And once his sight returned, he'd leave.

Still, she wanted him to see again, prayed nightly that God would grant that miracle. She'd lose him, but the world would regain a great surgeon and he'd stand at the helm of his speedboat again, plan his garden, and perhaps think of her sometimes.

She knew she'd never forget him.

A little after ten the next morning Lilly pulled her car into the parking space across from the medical center in downtown Shreveport and switched off the key. By the time she had gotten out of the car and gone around to the passenger door, Adam was already out of the car.

"You're sure you want to do this? Kristen won't like it," she warned, allowing Adam to take her arm.

"Jonathan deserved better than he's getting. He took enough crap from me not to have to take it from Kristen as well."

"Curb." Lilly waited until Adam stepped on the sidewalk, then continued down the sidewalk. "You had reason."

"I had an excuse. So does she." He squinted at the bright reflection of light. The medical center was thirteen stories of golden glass. "Jonathan's office building is dead ahead," he said, pleased with himself.

"In the center is the revolving door. We better take the outer one." She pulled open the heavy glass door. "I almost lost one of my pies that way."

"You sure you're not saying that to spare my feelings?" he questioned lightly, but she heard the disquiet beneath his words.

"What I'm sparing you is me tripping all over you while trying to get out of the thing." Crossing the lobby, she jabbed the button for the elevator. "The people behind or in front of me always go too fast. I bet you're the same way."

"Guilty." He heard the *ping* announcing the arrival of the elevator, the doors opening. Lilly stepped on first. He followed closely.

The elevator stopped on the third and fifth floors. People piled on and they were crowded like sardines. It annoyed him as it always did until he felt the pressure of Lilly's soft breasts pressed against his back. He'd bet her head was downcast, her cheeks flushed with embarrassment. He probably should be ashamed of himself for enjoying the sensation. He smiled. He wasn't in the least.

The elevator door opened and they stepped off. "That was interesting."

"I . . . I . . . guess so." Her hand trembling, she opened the door to Jonathan's office. Pale pastels and light greeted them.

"There's a small couch in the corner." Lilly led Adam to a light blue seat, then went to the receptionist, trying to forget the tingling sensation in her breasts and how she had wantonly wanted to press her body closer to Adam's.

"Hi, Sandy."

The pretty brunette glanced up from behind the partial glass enclosure. The welcoming smile on her heart-shaped face widened. "Hello, Lilly. Who ordered a pie this time?"

"No one," Lilly answered. "Could you please let Dr. Delacroix know that Dr. Wakefield would like to see him?"

The receptionist's hazel eyes widened perceptibly, then searched the waiting area before stopping on Adam in the far corner of the room. "Right away."

Lilly went back and sat on the love seat beside Adam. "Sandy, the receptionist, went to tell Jonathan."

He nodded, then leaned over. "I hope I'm not the only man in here."

"You aren't," she whispered, then glanced at the other two men. One wore a business suit; the other wore jeans and a T-shirt. They were probably husbands of the pregnant women they were seated beside. Instead of looking at the numerous fashion and parenting magazines on the table and in the racks, the couples were talking softly to each other.

A baby represented the completion and the beginning of a circle of a couple's love. Lilly had regretted that she hadn't gotten pregnant after she married Myron; she'd foolishly thought a baby might change him and prayed to get pregnant. Thankfully, God knew better.

The wooden door beside the glass-enclosed reception area opened and Jonathan came out. He spoke to his patients but never slacked his long stride toward Adam. Jonathan wore a starched, pristine white lab coat over a white shirt and silk tie. Tasseled loafers peeked from beneath tailored gray pants. He looked as tired and as miserable as Eleanor had this morning when she thought no one was looking, Lilly thought.

"Is she all right?" Jonathan asked the moment he stopped in front of them.

"About as well as you'd imagine." Adam stood. "Can we talk?"

"Come on." Jonathan took Adam's arm, then stopped to ask Lilly, "Will you be all right here?"

She picked up a fashion magazine. "I'm fine. Go on."

Jonathan didn't need any further urging to take Adam to his office. "No matter what you think, this is my fault and not Eleanor's," he said when he closed his office door.

"I'm not here to find fault, Jonathan," Adam said, extending his cane. "I've known you all my life. You've never committed a single act that would make me doubt your integrity."

Jonathan paced away, then returned. "I love your mother."

"If I thought otherwise, this cane would be on your head instead of the floor," Adam said calmly.

Jonathan's lips curved slightly upward for a brief moment. "How does Kristen feel?"

Adam wouldn't lie. "At the moment she can't accept the idea of you and Mother together."

"Oh, God. What a mess." Jonathan went to the window to look out toward the sprawling Shreveport Memorial Hospital. "Eleanor loves her children more than her life. She'd cut off her arm with a smile on her face before willingly hurting either of you."

"That doesn't mean she doesn't love you."

"It means I don't have a chance. I'd fight for her if I thought I'd win, but I wouldn't, and Eleanor and Kristen's relationship would be damaged irrevocably."

"I'm sorry." Jonathan knew Eleanor as well as Adam. "Kristen is going through a rough time now. She and Eric broke up. She's not talking, but it's obvious she's hurting badly. It's my bet there's another woman involved."

Jonathan turned from the window. "The little bastard."

Adam wasn't surprised by the venom in Jonathan's voice on behalf of Kristen. She may have tried to cut Jonathan out of her life, but she'd always be a part of his. "Kristen thinks you loved me best; I always knew it was her."

Jonathan nodded. "She needed me. You were always independent and cocky."

"She still needs us, Jonathan," Adam said, his hand clenched on the cane. "She's still trying to find her place in this crazy world."

"You think I don't know that?" Jonathan asked heatedly. "I won't make it any more difficult for her. I told you I'm out of the picture. If that's all you came to tell me, you can go. I have patients to see."

Adam took a step toward the shadow that moved through the bright light. "I came because I admire you and I don't think there's a better man in the world for my mother or to be a friend to this family. I came because I wanted to let you know that my surgery is scheduled for eight in the morning."

Strong fingers closed around his upper forearms. "I . . . I wish I could be there with you."

"I'll have Lilly call when we know."

"You do that." Jonathan's hands fell; he stepped back.

Adam extended his hand. "I'll be gone for several weeks, but I'll see you when I get back."

Jonathan's hand closed around Adam's; then he pulled him roughly against his chest. Adam had come a long way. Seeing no longer just meant visually; it meant being with a person. "You take care of yourself and tell Scott he had damn well better live up to his reputation."

"Is that the only message you want me to deliver?"

There was a long silence; then, as if the word was dragged from the depth of his soul, Jonathan said, "Yes."

The jet was waiting for them on the runway. Lilly followed Adam up the stairs and into the plane. Eleanor and Kristen were already aboard and seated side by side.

"You saw him, didn't you? That's the errand you had to take care of, isn't it?" From her window seat Kristen peered around her mother's suddenly tense body. The magazine in Eleanor's hand shook.

Adam allowed Lilly to take her seat, then sat beside her and buckled his seat belt. "I saw Jonathan. I wanted to let him know about the surgery."

Kristen's gaze flew to the door. "He's not coming, is he?"

"No, Jonathan doesn't want us to take sides," Adam said.

"Meaning I do," she tossed back.

"Meaning he loves you." Adam removed his glasses, trying to will himself to see through the smoky haze. It was useless, as useless as trying to get his sister to understand that the love between Jonathan and their mother didn't diminish what she and their father had shared. But he wasn't giving up on either.

"We all do. Love is what has kept this family together through the bad times. That's not going to change. Did you stop loving me when I was going through my depression and being an ass?"

"Adam."

He ignored his mother's outrage. "Did you, Kristen?"

"No."

"Then why would you think we'd stop loving you?" He didn't wait for an answer. "You're hurting and you may want to hurt. I can handle that because I know deep down the capacity for love you have. I remember the little girl who always wanted to include everyone at her party, went out of her way to help others. That person understood love and loving."

"I'm not a little girl anymore."

"No, you aren't. You're an adult, so act like one."

Kristen looked at the window; then a sound made her turn. She glanced around. Her mother's head was bowed. Kristen heard the sound again. Frowning, she saw the teardrops splatter on the page of the fashion magazine in her mother's hands.

Quickly Kristen glanced away, fighting her own tears.

There was a steady procession of hospital staff in and out of Adam's room the next morning. Although vitrectomy surgery was usually done in day surgery, Dr. Scott had decided to keep Adam overnight for precautionary measures. Thus he'd been given a private room instead of a cubicle in the day surgery area. The fragrant scent of flowers lingered in the air. Flowers had been in his suite when he checked in, and more had arrived as the morning lengthened.

"You ready to do this?" Dr. Scott asked, coming to Adam's bedside.

"You should be in the OR scrubbing up," Adam said playfully, grasping the hand that took his.

"Still giving orders." Dr. Scott turned to Eleanor and glanced around the room. "Where's Jonathan?"

"He couldn't make it," Adam answered into the growing silence.

"Must have been mighty important," Dr. Scott said. "I thought he'd want to scrub in and watch over my shoulder. He's hovered over you like a guardian angel in the past."

"You'll take care of Adam, won't you, Louis?" Eleanor asked from the other side of the bed.

"I've got the best team in the country. We'll be in about two or three hours, depending on what we find. I'll keep you posted," he said, then nodded to the orderly standing just inside the door.

The man opened the door and pulled in a gurney. A middle-aged woman came in behind him wearing a pink smock.

"The volunteer will show you where to wait."

Eleanor leaned over and kissed Adam on the cheek. Kristen followed suit. "We'll be waiting and praying." They left with the volunteer.

"I'm missing a kiss," Adam said lightly.

Lilly flushed.

"I don't think you meant me," Dr. Scott said with a broad grin. "I'll herd everyone outside and give you one minute."

"Lilly," Adam said as soon as he heard the sound of the door swinging open, then closed. "Did I embarrass you?"

"No. I wanted to kiss you," she admitted truthfully. It would be one more memory.

"Then kiss me." Her mouth brushed against his, a gentle pressing of lips; then her cheek was against his. He felt the wetness. "I'll be all right. Either way. I'll be all right."

"I know."

"Do me a favor? You'll know before I do. Call Jonathan for me."

"I will."

The door opened and Dr. Scott and the orderly came back. "They're waiting for you outside, Ms. Crawford."

Squeezing Adam's hand, she started from the room. Opening the door, she heard the doctor say, "You sure know how to pick 'em, Adam."

Her heart in her throat, she paused in spite of herself and listened for a response from Adam. "You don't have to tell me she's beautiful, Louis; I already know."

Letting the door swing shut, Lilly fought the stinging in her eyes. More than anything she wanted Adam to regain his sight. What she didn't want was to see the disappointment on his face when he saw her for the first time.

Chapter Twenty~Three

Adam drifted in and out of consciousness on the operating table, catching bits and pieces of conversation about a golf tournament, needing more suctioning, the high cost of malpractice insurance, the cute 11–7 nurse in ICU. He tried to remain conscious, but the anesthesia was taking him down under a black layer of clouds. His last conscious thought was a prayer that when he awoke the clouds would have lifted forever from his eyes.

Waiting had never been easy for Eleanor. With each dragging minute, she prayed for Adam and wished Jonathan were with them. The day surgery waiting room was empty except for her and Kristen. Lilly had gone to the chapel. Kristen had wanted to stay, and Eleanor had stayed with her. The door opened and Eleanor turned and blinked.

"Jonathan!" Eleanor cried and started toward him, then stopped abruptly as if she had run into a solid wall. She turned away, her eyes shut.

Jonathan's gaze hungrily followed Eleanor; then he saw Kristen sitting in a straight chair looking at him with narrow, watchful eyes. Despite her phone call to him early that morning asking him to come as quickly as possible, she obviously hadn't forgiven or accepted him. How much pain was a man supposed to take in a lifetime? He started to back out of the room.

"Where're you going?" Kristen asked casually, her long legs crossed at the ankles, her hands loosely linked in her lap.

"Is this your idea of a sick joke?" Jonathan asked, his jaw clenched.

She shrugged. "I thought when a man really cared about a woman, he'd fight for her. But I see you don't deserve my mother."

Jonathan stalked across the room until he towered over the young woman he loved like a daughter. After two sleepless nights he'd been pushed to his limit. "Don't you dare tell me I don't love your mother. I've loved her from the first time I saw her. I loved her through her pregnancies with Adam and you, felt blessed and tortured that she and Randolph allowed me to be a part of your lives. But I know what you and Adam mean to her. I won't make her choose."

"Afraid you'd lose?" Kristen taunted, her gaze intent.

"Eleanor would lose. When she hurts, I hurt. Maybe one day you'll be the woman I thought you were and realize that." He whirled to leave.

"Jonathan, wait," Eleanor said. "Kristen, I told you I wouldn't see Jonathan again. But what you've done is reprehensible."

Kristen studied her mauve-colored manicured nails. "I had to see something for myself."

"How badly you could hurt us?" her mother asked, fighting the stinging moisture in her eyes.

"No. How much you loved each other," Kristen said quietly and looked up. "You've been miserable since the other night, but you would have let him walk out again, and he would have given you up to keep from hurting you further. It seems I didn't know what love is any more than Eric did."

"He hurt you." Jonathan's eyes went flint-hard.

"I'll get over it." Kristen came to her feet. "Now, give my mother a kiss and we can go join Lilly in the chapel."

Jonathan didn't move. "I have to know something first." He faced Eleanor. "I can't go through losing you again. If Kristen suddenly decided she didn't want me around, would you walk out on me again? Before you answer, be sure."

"Don't I have anything to say about this?" Kristen asked.

"No," Jonathan and Eleanor answered at the same time.

Hope shone in his eyes. "I love you, Eleanor. I loved you yesterday. I love you today. I'll love you forever."

"I love you," she repeated, then rushed into the shelter of his arms. She was lifted and held tight against his wide chest. When her feet touched the floor his lips were on hers. The kiss was full of need and promises that would never be broken.

Eleanor's shaky fingertips replaced her lips. "I couldn't stand to lose you again." She turned to Kristen. "You have to live your life just as I have to live mine. I love him."

Kristen glanced from her mother to Jonathan. It didn't take much effort to remember a similar look between her mother and father. Her father had loved her mother unconditionally. Adam was right. He wouldn't have wanted her to be alone. "So when's the wedding?"

Eleanor flushed again. "He hasn't—"

"Will you marry me, Eleanor?" Jonathan asked, cutting her off.

Eleanor beamed. "Yes. Yes. A thousand times yes."

Kristen smiled, her own heart lighter. "I'd say we have a big surprise for Adam when he wakes up."

The instant Eleanor saw Dr. Scott's face she knew. Tears flooded her eyes. She leaned into Jonathan. Lilly and Kristen rose in tandem from the leather couch.

Grinning broadly, Dr. Scott stopped in front of Eleanor. "He came through the surgery just fine. Optic nerve and retina intact in both eyes. Macula looks healthy. I removed the hemorrhage without any problems. Barring complications, he should be back to twenty-thirty within a couple of months."

Jonathan clapped the surgeon on the back. "I always heard you had the best hands next to God."

"That's a compliment I don't take lightly," he said. "Glad you showed up."

Jonathan glanced down at Eleanor. "My family needed me."

Adam woke slowly. He heard voices. He blinked. Blackness surrounded him. His heart booming, he tried to send a message to his brain. He needed—

"Dr. Wakefield, you're in the recovery room." A gentle hand restrained his hand from touching the bandages on his eyes. "You came through just fine. Optic nerve intact, retina intact, macula intact, hemorrhage removed," continued a calm, soothing voice that understood what he'd want to know. "You're probably a little groggy. Dr. Scott went to talk to your family. You're going to be fine. Try not to touch the bandages on your eyes. You're fine. You're fine."

With a litany of thanks going though his brain, Adam drifted back to sleep. He was going to see again.

The next time he woke up, they were moving him to his room. He barely got inside before he heard the women, then Jonathan's voice. Kristen explained how she had called him and finished by telling of their mother and Jonathan's plans to get married.

Adam knew Kristen had it in her. But one person had been quiet.

"Lilly?" He lifted his hand.

Hers quickly closed around his. "Rest. I'm here, Adam."

He went to sleep vowing that by his side was where she'd remain. His life was finally getting back on track.

"You should have told me." Arms folded, Adam sat on the couch in his home in Sausalito Saturday afternoon. "I could have postponed the surgery."

"No." Lilly knelt in front of him and placed her hands on his denim-covered knees. They'd only been home from the hospital a couple of hours and had been arguing half that time. "I told you I have to take care of this myself."

"You need a character reference. I could have gone with you."

"Adam, you aren't listening," she said patiently. He'd been upset since she told him that her court date was Monday and she was flying to Dallas the next afternoon. "I need to do this on my own. I have to face Myron, look him in the eye, and be unafraid."

"What if he tries to harm you?" Adam asked, unfolding his arms.

Her hands trembled, then steadied. "I'll be in a court full of people. Nothing is going to happen to me."

"You can't be sure. If that scum touches you—"

"He won't," Lilly said quietly. "Please don't get upset about this. Don't make me regret telling you."

"Scott won't allow me to fly, dammit!"

"Neither will I. Please let me do this on my own. Trust me." She needed him to understand. "Please."

Suddenly his hands reached out and closed around her forearms, then lifted her. She tensed, then relaxed as she landed in his lap. The arms locked around her were fierce and protective. "You aren't going alone and that's final. If Mother or Kristen can't go with you, I'll hire someone. Your choice."

"Were you always this dictatorial?" she asked, her voice unsteady.

"Yes."

It took all of her willpower not to kiss his stubborn chin or lean into the shelter of his arms. "In that case, I'll ask Eleanor. Now, if you'll let me up, I need to pack."

"Call Mother first." His hold loosened.

Reluctantly she came off his lap. "All right. Any other orders?"

"Just be safe and come back to me."

Warmth and love swept through her. If only he loved her instead of needed her she'd be the happiest woman in the world.

"I will," she said and walked from the room.

The private jet landed at Love Field in Dallas, Texas, at nine-thirty Monday morning. A car and driver were waiting for Lilly and Eleanor. Lilly was grateful. She wanted to be able to get back to Adam as soon as the hearing was over.

She and Eleanor got inside the stretch limousine, and the driver hit Carpenter Freeway and headed south toward Highway 45 and Little Elm. Less than an hour later, Lilly saw the city sign and fought against the fear creeping through her. Opening her purse, she took out Adam's medical school graduation ring. He'd given it to her that morning since he couldn't be with her. Nothing could have pleased or encouraged her more.

Arriving at the red brick courthouse, Lilly stepped out on the brick pavement. Eleanor followed. A hush fell over the gathered crowd. Lilly knew that her white Armani suit (purchased at Adam's and Eleanor's insistence after a trip to Neiman Marcus Sunday afternoon) and the limo were going to cause speculation. She no longer cared.

She wanted Myron to know that no matter how the hearing went, he hadn't beaten her down; he hadn't won. Her life was better after leaving him, not worse.

She recognized several faces in the crowd. None of them returned her greeting or smile. A heaviness centered in her chest. "They act as if I'm a stranger."

"Come on, Lilly; let's go inside." Eleanor took her arm and they had started up the walkway to the steps of the courthouse when she heard her name.

"Mrs. Crawford."

She turned to see her lawyer, Kent Powell, rushing toward her. He wore a conservative three-piece blue suit with a striped silk tie and a pearl gray Stetson. In his hand was a leather briefcase. He looked young and inexperienced. Her flagging courage wavered.

"I almost didn't recognize you," he said, his gaze drifting to Eleanor.

"Mr. Powell, I'd like you to meet Eleanor Wakefield, a friend of mine."

Eleanor inclined her head. "Mr. Powell."

He quickly tipped his hat, his shrewd eyes taking in Eleanor's tailored suit, the expensive but tasteful jewelry, the sophistication that came from years of wealth and privilege. "Mrs. Wakefield."

Lilly could see the questions in his face. "Why don't we go inside and talk?"

"Certainly."

Inside the courtroom that had remained unchanged for the past fifty years, they took their seats on the hard, solid oak chairs in front of the scarred wooden table.

"If you don't mind, I'd like to know how you know my client."

Lilly told him everything.

"I'm glad you could come, Mrs. Wakefield. The story has been circulating that Mrs. Crawford ran off with a man."

Lilly's mouth thinned. "I guess we know who's behind it."

"Yes, but he has a lot of friends. They're all set to testify at his behest," the lawyer paused. "Perhaps you should reconsider changing the wording on your divorce decree. You could walk out of here today a free woman."

"No. Myron took enough from me; he's not winning this."

"All right, but remember this could get messy."

Lilly didn't realize how accurate her lawyer's words would be until Myron's lawyer began calling witnesses to the stand. She listened as three men told how she had tried to seduce them. Her lawyer's objections and the fact that they were fishing and hunting buddies of Myron didn't matter.

Her lawyer's cross examination did little to shake their story. Myron's lawyer paraded witness after witness who sullied her reputation and depicted her as being as free with her body as her mother had been. Not one person spoke in her defense. She looked at the women who had stood shoulder to shoulder with her in her kitchen after Mother Crawford's death. Each one turned away. Shayla's testimony that Lilly had been uncaring and cold damaged Lilly's case even more.

"Your Honor, I call Myron Crawford to the stand."

Lilly closed her eyes. She wanted to run from the room. Instead she gripped Adam's ring and opened her eyes. Myron might win in court, but she'd never cower before him again.

"Do you swear to tell the truth and nothing but the whole truth?"

"I do."

"You may be seated."

"Mr. Crawford, you've heard the witnesses in this courtroom say some pretty bad things about your wife. If they're true, why didn't you divorce her?" his lawyer asked.

Myron, in a black suit, looked handsome and tortured, the picture of a wronged husband. But he was a man whose good-looking face hid his evil heart. Briefly he hung his head. When he looked at Lilly, there were tears in his eyes. "I loved her. God help me, but I still do."

The lawyer turned and stared hard at Lilly. "You love her? You love a woman who would make Jezebel look like a saint?"

"I object." Kent Powell shot up from his chair.

"Objection sustained."

Myron's lawyer continued looking at Lilly. "I'll rephrase the ques—"

A hush fell over the courtroom as a tall, broad-shouldered man entered. He looked neither to the right nor to the left as he made his way down the aisle.

On the stand Myron's eyes widened, then narrowed with hatred.

Lilly knew that look of rage. When she looked behind her she knew the reason. She was up and on her feet in seconds. The young man's arms closed securely around her. Conversations broke out over the room.

Judge Lowell's gavel banged for the courtroom to be quiet. Kent Powell watched with a sinking heart as his case went down the drain. He'd actually believed her.

"Order. Order in the court," the judge demanded, banging his gavel. "Mr. Powell, control the exuberance of your client and have her take a seat," he said, his lips sneering.

"Mrs. Crawford, you and the man please sit down," Mr. Powell pleaded.

Neither moved to obey him. "I heard you needed me as a witness to my father's cruelty to Lilly," the man said.

"Your father?" Powell looked from the strikingly handsome young man to Myron Crawford on the stand.

The body build was similar, but there the resemblance ended. The younger man's features were softer, but the eyes were just as hard. He was dressed in freshly pressed jeans and a denim shirt and jacket. His hair was in a foot-long ponytail.

Myron came out of his chair. "He's a liar! Just like she is!"

"And I suppose these are lies." Rafe ripped off his T-shirt and shirt. Women and men gasped. Welts and loop marks made from belts and extension cords criss-crossed his muscled back.

"Bailiff, bring that man up here."

Rafe was already moving. "You want to see what a loving father I had? Take a good look."

"You were willful. A man's got a right to chastise his child. It says so in the Bible."

"Not beat," Rafe told him. "Lilly tried to stop you once and you beat her. If it hadn't been for Grandma, I would have killed you."

"See!" Myron gestured toward his son. "See what a devil I had in my house!"

"Is she a devil, too, Myron? Lilly never did anything except try to be a good wife and mother," Rafe said, his fists clenched. "But that wasn't good enough for you. You treated her like a hired servant instead of a wife. Wives are supposed to be submissive to their husbands, you always said. You could quote the Bible when it suited you in your wrongdoing."

"I based my life on the Bible."

"You based your life on cruelty and deceit," Rafe said contemptuously. "You hurt her in the cruelest way a man can hurt a woman, you bastard."

Myron's nostrils flared with fury. "That's a lie! If I'd treated her so badly, she wouldn't have stayed!"

"She stayed because she wanted to help me and Shayla, even though my sister was too selfish to realize it then and apparently that hasn't changed." He shot a glance at his sister, then turned back to Myron. "But Grandma did."

With an enraged cry, Myron came out of the witness stand. The bailiff finally moved to stop him. The judge shook his head.

"You shut your mouth!"

"Grandma moved in with you to try and help. She told me so."

"To help?" Lilly said.

Rafe whirled. "Didn't you ever wonder why an independent woman like Grandma would move into another woman's house?"

"She was sick," Lilly reminded him.

"She wasn't that sick, not at the beginning, but watching Myron's hatred took its toll on her. There was a darkness in him that all her praying couldn't eradicate."

Tears pricked Lilly's eyes. She thought she had sacrificed her happiness for Mother Crawford the past five years. It had been the other way around.

"You're lying!" Myron yelled. "You weren't even here for her funeral."

Rafe faced his father. "Because I swore I'd kill you if you ever laid a hand on me again and I didn't want Grandma's funeral to be the place."

His expression murderous, Myron stepped closer. "Well, you're such a big man. Come on."

"Gladly."

"Bailiff!"

The uniformed guards moved swiftly to separate the two men before the blows started. It took two additional men from the court next door to accomplish the task. The judge banged his gavel although the courtroom was eerily quiet. "Everyone sit down. I'm ready to give my verdict. Young man, put your shirt back on. Take a seat, Mr. Crawford."

Glaring at his son, Myron straightened the coat of his black suit and went to his seat. His lawyer refused to look at him when he did.

Lilly grabbed Rafe's hand and pulled him down into the chair beside her. "No matter what, I'm glad you came."

"In view of the testimony I've heard here today and in view of the fact that there are no assets to divide, I hereby grant Lilly Crawford the divorce from Myron Crawford on the grounds of mental cruelty."

"What!" Myron surged from his seat.

"Sit down, Mr. Crawford, unless you want to be held in contempt of this court." Judge Lowell stared at Myron until he sat down. "Let me say that although your son is a grown man, your treatment of him is reprehensible. To call yourself a Christian is a disgrace to God and fellow Christians. As for the three men who testified here today, if I find they lied they'll be held for perjury. Case closed." He banged his gavel.

Lilly hugged Rafe. "Thank you."

"Thank you for taking care of Grandma." Briefly he lowered his head. "I couldn't take it."

"She understood."

He nodded and pulled out a white card and gave it to her. "If you ever need me, you can reach me at this address."

Lilly clutched the card in her hand without looking at it. "I'm glad the investigator found you."

"Me, too." He glanced away briefly, then centered his gaze on her. "I never thanked you for taking care of me and Shayla."

Her hand closed on his muscled forearm. "You didn't have to. I wanted to." Her eyes saddened. "I know it wasn't easy coming back here. I appreciate it."

"That's what families are supposed to do. Help each other," he said simply. "We got it right even if they didn't."

Lilly wasn't sure if he meant his father or her mother, then realized it didn't matter. "We certainly did." Opening her purse, she took out pen and paper and wrote down her Shreveport address, then, after asking Eleanor, wrote down Adam's Sausalito address and phone number and handed the slip of paper to Rafe. "You'll be able to find me at one of those addresses."

Rafe glanced at Eleanor, then back at Lilly. "I'm glad you found friends and happiness."

The hint of sadness in his voice troubled her. "Rafe, don't let your hatred of Myron ruin your life."

There was a brief flicker of something in his dark eyes; then it was gone as quickly as it had come. "I won't. Stay safe and be happy." Kissing her on the cheek, he turned and walked from the courtroom.

"Good-bye, Rafe," Lilly mumbled to his retreating back.

"He's quite a young man," Eleanor said, watching Rafe walk away.

"We would have lost without him," Powell said, gathering his papers and putting them in his briefcase. "I don't guess you'll be staying on in Little Elm."

"No. I realize now I could never be happy here. People and circumstances wouldn't let me." Lilly extended her hand. "I'm leaving, but there's a couple of things I have to do first."

Outside the courthouse, she ignored the whispers and stares and searched the crowd. Seeing Myron in the parking lot with the three men who had lied about her on the witness stand, she headed in that direction. The crowd parted as if they were the Red Sea.

"Lilly, don't do this," Eleanor pleaded, worry in her voice.

"I have to. Wait here. Please."

Leaving Eleanor on the sidewalk, Lilly didn't stop until she stood in front of the man who had made her life hell for six years, and she had been coward enough to let him. "Myron."

He spun; contempt and hatred flared in his eyes. The three men who had testified against Lilly refused to meet her gaze and quickly scurried away.

"Come back here!" Myron yelled. The men practically ran to their cars. Motors roared as they sped away. Myron swung back around and glared at Lilly. "If it's the last thing I do, you'll pay for what you did today."

"You did it to yourself." She was unfazed by his anger or threats. "There's over a hundred witnesses this time. Hit me again and you'll go to jail. I guarantee it."

His head jerked up and around. He glared at the watchful crowd, then brought his furious gaze back to her. "They won't always be around."

She refused to cower. She'd done that too many times. "You are a sneaky, vindictive coward, Myron. Mother Crawford knew it, Rafe knew it, and now the whole town and Shayla know it."

Rage distorted his features. Shayla had always been his Achilles' heel. He drew back his balled fist.

Eleanor screamed Lilly's name.

People gasped.

Instead of raising her hands protectively over her face, Lilly did what she had always been afraid to do. She kneed Myron in the groin.

His eyes bugged in pain and surprise. Clutching himself between his legs, Myron moaned and fell to the ground, hurling curses at her from between clenched teeth.

"You'll never hit me again, Myron," she told him, her voice surprisingly calm. "I'm free of you and I'm going to be happy. Somehow I don't think you will be, and you only have yourself to blame." Turning, she started back to the limousine.

On the way out of town they stopped by a florist shop. At the cemetery Lilly laid the dozen deep red roses on Mother Crawford's grave beside the dozen already there. Rafe.

"You won't be forgotten. I promise. Thank you for looking after me." Standing, she went back to the limousine where Eleanor waited.

Aboard the plane Eleanor had the stewardess open a bottle of champagne and toasted Lilly. After a couple of sips, Lilly put in a call to Adam. Disappointment slumped her shoulders when the housekeeper informed her that he wasn't there. He and Kristen had gone out. No, she didn't know when they planned to return.

Slowly, Lilly hung up the phone. She had so much to tell Adam. He'd be so proud of her.

"You love him, don't you?" Eleanor asked quietly from beside her.

"Yes." Lilly didn't even think of lying.

"I'm glad." Eleanor smiled warmly.

Surprise widened Lilly's eyes. "You don't mind?"

Eleanor's smile widened. "Why should I mind that my son is loved by a wonderful, caring woman who makes him happy?"

Lilly was stunned . . . and overjoyed.

"Now that that's settled, how about some more champagne?" Eleanor plucked the bottle from the ice bucket.

Grinning wildly, Lilly lifted her glass.

Arriving at Adam's house a little after three that afternoon, Lilly was disappointed to learn that he and Kristen were still out. Since the housekeeper wasn't sure when they'd return, Eleanor invited Lilly to go shopping with her to search for a wedding dress. Certain she'd worry and watch the clock if she stayed, Lilly accepted the invitation.

"Lilly, how about this one?" Eleanor asked two hours later.

Lilly glanced up from the chair in the fitting room of the couture salon in Neiman Marcus. Eleanor's face glowed with happiness as she slowly pirouetted in a Valentino ivory suit with a long-sleeved, side-tie jacket and tea-length skirt. She looked beautiful and deliriously happy. Lilly couldn't help wondering if she'd ever get the chance to wear something so exquisite and feminine for Adam.

"Jonathan will be speechless," she assured Eleanor, letting the joy she felt for her push aside any doubts about her own unsettled situation with Adam.

"I saw another suit in lilac, and if I'm not mistaken there's the most darling hat you ever saw in Accessories that would match. The combination would be perfect for the garden wedding we plan." Eleanor stepped off the platform and reached for the side tie. "I think I'll just slip this off and try it on. Do you mind?"

Lilly stood and pushed the button for the saleslady. "Not at all."

Darkness had settled over Sausalito when Eleanor opened Adam's door. "Thank you for going shopping with me."

Lilly's gaze went up the stairs before she gave her attention to Eleanor. There had been no word from Adam since they returned to San Francisco. "Of course. I enjoyed it. Thanks for letting me tag along."

Eleanor hugged her. "You're welcome. I had fun."

"I just hate you didn't find anything," Lilly said. "I think the problem was that you looked great in everything you tried on."

Eleanor's smile was quick. "Thanks for the compliment. I still have seven weeks. You sure you don't want to go with me to the art council meeting?"

"No," Lilly assured her. She preferred to wait for Adam. "I'll be fine."

"He and Kristen should be finished with their errands shortly. Good night." Eleanor shoved the silver chain strap of her purse farther over on her shoulder, then turned toward the door, stopped abruptly, snapped her fingers. "I almost forgot. Adam left a list of books he wanted me to get on his nightstand. Do you mind getting it for me?"

"Of course not." Lilly swiftly climbed the stairs. Her thoughts were on Adam when she opened the door and gasped.

"I take it you're surprised?"

Lilly whirled sharply to see Adam merge from the shadows in the room filled with the mellow sounds of jazz and bathed with the soft, warm glow of flickering vanilla-scented candles. The effect teased the senses.

"For you."

With hands that trembled, Lilly took the single red rose he held out to her. "Thank you."

"My pleasure," he said. The back of his knuckled hand grazed her cheek. Heat spiraled through her body at his touch, the husky timbre of his voice. She swallowed.

"Mother said you'd already toasted your freedom, but I hope you'll have dinner with me and toast again."

Lilly finally pulled her hungry eyes away from Adam's compelling features long enough to see the table setting for two on the balcony. The white tablecloth and crystal glowed in the moonlight. "Oh, Adam. It's beautiful." She brought her gaze back to him. It was impossible not to. The candlelight illuminated his handsome face and made her spin foolish fantasies.

"I'm glad you think so." He chuckled. "I had to threaten Kristen to leave me in here with the candles. She went out the back door when we heard Mother's car."

Lilly's gaze went back to the groups of candles scattered around the room. They sat far enough back for Adam not to accidentally knock any over unless he fell, and he was too self-assured for that. "This was all planned, I take it."

"I wanted to give you a beautiful memory by candlelight. Couldn't very well do that in the daytime." Taking her arm, Adam led her to the balcony and expertly poured each of them a glass of champagne. "To second chances."

"Second chances," Lilly repeated and drank, her eyes on Adam. The dinner might be a celebration, but the candles moved into the realm of romance. Her pulse raced.

He reached for her glass and set it on the table, then stepped closer until their body heat mingled. "Are you hungry?"

Her breath seemed to clog in her throat. "N—Not very."

"Good. I've wanted to do this for so very long." Pulling her into his arms, his mouth brushed gently over hers, once, twice.

Transfixed, Lilly stopped breathing and let herself feel the gossamer touch of warm, mobile lips shaping themselves to hers as hers heated and softened in return. A moan came from deep within.

"So sweet. Sweeter than I imagined."

"Yes," she murmured; her arms slipped around his neck. The flower dropped unheeded from her fingers to the floor. So this was what a kiss was like. A mating of tongues and spirits. Sweet. Tender. Powerful.

Adam's hands explored the gentle slope of her back, the rounded curve of her hips, the proud thrust of her breasts, as he had wanted to do so many times and discovered each touch fueled the need for another, then another. She shivered in his arms and clung to him, fitting her softness to his hardness.

She held nothing back. There was no hesitation. She simply gave and in so doing received more pleasure than she had imagined. The kiss, the touch, the soft sighs, and the ragged moans seduced her. She sank deeper into the kiss, into passion, and Adam sank with her.

His head lifted, his breathing labored. "I want to carry you to bed, but I'm afraid I can't remember exactly where it is."

His words sent a shaft of heat pulsing through her. In this room he never hesitated, never faltered. To know that she made him forget even for a moment excited her in a way that she never thought possible.

"Why don't we save it for the next time?" Boldly taking his hand, she led him to the bed and pulled him down beside her.

Without another word, she met his mouth again. They tumbled back onto the wide expanse of softness. His hands on the buttons of her suit jacket were quick and agile. Hers faltered on his shirt. She shivered as he slipped the jacket off her shoulder and trailed kisses to the valley of her throbbing breasts.

Shivers gave way to shudders as his lips took her nipple in his mouth, suckled gently. She felt the exquisite pull deep in the core of her womanhood. Her hand at the button of his slacks fisted.

"You're getting behind." Adam dragged her skirt over her feet, then followed with pulling her stockings down her legs with a trail of kisses to the instep of each foot.

Pleasurable sensations swept over Lilly in waves. Need trailed in its wake.

To touch and be touched; to love and be loved. She hadn't known that pleasure could be so sharp it bordered on pain, on insanity.

Her hands went to his shirt again. When the last button proved stubborn, she jerked.

Adam laughed. His rough laughter turned into a moan as her mouth dropped kisses over his chest. Then her teeth and tongue sought out the dark nipple on his chest and swirled her tongue around it. Soon she discovered that wasn't enough. She wanted him as naked as she was.

Straddling him, she undid the button on his pants, then drew them and his black briefs off. Looking up, she saw the proof of his desire, hard and proud.

"I won't hurt you, Lilly."

She smiled in the semidarkness with a woman's power. Her body had tightened, but not in fear. "I won't hurt you, either."

They each reached for the other at the same time and came together in the center of the bed, their knees touching, their arms around each other, their faces inches apart. "I was afraid you'd remember him."

"Once. No more." She glanced around the room. "Thank you for this."

He kissed her forehead, her cheek, brushed his lips across her mouth. "You deserved so much. When my vision returns, I'll show you the world."

Misery lanced through her. She could be greedy or accept the remaining time they had together. "Love me."

"Always."

He fastened his mouth on hers. Lifting himself over her, he nudged her legs aside. With one stroke he joined the two of them. Her heat welcomed him, closing around him like a hot velvet glove. Adam sighed with the pleasure of it, with the rightness of it. Then he began to move.

Lilly locked her legs around his back and met the thrusts of his body. So this was what it felt like to be loved and loving. Lilly held nothing back, not sure if Adam would have let her.

Hearing her soft cries of pleasure soothed the jagged edge of his need . . . just barely. He had never wanted this way. She was so responsive, so demanding. He didn't flinch when her nails dug into his back. He surged deeper, more powerfully into her, meeting her demands and reveling in the rightness of this woman.

He felt the little quakes inside her body and knew she'd go over soon. He planned to be there with her. Fastening his mouth to hers, he lifted her hips in his hands and thrust into her again and again until the world blurred and shattered.

Together they fell into the deep abyss of passion locked in each other's embrace.

Lilly watched the dawning day take the shadows from the bedroom and from Adam's face on the pillow beside hers. He was so utterly handsome and so hopelessly lost to her. She had lingered when she should have gone. Just one more touch and then she'd have the courage to slip away.

"Good morning."

She started; her hand paused near his face. "You're awake?"

He laughed at the obvious answer to her question. The sound caused her heart to skip a beat. How could just hearing his laughter make her want him?

His mouth brushed across hers; then he tugged. "Come here."

She went willingly, greedy again for his mouth, his hands on her body. He brought them together in one smooth motion. Just as Lilly sighed in contentment, he reversed their position and she found herself on top.

Pleasure rippled through her. He filled her completely. Deliciously.

"You're all that I desire."

Lilly heard the words but, more important, felt them in her soul and the most intimate part of her body where he touched her. She couldn't hold the words back any longer: "I love you, Adam."

"Lilly." Her name on his lips sounded like a reverent prayer.

Lilly locked her hands with his and began to move her hips. The pace was fast, and when completion came his name was on her lips. He took the word into his mouth and locked his arms around her and followed her over.

Her head on his shoulder, their bodies beaded with perspiration, their breathing labored, Lilly listening to the unsteady beat of his heart, storing another memory. Then she threw a glance at the clock and realized she had lingered too long. Seven-forty-seven.

"I better get up. Mrs. Howard will be here soon." The housekeeper arrived promptly at eight Monday through Friday.

Adam pulled her closer. "It's not unusual for a man and his fiancée to sleep together."

She jerked upright. "What?"

Adam felt under the pillow, pulled out a little blue box, then opened it. Inside, a two-carat heart-shaped diamond gleamed. "Besides planning the dinner, I had to find this. I'd get down on my knees, but I suddenly have the feeling if I did, you'd run."

Her heart breaking, she forced the words out. "I–I can't marry you."

"Why?" The quiet intensity of Adam's voice told her how important her answer was to him, how badly she could hurt him.

"Several reasons," she told him, dragging the sheet up to cover her breasts.

"I'm listening."

He deserved the truth. "I didn't want to fall in love with you, but I couldn't help myself. I kept telling myself I wasn't good enough, smart enough, pretty enough."

"That's idiotic."

She kept talking as if she hadn't heard him. "I know that I'm a worthwhile human being and I'm stronger than I thought I was. All my life I've depended on someone or something to make me happy. That's changed. I have to depend on myself for my happiness, and I have to be able to stand on my own. I have to come to you because I want to, not because I have no choice."

"Then you aren't leaving me?"

"I'm not that big of a fool." Smiling, she wrapped her arms around his neck. "There are plenty of colleges here, and I'm getting my degree and I'm going to get my business going again."

"I don't suppose arguing will do any good?"

She kissed him on the mouth. "Not this time. This is the way it has to be."

"I couldn't agree more." Taking her hand, he slipped on the engagement ring. "You have your conditions and I have mine. You're wearing my ring, and the second that diploma is in your hand we're heading to the church."

"I could keep your medical ring instead." she offered.

"Fine, but you're wearing this one," he told her flatly. "I want the entire world to know I love you."

"Adam, you're arrogant, dictatorial, obs—"

His mouth stopped her words. "And you're hopelessly in love with me the same way I am with you."

"Absolutely," Lilly answered with a smile as big as his.

His hand moved possessively over her hips.

"Adam, the housekeeper," Lilly reminded him, but she nipped his ear, already feeling her blood heat.

"I gave her the week off." He eased into Lilly's moist heat. She took him completely. He eased out, then back, stroking her inner walls as she stroked his. Rapture waited, but not yet. Not yet.

Lilly tried to speak, but the hard length of him inside her stole her thoughts. All but one as she matched his lazy rhythm: She'd found something else she was good at. Loving Adam.

Epilogue

He watched her come down the aisle toward him. Their family and friends were gathered to share in their happiness, but he had eyes only for her on this, their wedding day. He'd fretted about the flowers in the garden being just right, worried that it might rain.

She hadn't worried. As always, she had been his rock, his salvation. He'd waited so long for her, and now his wait was over.

"If any person can show just cause why this couple should not be joined in holy matrimony, let them speak now or forever hold their peace," intoned the minister.

Adam shot the minister a hard glare. He could have left out that part. When Adam turned back to Lilly she was smiling as if she knew exactly what his thoughts were. He grinned. God, how he loved her more each time he saw her. He'd catch himself sometimes just staring at her, the same way he'd stared the first morning the gray haze cleared from his eyes.

He thought she was the most beautiful woman in the world then; in the ten months that had followed, he hadn't changed his mind. It wasn't just her beauty on the outside, although her almond-colored eyes, high cheekbones, and lush lips got his blood pressure up just by looking at her; it was her inner beauty that had captured his heart.

His heart had known even before his eyes saw her that he'd love her forever. He didn't know what life held, but as long as Lilly was by his side, he could handle it.

Rafe released her hand and Adam stepped down to take it and lead her back to the minister. He'd waited a year for this day.

Life was good and he planned to enjoy each day to the fullest with the woman he loved, the woman who had been his turning point.

Letter to Readers

Dear Readers:

Trouble Don't Last Always will always have a very special place in my heart. Several years ago, when my writing career was just beginning, I began to see blank spaces where letters should have been. Concerned, I had my eyes examined and was told I needed bifocals. I insisted on a second opinion. Two weeks later I sailed through a more intensive vision exam, or so I thought. Imagine my horror when I was informed that I had a macula hole in each eye and surgery was needed immediately.

The first retina specialist advised surgery the next day, but he was professional enough to tell me that his last patient lost her sight as a result of that surgery. Needless to say, I wanted to see another specialist. A week later I was in the office of Dr. Parks, who gave me hope, but eventually the macula hole repair was needed. Instead of six weeks face down for twenty-two hours out of twenty-four, I had eight weeks. I was never so frightened in my life when my vision didn't clear on the exact day and hour that Dr. Parks thought it would.

I'm now blessed with 20/25 vision in my left eye. But what if the surgery had failed? What if the hole in the right eye had not resolved by itself? What if the complication of cataracts materialized? Those "what ifs" became the starting points for *Trouble Don't Last Always*. As in all of my thirteen previous published titles, I wanted to show the miracle of faith, the healing power of love, and the special bond many families are blessed to share. I hope you feel I succeeded.

If you know of anyone who needs more information for the visually impaired, please call Lighthouse International at 1-800-829-0500. The National Domestic Violence hot line number is 1-800-799-7233. Before you go to bed tonight please hug someone you love and count your blessings.

Have a wonderful life,
Francis Ray
E-mail: francisray@aol.com

Reading Group Guide

1. Did Lilly pay too high a price by staying with Myron? Do you agree with her reasons for staying? Why or why not?

2. What is the one thing that you feel you could never forgive your significant other for?

3. Should Adam share the blame with the carjackers for his blindness?

4. How did Lilly's and Adam's families influence their lives?

5. What part did faith play in the lives of Lilly and Adam?

6. What lesson about life and love did all the characters have to learn?

7. Has there been a turning point in your life, and if so, who or what influenced it and how has it changed your life?

8. With no definite plans and little resources, Lilly stepped out on faith to find a better life for herself. Do you think you would have the same courage and determination in her place? Why or why not?

9. When life gets tough, what helps you to remember that trouble doesn't last always? What helped Lilly and Adam to remember?

10. Domestic violence is often viewed as a family crime and not reported. If you were aware of someone in an abusive relationship, how would you handle the situation?

11. When Lilly first met Myron he was cordial and caring. Adam was harsh and rude to her. Both men said they loved her. Only one told the truth. Can a woman always tell if a man loves her? Explain your answer.

**For more reading group suggestions visit
www.stmartins.com**

Get a **Griffin**

St. Martin's Griffin

Here's an excerpt from Francis Ray's next book

Like the First Time

Coming May 2004

There was no man in her life, and never had been. She'd always been shy and a loner. One of the reasons she had chosen to major in Computer Science was that she dealt with machines better than people. She had viewed working overtime and on holidays as a way of reaching her goal of being financially independent by the time she was fifty. Marriage and family would come, but she was too busy trying to rise in her profession to date. Now, at thirty-nine, she had done neither.

Standing to go to the kitchen, she caught a glimpse of her reflection in the mirror over the dresser in her bedroom. Everything about her was ordinary: her face, her eyes, her mouth, and her nose. She'd never stop traffic the way Brooke did and certainly didn't have the air of confidence or poise that Lorraine possessed. She didn't have that sparkle, that zip.

For some odd reason she thought of Brooke's comment about her missed opportunity with Gray. It would be laughable if it weren't so implausible. By the time he turned thirteen and was almost six feet tall, girls were always after him. He could have had his pick. The daughter of the cook and the chauffeur wasn't even in the running . . . not that she wanted to be.

Annoyed with herself for letting her mind wander to something totally off base, she left her bedroom and headed for the beach. Perhaps a walk would clear her head.

Her hand clamped around the cell phone, Brooke paced the floor and waited for Randolph to pick up. It was barely ten minutes after four Saturday morning. This was her third time trying to reach him since she'd set her alarm clock for four. Last night she kept getting his machine. Every time she'd think he might be out with another woman, she'd glance at her gold bracelet on her wrist. He must have been too tired to check his messages last night and simply forgotten this morning.

Randolph loved her. He'd told her that numerous time. Once she talks to him everything will be all right. Perhaps he'll even ask her to marry him now and she wouldn't have to worry about finding a new job at all. She'd be too busy planning her wedding.

"Peterson."

Hearing Randolph's voice Brooke felt tears sting her eyes and blinked them away. Randolph didn't like emotional women. "Randolph, thank goodness. I've been trying to reach you since yesterday."

"I had a lot of work to do and I had the machine on. I was trying to finish this morning, but the phone kept disturbing me," he grumbled.

Brooke tried to remember how Randolph hated being interrupted. "I'm sorry, but something terrible had happened."

"You're dumping me?"

Brooke blinked. "No, honey, you know I love you . . . it's something else. Yesterday I was laid off."

"What! What did you do?"

She was almost as shocked by his second question as she was by his first. "I didn't do anything! It was my supervisor, Opal Seevers, she's always had it in for me and because Middleton is going through restructuring, she probably put my name at the top of the list to go. The hag."

"Restructuring doesn't work that way, Brooke. Upper management has some say so in the leveling process, but consultants usually have the final say on the positions that are expendable."

Her hand tunneled though her hair in rising irritation. Randolph could be so . . . so analytical and logical at times. "Randolph, we're talking about my job. They only gave me two weeks severance pay."

"You'll find another position. You're smart, savvy, and gorgeous. I can think of several companies that would snap you up."

She perked up. "Which ones? Can you call them?"

"You don't need me to do that, dear. One of the reasons I'm so crazy about you is your resourcefulness. You'll find another job and be back in management before I get home. Now, I have to run. These reports are due Monday morning and I want to make sure they're on time and correct. The bank president and the board will be there. I need to make a good impression."

"But Randolph—"

"You'll do fine. I really must get back to those reports. I'll call later. Bye."

"But . . ." Her voice trailed off as she realized he'd hung up on her. How could he have done that to her? Cell phone in her hand, she swallows the growing knot in her throat. She'd thought he'd be sympathetic, offer encouragement. He'd done none of those things. She tried to hang on to his promise that's he call later. Laying down in bed, she snapped out the light, put her arm over her eyes and wished she could call her mother.